BARLOW
BY THE
BOOK

OHN
STER

BARLOW
BY THE
BOOK

Portnoy
PUBLISHING

To Trish,
Who strikes the right chord in my life.

And to Kevin Hart
who spotted the potential of the Barlow character long before I did.

First published in 2015 by Portnoy Publishing

1

Copyright © John McAllister, 2015

The right of John McAllister to be identified as the Author
of the work has been asserted by him in accordance with the Copyright,
Designs and Patents Act 1988.

ISBN: 978-1-909255-11-1

Printed and bound by: CPI

Cover design: Cory Clubb – @coryclubb
Typeset in: Bembo by Sheer Design and Typesetting

Portnoy Publishing
www.portnoypublishing.com   Twitter: @portnoypub

1

The rain shower had eased off after softening the ground for the next day's point-to-point meeting.

Going good, thought Station Sergeant Barlow, but whether for the point-to-point meeting or the slope that eased his bicycle through the streets, or from a pleasant day spent in the station kitchen catching up on paperwork, he couldn't say. His thoughts lingered on a chilled pint to wash down a chip tea. Meantime, he chewed on an imaginary Mint Imperial.

A flapping greatcoat caught his attention. The owner of the coat stood in the recessed doorway of an unlit shop.

'What the devil?'

He slowed the bike as he came level with the doorway. Edward Adair came bouncing out. Edward was Major (wartime hostilities only), the Honourable Edward Adair, GC, MC. Gentleman, and tramp by profession.

Edward looked indignant. 'You're running late, Mr Barlow.'

'What no good are you up to?'

Barlow didn't stop the bike, forcing Edward to march double-time to keep up. By the second lamppost, he was puffing for breath. 'One has need of one's services.'

'Your hut's under water?'

'My accommodation is perfectly habitable, thank you.'

Under the third pool of light Barlow gave him a quick up and down. Edward's face and hands were clean, though he hadn't shaved in days. His eyes red-rimmed, his hair long enough to flop about. Even in his late fifties he remained scrawny.

Barlow stopped the bike and put a foot on the ground for balance. He waited for a couple to pass by before he said, quietly, 'Edward, move into digs before you catch your death.'

Edward grasped the lamppost for support. 'Grace is coming.'

'It's not like you to get religion.'

'She's coming.' Edward's words lingered painfully in the air.

'You said that before and nothing happened.'

'But now she's bought the ticket. She's flying into London next month.'

He continued to grasp the lamppost as if the world was about to fall in on him.

Barlow saw tears start and asked. 'What, hoity-toity Lady Muck, too-good-for-the-likes-of-you, Grace?'

The threatening tears retreated. Edward's head came up, his nose pinched in indignation. 'The Honourable Grace Alexandra Elizabeth Montmercy née Adair.'

'She's going to kill you,' said Barlow.

A startled 'Hey!' cut the air. A scuffle had started among a group of youths ahead.

Barlow wheeled his bike into the darkness between the pools of light. *Bugger it,* but he'd already done a thirteen-hour day and District Inspector Harvey didn't allow him any overtime. Get involved with that lot and there'd be another five hours of paperwork.

The scuffle spilled over into the street. It needed sorting out before it got serious. 'Edward, I'll meet you in the Bridge Bar. Tell the barman to pour the usual.'

He leaned the bicycle against a wall and hitched up his belt two-handed. The shouts and scuffles became interspersed with the thud of heavy blows. Barlow had another chew on an imaginary sweet, this time a bitter mint. Those boys were spoiling his Friday night pint; they'd soon feel the sharp edge of his tongue.

'Has one need of one's assistance?' enquired Edward.

'Just make sure that pint's waiting for me.'

Barlow walked on, gathering his breath for a purposeful, 'Listen you lot.'

The couple who'd passed him a few moments ago stopped short of the Provincial Bank. The man held a lodgement pouch in his hand. They looked at Barlow in relief as he came level.

'Put your money in and go back the way you came,' he said.

They nodded, grateful, and walked with him.

The man said, 'You're Sergeant Barlow.' He held out an envelope. 'Would you mind giving this to Vera? It'll save a stamp.'

From up ahead Barlow heard the smash of glass as a window went in. 'Oh shite!' There went his pint and the night off. 'Sorry for the bad language.'

He put the envelope in an inside pocket. Escorted the man and the woman to the gate leading to the overnight safe, and then continued on his way, this time with a purposeful stride: someone was going to get his collar felt. The scuffling now extended to the far pavement, as the combatants tried to distance themselves from the damage to the shop window.

Vehicle lights swept the street, putting the youths in stark contrast to the near darkness beyond. Barlow heard the engine rev harder. He whipped his head around to get a closer look. *A van of some sort.* The last thing he needed was for the truck to plough through those young idiots.

The van didn't slow. The driver clicked on full beam headlights, blinding him. Barlow stepped into the street and held up his hand. The lights grew stronger, almost burning in their intensity. *It's not for stopping.* He jumped one way, the van swerved the other and roared past him, horn blaring. The wash of air sent him staggering, the wing mirror missing his head by inches. The van roared through the group of youths. They yelled their indignation and hurled beer bottles after it. The bottles fell short, shattering along the ground. The afterglow of the van lights showed no bodies lying in its wake. *Only God knows how.*

Barlow tried to get the number of the van but the number plate was dirty, the bulb illuminating it weak. *TZ something.* Tyres screamed as the van side-slicked around a corner and sped out of sight.

Barlow found himself out of breath from shock. His heart pounded as he ticked off what he knew: dark-coloured van, possibly green. An old Bedford by the look and sound of it. Belfast registration. *Bloody foreigners.* Three men in the front. *Now I'd do those bastards with pleasure.*

The youths still squared off at each other even as they separated into their respective groups.

'Hold it you lot.' Some of them tried to drift up a side street. 'Right there!'

They stopped because he knew most of them and their fathers by name. And they knew it.

He gathered them around him. They stood in two groups: Boys from the Galgorm Road, down from university for the summer. The others, young men nearing the end of their apprenticeships, their bodies thickened and hardened from heavy lifting. He saw some blood, one or two obviously in pain. *Serves them right.* The scent of testosterone hung in the air, hands remained fists. *Still ready for a fight.* They closed in on him, the common enemy.

Edward gave a quiet cough behind Barlow.

At least my back's secure.

'What's this kerfuffle all about,' he asked.

'Did you see that bloody van?' asked someone.

'Did you see you bloody lot?'

At least they were talking. He needed to keep them at it. 'Anyone get the number?'

Silence. A few heads shook. Tensions eased.

'So what happened here?'

'They attacked us,' said a languid voice.

Barlow knew him. JD his friends called him, the judge's son and supercilious little git even if he was six foot three.

'He knocked my fish supper out of my hand,' said one of the apprentices.

'For no reason,' confirmed one of his friends.

Right enough, the remains of a fish supper lay scattered on the pavement. A brown bottle ... a wine bottle, noted Barlow, had gone through the plate glass window and lay among the display clothes in Kirker's shop. A menswear shop that sat sandwiched between two local emporiums.

'Who threw that?'

A finger pointed at JD. 'It nearly took my head off, only I ducked.'

'Never,' said JD. 'It was one of you lot.'

The stupid denial irritated Barlow. JD was trouble, always had been, but he was a mere novice compared to his father. 'Everyone down to the station. We'll sort it out there.'

'Look,' said JD. 'What if we pay? Make good the damage?'

He sounded anxious.

Too late.

One of JD's friends said, 'I could fetch some four by eights out of my father's timber yard.'

An apprentice said, 'My tools are nearby.'

Edward whispered in Barlow's ear, 'Don't make it personal.'

'Clear off,' snarled Barlow, but he knew Edward was right. He wanted to see the look on the father's face when he heard that JD had been charged with malicious damage and incitement.

He gave a long, purposeful sigh. Letting everyone off with a bollocking might save trouble with District Inspector Harvey. The Galgorm Road lot were related to half the members of the City Club. Thanks to Barlow, Harvey's application for membership to the Masonic Club had been blackballed. He'd be unliveable with if the same thing happened to his application to join the less prestigious City Club. Not that Ballymena was a city, but it had aspirations beyond that of a mere county town.

Barlow compromised. 'It's up to Mr Kirker whether he wants to press charges or not.'

And good luck with that, he thought, because Unwin Kirker was an irritable little man, who had started his business life with nothing and was now doing rightly, selling inexpensively priced clothes to youths and workers.

'You lot!' thundered a voice beyond the group.

The youths parted as a stout policeman came running towards them. The policeman saw Barlow and his run suddenly developed a limp.

'You took your time,' Barlow hissed.

Constable Gillespie breathed indignation and rubbed his back as if in pain.

'You'll live,' said Barlow and gave him a quick briefing. He finished with, 'Get the names and addresses of everyone involved.' He pointed at the window. 'Secure that bottle. We may need it as evidence.'

Barlow returned to the station where he rang Unwin Kirker at home and took the initial blast of outrage from the small shopkeeper. Kirker was on his own. The family were at Portrush for the weekend. He'd been planning to join them tomorrow night, and now this. He'd be straight down to the station. Of course he wanted to prosecute.

So did Barlow, but he was thinking more of the driver of that van. It was late by the time he'd written up his police diary regarding the incident. The pubs were long since closed and he'd missed his weekend pint. He headed home.

2

Conscious of the late hour and of the near neighbours already asleep, Barlow quietly opened the front door and stepped into his living room. Clicked on the light. Vera, his daughter, lay curled into a two-seater settee, her head on Kenny Cameron's legs. Kenny's hand rested inside her blouse, cupped around a too-generous breast.

'By God!' Barlow said.

Toby, the Jack Russell dog, snarled at Barlow from Barlow's fireside chair.

'Go on, you cur.' Rather than take Kenny by the throat he gave Toby a pat on the back to keep his hands busy. Got one brief tail wag in return. The young couple jerked awake. At least nothing important had to be done up or pulled up, he noted, as they shot apart.

Vera got to her feet, her face flushed with sleep and embarrassment. 'Da.'

'Aye.' He pointed a finger at Kenny, then thumbed towards the door. 'Shut it on your way out.'

Equally flushed, Kenny edged around Barlow in the tight little room. 'Yes, sir. Goodnight, sir.' Hesitated with his hand on the door catch. 'Nothing... I mean... we didn't... I mean...'

'Good night,' snapped Barlow.

The front door opened and closed behind Kenny.

Vera squared up to Barlow. She had his thick build that no amount of dieting could reduce. 'I'm nearly eighteen. I've left school and I can do what I want.'

They'd had this discussion before and he'd learned to keep his temper. 'What if you get pregnant?'

'Kenny loves me.'

'But do his parents? And they'll be the ones footing the bills.'

'Da...'

'Kenny's going to university, love. Things could change.'

Her face worked a denial that didn't come.

Rather than remind her that Mrs Cameron disapproved of the relationship, and have Vera in tears, he pointed to the two-seater settee. It was covered in a dark blue fabric and had wooden arms. 'Where did that come from?'

She patted the cushions to show their springiness, her eyes nervous. 'I bought it.'

'Bought it with what?'

'Money I'd saved ... well some of it.'

One anger built on top of another. He kept his voice low, so as not to waken the neighbours through the thin walls. 'You're into those loan sharks. I warned you about them.' He shook his head wondering what to do with her, what to do with kids in general, short of locking them up until they got a bit of sense.

'It's not like that,' she said. 'I'm in the credit union.'

She'd kept that from him as well.

He remembered the envelope for her in his pocket and pulled it out. 'So that's what this is all about, borrowing money?'

'My book.' She snatched out of his hand. 'I got so excited I left it behind me.'

He stayed back from the settee as if by touching it he implied acceptance. 'How much did you borrow?'

'Twenty-five pounds.'

The thought of the neighbours knowing their business throttled the roar in his throat. 'You get five pounds a week from Woolworths, and half of that goes on clothes.'

'I'm paying it off at ten bob a week. I'm saving more than that already.'

She was shaking.

'And the interest?'

'A quarter percent per week.' She showed him her credit union book. 'Look, Da.'

On one side was the sum of twenty-three pounds ten shillings and three pence. On the other the twenty-five pound loan.

She pushed him into his usual chair. Barlow hiked Toby onto his hip rather than sit on him. Vera ducked down beside them. She smelled of perfume and of a day's sweat and something male. 'I've twenty-three pounds odd, saved. Ten of it is for my holiday in Portrush with the Camerons. I'm allowed to take that out.'

'What do you mean "allowed"? It's your money.'

'Da, if I take out the thirteen pounds against the settee, I'll have nothing left. This way when the settee is paid for, I'll still have my savings.'

It had been a long day. He'd missed his Friday night pint and complicated thinking about money always left him confused. He'd call into the credit union people at the start of the week and have it out with them. The quarter percent interest per week couldn't be right. He knew loan sharks who charged one percent a day, and they were the good ones.

Meantime.

'Why the settee? What's wrong with what we've got?'

She snapped to her feet. 'Da, this place is a dump. An outside toilet and you have to go through my bedroom in order to get to yours.' She drew back, distancing herself from his life. 'Everything we've got came out of auctions.'

Okay, the furniture was a bit faded and he needed a cushion under him to make his chair comfortable, but he'd started out with less. *A hell of a lot less.*

'It was wartime. There was no new furniture to be got.'

'And this is nineteen bloody sixty.'

'Mind you language.'

She stayed stubborn, unrepentant. 'I'm sick of my friends laughing at me for the way we live. One cold tap for everything and lifting the dirty dishes out of the sink, so that we can wash. Having to boil the kettle for hot water and washing ourselves in a tin bath.'

A tear came. Then another. She fled upstairs to her bedroom. He heard her muffled sobs and the crash as she threw herself into bed. The sobs faded.

He reached out and flicked a switch, so that the light spilling up the stairway wouldn't disturb her sleep. The dog jumped onto the floor, its nails clicking on the linoleum as it ran up the stairs. He heard the jump onto Vera's bed.

'You're supposed to be my dog,' he said to himself and sat on, his head resting against the high-backed chair. Maggie, his wife, in hospital, homicidal, and now this. He felt the scar on his chest where Maggie's knife had slashed the skin. Funny the way that wound still hurt, but not the stab to the upper arm that had nearly killed him. He couldn't change the house in any way, literally couldn't move an ornament without her throwing a fit. When decorating, he always had to use the same dark green paint.

The living room window shattered. Something blurred past his eyes, hit the far wall. Ricocheted.

3

Barlow found himself lying on the floor. Instinct, he realised. A hangover from his wartime days when a quick dive into a trench could make the difference between life and death. His heart started to pound.

Another smash of glass. Something whanged off the cast-iron range, smacked into his chair.

He scrambled to the stairwell for cover. Toby flew down the stairs and barked wildly at the front door. Vera came tumbling after him. 'Da, are you all right? Da?'

'I'm fine.'

He heard footsteps running off. Stood up and gave his trousers a quick dust down. 'You stay here.' Headed for the front door, wishing he had his gun. It was safe in his locker at the station. Right then he was mad enough to send a couple of bullets after the attacker, burn his backside to a frazzle.

He flung open the door and ran straight into something, crashed to the ground. *My knee's bust.* His elbows scraped over the pavement and he banged his head. Toby jumped onto his back and off again. Headed down the road barking like fury.

Vera stood in the doorway. 'Da, are you all right?'

'No I'm bloody well not all right.'

Lights came on in the houses around them. He found himself lying entangled in his own bike. The attacker had moved it across the doorway to block a quick pursuit. He hauled himself to his feet. The handlebars were crooked. He wrenched them straight and flung his leg over the bar. His foot found the far pedal. His knee hurt, his elbows hurt. So did his head and the bike screeched metal. The gunman or whatever – he hadn't heard a shot – had let down the tyres. Barlow flung himself off the bike in a fury.

Neighbours came to their doors, blinking sleepily.

He buried his anger. 'Nothing to worry about. Go back to your beds.'

The damage to the window needed examining but Vera was standing, shaking, hands over her face.

He put an arm around her. 'No harm done, love.'

She wore a short nightie, pink, with a lot of leg showing. She'd be embarrassed when she realised. He led her indoors and closed the door firmly against the curious neighbours, held her until the shaking stopped. Then lifted her onto the first step, and sent her upstairs to dress and put shoes on before she stepped on broken glass.

Toby came back and yelped at the door to be let in. He looked desolate: no blood on his teeth, no torn material clenched firmly in his jaws. The attacker had evaded him somehow.

Barlow lifted him off the glass-strewn floor and put him on the settee. Toby immediately jumped down and stood tight against Barlow, eyes fixed on the window, hackles raised.

'Oh now you're my friend.'

He put Toby on the settee again and this time made him stay while he brushed up the broken glass and looked for whatever had come through the window. He found two steel ball bearings: one under the table the other on the seat of his chair. The back of the chair had a dent in the wood where his head normally rested. *Lucky or what?*

He scooped up the ball bearings with a sheet of newspaper and rolled them into an empty jam jar.

Vera came down dressed in jeans and jumper. She poured still warm water from the kettle into a bowl, added a generous splash of Dettol to the water and stirred with her finger to blend them into a creamy wash. Then she made him take off his shirt while she swabbed his cuts with cotton wool dipped in the bowl. He simulated more discomfort than he actually felt and complained about her torturing him. She giggled and colour came into cheeks white with shock.

'I was thinking, Da...'

'Aye, now when you've me down and helpless.'

'The film, *South Pacific*. When the heroine takes a shower, it's under a bucket with holes in it.'

She was still on about a bathroom of sorts. He had to admit to himself that she'd got to an age where things became difficult on bath night.

'So, you want to stand under a bucket in the yard? The neighbours will enjoy that.'

She gave him one of her well-practised looks. 'No, Da, the coal shed.'

He pretended indignation. 'And where will the coal go?'

She didn't say anything, just smiled. Her mother used to be like that. The more objections he came up with the more she knew he was thinking about it.

A car pulled up at the door. Duty Sergeant Pierson and Constable Gillespie knocked and came in. Toby allowed Gillespie to pat him, but snarled at Pierson until Barlow ordered him to be silent. Toby retreated under the settee, throat still rumbling.

Sergeant Pierson kept his bulk close to the door, ready for a quick exit if the dog came at him. 'We received a report of an incident.'

'Aye, attempted murder. And it wouldn't be "attempted" if I'd got my hands on the wee bugger.'

He told them what happened. Didn't let on about the ball bearings, let them assume it was a couple of thrown stones. Ball bearings and no noise meant a catapult, and somebody young enough to use a catapult was likely daft enough not to think of fingerprints. *I'll sort you myself, sunshine.*

The formal interview finished, Pierson closed his notebook. 'Barlow, we need a list of known enemies. People who've made threats against you.'

'A list of friends would be easier and much shorter,' muttered Gillespie.

4

'You're early,' said Sergeant Pierson when Barlow arrived at the station. It sounded like an accusation because the minute hand of the clock hung short of seven-thirty and Barlow wasn't due on duty until eight.

'A quiet night, going by you two,' said Barlow, glaring at Gillespie for making the place look untidy.

Gillespie was leaning on the counter, staring longingly at the empty fire grate on the far wall. On April first – no better day in Barlow's opinion – District Inspector Harvey had declared the arrival of summer and forbidden all forms of heating in the station. Even in July, the stone walls of the old building held the chill of winter.

'We had Kevin and Darran Hart in for a while,' said Gillespie.

'What were they up to this time?'

'Directing traffic at the Town Hall, and the two of them as drunk as lords. We had to haul them in for their own safety.'

Barlow finished the story for him. 'So they sat in the cell and sang their wee hearts out.'

Gillespie groaned. 'And not a note between them.' He nodded at Pierson, 'Your man here threatened to kick their heads in if they didn't stop.'

'So a quiet night then.'

Pierson became indignant. 'Last night quiet? Mr Hunt's house was robbed.' He preened himself. 'Mr Harvey put me in personal charge of securing the scene until DS Leary and his team arrived.'

'No better man for the job,' said Barlow.

He and the rotund detective had never seen eye-to-eye. It had nothing to do with Leary being looked at with suspicion by both sides of the religious divide. Leary was a Protestant with a Catholic name. A "Sooper" whose family had exchanged their religion for food during the Great Famine.

Barlow spun the Incident Book around to have a look. The burglary had been reported at one forty-three, just after he'd left the station for the night.

Gillespie straightened himself off the counter, sighing and rubbing at his back. 'Mo Hunt was out all evening finalising the arrangements for today's point-to-point meeting. He got home from the club to discover that the house had been gutted of anything valuable.'

'Gutted?'

'Paintings, bric-a-brac, furniture. A lorry load of stuff.'

'Query green van, query Bedford with a Belfast number plate,' Barlow said, looking hard at Gillespie. 'That back of yours. You're not fit to police the point-to-point. Think of all that lovely overtime you're going to miss.'

Gillespie gave himself a shake. 'I'm feeling better already.'

'Aye, I thought you might.'

Pierson became all excited. 'The getaway vehicle, you saw it?'

'Possibly.'

'Then you'd better tell Mr Harvey. He's dealing with the case personally.'

Barlow bit off his surprise at Harvey being in that early. Harvey tended to be a nine to six, Monday to Friday man. The previous District Inspector had haunted the place, never seemed to go home. One reason why he'd died at his desk, his head buried in a pile of files he hadn't the energy to process, yet couldn't bring himself to delegate.

Barlow walked down the corridor to the back offices. Grit on the wooden floor spat out from under his feet. Someone was going to get a brushing job. Something Pierson should have seen to, but then Pierson spent more time scheming than doing actual work.

Pierson was Harvey's blue-eyed boy. Pierson wanted Barlow's job as Station Sergeant and Harvey wanted to give it to him. Only a bit of luck and some quiet support from Captain Denton, the civilian Chairman of the Local Policing Board, had stopped that from happening. Barlow could, of course, retire on a full pension, but then what would he do with himself all day?

The detectives' office door lay open. That surprised him. Usually, they kept it shut, so that no one could see them studying form or salivating over photographs of buxom women in the *Daily Mirror*. Not only that, but all the detectives were on duty. *And at this early hour?* He had to find out why. *Isn't that half the fun of being a policeman, being able to ask nosey questions?*

He stepped in, pretending to duck under a hanging cloud of cigarette smoke. He spotted a uniformed constable among the cheap suits and half-mast ties. A man he'd never seen before. 'And you are?'

The constable jumped to his feet. 'Constable Frank Wilson, Sergeant.'

About mid-twenties, Barlow thought. Wilson had a shock of dark curly hair and an air of surliness.

'When did you arrive?'

'Last night, Sergeant.'

'And you went straight to the Section House. Didn't think of making your number at the front desk?'

'No, Sergeant.'

He was right about the surliness. He'd sort that PDQ.

He looked at the paperwork spread over the detectives' desks. 'That looks good, very impressive.'

Detective Sergeant Leary scowled. He was a short, fat man and one of the best customers of Matthews Bakery. Right then he looked haggard from lack of sleep. 'That burglary at Mo Hunt's house was a professional job. They wore gloves, but Harvey wants every fingerprint we find there checked out.'

Barlow nodded with false sympathy. 'That'll include finger-printing half the members of the City Club. Harvey won't like that, not with him up for membership.'

He told Leary about the van nearly knocking him down. Leary became interested because its appearance in the town fitted into the timeframe for the burglary.

'Pity you didn't get the full number.'

'You want jam on it as well?'

'You had your own problems last night.' Now Leary was smiling as he pointed to a four-drawer filing cabinet in the corner. 'Go through that lot. There's bound to be someone there who especially hates you.'

5

Barlow knocked at the door and stepped into Harvey's office. He thought that Harvey, like the magnolia paint and modern furniture, did not blend with the Victorian cornicing and wooden panelling. Nor did Harvey's newest addition fit in, a drinks cabinet. *The bottom drawer was good enough for the old DI.*

Harvey had been asleep, his head resting against the wall. He jerked awake. 'Barlow, I've told you before. Do not come in until I say "enter".'

Barlow snapped to attention, honouring the portrait of the Queen on the wall behind Harvey, rather than Harvey himself. 'Sorry, sir, I thought I heard you.'

Harvey buried his head in a file, made a squiggled note and then looked up. 'What do you want?'

Barlow told him about the suspicious van.

'And you didn't get the number?'

'Defective rear lights, sir.'

'Not good enough, Barlow. If you'd phoned in immediately we could've recovered Mr Hunt's goods before he even knew they'd been taken.' He sat back and squared his shoulders. 'That would have made me look good with the club members.'

'Indeed, sir, you deserve to be among men of your own ilk.'

Harvey looked suspicious at the over-fulsome reply. Just then his phone rang. He took the call. 'Helen, removal men or no removal men, the children are your problem.' He hung up and consulted some files. Squinted at the handwriting and put on his reading glasses. Took them off again because he was vain.

The phone rang again. Harvey snatched the receiver and barked, 'I told you, no calls until I say otherwise.'

The WPC on the switchboard said something, her voice tight with nerves. Harvey held the receiver out to Barlow. 'It's for you, a Mr Unwin Kirker, and apparently he's very annoyed.'

Barlow couldn't figure what was annoying Kirker. According to Gillespie, Kirker and the youths had come to a settlement: JD and his friends were to pay for a new window. The apprentices had shaken glass shards out of the display clothes and agreed to buy them.

'I'll take it outside,' he told WPC Day.

'You'll take it here,' said Harvey. 'If there's a complaint against you Barlow, I want to know about it.'

Unwin Kirker's annoyance sizzled down the phone. While he'd been down at the shop sorting out the damage someone had broken into his house and stolen a week's takings.

'That's a powerful amount of money to leave lying around, sir.'

Kirker's reply was sharp and to the point. With the family away on holidays there was only himself to run the shop. He'd been too busy serving customers to go to the bank.

More like begrudged closing the shop for ten minutes, reckoned Barlow, but didn't argue. He promised he'd come straight out to Kirker's house with the detectives and hung up.

Kirker's voice had been loud enough for Harvey to hear both sides of the conversation. 'This broken window, can we expect some prosecutions? Send a message to certain elements that loutish behaviour will not be tolerated?'

Barlow knew exactly which element Harvey had in mind.

'The university lot started it and it was one of them who broke the window.'

Harvey grunted his annoyance and changed tack. 'This new constable, Frank Wilson. He's the modern breed of policeman:

first class honours from Queen's, glowing reports from his superiors. I want him to shadow you, learn a Station Sergeant's job from the ground up. When you're on duty, he's on duty. Where you go, he goes. Is that perfectly understood?'

'Indeed, sir.'

'No exceptions, Barlow. None.'

Barlow took a turn around the station. Chivvied the new shift out of the locker room. 'Any man who doesn't.hit the streets this morning doesn't get dossing at the point-to-point this afternoon.'

Allegedly pressing paperwork lost its appeal and there was a general exodus.

He put his head around the detectives' door and told Wilson they were going out. Informed Detective Sergeant Leary that he had another burglary to investigate.

Back in the Enquiry Office he found Pierson breathing fire. 'That new man, who does he think I am?'

He held up a letter for Barlow to see. 'He wanted to know if I would put it in with the rest of today's post. And...' He jabbed the envelope at Barlow's face. 'Look at the address.'

The letter was addressed to a Mrs J Wilson, Malone Park, Belfast. Arguably the most prestigious address in Northern Ireland. People who lived in Malone Park didn't work in factories – they owned them.

'Very nice,' said Barlow.

'But don't you see what that means?' demanded Pierson. 'An address like that, Wilson's family hobnob with people like the Chief Constable.'

'They have to let the Chief Constable out sometimes,' said Barlow, still sounding unconcerned. Then he added, 'Mr Harvey wants Constable Wilson to shadow the Duty Sergeant. Every shift he's on, with no exceptions.'

'I don't want that toffee-nosed git anywhere near me,' said Pierson.

'Oh?'

'Didn't you hear? At his last posting, he got the Station Sergeant jailed and a senior constable fired. They lost their pensions.'

Gillespie smirked. 'I meant to tell you, Sarge. DI Harvey asked Wilson's friend, the Chief Constable, to send him here as a special favour.'

Barlow volunteered Gillespie to run him and Constable Wilson up to Unwin Kirker's house.

'Wait a minute, Sarge, I'm just going off duty.'

'Another couple of minutes won't kill you. And go round by the shop, I want to see what's happening to that window.'

Gillespie went off muttering to fetch the car.

'Sergeant, that man has just finished a twelve-hour shift and he's on duty again tonight,' said Constable Wilson.

Barlow sensed the notebook out ready to record his reply before he even spoke. 'It won't kill him.'

He turned to Pierson. 'Last night, I thought Gillespie was supposed to take the DI to Belfast?'

'The DI said the meeting might run late, so he drove himself.'

'Indeed.'

Barlow waited at the front door for Gillespie to bring the car around. He could have offered Pierson a lift home, but didn't, and Pierson didn't dare ask.

Even at that early hour, traffic was building in anticipation of the point-to-point meeting. Sunlight stretched deep shadows across the street and Barlow sensed a colour and airiness about the town that he hadn't noticed before. *It's myself*, he realised. *I'm getting over things.* That was the closest he'd allowed himself to dwell on a spring when he'd been in hospital twice; Maggie, his wife, in the "mental", on suicide watch, and the death of a woman who had given Barlow's life purpose and hope.

Gillespie pulled up opposite Kirker's shop. The temporary four by eight plywood lay in the back of a lorry while workmen measured up for a new window.

Gillespie chuckled. 'The apprentices demanded a discount on the damaged goods. Kirker said they should pay more for the glitter, even if it was broken glass.'

Barlow grunted. 'He's singing a sourer tune this morning.'

And, so he was, when they arrived at his house, a four-bedroom stand-alone overlooking the town. Two cars stood in the gravelled drive. Barlow recognised Kirker's Rover from the night before.

He nudged Gillespie. 'You're the car man around here. The Jag, who does it belong to?'

'That Jaguar,' Gillespie put emphasis on the full word, 'belongs to Shalko Adair, Auctioneer, Valuer and Estate Agent. Distant cousin of the Adairs of the Castle, he'd have you know. Former Secretary of the golf club, stalwart of the City Club...'

'I wanted to know who owned the Jag, not his life history.' He climbed out of the squad car and held the back door shut against Wilson following him. 'I'll get a lift back with one of these two gentlemen. Mrs Harvey's moving house today. There are a lot of wide boys in town for the point-to-point, so go keep an eye on her stuff.'

Wilson looked like he'd protest. His mouth formed the words, 'Mr Harvey...'

Barlow got in before the young constable could finish his sentence. 'Imagine the embarrassment if the DI got robbed.'

Gillespie's voice vibrated indignation. 'I need my sleep.'

'You'll be dead long enough. Anyway, you'd planned to go fishing this morning and it's too sunny. The fish won't rise.' He raised his voice. 'Give the woman a hand while you're standing there doing nothing.'

The front door whipped open. Unwin Kirker's squat shape filled the doorway. 'Where are the detectives?'

'On their way, sir.' At least he hoped they were. 'Meantime, if you'd show me things were.'

Barlow realised that Kirker wanted an instant solution to his loss. Things didn't happen that way. He motioned and eventually Kirker led him into the house.

The house surprised Barlow. Externally, it was Georgian, renovated and well maintained with lawns and shrubberies. Internally, he'd expected heavy furniture, embossed wallpaper and uncomfortable chairs. Instead, he walked into lightness of colours that started subtly at the front door and used the hallway as a prism to send individual shades curling into the rooms leading off the hallway.

'Good Lord,' said Barlow, his surprise leaving him unsure whether he liked it or not. He focused in on a lamp on the hall table. A Tiffany or he'd eat his cap. Rather than risk putting his cap near a small fortune he tucked it under his arm.

'Now where did you keep this money?'

Kirker led the way down the hallway and under the stairs into his study. There, Barlow found practicality: a modern desk and chairs, filing cabinets and a shelf of spring-clip files bursting with papers. And Shalko Adair, who sat at a desk littered with cashbooks and ledgers.

Barlow's teeth were on edge as if he'd bitten into ice. 'This is a crime scene. Mr Adair shouldn't be here.'

'He's working out how much I've lost.'

'You don't know, sir?'

'Six hundred and thirty-four pounds, eleven shillings and four pence halfpenny,' said Shalko. He smiled. 'Approximately.'

'Indeed, sir.'

'However,' said Shalko, enjoying his moment of importance. 'There are some cheques among that figure which can be cancelled and replaced by the payers. The true loss in cash terms is four hundred and eighty-nine pounds, five shillings and four pence.'

'And the halfpenny, sir?'

'And a halfpenny,' agreed Shalko, with an edge of annoyance.

Barlow turned to Kirker. 'Where was the money kept?'

Kirker indicated a grey four-drawer filing cabinet. Barlow breathed a sigh of relief that it hadn't been the desk. He examined the filing cabinet and could see no sign of a forced entry. 'It wasn't locked then?'

Kirker flushed with annoyance. He'd been working out of the cabinet, getting his month-end books up to date, when the call came about the broken window. He never thought. Just grabbed the car keys…

Barlow interrupted. 'Fingerprints, sir. We'll need your fingerprints and Mr Adair's for elimination purposes.'

'I'd more sense than to go near the filing cabinet,' snapped Shalko.

'And all your family's fingerprints too,' said Barlow to Kirker.

Kirker sighed, 'They're at the caravan. I'm going down there tonight. I'll bring them all back tomorrow. Would that do?'

Barlow thought of all the fingerprints scattered across the detectives' room from the Mo Hunt's break-in. 'Monday morning would be fine. Now, if you'd show me how the burglar got in.'

The burglar had got into the house through an open window in the utility room. The utility room itself held a year's worth of Barlow's pay in fridges and freezers alone. He scowled at the now closed window. Kirker explained about coming home and closing the window and going to bed and not thinking about the money until the morning, while getting ready for work.

'You've done well for yourself,' Barlow said as he led the way back. He intended to get Shalko out of the study, and out of the house altogether if at all possible. He indicated a bronze statuette of an out-of-proportion woman stretching in a pose of lustful abandon.

'It's my hobby,' said Kirker. 'I go to house auctions looking for bargains.'

'I've never seen you at any around here.'

Kirker gave his first laugh of the day. 'Shalko grabs any bargains going before they reach the auction room.' He indicated the statuette. 'But occasionally I beat him to it. It's an original Bergman. He thought it was a copy.'

Barlow chivvied Shalko into stuffing his working papers into his briefcase, and kept chivvying until he and his briefcase were out of the study and down the hall to the front door. 'Now, if you'd wait in your car for a couple of minutes until the detectives arrive.'

Just then they did, two detective constables. It's not that they didn't know their job, Barlow said, as he accompanied them around the house, making sure their points of interest corresponded with his.

As an afterthought he asked Kirker. 'Did you notice anything moved, things out of position?'

'Now that you mention it.'

Kirker moved towards a table covered in bric-a-brac. All three policemen shouted as one. 'Don't touch anything.'

Barlow left one detective on watch while Kirker identified things out of place. He took the other detective outside again and between them they persuaded the reluctant Shalko to give them his fingerprints. 'Purely for elimination purposes,' he was assured.

The fingerprints taken, Barlow got into the Jaguar and asked for a lift back to the station. He loved the way the pleated-leather seat eased around him.

'It's Saturday morning, sir, and hardly breakfast time. Even so, I find you at Mr Kirker's house, filling out forms for an insurance claim.

'All part of the service, Sergeant.' Shalko frowned in annoyance. 'In this town money counts before breeding. It's people like Unwin Kirker who give me my living. All the nouveaux riches go to the big city firms. I get the crumbs off their table.'

'Now isn't that a shame,' said Barlow.

A smug look replaced Shalko's frown. 'But they're beginning to learn the error of their ways. I'm getting there, Sergeant. I'm getting there.'

Barlow said nothing. In his opinion, anyone who drove a brand new Jaguar had already arrived.

8

The point-to-point meeting got off to a good start with a couple of local winners. When questioned, the owners and trainers admitted to having placed a 'substantial' bet.

Barlow wandered through the colourful crowd with Wilson tripping at his heels. Occasionally, Barlow stopped or slowed without warning, causing Wilson to brake sharply to avoid a collision.

He stopped again. Wilson breathed down his neck. 'Look, son, you're here to watch out for ne'er-do-wells and other riff-raff, not to make sure I don't get lost.'

'Yes, Sergeant.'

'And, in particular, pickpockets.'

'Mr Harvey told me that a City Club member got robbed at the March meeting, and in the Owners' Enclosure at that.'

'So we're probably looking for a Red under the bed,' said Barlow, noting the "Mr Harvey told me".

'Yes, Sergeant,' said Wilson dutifully.

The Tannoy whistled and crackled. A man's voice carried tinny over the hubbub of the race crowd. 'Sergeant Barlow, please report to the Owners' Enclosure.'

'They're looking for you,' said Wilson.

'So they are.'

Barlow chose a curving walk in the direction of the Owners' Enclosure. Annoyance at being called made each step parade-ground fashion: leg up, toe out, foot crunching down on the reds, whites and yellows of that day's already beaten dockets.

The threat of his shining toecaps and the bulk of his looming figure left a swirl of people regrouping in his wake.

The Tannoy crackled again. 'Would Sergeant...' The words echoed and re-echoed from the near hills.

He spotted JD and his university friends.

JD looked startled to see him, then relaxed and smiled. He pulled a wad of notes from an inner pocket. 'Sergeant Barlow,' he said in a tone that put Barlow's teeth on edge. 'I made enough on the second winner to pay for Kirker's window twice over.'

JD's friends flashed their own, much thinner, winnings. One of them said, 'He put a pound on for each of us.'

Another said, 'I'd have put a fiver on myself if I'd known.'

'And that's why I didn't tell you,' snapped JD. 'You'd have ruined the price for the owner.' He cupped a hand and whispered into Barlow's ear. 'Number six in the sixth race.'

Barlow nodded dutifully and walked on. After a few steps he glanced back at JD and his friends. They were looking in his direction and laughing in way that made him doubt the tip for the sixth race.

The Tannoy called for him again as they neared the Owners' Enclosure.

Barlow pointed, first at Wilson and then in the general direction of the Call Box. 'Tell that daft idiot to shut up. I'm here. After that, take up position on the far side of the enclosure.'

Wilson didn't like them being separated but only dared ask, 'What are we looking for, Sergeant?'

'The usual not happening,' growled Barlow and sent him on his way.

Barlow eased himself back through the crowd until he was hard up against the rough canvas of a beer tent. From where he stood he was able to watch the Owners' Enclosure and the people coming and going around it. The smell of roasted hops came through the canvas screen and fortified him against a long stand.

The whole thing about the nobs being robbed at previous point-to-points puzzled him. Something he could never get his head around. In the scuffle of people along the line of bookies, those placing bets or collecting their winnings, the odd missing wallet was understandable and did happen. But from the Owners' Enclosure where everyone knew everyone else?

Barlow passed an enjoyable hour standing in the sun. When he cared to look he could see Wilson at the far side of the enclosure, always on tiptoe, always checking to make sure he hadn't slipped off by himself. On the other side of the canvas, drinkers celebrated or cursed various horses and jockeys. Barlow sensed a rhythm build in the unconnected movements of people as if something was about to happen.

He forgot all about duty and pickpockets when the corner of the canvas tent parted and the barman passed out a complimentary pint. Barlow found something satisfying about a pint in hand and the warm glow of a summer's day on his chest. Not wanting to compromise his authority and be seen drinking in uniform he removed his cap and tucked it under his elbow. After some thought, he took off his jacket as well and hung it over his left arm. All he needed, he felt, was a deckchair to sit on, a handkerchief over his face and life would be perfect.

'There you are,' said a sharp little voice.

Barlow turned to see District Inspector Harvey approach. As if by a miracle, Edward appeared at Barlow's elbow. Edward's face was flushed and his gait unsteady. He looked dishevelled, and mud stained the edge of his old army greatcoat. He'd probably spent the previous night lying under a hedge.

Barlow passed him the beer. 'Hold that for me.'

Harvey reached him, gasping with excitement. 'Barlow, he's struck again, the pickpocket. I ordered you to catch him.'

Buck passing little git, thought Barlow.

Harvey finally registered Barlow's state of undress. 'What are you doing out of uniform?'

'Sort of undercover, sir. I'm less noticeable this way,' said Barlow, his eye on Edward who was making short work of Barlow's pint.

Edward's sip turned into a long drink, the bottom of the glass rising higher and higher. Barlow didn't dare glare in his direction, in case Harvey took it as a personal insult.

'Humph!' snorted Harvey. 'You'll be in civilian clothes permanently if you don't smarten your act.'

Edward placed the glass on a beer crate, gave a salaam of thanks and wisely slipped away into the crowd.

'And let me tell you, Barlow, the Mayor is not amused. The roasting I got, you'd have thought I'd taken his bloody wallet myself.'

The Mayor! Barlow suppressed a smile. Currently, the mayor, Alderman Fetherton, was listed for hearing in the High Court on a charge of watering down milk supplied to schools.

Instead, he nodded in apparent sympathy at Harvey's embarrassment and watched with interest as colour flowed across his normally sallow cheeks. The Mayor had a voice that could be heard over the roar of six diesel engines revving on a frosty morning. Everyone within a hundred yards must have heard Harvey being told off. Barlow put a mental tick against the Mayor's name. Nobody was ignorant to his men and got off with it. Not even with the District Inspector.

9

District Inspector Harvey popped an antacid tablet. A bad sign.

'Barlow, you are to identify and apprehend the pickpocket. No excuses. In the meantime, I will personally guard the gate leading into the Owners' Enclosure and stop all unsavoury characters from entering.'

'Aye,' said Barlow, watching Edward being saluted into the Owners' Enclosure by the gateman. 'That would be about half the people in there already.'

Harvey glared. 'I'm quite aware of your socialist leanings Barlow.'

'A policeman with an opinion? What's the world coming to?' asked a man approaching from the side.

Harvey almost saluted. 'Colonel Packenham, sir.'

Colonel Packenham gave Harvey a friendly poke in the chest. 'Bertram, old boy. Call me Bertram.'

Harvey glowed under the compliment of a budding friendship. Barlow remained at easy attention but he gave Packenham a good up-and-down look out of the corner of his eye. The colonel was of medium height and thin for his age, almost whippet gaunt. Like Harvey, he wore cords and a jacket. Harvey's were brand new. The Colonel's were old and faded, the jacket made shapeless by the weight of this and that in the pockets.

The Colonel acknowledged Barlow's look with one of his own. 'I see you were in the service yourself, Sergeant?'

'The Rifles, sir, but I was seconded to REME as a Technical Officer.'

'You had a commission? Well done.'

'Warrant Officer, sir.'

'Second class,' said Harvey with some degree of satisfaction.

Barlow was torn between talking to the Colonel and watching how Edward's disappearance into the free beer tent occasioned the rapid exit of some of the ladies.

The first one Barlow took note of was Mrs Carberry. Mrs Carberry was a divorcee with a certain reputation. A reputation based more on whispered guesses than hard facts. Even so, wives instinctively put their husbands on a short leash when she was around.

A fair-haired woman followed Mrs Carberry out of the tent and took her arm. The newcomer, a thin woman, a touch below average height, wore a muted red and black dress and sensible court shoes. She was Mrs Harvey, the District Inspector's wife. Even now, her eyes looked for him, forever seeking his approval.

In Barlow's opinion she needn't have bothered. Over Christmas Harvey had done more than give Mrs Carberry a lift to the Round Table Ball. A lot more.

The Colonel was making moves to leave, and Barlow wanted to speak to him. As a fellow member of the British Legion, not that Barlow ever bothered going, it gave him the right to relax and become chatty. 'I presume you were in the Guards, sir?'

'General Service, old boy. One of those funny, whizz-bang units where we got up to things one is still not supposed to talk about.'

'Indeed, sir,' said Barlow with the greatest respect in his voice. 'Home service or did you...?'

'Really, Sergeant,' spluttered Harvey.

Packenham gave Harvey's elbow a friendly squeeze. 'Not a problem, Laurence, old boy.'

Harvey almost cooed with pleasure. Being on first name terms with someone of the Colonel's antecedents meant a lot to him. The Packenham estates on Kells Water dated back to the land grants of the first King James in the early 1600s. Barlow ached to know what had happened to the previous owners, other than rape, murder and pillage.

Wilson came hurrying at a pace just short of a run. 'Sir, the pickpocket, he's struck again. It's Captain Denton, He went to pay for a round of drinks and found his wallet missing.'

'He won't like that,' said Barlow.

His eyes were drawn back to the Owners' Enclosure in time to see a third woman bustling over to join the other two. She was big, buxom and bloated from too much self-indulgence: Mrs Fetherton, the Mayor's wife.

Barlow frowned, puzzled and uneasy. Those three woman together was like bad karma, and where had he heard that expression? Vera probably; she even read books by foreign writers.

And now that he thought about it, where was Vera? Why hadn't she come to the races? Surely, not because of a broken window. Around Mill Row front doors remained unlocked day and night because crime in Ballymena was mostly drunken brawls, *and the Dunlops of course.*

10

Harvey had gone grey faced. The Mayor being robbed was one thing, but the Chairman of the Local Policing Board? Such a loss could blight Harvey's career, stop all future promotions.

Harvey rushed back to the Owners' Enclosure. Colonel Packenham left at the same time.

Barlow frowned as he watched the two men: Harvey heading for the Enclosure, the Colonel taking a stroll through the thickening crowd. The Colonel walked with the easy stride of a man used to the fields, whereas Harvey had the stiff, jerky movements of a mynah bird.

Barlow nudged Wilson. 'Go and see if the DI needs you.'

Wilson hurried after Harvey.

'Come the revolution,' muttered Barlow, looking at the beer glass that Edward had drained to the last dregs. His legs were cramped from standing. He stepped away from the canvas wall and imposed on the barman to keep his jacket and cap safe under the counter.

His route matched that of the Colonel, who walked with his hands clasped behind his back and a smile on his face. Excitement was building for the next race. People were scurrying to the bookies to place their bets or manoeuvring to secure a good vantage point. The bookies' shouted odds took on a high-pitched note. Barlow didn't notice the girl in the pleated skirt and court shoes until she bumped into the Colonel. They exchanged greetings: an apology from her, a pleasantry from him, and they parted.

Barlow followed the girl, picking up his pace to keep her in sight.

She stopped and seemed to take pleasure in watching last-minute punters swirl around the bookies. A young gentleman spoke to her. She looked through him and walked on. She stopped again, obviously looking for someone in the crowd. This time she stared in Barlow's direction.

Barlow bullied up to a bookie. 'Neeson's of Ballymena' it proclaimed in scrolled lettering along the top of the board. He snatched a coin out of his pocket. 'Half a crown on number six.'

'My fortune's made at last,' said Jim Neeson, handing over a docket in return.

'A bad day?' asked Barlow, his eye still on the girl with the pleated skirt.

'It *is* when Geordie Dunlop gives his tenners to another Bookie. Obviously I'm only good for his sixpence each way.'

'A tenner?' said Barlow. He made his voice sound surprised, enticing more information out of Jim Neeson even though other punters were crowding around, waiting to place their bets.

Jim Neeson waved in the direction of the hill overlooking the racecourse. 'Didn't he come hurrying down from there to give it to the Toals?'

'Indeed,' said Barlow as his eye continued to follow the girl and his mind stored two pieces of information. One that Geordie Dunlop was seen heading down the hill. Two that, through the boundary hedge, Barlow could see a line of car windscreens glinting in the sunlight.

The girl now angled across the field, away from the racing. Her imposing height and the bounce of her dark hair made her easy to follow. She crossed the racetrack and used the old pillared gateway to get into the official car park. Barlow edged around until he was between her and the exit.

A group of youths sat on a tartan rug. A hamper lay open in the boot of their Rolls-Royce. The youths were brandishing glasses of champagne and plates of finger-sized bites. Barlow wouldn't have minded some. It had been a long time since breakfast.

Nobody else was near, nobody looking his way. Barlow crouched in order to keep his height below the roofs of the surrounding cars and slipped past the youths without being spotted. Kenny Cameron was one of the crowd and a girl in blue, not Vera, lay with her head on his leg. Barlow remembered Kenny from the night before, asleep with his hand inside Vera's blouse. He poised, ready to charge in and kick the lining out of him.

A hand tapped his shoulder. He shot upright, a curse struggling through clenched teeth. Wilson stood there. 'I nearly lost you, Sergeant, when you moved off. And DI Harvey said…' He clearly didn't want to quote Harvey's exact words.

Barlow knocked Wilson's cap flying. 'And get that bloody jacket off before we're spotted.'

Wilson ducked down with him. 'Who are we after?'

'Shut up and learn.'

He peaked over a bonnet while Wilson struggled out of his jacket. The youths were metronoming the champagne bottle at the girl as an inducement. 'Come and join us,' they called.

She shook her head and walked on, cutting across the lines of cars until she came to an old Humber Pullman. Its rifleman-green paint sparkled from soapy water and elbow grease polishing. However, rust edged the rims of the wheel arches and the tyres were worn down.

Barlow kept watch from a safe distance while the girl did something inside the car.

Wilson joined him, sans jacket. 'Why are we watching her?'

The girl finished doing whatever it was in the car, closed the door carefully and started back the way she had come. Her hair swung and she looked carefree.

Wilson quietly whistled. 'I wouldn't mind getting to know her.'

Barlow supposed she was good looking. And something beyond that: blood, breeding and class.

Still crouched, Wilson struggled into his jacket. 'Do you want me to get her name?'

This modern lot are all the same, sex mad. 'No I don't.' He pointed at the Humber. 'Note down the registration number, then meet me back at the beer tent.'

'Great, that'll give me her address as well.'

Barlow sighed. 'Son, that one could have you for breakfast and wouldn't even spit out the pips.'

11

Barlow held back Wilson's enthusiasm until the girl with the bouncy hair was well past them.

'Now you can go. Don't get too close, don't let her see you following her. Don't just accidently-on-purpose make her acquaintance, and be at the beer tent in ten minutes.'

Wilson was gone in a flash. Barlow noted that there were no worries this time about orders to dog his Station Sergeant's heels. Not that the girl needed following, but he wanted a bit of private time with Kenny Cameron.

He chose a curving route back to the racecourse that took him past the Rolls-Royce. Kenny saw him coming. He slid out from under the girl's head and got to his feet. He stood uneasily before Barlow, his face flushed.

'Where's Vera?' asked Barlow, making his question as pointed as possible.

'She didn't come.' Barlow frowned and Kenny hurried his explanation. 'She rang and said something had come up.'

Vera ring? They didn't have a phone in the house, so she must have gone to the call box. 'Did she say what?'

'No. I was out, you see. Mother took the call.'

Kenny's friends were watching, expecting a row. The girl in blue had got to her feet as well. She wore a matching blue ribbon in her hair and had the same name, Angela, and the same pouty face of her grandmother. A grandmother so "grand" she'd walk through a policeman rather than walk around him.

Vera's problem and she has to deal with it.

Rather than say the wrong thing, Barlow walked on. A race was just starting. He hurried across the racetrack and went back to the beer tent.

Barlow collected his uniform from under the bar counter. Pulled on his jacket, buttoned it carefully and tugged it straight. Squared the cap on his head. Not for him the guards' slope of the brim as favoured by the younger men. They sported it when they thought he wasn't looking.

The offer of a free drink was refused even though the glass was already under the nozzle.

'Not when I'm wearing my cap,' he told the barman. 'It puts a man on duty, but thank you kindly.'

Wilson was already at his heel, gasping like an eager puppy. 'Sergeant, do you want me to keep following her?'

'Just follow me,' growled Barlow and led the way back through the car park. They took up position on either side of the gateway leading onto the main road.

'What are we doing here, Sergeant?'

'Waiting,' said Barlow and listened for the result of the race.

The Tannoy crackled. 'Here is the result of the sixth race. First, number six…'

The price had been five to one, against. That's five half-crowns and my half-crown back, and a free pint waiting for me at the Bridge Bar.

JD had given him that tip, he remembered, and he'd been suspicious of it the way JD and his friends had acted afterwards. He wished now he'd bet a fiver. *That would be…* The missed opportunity was too much to bear thinking about.

People started to drift to the car park, anxious to get away before the rush home began. Wilson was on his toes again, this time his gaze fixed on the Humber Pullman. Barlow put him on point duty.

'It isn't busy enough, Sergeant.'

'It'll stop you from acting daft.'

Barlow was hardly back at his post when he spotted the Humber come edging out of the field. He flagged it down and walked around to the driver's side. Gave a rolling signal with his hand for the window to be lowered.

The driver smiled pleasantly as he obliged. 'Yes, Sergeant Barlow?' It was Colonel Packenham.

Barlow looked at the young lady in the passenger seat. The girl with the bounce of black hair and the pleated skirt.

'Tell me, Colonel, would this young lady happen to be your daughter?'

'Why do you ask?'

'She's a well-finished young lady with the prospects of a good marriage.'

Packenham frowned. 'I fail to see the point you are trying to make.' He put the car into first gear. 'Now if you will excuse me.'

Barlow drew his truncheon. 'We don't want any unpleasantness, do we, sir?'

Packenham pointedly released the handbrake. 'The unpleasantness will be between you and Mr Harvey if you delay me any longer.'

The driver of a Ford Popular stuck behind the Humber blew his horn. More drivers took up the protest.

Barlow shouted for Wilson and pointed at the Ford. 'We know his horn is working. Make sure everything else is.'

He turned back to Packenham. 'Colonel, wartime volunteers are a fairly ignorant bunch. Even so, you'd think that someone connected with whizz-bangs would know that an "army technical officer" is a status, not a rank. I was part of the UXB section, a bomb disposal expert.'

Packenham didn't even blink. 'I was just being polite.'

'Just as you were when your daughter bumped into you on the field. You were so polite you pretended not to know each other.' He leaned in closer. 'While you passed her Captain Denton's wallet. That way, you can never be caught with more than one on you.'

He opened the door and indicated for Packenham to step out. 'That's why you always steal from other nobs. People you know. People who'd want to believe that you found the wallet lying on the ground and picked it up.'

Packenham had gone white. 'You've no proof.'

Barlow pointed. 'If the young lady would care to open the glove compartment?

'Daddy!' said the daughter. She started to cry.

'Sergeant, we needed… This last few years… things have been very difficult.' He reached over, took his daughter's hand and squeezed it. 'She's been very loyal.'

He got out of the car and closed the door. Dropped his voice. 'Have you a daughter?'

'What's that got to do with it?'

'If you had, you'd understand.'

Barlow didn't reply but sent Wilson to a nearby house to ring for a patrol car. Meantime, he had the Colonel and his daughter to step out of the car while he searched it and found the missing wallets in the glove compartment. He put them in his pocket, then thought to tell the Colonel and his daughter to stand apart. The Colonel stood with one hand on the roof of his car, looking across the fields. The daughter's body shook hard and she fought back tears with a miniscule handkerchief. Barlow offered her his handkerchief. She refused with a look of scorn accumulated over multiple generations of lording over tenant farmers.

Wilson came back. 'A patrol car's on its way.' He saw the daughter with the sodden handkerchief and offered his own. This time, she did not refuse.

He sidled up to Barlow. 'Sergeant, how did you know it was the Colonel?'

It was the end of a sun-laden day. Barlow had free pint waiting for him in the pub and winnings to pick up from Jim Neeson, the Turf Accountant. He exhaled slowly for effect. 'Like I told you, son. It's when the usual doesn't happen. When girls and boys meet, they eye each other up, chat. The Colonel's daughter avoided people of her own age. She cut them dead or made an excuse and walked on. The rest was guesswork and good luck.'

'What has the daughter got to do with it?' asked Wilson.

Barlow could have cut his tongue out. 'Nothing, son. Absolutely nothing.'

12

Barlow settled Colonel Packenham in an interview room. Then he asked WPC Day to bring the Colonel a cup of tea and to sit with him. The man had admitted to stealing, so there was no need to be discourteous in their dealings with him.

Harvey nearly had a fit when he heard that the pickpocket was none other than his newest best friend.

'Not a word, not a syllable are you to speak to the Colonel, until I get there,' he spluttered down the phone. 'Colonel Packenham a pickpocket? Ridiculous! He's a deputy Lord Lieutenant of the county.'

Barlow had driven the Colonel to the station in the Humber while Gillespie brought in Wilson and the daughter in the patrol car. Separating suspects was normal procedure. It prevented them from concocting a cover story. Wilson and the girl had now arrived.

Her patrician disdain echoed throughout the building. 'You're an ignorant flatfoot even if you do have a university degree.'

'And you're one spoiled…'

At that point Barlow hustled Wilson into the kitchen. 'Shut up or you'll be accused of bullying a suspect.'

'Bullying! That one? Ha!'

Barlow closed the door on him and asked a WPC to escort the girl into another interview room. At the sight of the cramped room and the old deal table, scuffed chairs and the high window, much of her temper drained away. Even so, she sat poised, as if attending a function at Hillsborough Castle: knees together, legs at a slight angle.

'We'll get you a cup of tea,' said Barlow.

'I don't want tea. How dare you insult my father in this way; humiliating him. He's an old man and he's not well.'

Her lips trembled and her eyes filled with tears.

He closed the door on her. Turned to find Gillespie standing with a grin on his face.

'You should have heard them, Sarge, the whole way in. They sounded like me and the wife on a Saturday night.'

Barlow grunted. 'The last time you raised your voice to your wife she clocked you one. And that was on your honeymoon.'

He went back to the kitchen and let Wilson out. Wilson's jaw was set hard. He was still in a temper at Barlow accusing him of bullying the Colonel's daughter.

Barlow handed him a brown envelope. 'The stolen wallets are in that. Your case, so start the paperwork.'

'My case?' Wilson's temper faded. 'Thanks Sergeant, I won't let you down.'

He rushed off to find a desk to work on. Barlow stopped him with a shout. 'Son, if you ever treat a suspect like that again. I don't care how annoying they are, I don't care what they're alleged to have done or not done...' He jabbed a finger at Wilson to emphasise his annoyance. 'You'll be off the force.'

He turned on Gillespie. 'And you should have known better.'

'I wouldn't mind that Judas copping it.'

'What do you know about it?'

Gillespie's face flushed with temper. 'He blabbed on fellow coppers, that's what he did. The sergeant's in jail, and he'd already spent five years in Changi as a prisoner of war.'

Barlow said, 'Where he learned about battering people on the soles of their feet. They nearly killed the man.' He heard

Harvey's voice coming from the front desk and thought he should get there in a hurry. 'I'd have turned you in for the same thing.'

'But we know you're a bastard,' said Gillespie. He hurried away, his voice trailing back. 'Sorry.'

'You owe me a salmon for that crack,' shouted Barlow.

Gillespie glanced around. 'Poached?'

'When did you ever spend money on a licence?'

13

Harvey was having one of his tantrums. His face looked like boiled lobster, bright pink shading to purple.

'Barlow, this is ridiculous. Colonel Packenham of all people.'

Barlow's hand twitched to smack the man. 'Talk to him yourself, sir.'

'Believe me, I shall.'

Harvey bustled off. Barlow decided that a long, thoughtful sit was in order and wandered down to the kitchen. He poured himself a cup of tea, and sat swaying to and fro in the old rocking chair he'd recovered from a pile of builder's rubble.

WPC Day joined him.

'What about the daughter?' he asked.

'The DI sent Miss Sweet Innocence home.' She grimaced and pretended to throw up. 'Honest to God, he acted like a lapdog around her.'

'And the Colonel?'

She scraped crumbs off a digestive biscuit with a fingernail. 'Papa Bear, I don't want you getting into trouble with the DI.' Hesitated. 'But I think you should take a look at the Colonel.'

'You think?' He trusted WPC Day's instincts, in spite of her having men, marriage and children on her mind instead of the job. The man she was supposed to marry, a second-hand car salesman, had "postponed" the wedding while he settled himself into a new job in England.

He concealed his sympathy with a scowl. 'You are studying for that sergeant's exam?'

'Sort of.'

She left and he finished his tea. Washed the cup, wiped it dry and put it back on its hook. Delaying tactics, he knew. His walk to the interview room was equally slow, his knock gentle.

A voice snapped, 'Come in.'

He opened the door.

'What do you want, Barlow?'

'If you could spare me a minute, sir.'

He pointedly held the door open. Harvey rose to his feet reluctantly. The Colonel was sitting bolt upright in his chair. He acknowledged Barlow's presence with a nod.

He appears to be all right, Barlow thought. Perhaps a shade of too much colour on his cheeks? But, like WPC Day, Barlow had this instinct for anticipating trouble. Especially when he remembered how the Colonel had balanced himself against the car after his arrest.

'What?' asked Harvey when they moved out into the corridor.

'Sir, Colonel Packenham is an old man and an important one at that. Right now he's under a lot of stress. I was wondering if we should call in the police doctor. Just to be sure, if you see what I mean?

Harvey looked pleased. 'You're right. Show people that we care about those in our charge.'

'I'll do it straightaway,' said Barlow and headed off to the Enquiry Office and the phone before Harvey could have second thoughts.

The police doctor arrived. Police doctors tend to be uncaring butchers and this one was worse than most. However, he looked pensive when he emerged from the interview room.

'I'm not happy about the Colonel,' he told Barlow. 'He's got a fairly high temperature. The Colonel says it's his monthly bout of malaria and he has tablets at home. I'd like to admit him to hospital for observation, but the stubborn old goat won't go.'

'What then?'

'Get him out of here before he croaks on us.'

Easier said than done, Barlow discovered. The daughter must be still on her way home – no one was answering the phone there. The Colonel's house was miles outside Ballymena, which meant coordinating police cars from different districts in order to transfer the old boy.

Wilson snapped to attention. 'Sergeant, I have a car. I could take Colonel home.'

Constables with their own cars? *What's the world coming to?*, wondered Barlow.

He looked at the clock. Eight already, knocking off time and he still hadn't heard from Vera. He signed himself out and hurried home.

14

A wall of hate hit Barlow as he walked in the door of his own house. Vera sat scrunched up in a corner of the new settee, shoulders rounded, arms folded as if in pain.

'Da,' she said, her voice almost a whisper. 'Ma's home.'

Maggie? Home?

He went so tight with tension he had to turn his body rather than his neck to look at his wife. She sat on a wooden chair at the window. Upright, with ninety-degree bends at knee and hip. Her face held – he could never describe it other than a blackness. As if her face betrayed her mood in shades that varied between cream and heavy grey. Today's colour burned acid in his stomach.

'Maggie, love, it's great to have you home again.'

He stared at her hands. They sat folded on her lap, the fingers working in and out of each other. Nothing there and no knife on the table. She was wearing her old black coat and it a June evening. *Could she have a knife concealed in that?*

'Isn't it great, Da, they've let Ma home.' Vera's words rang with false enthusiasm.

Great nothing. His wife's very stillness chilled him. How did she get out? *She must have escaped.*

'On a visit?' he asked his daughter.

'No Da, to stay.'

'To stay? Wonderful!'

He went over to give Maggie a welcome home hug. She shrank away from his touch. *Oh dear God, she's no better.* 'Maggie, love, let me take your coat.'

He stepped back to give her room. Maggie slowly stood, her eyes fixed on something past him. He didn't dare turn and figure out what she was looking at. Maggie unbuttoned her coat and ignored his hand already out to take it. Folded it over a chair instead. *No knife hidden in the coat and she wasn't sitting on one either.*

Now he dared turn around. Vera looked like she'd been glued to the seat for hours. Poor kid. *If only I'd taken the hint.* That call to the Camerons was a cry for help. Of course she couldn't tell Mrs Cameron what was really wrong. She'd enough problems dealing with the woman already.

And as for the flaming Jack Russell. Instead of being on guard to protect Vera, Toby was stretched out on the other half of the settee, snoring, his head resting in Vera's knee. He seemed to sense Barlow's glare because he opened one eye, bared his teeth and went straight back to sleep. *Some flaming guard dog that.*

'So they've let you home?' He asked Maggie.

He knew he was fixated on that, but Maggie was back to sitting upright in the chair. With evening already drawing in, he dreaded the night ahead. Wouldn't dare sleep.

'A water tank burst in the ment… the hospital. It brought down ceilings and things. They had to close some wards,' said Vera.

He made himself aim the question at Maggie rather than talk about her to Vera. 'So you're finished at the hospital?'

No reply.

'Starting Monday, Ma's to go to the outpatients every day for occupational therapy.'

Monday! That left Sunday and two nights without sleep before the hospital realised they'd made a mistake and read-mitted her. And him on twelve-hour shifts at work. 'You'll be bringing home trays next and those crocheted things you put on armchairs.'

No response.

Outside a car horn beeped.

Vera stood up. 'That's for me.' She seemed relieved, yet afraid to go. If she hadn't been there that last time he'd have died, bled to death right where he now stood. Even the thought of Maggie with a knife made his wounds itch.

'I'd forgotten. You're babysitting tonight for the Dentons.'

Thank God for that. If anything happens, at least she'll be safe.

He looked at Vera properly for the first time. She wore a three-quarter length lime green dress, with her hair brushed back bouffant style. It gave her height, made less of her chunky body.

'Dressed up like that?' he asked.

'Camilla wants me to join the guests once the children are settled.'

'You call her Camilla?'

'She told me to.'

His daughter a guest at a party run by the Dentons? An invitation half the blue-rinse brigade in the town would kill for. And on first-name terms with Camilla Denton, whose family had reached the upper echelons of society long before they built their Georgian mansion in 1805. Camilla Denton, married to Captain Charles Denton, owner and managing director of the Ballymena Brewery Company, Chairman of the Local Policing Board. For a moment, Barlow forgot about Maggie and wondered at the hidden life of his teenage daughter.

The car horn sounded again. A double beep this time.

Vera scooped up an overnight bag. 'I'd better go.'

He went to the door with her. Whispered. 'Your Ma…' And didn't know what to say.

Vera seemed to read his mind. She whispered back. 'I don't know, Da. She seemed okay at the start, then all of a sudden she went funny.' Her voice dropped even lower. 'There are six sharp knives in the scullery. I've hidden them under the dishcloths.'

God Almighty, what are we doing with six?

He wanted to hug her worries away, to rumple her hair and tell her that she had an overactive imagination. 'Vera, burst water tanks or not, they wouldn't have released your mother if they thought she was a danger to herself, let alone to anyone else.'

'I suppose.'

At least he'd given her a doubt to hold onto. Wished he believed it himself.

15

Captain Denton stepped out of his Rolls-Royce and held the front passenger door open for Vera. When she had settled in and the door was closed, Denton leaned towards Barlow, and in an almost-whisper asked: 'Colonel Packenham is the chief suspect…are you absolutely sure?'

'Positive.'

'Is there any possibility it might not be him? It could prove very helpful, if that were the case.'

'In what way?'

'Packenham is on the County Council.'

'So?'

'Some big contracts are coming up shortly. He'd make sure they were allocated honestly.'

Barlow shrugged. 'It was your wallet.'

Denton nodded and got into the Rolls. Barlow watched as the car disappeared over the brow of the hill. *Done honestly and you gain,* he thought.

Maybe Denton wasn't the most honest man in the world, but he was by no means a crook. Anything he did benefited the town and his workers.

16

Barlow drew breath and turned to go back into the house. He noticed for the first time that the smashed front window of his house had been replaced. Terry Esler, he guessed. A near neighbour. He'd owe him for the cost of the glass and the putty. No charge for labour. A word of thanks, a pint at the weekend and they'd be square. What with Edward's weekend pint still to be paid for, Barlow's next visit to the Bridge Bar would cost him a fortune.

If I'm still alive.

He went back into the house to find Toby sitting at Maggie's feet. Her hand rested on his head. Toby again bared his teeth, this time a faint growl rumbled.

'I should have put you in the Dog Pound,' said Barlow glad to find something to say. Not that he would ever think of getting rid of the dog. It had saved his life, if only by accident, when he was about to be shot by its owner.

Barlow sat in his own chair but remained alert because Maggie had been in the house on her own while he was out talking to Captain Denton. He'd have to check the where-abouts of the six knives before he dared turn his back on her.

Maggie's gaze was as intense as ever. It came straight at him.

'The weather's been pretty good recently,' he said.

No response.

'And there were several local winners at today's point-to-point.'

As if he'd never spoken.

'I got a tip for the sixth race, so I won a few bob.'

Still nothing.

'I thought we could blow it on a dinner – to celebrate you getting home.'

Her gaze, he realised, wasn't aimed at him as such, but seemed to curve around him. *That bloody settee Vera bought. Maggie hates change.*

'Maybe try out the new Chinese at the State cinema? You, me and Vera?'

Not a sound, not a movement. The dog bared its teeth again. *Two against one.*

Outside, dusk settled in, making Maggie's movements indistinct. He rubbed at his wounds. *Like that last time.*

'Look, Maggie love, Vera didn't mean any harm. She bought the settee as a coming home present for you, didn't even tell me. She borrowed the money from the Credit Union, every penny, and now she's got to pay it back.'

Somehow or other he'd caught her attention. He could understand her being worried about Vera getting into debt. He didn't like it either.

He got down the Credit Union book from behind the candlestick on the mantelpiece. While on his feet he slid the kettle onto the hotplate, to make them a cup of tea. Sat across the table from Maggie and tried to explain the workings of the Credit Union. How they made you borrow money instead of taking out your own.

'Their idea seems to be that if you empty out your savings, you'll never put it back. But, if you borrow money, you'll make a point of repaying it.' He scratched his head. 'So you're paying interest on money that's already yours.'

It made sense to him in an oddball way that he couldn't explain. His formal schooling had ended at age twelve when he ran away from the Workhouse. He'd lived unnoticed, as he thought, in a ruined gate lodge on the Adair estate. But Edward knew he was there and made sure the estate workers left him in peace.

'Does it make any sort of sense to you, Maggie?'

It would if she was paying attention. Before their marriage and Vera's birth, she'd worked in an office. He knew she was listening because the dark aura around her eased even as night settled into the small room.

He got up and switched on the light. Sat down again at the table. *What else to talk about?* Vera was always a safe subject.

He told her that Vera had finished school. That she was waiting for her Senior Certificate results. 'She'll do well, you wait and see.' Meantime she was working in Woolworths.

Without intending to, he drifted on to talking about Kenny. He left out about finding them in intimate clutches and his worries about Vera getting pregnant. Instead, he talked about Mrs Cameron's attempts to break up the romance. How it was bound to happen anyway when Kenny went to university.

'Our wee girl's going to be hurt, and there's nothing we can do about it.'

His voice shook with fear for Vera. At least he blamed it on that rather than the coming night with Maggie home. He made the forgotten tea and gave Maggie her own special mug, one Vera had bought for her in Hogg's china shop.

Maggie took a sip and then stood up. Spoke for the first time. 'I'll go to bed.'

Her aura really had improved, he could almost see a bit of colour in it.

'Aye, you must be tired. It's been a long day.'

She used the outside toilet. He heard pills rattle in the scullery and a tap run. Then she came back and went up the stairs without another word. He wondered about the pills. Could she be trusted with them? What if she slipped a handful into his tea? *Bumped me off that way.*

He sat and listed to the creaks of the old wooden floorboards in the house. Her feet on the stairs. Her footsteps as she crossed Vera's bedroom – more a large landing – to get to their bedroom. The singing of the springs as she crept into bed.

He went and checked the knives under the dishcloths. Still six and they looked undisturbed. Opened the front door to let Toby out. Toby ran up and down the millrace across the way, seeking out rats. Gave up and came back into the house, slipped past Barlow and ran up the stairs, nails click–clicking on the linoleum.

'Don't you disturb her,' whispered Barlow, furious.

The dog scampered across Vera's room into the bedroom. A scrabble of a jump, then silence. Barlow waited for Maggie's protest at the dog's arrival, but none came.

'Bloody brute.'

Toby had never shared his bed. But that night Barlow had no objection to the dog providing a barrier between him and Maggie.

The night was warm. The house fuggy from the heat radiating off the range. He was dreading the hours ahead. Vera was overnighting at Denton's, so he could always sleep in her bed. But what about the next night and the next and the one after that? *Maybe we could rent another house: one with three bedrooms and locks on all the doors.* But also knew the change would upset Maggie too much.

He closed the front door behind him and walked away from the house and his fears. Not too far and not too fast. *A bit of a dander.*

The odd vehicle passed. One caught his attention, cut through his drifting thoughts. A green Bedford van.

17

Barlow could only watch as the Bedford van drove past him and on down the street.

Where's it going? Where's it coming from? He looked around, unfocused. *Where am I?* Everything looked familiar and yet…

A name above a doorway caught his eye. McCann's. He was at McCann's pub on the Galgorm Road. He watched the Bedford sweep past the police station. 'Cheeky buggers.'

He took to his heels. Ran past Morton's Mill and burst through the front door of the police station. Pierson was in the Enquiry Office, head in a newspaper. Pierson swept the newspaper under the counter before he looked up, a "yes?" forming on his lips.

The newspaper issue Barlow would deal with later. Right now. 'Where's the nearest patrol car?'

'Out near Broughshane, at a minor shunt.'

Totally in the wrong direction.

'And the other one?'

'Gillespie took the DI to Belfast. He's not back yet.'

'Shite!' roared Barlow even as he wondered what had taken the District Inspector to Belfast on a Saturday night.

He pointed to the phone. 'That Bedford van passed me again, heading towards Galgorm. Get on the phone. See if some other station can pull it in.'

He stopped talking, frustrated at not being in on the chase. Pierson, he noticed, had to consult the phone book for the numbers of the local police stations. *He should know those off by heart.*

Barlow suddenly remembered something. 'There's an old Austin A5 outside the door. Who does that belong to?'

'Wilson,' said Pierson, like it was a bad word.

Barlow put his head around the counter and roared down the corridor. 'Wilson!'

Wilson's head appeared at a door, a "what now?" expression on his face.

'Come on.'

Wilson scowled.

'Bring your car keys.'

Wilson's face brightened.

'And take that look off your face.'

'What look, Sergeant?

'All of them.'

He hurried Wilson out the door and into his car. At least the car was faced in the right direction. He pointed up the road towards the railway arch. 'Now drive.'

Wilson indicated and pulled out, changed smoothly through the gears.

Barlow gritted his teeth. 'This isn't a driving test. Put the foot down.'

'We're in a speed limit.'

His hands itched to take the young officer by the throat. Instead he roared. 'Drive!'

He watched the needle as the speed climbed. Forty. Fifty. At sixty the needle quivered to a halt. 'Can't this thing go any faster?'

'Not with a heavy load.'

He let that crack pass and stared out into the darkness ahead. Still no sign of the van. Mature trees and the odd house showing lights sped by. This was where many of the City Club members lived in their grand houses. He hoped the hole in

Wilson's exhaust had created enough noise to disturb their sleep. *Maybe even waken them up.*

Dan's Road came up.

He made a quick decision. 'Go left.'

"Go left" because any Belfast man trying to avoid the main road back to the city would have to take Dan's Road. Either that or be half way to Derry before they could cut around the far side of Lough Neagh.

Dan's Road, then the Toome Road. Now they were deep into the countryside, and still no sign of the van. Cars passed them going in the opposite direction. He wished he'd a way of asking them if they'd seen anything.

Toome, he remembered, had the Bann River flowing through it and the police station was set right beside the one and only bridge. At Slatt he pointed for Wilson to turn off the Toome Road and take the bog road to Randalstown. The A5 shook and its springs squealed as it bounced from bump to bump.

'You haven't asked me who or what we're chasing,' said Barlow.

'Sergeants tell me what they want me to know. Usually, they tell me to mind my own business.'

The boy had had a rough time at other stations. Nevertheless, Barlow intended to sort that attitude. But later. Now wasn't the time. 'We believe that a green Bedford van with a Belfast registration was involved in the robbery of Mo Hunt's house.'

Wilson looked his way, ready to say something, but the car hit a pothole and he had to fight a vicious swing to the left. They scraped a high grass bank, yet somehow managed to stay on the road.

Barlow ostentatiously wiped sweat from his brow and continued. 'The van's in town again tonight, so the chances are they've robbed some other poor sucker.'

'But no one's reported a robbery.'

'Half the town's away on holidays. So half the town wouldn't know about it until they got back.'

And that was something that puzzled him. The men in the green van had robbed two empty houses on two consecutive nights. That went way beyond luck. He selected an imaginary sweet – an antacid tablet to counter Wilson's driving – and had a good think about it.

Wilson sat humped over the steering wheel, fighting to keep the car on the road. They crossed Kells Water, their speed dropping to below forty. Chugged up the next hill in third gear. The speed dropped even further.

Barlow said, 'That rich father of yours. He might have bought you a decent car when he was at it.'

Wilson glared back.

Up ahead of them the lights of an oncoming car illuminated a high-sided vehicle. Barlow said a private prayer that he'd been right, that it was the van.

Wilson said, 'How did you do it, Sergeant?'

'Do what?'

'Guess which road they'd take.'

'I thought you didn't ask questions?'

The engine roared as the car crested the hill. Wilson slammed the gearstick into fourth and stamped the accelerator to the floor. The speed climbed agonisingly towards fifty. The oncoming car passed the van. The van was the right shape for a Bedford, but Barlow and Wilson were too far back to see what colour it was. The oncoming car blurred past them. Now it was just Wilson's car, the van and a straight road ahead. The humps and bumps rattled the A5 in every direction. Barlow kept his jaw clenched tight to avoid chipping teeth on the ricochets.

The van was travelling at less than thirty miles an hour. *God help them, but they're afraid of breaking the china and glass they stole.* Wilson slowed and gave it full beam. Definitely a green Bedford. They still couldn't read the number plate, not even the first letter this time.

Barlow unclenched his jaw to say, 'Blacked out, the crafty buggers.' He nodded ahead. 'Pull out. Get level with the driver.'

Wilson obediently swung the car to the right. The A5 accelerated slowly.

They came level with the van's rear wheel, then the van driver accelerated away from them.

'Faster, son.'

'It's going off a cylinder.'

Right enough, the A5 was shuddering like it had St Vitus Dance.

The van was getting away from them. Barlow heard the smash of something fragile as it hit a particularly bad pothole.

Wilson hauled in fast to avoid an oncoming car. Then moved out again.

The van was now outlined against the street lighting of Randalstown. The cylinder came back on line and the A5 surged ahead. Caught up with the van. Repeated flashes of full beam and beeps on the horn were ignored.

'I'll get ahead of them, Sergeant. Force them to stop.'

Barlow shuddered at the keenness of youth. 'Don't even think about it.'

'Easy peasy,' said Wilson. The A5 surged again. They came level with the rear wheel, then halfway along its side. The van went into a vicious rear-wheel skid and slammed into the A5, then straightened and drove on.

Hit by the heavier vehicle, the A5 reared up and mounted a ditch. Barlow didn't have time to brace himself as they crashed through a hawthorn hedge, with barbed wire whipping and snapping around his open window. The car crunched into a ploughed field and came to a halt with the wheels buried in soft earth.

Barlow was sure he had died. Then pain from bruised arms and legs exploded across his body. *Death no.* He looked over at Wilson. *Murder maybe?*

Then he remembered that crack about heavy weights in the car. 'I'll tell you something for nothing, son. You're driving is shite.'

18

Barlow and Wilson trudged the two miles to Randalstown police station. Battered at the door until the Duty Constable woke up and let them in. No, the Randalstown police didn't know anything about a Bedford van, green or otherwise. If the Ballymena station had rung, they'd have been on the lookout for it.

'If we'd the time,' said the Duty Constable, an old cynic with more years served than even Barlow himself. 'Things never stop around here, what with speeding tractors and unlicensed cows on the road.'

So Pierson hadn't rung Randalstown, *the idiot*. Where else had he missed? *Had he bothered his head ringing anyone at all?*

Wilson hardly spoke while they waited for the duty car to come and pick them up. Sat and sulked.

The old constable raised an enquiring eyebrow at Barlow and didn't offer Wilson a second cup of tea. Tactfully, he'd made tea instead of producing the customary bottle of poteen.

'You'll be sore in the morning,' he told Barlow.

'This is the morning,' said Barlow, listening to the birds' uncertain start to the dawn chorus.

Constable Gillespie picked them up at four. They stopped at the crash site on the way past. 'You've a broken axel,' said Gillespie cheerily. 'Probably the sump as well.'

Wilson's bad mood deepened. He told Barlow. 'It's your fault. Only qualified police drivers are authorised to take part in high-speed pursuits.'

Barlow spat out the imaginary sweet he was chewing. 'I didn't hear you objecting too much at the time.' He pointed at Wilson's waist. 'And where's your Webley pistol? Outside the station, in uniform, you carry your gun at all times.'

Wilson said, 'I don't see yours either.'

'Son, I'm off duty, in bed sleeping the sleep of the just.'

'Girls, girls,' said Gillespie.

They climbed into the police car. Wilson in the back. Gillespie drove slowly along the bog road.

'I'd like to get home before lunchtime,' Barlow said.

Gillespie ignored him and twisted around in the seat until he could see Wilson. 'You're on morning shift all this week. What were you doing in the station anyway?'

'Paperwork on the Colonel Packenham case,' replied Wilson, his voice devoid of enthusiasm.

Barlow nudged Gillespie to continue with the questions.

'You were at that all evening?'

'I was back late. I couldn't sleep.'

A twitch of worry started in Barlow's stomach. He sucked on a Mint Imperial for a moment to steady his thoughts. 'It took you all evening to drive to the Packenham estate and back?'

'The Colonel, he insisted that I have a cup of tea before I started home.' Wilson sounded defensive. 'Eleanor had dinner ready and... well they made it impossible to refuse.'

Wilson associating with a known criminal? Mr Stickler to the Rules Wilson risked compromising the Packenham case by ... He'd only do that if he was after bigger fish. Like Barlow himself for not charging the daughter with concealing the stolen wallets.

Barlow realised something else. Wilson had referred to the daughter as "Eleanor" which meant they were now on speaking terms. Which meant that Wilson now had his feet under the Packenham table. Which meant that the case against the Colonel could be dropped and the daughter guaranteed immunity from prosecution, in exchange for testifying that Barlow knew that the daughter was involved in the theft of the wallets and had failed to report it to his superiors.. He'd be in all sorts of bother, and this time he couldn't depend on the tacit support of Captain Denton. Denton needed the Colonel on the County Council board. How else could he ensure that he and his cronies made another fortune on the backs of the ordinary people?

He said, 'I hope the wine wasn't corked.'

'Of course not. It was vin…' Wilson went suddenly silent.

Barlow said, 'Watch yourself with that Packenham woman. There are well-honed teeth behind that smile.'

Gillespie dropped Barlow at his door. He stumbled upstairs, undressing as he went. Maggie was at the far end of the bed, turned away from him. The dog lay curled into the bend in her knees. It growled softly. Barlow ignored it and crawled between the sheets. Even lying down his head spun from tiredness.

The knives! I never checked.

In a minute, he told himself. Just a minu…

Liquid poured down Barlow's face and bubbled around his mouth. A weight crushed his chest. *She's stabbed me again.* He forced an eye open against death. A tongue slobbered his face and he quickly shut it again. Toby was standing on his chest.

'Get off, you bugger.'

He put an arm up to protect himself from more licks and pushed the dog off. Toby retreated back to Maggie's side of the bed and lay down.

Barlow patted his pounding heart calm. 'Do that again and you're for the pound.'

The dog bared teeth.

Barlow listened to Maggie's breathing: deep and even, so she wasn't pretending to sleep. He couldn't remember the last time she'd slept through a full night. Realised something else. Going by the way the sun angled through the window, sparkling the old iron bedstead it was... His head whipped around to the bedside clock. Nearly seven-thirty, he should be at the station for the changeover. The main working sifts in the police were from eight to eight. Incoming shift sergeants came in early and the outgoing sergeant stayed late to ensure a smooth changeover.

He rolled out of bed, every muscle in his body complaining about having to move. *Wilson and his flaming driving.* Collected his clothes and slipped downstairs. Toby followed him and accepted a pat. 'Oh now we're friends,' he said, wondering how the dog knew his shift hours and when he should be up. 'Don't get it wrong tomorrow morning,' he informed Toby as he let him out. Tomorrow he was off duty. He didn't want to see or hear from anyone before nine o'clock at the earliest.

Washed, dressed and shaved and feeling every day of his age he cycled to work. Pierson looked pointedly at the clock as he came through the door. It read seven forty-eight.

'Do we know yet who's been burgled?' asked Barlow.

'No, and let me tell you, the DI is not amused.'

'Then stop telling him your lousy jokes.'

It had been a quiet night, the cells, for once, mercifully empty. Barlow nodded. He liked the idea of a nice quiet day.

The Incident Book said that Pierson had telephoned Antrim station and asked them to keep a lookout for the green van.

Barlow pointed at the entry and, with anger carefully controlled, asked. 'Why only Antrim?'

'Going to Belfast from here you have to go through Antrim.'

Barlow pointed at a map of Northern Ireland on the wall and made a sweeping gesture with his hand. 'If you ever got a brain you'd be dangerous.' He drew breath, ready to give Pierson a roasting.

The phone rang. Pierson dived for it. 'Police, Ballymena.' He listened and handed it over to Barlow. 'It's your daughter for you.'

'Hi love.'

In the background he could hear Camilla Denton's voice raised in exasperation and the argumentative voices of four lively children.

'Da, I rang earlier, you weren't in.'

Vera's voice shook and he sensed tears close. She'd had him dead, murdered in his own bed.

'I slept in,' he said like it was the most natural thing in the world.

'And Ma?'

He sensed the change in her voice, much of the tension gone.

'Still asleep when I left.'

'Did she take her tablets?'

'She did last night.'

'Did you watch her do it?'

He felt like a schoolboy caught out. He should have watched Maggie take her tablets. He'd caught her at it before, washing them down the plughole. *What was I thinking of?* And as for this morning's tablets? God only knew if she'd take them or not.

The front door snapped open. Harvey burst in, his face mottled with fury.

'Barlow, my office. Now!'

Harvey stormed on.

Barlow said, 'I've got to go, love,' and felt guilty. Vera needed to talk and she deserved the time.

He tugged his uniform straight and hand-brushed his hair tidy. Followed Harvey, wondering what had made the District Inspector so incensed.

The office door had slammed behind Harvey. Barlow knocked and waited until he heard the shout 'enter' before opening the door. Stood at attention before the desk. Wished he still had the old District Inspector and his Victorian furniture instead of this jumped-up pipsqueak and his trendy office trash.

'You wanted to see me, sir.'

'Last night.'

'Was very eventful, sir.'

'Was badly handled, a total overreaction by you.'

'Sir?'

'And let me tell you, Barlow. I should be preparing for church. Instead, I find myself dealing with another of your disastrous decisions.'

Barlow nodded to himself. So that was why Harvey was dressed in a fresh laundered suit and a shirt barely out of the box.

'On Friday night you saw a green van which *might* have been involved in a robbery, but you failed to get its number. Last night you saw a green van, assumed it was the same one, assumed that someone else had been robbed and started a wild goose chase.'

Rather than get into an argument and be accused of insubordination, he decided to play it safe. 'Sir, I hope I was wrong. I'd hate to have somebody else robbed blind, like Mo Hunt.' A neat reminder that Harvey's friends were the ones most likely to be burgled.

'You'd do better hoping that you're right.' Harvey's hand reached out, an instinctive gesture, as he usually had a separate file for each complaint against Barlow. 'As for that unauthorised and totally irresponsible car chase. You forced a young officer to drive in a dangerous manner. An officer who is not a trained police driver and is therefore forbidden under any circumstances to participate in fast pursuits.'

'Sixty miles an hour was hardly fast.'

Harvey scowled at being interrupted. 'You crashed. That young officer could have been killed and the car is badly damaged.' Now he paused, waiting for a reply.

Barlow said nothing. A yes could imply guilt and be used against him in a formal enquiry. If he said no, he was being argumentative, ignoring obvious facts.

'Well?'

'What does Constable Wilson have to say about last night?'

'That is irrelevant to the Duty Sergeant's complaint.'

An evasion which Barlow found interesting. Obviously, Wilson had already been questioned, but he appeared to have accepted personal responsibility for the damage to his car. *Not a buck passer. I like that.*

As for Pierson complaining. Some night, somewhere, he planned to meet that gabshite down a dark alley. Meantime, he kept quiet. Anything he had to say would be ignored anyway.

Harvey sat back in his chair. 'A total overreaction on your part, together with a misinterpretation of facts and a highly dangerous pursuit.' He started to look pleased with life. 'All you had to do – and should have done – was make a proper report to the Duty Sergeant. Instead, you gave a garbled report, told him to ring Antrim station and then went charging off across the countryside.' Harvey leaned forward again, hands firmly on the desk. 'This, Sergeant, is not the Wild West. There are laid down procedures for every eventuality. Procedures which you consistently and blatantly ignore.'

'I deny that,' said Barlow, thinking it better to say something. Anyway it was the truth. He didn't ignore standard procedures. They could be very useful at times.

'Deny as much as you want, but there will be an enquiry into both your actions and your competence.' Now Harvey looked like the church service would be a prayer of thanks for delivering Barlow into his grasp. 'The least you can expect is a censure and be ordered to pay for the repair of Constable Wilson's car.'

Barlow said his own prayer. A prayer that some house had been robbed down to the bare boards. Hopefully, the house of one of Harvey's friends. *If he has any.*

'Very good, sir,' he said and left.

20

By the time Barlow got back to the Enquiry Office Pierson had wisely signed out and disappeared off home. In the rain, Barlow noted with pleasure, heavy pounding rain. *Hopefully, that two-faced lick will get pneumonia.*

Frustrated at missing Pierson he spat out a sweet and went looking for Wilson. Found him working dutifully on the case against Colonel Packenham. Barlow crooked a finger and jerked a thumb towards the door. Wilson followed him out into the corridor. He looked both surly and uneasy, a combination of looks that Barlow found interesting.

'Right, son, you're going to have a busy day.' He ticked the items off on his fingers. 'I want that Packenham case done and dusted by home time. You have your car to recover. And…'

He led Wilson into the locker room and opened up his own locker. Lifted out the jam jar containing the ball bearings shot through his front window. 'Do you know anything about fingerprinting?'

Wilson started to look interested. 'I've done a course.'

'I want you to extract any fingerprints on these and then trace them through our juvenile records. There's a pint in it if you find the person they belong to.'

'But, Sergeant, we don't keep the fingerprints of juveniles. It's strictly forbidden by law.'

Barlow pointed to a room down the hall. 'In that room there's a cabinet full of juvenile fingerprints that doesn't exist. Now, when you're next talking to the DI don't mention the cabinet.

He wouldn't thank you for being told something he knows about, but doesn't want to know about officially.'

A flush of red rose above Wilson's collar. He stared studiously at the jam jar rather than meet Barlow's eye.

Barlow added. 'You can work in the Enquiry Office, help me man the counter.'

Satisfied that he had Wilson where he could keep an eye on him, he cruised the building. The rain looked like it was on for the day, so he restricted foot patrols but made sure everyone was gainfully employed, including the detectives. *On a Sunday?*

He put his head around the door. 'What are you lot doing in?'

Detective Sergeant Leary scowled up from his desk. 'Isn't Mo Hunt the Master of the Hounds and a friend of the DI? Harvey wants the family silver recovered, the thieves caught, tried and hung by tomorrow at the latest.'

'Think of all the overtime,' said Barlow.

'Bugger the overtime. Now clear off.'

Barlow looked at the piles of fingerprints lifted from Mo Hunt's house. 'If you need a uniform to help, just say. I've got a few sugar cubes who'd melt in the rain.'

'Not Frank Wilson,' said Leary. 'I don't like tell-tales.'

'No way, Harvey has us joined at the hip.'

'Be careful of that one,' said Leary.

'So everyone says.'

21

The slow Sunday morning wore on, the day darkened until lights became a necessity not a luxury. The rain pounded down, ricocheting off the roof of the Protestant Hall across the way. Formed streams that collided outside the police station and turned the car park at the Tower cinema into a pond. Barlow took it upon himself to light a fire in the Enquiry Office. Officers coming in from patrol left their boots in a semi-circle around it to dry out.

The front door banged open and slammed shut. A heavyset man in a dark, pinstripe suit dumped a streaming umbrella in a corner. The man tried to bypass the counter. Barlow stepped into the passageway and blocked him.

'Good morning, Mr Whithead.'

'What's good about it?'

Barlow let time work a pointed pause before he said, 'Can we help you, sir?'

'I want to see Mr Harvey. Now!'

Barlow made a play of looking back at Wilson for confirmation. 'I'm afraid Mr Harvey has left for the day.'

Wilson's neck bulged as he fought against nodding to confirm a lie. Harvey normally looked in after a post-church gin and tonic at the City Club.

'Well somebody else then.'

'I take it you've got a problem that you wish to bring to our attention, sir?'

'A complaint: theft, wilful damage, deceit. I never came across anything like it before in all my life.'

'And you an accountant?'

Whithead's face set hard. 'Are you trying to be funny, Sergeant, or merely insulting?'

Barlow looked at the floor around Whithead's feet. The varnished wood-planking was turning dark from the rivulets of water running off his trousers.

'You stay by the coal fire, sir, until you dry out. I'll get you a cup of tea to warm you.' He turned to give Wilson his orders but the young constable was already on his way to the kitchen. He called after him. 'The best china and bring a plate of biscuits for Mr Whithead. Those Cadbury chocolate ones that the DI likes.'

Whithead said, 'That's very civil of you, Sergeant, but it won't do you any good.'

'Sir?'

'Geordie Dunlop is a friend of yours.'

Barlow looked astonished. 'Geordie Dunlop? Begging your pardon, Mr Whithead, but I've had Geordie Dunlop in court more often than you've had hot dinners.'

'For what?' Whithead looked angry enough to storm out. 'My solicitor, Mr Moncrief, warned me about you. You've had Geordie up for minor misdemeanours, when everyone knows he's robbed half the county.'

'You bring me the proof, sir, and I'll fashion the noose.'

Barlow poked at the coals to get a better flame. Whithead's trousers started to steam in the heat. He had to move away from the fire to stop his legs from being scalded.

His story was the sort to boil anger in a man embarrassed by his impoverished beginnings. What Geordie Dunlop had done – allegedly, Barlow chose to remind him – would be remembered with a laugh every race day, even by Whithead's best friends.

Geordie had driven Whithead's herd of Ayrshire cattle into a field of winter wheat and then sign-posted the pastureland as a car park for the race meeting. Ten bob to park the car and free entry for the driver and all his passengers into the race-course. Access to the racecourse by a hole that Geordie had thoughtfully made in the adjoining hedge.

Barlow nodded. 'Maybe you should be grateful to Geordie Dunlop. Now you know it works, you could set up your own car park in future years.'

Whithead choked at the very thought.

'He's a desperate man, that Geordie,' said Barlow quickly to cover from appearing to belittle the man's complaint.

'I want him jailed,' said Whithead. 'A hundred cars he put in there and a whole field of winter wheat tramped into the ground.'

'Hearsay is fine, sir, but we need proof,' said Wilson, as he returned with the tray of tea things.

Whithead opened his mouth to protest, but Barlow got in first by adding. 'A couple of witnesses would go a long way.'

Barlow spotted the chocolate biscuits, realised he was starving, that he hadn't had time for breakfast.

'Witnesses I've got,' said Whithead, patting his pockets. He produced a small Woolworths cash book and cursed when he discovered it had got damp. Luckily, the page he needed opened easily. 'Two names and addresses. Men of irrefutable character.'

'You're a quare man, sir,' said Barlow. 'And that Geordie is a madman. The only time he wasn't in trouble was when he fought for King and country during the war.'

Whithead snorted. 'If I remember rightly, it was that or jail.'

Wilson served tea with milk and sugar. Whithead patted an incipient paunch and refused a biscuit. Barlow fetched paper and an old ledger to lean on. He sat across from Whithead at the fire and wrote down the complaint in a slow hand. Whithead had a china cup and saucer, Barlow his old mug. Between sentences Barlow chewed thoughtfully on the District Inspector's chocolate biscuits.

'Sir, let me see if I've got this right. Geordie Dunlop was seen in the field by one of your men. Mind you, at a fair distance and your man's eyesight mightn't be that great. Geordie was observed to escape through the hedge and run into the crowd just before the third race. Your man didn't see him make the hole in the hedge nor did he see him accept money from any of the car drivers or their passengers.'

'Sergeant, you're twisting my words.'

'No, sir, I'm reading what's on the page.'

'The two names I gave you, Smythe and Thompson, will verify it.'

'I'll speak to those gentlemen this very day, sir.'

'Make sure you do.'

With that, Whithead left.

Barlow stood at the window and watched him trudge through rain that continued to lash down.

It was a slow day anyway. With Gillespie off duty he could take one of the patrol cars without first getting into an argument. *You'd think he owned the blessed things the way he goes on about them.*

Barlow shook his head. 'That man.'

Wilson asked, 'Do you mean Geordie Dunlop?'

'No, Whithead. He started as an articled clerk in an accountant's office. Now he's got his own firm and lives on a sixty-acre farm.'

'So what's the problem?'

'His mother was a servant girl and his father a labouring man, so the county types blackballed him when he tried to join the City Club. Anything to do with them or their horses, and he sees red.'

Soon after Whithead had left the station District Inspector Harvey appeared, breathing gin and tonic. Straight off he spotted his good china cup and saucer, and the wrapper that had been his packet of biscuits.

'What's going on here?'

'Mr Whithead, the accountant, called with a complaint.' Barlow crumpled the biscuit packet and lobbed it into the fire. 'I'm afraid the gentleman must have skipped breakfast. Fair hungry he was.'

22

'Enquiries are proceeding, sir,' said Barlow in his most reassuring voice.

It was some time later and he was standing before Harvey's desk, his toes tight against the ash base. He leaned forward from the hips as if he had difficulty hearing. One slip and his entire bulk would land on top of his superior.

Harvey was reading Whithead's complaint while flicking through various directives from Headquarters.

'You're in my light,' said Harvey, without looking up.

Barlow moved back a pace.

'More.'

He obliged with a brief shuffle.

Harvey tried to glare him back further. Barlow returned the look: chin up, eyes following the slope of his nose. Harvey, he noticed, had a nervous tick in his Adam's apple. *That's new.* So his campaign to give his superior an ulcer was starting to work.

According to the sergeant in "Records" at Headquarters, Harvey had been a nod-through. He only made minimum height for the police because his uncle was the medical officer. Barlow thought he should ring that sergeant again. Confirm that the drunk and disorderly charge against the sergeant's cousin – a Linfield supporter objecting to a five-nil drubbing by Ballymena United – had been lost. See what else the sergeant knew.

Harvey broke the stare first and looked away. He leaned back in his swivel chair, poised his elbows on the arms and tapped fingertips together. 'Tell me, Barlow, what exactly have you achieved today?'

Barlow stood solid. 'I noticed that Constable Wilson hadn't listed the contents of the wallets stolen by Colonel Packenham…'

'I don't want to know about Colonel Packenham. Even the Chief Constable has been on about the case.' It came out as a squeak of embarrassment.

Barlow studied the portrait of the new Queen on the wall behind Harvey. He still missed the portrait of the old king in his sailor's uniform. A man's man.

Outside, the day got darker with renewed rain. Harvey pushed his swivel chair away from the desk. He went around the room switching on lights, frowning at the decor. Barlow found himself agreeing with Harvey that the flocked wallpaper should go. It had been there since before the war and hung heavy with layers of cream paint.

Harvey went back to his desk and picked up Whithead's statement. 'It's a disgrace that Geordie Dunlop encouraged people to get in without paying.'

'Aye, sir.'

'As for these witnesses?'

'I'm informed that Mr Whithead's cattle man, Alan Thompson, may have seen something. Then there's a Mr Smythe.'

'I want those people spoken to.'

'The problem is, sir, I'm given to understand that Thompson is more or less blind.'

'Today, Sergeant.'

'As soon as Constable Wilson gets back. He's away with the tow truck to recover his car.' Barlow looked at Harvey, all innocence. 'I promised him faithfully I wouldn't leave the station until he returned.'

Harvey looked uncomfortable and wouldn't meet his eye.

Barlow had no intention of going anywhere near Thompson or Smythe until he'd been home to check that Maggie was okay.

23

Barlow opened the door into his house and stood transfixed. Maggie sat on one half of the settee, Toby occupied the other. Maggie wore a dress, one she hadn't looked at in years, and proper shoes, not her battered slippers. Vera sat at the window, her nose in a book. The range glowed red through its open door and a pot of mince and potatoes simmered gently on the side.

The normality of the scene caught in his throat, his eyes felt moist.

'It's well for some,' he said, shaking the rain off his cape and hanging it over the banisters to drip-dry.

Vera busied herself serving lunch. Barlow noted two places set at the table and a tray set for Maggie as if she was still in bed. *So things aren't that normal.* He sat down in his chair and made sure his feet got in Vera's way.

She said, 'Da!' and pretended to tramp on them.

'Mr Barlow,' said Maggie.

Where did she get Mr Barlow from? Here she was not eating at the table with them and calling him Mr Barlow like they were strangers. *That hurts.* The only thing left of their marriage was the house they lived in and the bed that circumstances forced them to share.

'Mr Barlow, this dog has no collar or lead.'

He looked at her puzzled. He'd never put a lead on the dog. He and Toby started and finished a walk together. In between Toby ranged far and wide, only coming back every so often to check Barlow was where he should be, and then trotting off again.

Maggie sniffed her disapproval. 'Poor Toby was dying for a walk. I had to fashion a collar out of a piece of string.'

Toby wagged his tail at the mention of his name. Lifted his head and sniffed at the food being ladled out.

'I'll buy them first thing tomorrow, and a brush,' said Maggie.

What the hell tablets is she on?

He watched Vera dance around the room as she put things on the table. Here was her "Ma" talking and acting normal and going shopping. Everything was fine in Vera's little life. He found himself smiling as he levered himself out of his chair and took a seat at the table. Maggie stayed on the settee with the tray on her lap. Toby sat up, hopeful of being offered leftovers.

'Did you have a good night?' Barlow asked Vera between mouthfuls.

She glowed with pleasure. 'I did, and Clarissa Denton let me use the phone again. Aunt Daisy said she'd be delighted.'

'Delighted to do what?' he asked cautiously.

Sometimes when Vera "thought" he felt he was being hit by a steamroller. Having got the headlines out in a rush, Vera filled in the gaps. Barlow nodded as he listened.

Aunt Daisy was Maggie's elder sister. Daisy still lived in the family home near Donaghadee, where she worked as the senior clerk in a builders supply merchants. Daisy had planned to spend her holiday week decorating the house but, of course, she'd be delighted to come and, 'keep Ma company,' said Vera pointedly, while Vera was spending the week in Portrush with Kenny and his family.

Barlow tried not to think of the complications of Daisy coming to stay. She was such a lady and never complained. But Daisy was a spinster and used to her own privacy, especially when it came to… *How did they describe it in Army Regulations?* Bodily functions. He'd have to come and go through Daisy's bedroom.

No wandering about in his long johns in the middle of the night. *Maybe I'll buy myself one of those dressing gown things.*

He could see himself in a dressing gown, maybe get Vera to buy him a pair of slippers for his birthday. Take up smoking a pipe.

That thought brought him round to thinking about Vera and the Dentons. Mrs Denton regularly had Vera out to babysit and quietly, without any big thing being made of it, had taught his daughter style. Hints dropped, small gifts made. Like a scarf he had seen Mrs Denton wear last winter, now thrown casually around Vera's neck. It transformed jeans and a plain blouse into something elegant.

He looked across at Maggie to see what she thought of Daisy coming to stay. Maggie looked pleased but said nothing. She appeared to have run out of conversation. Gone back into her own thoughts as she picked delicately at her food. Barlow searched his mind for something to talk about that might engage her interest.

The only thing in his head was his ongoing feud with Harvey. He could hardly talk about that and worry everyone unnecessarily. *God forbid Vera ends up with a man like that.* Thinking of Harvey and marriage reminded him of Mrs Harvey and her surprising choice of friends.

Mrs Fetherton was the wife of the Mayor, which in Barlow's opinion, was cause enough to dislike her. And Harvey had *entertained* Mrs Carberry at Curles Bridge after the Round Table Ball. He knew Mrs Carberry vaguely to talk to and by reputation. "Nice" and "unfortunate" were the words he used to describe her. A real lady brought down by circumstances and a lot of bad luck.

'Tell me,' he asked Vera. 'Do you know anything about Mrs Fetherton and a Mrs Carberry?'

Vera said, 'Other than the fact that even Mrs Fetherton's friends run scared of her tongue and Mrs Carberry depends on a few rents to pay the bills. No. Nothing.'

He jerked around in his seat, surprised, and caught one of Vera's knowing smirks that both irritated and amused. He asked, 'How in God's name do you know all that.'

'Clarissa Denton and her friends. You should hear Clarissa when she's pretending to be Mrs Fetherton, ordering everyone around. She's a hoot.'

'Right,' he said, still startled at what she knew and hadn't passed on. *Close mouthed, not a gossip. Good girl*. 'And District Inspector Harvey's wife?'

'She always looks like she's lost a pound and found a penny.' He saw her hesitate, worrying about betraying a confidence before she added. 'I've heard Clarissa and the rest talk. Mrs Harvey's married life... Well, you know what he's like, Da.'

'Aye.'

Vera folded her arms and leaned forward, instinctively imitating Barlow when he wanted to put a suspect under pressure. 'Why do you want to know?'

So he told her about seeing the unusual combination of the three ladies at the point-to-point.

'And?'

'I want you to keep an eye out for them.'

'Why?'

He said, 'I don't know, but I trust my instincts.'

24

Barlow managed to stay busy in the station until late afternoon. He kept looking out the window at the rain. It had not eased up.

Every so often Harvey did a tip-toe walk through. 'Are you not away yet?'

'Just finishing up these reports' or 'Constable Wilson is on his break,' or 'In a couple of minutes.' He wished Harvey would go home. DS Leary and his team were quite capable of finding the men who had burgled Mo Hunt's house without his interference. Finally, Barlow admitted defeat. 'The squad car's here now, sir. We're on our way.'

'To the scene of the burglary that didn't happen last night?'

'Nothing's been reported yet,' said Barlow.

'And it won't be,' said Harvey.

Wilson said, 'Sir, we're off to Mr Whithead's farm. The stockman will be in about now to settle the cattle for the night.'

Harvey glowered at Wilson for apparently taking Barlow's side. 'Not in one of my cars, you're not. Not after last night. Use the bikes.'

'Very good, sir,' said Barlow, not letting Harvey see his annoyance. He led Wilson out into the yard and invited him to take his pick of the old boneshakers available. 'You do know how to ride a bike?'

'Of course, Sergeant.'

'You said the same thing about your driving.'

They set off. With cape on and head down, Barlow remained reasonably dry in spite of the driving rain.

Whithead's man, Alan Thompson, was wiry-thin and totally unphased by the headshakes and foot stamping of a Jersey bull coming into maturity. He gave the young bull a slap on the rump and told it to mind its manners. That type of man, Barlow knew, made a good witness.

Thompson led Barlow and Wilson into the comfort of a disused tack room. The lingering smells of saddle soap and damp leather were not unpleasant. Barlow stretched his feet towards a glowing stove and let Wilson conduct the interview.

Thompson could swear he'd seen Geordie Dunlop on Whithead's land and, no, there was nothing wrong with his eyes. In fact he had perfect vision. Wilson wrote down Thompson's statement.

Thompson had his Bic biro in hand, more than ready to sign the statement, when Barlow intervened.

'There's a bit of a problem,' he said. 'When you were in the pastureland, you might have been tempted to nip through the hedge to watch a race yourself?'

'I might have,' said Thompson, suddenly cautious.

Barlow sucked an imaginary wine gum while he talked things through. 'It's the sort of question the Defence Counsel would ask. They're like that, you know.' He tipped the chair back onto its rear legs and rocked himself to and fro, nice and relaxed. 'And if you did go through the hedge, then you could be in trouble yourself for trespass and possibly for theft. After all, you watched races from the racecourse itself without paying the required entrance fee.'

'Now wait a minute,' said Thompson.

'I'm only saying.' He looked over at Wilson. 'I think we should caution Mr Thompson formally before he signs that statement.'

Wilson looked uncertain.

Thompson put his pen down. Dropped it as if it had suddenly got hot. 'I need to think about this.'

'Do you?' asked Barlow.

He spent a couple of minutes trying to convince him to sign the statement. The best Thompson would do for them was to give the names of other people he'd seen in or around the field.

Barlow finally gave up trying to get the statement signed. 'Bad luck on you for dragging me out on a day like this, and for nothing.'

He and Wilson got on their bikes and creaked off to see the second witness on Whithead's list: a Mr Smythe.

Mr Smythe, a printer who did graphic design on the side, had made a success of a small family business. Starting in an end-terrace house, he now lived in an old farmhouse with five acres of land for his children's ponies. The old farm kitchen had been extended to make a large working area with a new bedroom above. Going by the soil pipe running down the outside wall, the new bedroom had its own bathroom.

He's got two of the things, and there's me with none.

Mr Smythe was expecting them and led them into the kitchen. Had a cup of tea in their hand almost before they could settle. Mr Smythe was more than willing to help jail Geordie Dunlop because Mr Whithead was both his accountant and his friend.

Barlow selected a custard cream biscuit to help wash down his tea, and nodded at Wilson to begin.

Wilson said, 'I must warn you Mr Smythe that anything you say will be taken down…'

'That's why you're here,' said Smythe impatiently.

'and may be used in evidence against you.'

'What?' Smythe looked to Barlow, angry. 'That's ridiculous.'

Barlow sighed heavily. 'It's a question, sir, of what you knew: An unofficial car park, a convenient hole in the hedge.'

Wilson added eagerly. 'And as a personal friend of Mr Whithead, the implication is that you knew you were on Mr Whithead's land and you were aware of his enmity towards the Hunt Committee.'

Suddenly, Mr Smythe wasn't at all keen to make a statement. Perhaps he should speak to his solicitor first, he said. After all, if one was going into court and swearing an oath to tell the truth, one ought to be one hundred percent sure of one's facts.

Having made up his mind on the matter, Smythe would not be budged. Barlow finished his tea and most of the biscuits before giving Wilson a nudge, and they left.

They collected their bikes from where they'd left them near the back door and wiped the worst of the wet off the saddles.

Barlow looked up at the pouring rain. 'Some days you win, some days you lose.'

25

Barlow and Wilson cycled back to the station. By the time they arrived, it was nearing eight o'clock and the end of their shift. Inspector Foxwood and Sergeant Pierson had been called in early to arrest Geordie Dunlop and question him about his alleged crimes. Harvey had gone home. 'It's my day off, after all.'

Pierson smirked as they walked in through the door. 'Still nothing about that big burglary last night.'

Barlow pretended not to hear and went to report to Inspector Foxwood. Wilson dutifully trotted after him. They found Foxwood picking through the files that cluttered his desk. Inspector Foxwood, Clarence to his friends, was an Englishman who had married a Northern Irish woman and transferred to the RUC. Barlow thought him a competent officer, though overly anxious to please Harvey.

'No joy, sir,' Barlow informed Foxwood, and explained that both witnesses had become uncooperative when their own culpability in the alleged crime had become apparent to them.

Foxwood looked to Wilson for confirmation.

Wilson nodded. 'They were keen to do down Geordie, but not if it meant risking their own necks.'

His voice resonated with an eagerness to support Barlow, which Barlow liked.

Foxwood shook his head wearily. 'Better release Geordie then. With a bit of luck, he'll catch pneumonia walking home in the rain, and die.'

'Now, sir, you wouldn't wish evil on our best customer.'

Barlow went down to the cells himself to discharge Geordie. Wilson accompanied him. Barlow could almost feel the notebook and pen handy, ready to note anything said out of turn.

Geordie Dunlop was a big, thick-built man nearing retirement age. Muscle was giving way to fat and Geordie's belt had stretched a couple of holes in recent years. Having said that, one blow from Geordie would put most men in hospital.

Barlow opened the cell door and leaned against the door frame. Geordie stayed stretched out on the bunk, scowling at the ceiling, and ignored Barlow.

'You're a bollox,' Barlow said.

Without looking around, Geordie said, 'That nasty bastard you sent. I'm going to do him some night.'

Wilson said, 'That's a clear threat against the person of Sergeant Pierson, and a chargeable offence under… '

Barlow told Wilson, 'Why don't you give him Pierson's address while you're at it?'

Wilson flushed and went quiet.

'So you robbed Mo Hunt's house,' said Barlow.

'I did no such thing,' replied Geordie.

'And damaged Mr Whithead's crops and stole money from the Hunt Committee?'

'I'm as honest as the day's long,' Geordie said, swinging his feet to the floor and flexing his back.

'It's July and the days, like your moments of honesty, are getting shorter,' said Barlow, as he moved back from the door. 'Come on, you're getting Police Bail.'

Geordie sat on. 'They came charging into the house like a herd of bullocks. That git of a sergeant – Pierson, isn't that what that young Rozzer called him? – tramped over the grandchildren's toys. Deliberate. I saw him do it. "You can claim, he says".' Geordie's face set hard and he imitated a spit on his knuckles. 'I'll deliver the claim myself, personal like.'

'That's enough,' said Barlow sharply.

'And he insulted the wife.'

Barlow tapped his watch. 'I'm off duty in two minutes. If you're coming, come, because we're not feeding you.'

Geordie finally heaved himself off the bed and walked out of the cell. 'Told her she was no better than a tramp, married to the likes of me.'

'Well he's got you right,' said Barlow, jerking a thumb towards the stairs and the way out.

Pierson stood in the Enquiry Office organising things for the late shift. As soon as Geordie saw him he again spat on his knuckles.

Barlow tapped Pierson's arm to get his full attention. 'Don't walk anywhere in the dark on your own.' He nodded meaningfully at Geordie. 'For a while, that is.'

Pierson's face lost colour.

Wilson prepared the papers to grant Geordie police bail. With nothing better to do, Barlow gave him a formal warning about his "violence of the mouth." Enjoyed the looks of hate Geordie directed at Pierson, who found an excuse to disappear deeper into the building.

With the paperwork completed and Geordie thrown out into the downpour, Barlow headed off to the locker room to secure his gun for the night.

Wilson followed him. 'Sergeant, about those fingerprints.'

'When you've time,' said Barlow. 'When you've time.'

Now that he'd time for himself he'd begun to think about Maggie and wonder how he would find things at home.

Wilson opened his own locker and produced a sketchbook. 'When I put the powder on the ball bearings, you could see partial prints.' He slipped some photographs out of the back of the sketchbook and showed them to Barlow. 'If you look, you'll see that the images are incomplete because of the curvature of the ball bearings. I don't think you could use them in evidence.'

'Aye,' I see what you mean,' said Barlow, not letting on that he'd intended to treat the offence as a private matter, and clip the perpetrator around the ears.

Wilson opened the sketchbook and showed Barlow the first page. It held larger than life pencil drawings of a thumb and forefinger. All the whorls showed up clearly. The image of the thumb was interesting. Right in the centre was a jagged scar. The sort you got when trying to open a lemonade bottle without a proper opener.

Barlow looked at Wilson. 'Tell me, son, did you go to bed last night?'

'Well... I wanted... and... '

'You're no good to me square-eyed.' He closed the book and handed it back. 'But good work.'

Wilson looked almost puzzled. As if he hadn't heard praise in a long time.

The slam of the front door closing echoed through the building. Voices were raised, one almost screaming in fury. 'It's gone, all gone. They've cleaned me out. Not a thing left, not even the old iron doorstopper.'

Wilson went to run to the Enquiry Office.

Barlow grabbed him and held him back. 'Son, you don't want to get involved. That's Unwin Kirker in complaining, and he'll keep you here till midnight.' He swung Wilson around and shoved him ahead of him. 'This way for the back door and the Section House.'

Even as he retreated from the row developing in the Enquiry Office, Barlow looked back and wondered. *Two empty houses in two nights?*

26

'Daisy, you look a treat,' said Barlow. The Belfast to Derry train breathed steam in their direction as they touched cheek to cheek in greeting.

His sister-in-law was the same height and build as Maggie, but Daisy's face had a bloom of contentment. Any crease marks came from constant smiling. Today, Daisy wore a blue and white polka dot dress and carried a light raincoat over her arm.

Daisy gave the waiting Vera a hug. Picked up her case again and then looked around. 'She didn't come?'

'No.'

It came out shorter than he'd intended. Maggie had taken Toby for a walk in the People's Park rather than come to the railway station to meet her sister.

'Then things are...?' ventured Daisy.

'Fine,' he said.

At least he hadn't been murdered in his bed. But every turn, every movement of Maggie had him snapping awake in the middle of the night, heart pounding.

He took Daisy's suitcase, slipped it from a hand creamy with good health – in sharp contrast to Maggie's skin, which looked even more dry and brittle than usual, especially since her most recent stay in the hospital.

The guard started up the length of the train, slamming carriage doors shut.

'I'd better go,' said Vera. She gave him a quick kiss and her Aunt Daisy another hug and jumped into a carriage.

Vera was flushed with excitement. A week away from home – in Portrush. He'd heard the itinerary a dozen times. She planned to get off the train at Coleraine. Kenny had promised to meet her there and they could catch the bus to Portrush together.

What with Maggie's illness and one thing and another, Barlow couldn't remember the last time they'd managed a day away as a family. He felt sad for Vera that she'd missed out on so much.

'Da, don't forget the Credit Union. The envelope's behind the clock on the mantelpiece.'

'Yes, dear. No, dear.'

He was to call on the Friday night and make her weekly payment against the settee. Right at that moment Barlow was more concerned about Vera herself. This wasn't a child heading off to the seaside with a bucket and spade. This was a young woman going to spend a week with her lover.

He wanted to say 'Be good. Be careful', but instead found himself saying 'Have a good time.'

Chains rattled and buffers clashed and jerked apart as the train pulled out. He stood and stared until it was out of sight. Vera had never before been away from home without either him or Maggie going with her.

'She'll be fine,' said Daisy.

'Aye, with Mrs Cameron and her "napkins with breakfast" lifestyle.'

'That's not what I'm talking about. Vera's got gumption, trust her.'

He looked at her. 'Do you tell fortunes as well as read minds?'

He found Daisy staring straight into his eyes. Her stare felt warm and friendly, something he found easy to return.

'How is Maggie really?' she asked.

'I don't know. Brittle? I don't know.'

'I never wished this on you,' she said. Which puzzled him.

'Come on,' she said, and they started down the slope to the exit.

The suitcase wasn't heavy and the weather was good, so they walked rather than take a taxi. On the way he told her, as best he could, about Maggie and her condition. Not much talk out of Maggie and she picked at her food. In bed at night, Maggie kept well to her own side. Moved further away if he happened to turn in her direction. Not that he said that because… well Daisy had never married, never had a beau so far as he knew, and he didn't want to embarrass her with intimate details.

Still, there was something – he looked for the right word and settled on "bracing" – something bracing about walking through the town with a good-looking woman at his side. Occasionally, on the narrow footpaths, with people passing, their bodies bumped. And that felt good as well.

At the bottom of Mill Row, he hesitated. 'The house isn't up to the standard that you're used to. Any other time you came to visit, you stayed in Mrs Anderson's guest house.'

'John Barlow, it isn't just a house, it's *your* home, and I'm proud to be *your* guest.'

She sounded so positive that his own embarrassment annoyed him. He led the way to the house and opened the door. Felt a tinge of anxiety, *No Maggie and no dog.* Stepped back and let Daisy enter first.

She stood in the centre of the living room and turned around slowly. 'Well, John Barlow, this place is shining.'

It was. He and Vera had spent the previous evening scrubbing and dusting. He'd even taken a knife and boiling water to the weeds growing in the yard.

Her eyes, he noticed, settled on a point at the bottom of the stairs where he had lain bleeding to death. Would have died if Vera hadn't talked the disturbed Maggie into handing over the knife, and then run for help.

He tried to think of something more cheerful. Jumped to the problems of a guest in a house with only an outside toilet, or of him walking in unannounced and finding Daisy just stepping out of the tin bath. *It has to be a worry for her.*

The front door opened and Maggie came in. Toby went up to Daisy, sat and held up his paw in greeting. *Bloody show-off.* Maggie stood stock-still and stared at them. He found himself comparing the sisters. Maggie had the bone structure for beauty. Daisy had the flesh that turned the bone into a real human being.

He disliked what he was thinking – one woman half-dead and the other very much alive – and made a show of looking at his watch. 'I've got to go. I'm on a late lunch break.'

He escaped the house as the sisters hugged in greeting. Maggie was talking. Laughing even.

She seemed to relate to everyone but him.

27

Barlow arrived home from work shortly after eight o'clock. The day had turned cold, the clouds threatening and bringing dusk early. Muted light showed through the drawn curtains. He knocked on the front door to alert Daisy to his arrival.

Dance music from the BBC Light Programme filled the air in the living room, where Daisy and Maggie were sitting on the settee, apparently in mid-chat. Maggie almost smiled a greeting. Toby bared his teeth but didn't snarl – obviously on his best behaviour with a visitor in the house. Barlow sat in his usual chair while the two sisters fussed around setting out the dinner.

They ate – he wasn't sure what – as his full attention was focused on Maggie. Maggie behaving like a new person. Normal even. She ate, she spoke. Even to him, without prompting, wanting to know if he needed the salt.

After dinner, Daisy and Maggie retreated to the scullery to wash up. Barlow sat content and watched the glow from the fire. The way things were he could sleep that night, confident that he was safe.

He dozed off and awoke some time later to find Daisy standing over him, holding out a bottle of scotch. 'For the man of the house.'

'Now there was no need to be doing that.'

'John Barlow, I like to pay my way.'

She always called him "John Barlow", halfway between friendship and formality.

He heaved himself out of the chair. 'Well if you're paying your way, I hope you brought some cloves as well.' He unscrewed the top and sniffed appreciatively. *Good stuff too.* 'You'll have to join me, ladies. A man drinking alone in his home is bad news.'

Maggie looked doubtful. *Maybe with all those Valium tablets, she shouldn't.* Daisy put the kettle on and went looking for sugar. *Now there's a woman after my own heart.*

As they sipped their hot whiskeys, Daisy asked, 'And you have a television now as well?'

He could read people; moreover, he'd known Daisy for years. In fact, she was the person who had engineered his first meeting with Maggie. So, he sensed an edge to Daisy's question. An edge that unsettled him. *Like I'm a tightwad or something?*

Rather than shrugging off of the question – but also in order to get a conversation going – he gave a fulsome response. 'Last Christmas, I had to go into a house where a man had been murdered. The family lived in a damp hole of a place, with only bread and potatoes for food. Their radio was a pre-war monstrosity, bought second-hand.'

He found himself embarrassed at the way the sisters looked at each other, as if wondering what made him think his house was any better.

He ploughed on with the explanation. 'There was all this talk at the time about the new Ulster Television channel starting up, and I'd a bit of spare cash... Maggie's in the house all day by herself. I thought it might give her a bit of company.'

He stopped there, wondering why he felt so embarrassed at buying a treat for his wife.

Daisy nodded across to him. 'You're a good man, John Barlow.'

'There's some as would say different,' he growled, and they all sipped in unison.

He tried a bit of tell-the-truth-and-shame-the-devil on Daisy. 'It's your week's holiday. You don't mind spending it all here?'

'No.' Daisy held up her glass, hinting that it was empty. 'It's great having company instead of sitting in an empty house at night. In fact…'

Without consciously thinking of it, Barlow sensed a change in tone.

'In fact, Mr Gardiner Senior couldn't believe that I planned to take the whole week off. He said the last time that happened was when he was still Young Mr Gardiner.'

They laughed at Mr Gardiner Senior's surprise. More than once he'd accused Daisy of being a workaholic, coming into the office when she should be on holidays.

'We do more talking than Debt Control,' she admitted.

Surprisingly, Maggie became almost garrulous. She talked of growing up in Donaghadee. Of going to the little school down the road. How it felt funny having a teacher who was also their father. Of calling him "Papa" at home and "Sir" in the school. How good he'd been to them after Mama died.

'We were children then,' she said, a tear of regret in her eyes. 'Hardly more than babies.'

Daisy said little other than to confirm some part-remembered fact.

Barlow kept an eye on the clock. He wanted to pop down to the Bridge Bar and have a word with Edward. Colonel Packenham's case was listed for hearing on Thursday. Edward, being a nob himself, might be able to answer something that was niggling Barlow.

He also got the impression that Daisy was uneasy about all this talk of the old days, though he couldn't figure what harm it could do. *It's certainly doing Maggie a power of good.*

28

On the Thursday morning, Barlow attended Court as a material witness against Colonel Packenham. With him went Frank Wilson, the designated arresting officer.

'That means you do all the paperwork,' Barlow had told the young constable.

Wilson also had to deal with District Inspector Harvey. Harvey's wrath at being taken in by his new friend had gradually replaced his initial embarrassment. The District Inspector wanted no deals done, no concessions made. Every possible clause of the criminal code listed was to be used against Packenham. The Colonel was for jail, and that was that.

Virtually every decent town in Northern Ireland had a courthouse with colonnades and porticoes. Ballymena, on the other hand, had to make do with a dark-stoned building jammed between the Presbyterian "West" Church and the Castle Arms Hotel. Barlow met Colonel Packenham on the first of the three steps leading up to the courthouse. Packenham was dressed to the nines: rolled umbrella, bowler hat, the lot.

Barlow dispatched Wilson to speak to the Clerk of the Court about the case. Once he was safely out of sight, he stepped in front of Packenham and saluted.

'Hardly appropriate, old boy,' said Packenham.

He looked shaken and had lost weight.

'What happened at Oxford?' asked Barlow.

Packenham nodded his defeat. 'I knew you'd find out.'

'And?'

'In the beginning it was fun. A game I was particularly good at.' Packenham's eyes went unfocused, his mind back in the thirties. 'At first we returned the wallets... and then I didn't.'

'You got a month.'

'And sent down from my college. When the war came, I joined the Rifles. They kept insisting that I take a commission.' He sighed. 'I had to tell them the truth. They didn't want me after that, and the doctor diagnosed a heart condition to have me discharged.'

'And afterwards, sir, you went to the Far East?' he said, noting blotches on the Colonel's fingernails, his eyes yellow with malaria.

'The Marshall Islands, sir.'

'Was that before or after the Japanese?'

'During. I was a Coast Watcher, but please...'

Barlow didn't understand how Packenham had been able to do it. Days and months on his own, never knowing when the Japanese would find him. At least, when he, Barlow, stood over a bomb, there was always someone at the other end of the telephone line to talk to, to encourage him on. For him to know that he wasn't alone.

A group of men swirled around them. They wore pinstripe suits and high collars, and all of them carried a cloth bag. Counsels and their Juniors.

Barlow dropped his voice. 'But why the "Colonel"?'

Packenham took him by the elbow and pulled him to the side. 'My mother had Dementia. She didn't understand about me not being in the army. She thought I'd been posted to the Far East.' He stopped speaking.

'Go on,' said Barlow encouragingly.

'I was working with the Americans and they laughed at my British accent.' An old memory caused a smile to flicker across

Packenham's lips. 'So I played up to it: la–di–da accent, mono-
cle, cravat, walking cane. They said anyone that grand couldn't be
anything less than a colonel, and the title stuck. I told my mother
about it – I thought it might amuse her a letter. She didn't understand that it was a joke, and she told everyone I'd been promoted.'

Just then Packenham's daughter rushed in the gate. The
look of concern for her father turned to pure hatred when she
recognised Barlow.

Packenham said, quickly, 'It's hell when your mother's mind
goes. But what if it's hereditary?'

'Tell me about it,' said Barlow. He spotted District Inspector Harvey's car on the roundabout and started to move off.
'About our agreement, sir.'

Packenham stiffened in annoyance. 'I gave you my word
that I would plead guilty and ask for previous offences to be
taken into account.'

Barlow said, 'Forget your word of honour. When you go in
there,' He jerked a thumb in the direction of the courthouse.
'It's every man for himself.'

Some of the weight of worry eased off Packenham's shoulders. 'Thank you, Sergeant.'

'Nah, sir. We old soldiers have to stick together.'

'Like bloody glue,' said a voice. That of the Mayor, Alderman Ezekiel Fetherton.

Packenham stepped away. Barlow stood on. The Mayor was
a head shorter than Barlow and was becoming increasingly
bald. He also had a glow to his cheeks, which had more to do
with evenings spent in the City Club than the milk he sold.

The Mayor gave Barlow a long, hard stare. 'I was wondering,' he asked, 'how I lost a wallet with two hundred quid in it,
yet when I got it back it there was only one hundred and fifty
quid left. Fifth had gone missing. Nicked!'

Barlow was at his blandest. 'Is His Honour sure of his figures?'

'Yes,' snarled Fetherton. 'And don't you deny it, Barlow.'

'You can, of course, prove that you had the money in the first place?'

Fetherton tried to stare him down, but he didn't have the height. 'My secretary can. She gave it to me in dry cash.'

Just then District Inspector Harvey paraded through the front gate of the courthouse. He was in uniform, with black gloves – one worn, one carried – a swagger stick and boots that shone like mirrors.

Fetherton saw him and waved him over. 'Here, Harvey.'

Harvey jerked with annoyance. Barlow didn't blame him. Policemen expect to be treated with deference, not shouted at like some messenger boy. He decided to teach Fetherton a lesson about police work.

He said, 'An accusation like that, of money missing while in police custody, is a very serious matter. First off, Mr Mayor, we would have to verify its very existence against the books of your company.'

Fetherton's eyes shifted uneasily. He almost seemed relieved when Harvey made a point of stopping to speak to a senior counsel.

Barlow egged Fetherton on. 'Of course, if you made an accusation like that to Mr Harvey, and couldn't prove you had the money in the first place… '

'Yes? What?'

'Well, seeing that Mr Harvey is so keen on this "no crime tolerated" thing, sir, he might feel obliged to inform the taxman that not all the money your men collect gets recorded in the Cash Book.'

Fetherton blustered with indignation. 'Are you accusing me of not paying my proper taxes?

Barlow looked pained. 'I'm only saying.'

Just then, Harvey excused himself from the senior counsel and began walking their way. Fetherton looked ready to bolt.

'I'll leave you to it, sir. I'm sure you and the DI have a lot of important business to discuss,' said Barlow, and he walked off.

Fetherton hissed after him. 'I won't forget this, Barlow. I'll get you yet.'

Barlow said nothing but chewed on one of his imaginary sweets, a wine gum this time, and went in search of Frank Wilson. He found Wilson at the back of the building, standing guard over a sheaf of papers the thickness of Volume 2 of Arthur Mee's Encyclopaedia.

'Tell me, son, is it a pickpocket or Crippen the murderer you're taking to court today?'

'It's my first big case and I need to be sure of my facts,' said Wilson, looking more nervous and unsettled than Colonel Packenham.

'So you stayed up all night rewriting everything, you daft eejit.'

He took a good look at Wilson. The young constable was pale under his cheekbones and his writing hand looked swollen. Barlow shook his head at the memory of the eager young constable long become a cynical Station Sergeant.

All the same he couldn't help ribbing Wilson. 'You'd make a great sob sister for the likes of Geordie Dunlop.'

Wilson's face set stubborn. 'I always wanted to be a policeman.'

'And so you are. And some day you'll make Inspector, God help us.'

Barlow took the papers out of Wilson's hands. He had to pull them clear, they were held so tightly. 'Meantime, if I don't reduce your paperwork, Judge Donaldson will feed us both to the hounds.'

He flicked through the file and pulled out four sets of stapled papers. 'There you are, son. Leave the rest in the Clerk's office.'

There was a sudden bustle of people around them. Everyone seemed to be heading for the courtroom.

Barlow checked his watch. 'You should be in there.' He hesitated. 'Tell you what, I'll put the folder in the Clerk's office for you.'

He nodded at Wilson and walked on. At the point in the passageway, where it narrowed and turned towards the rear of the courthouse, he stopped and looked back.

'I'll be in the tea room if you need me.'

29

The row involved Sergeant Barlow long before he heard about it. He had his egg and bacon bap finished and was on his second cup of tea when Frank Wilson came bursting into the tearoom and skidded to a halt beside him.

'Never run unless you're in hot pursuit,' said Barlow.

'Yes, Sergeant. Sorry, Sergeant.'

'It looks bad and it tends to panic innocent citizens.'

'But Sergeant… '

'Don't let it happen again.'

Wilson burst out. 'The Colonel Packenham case, it's gone belly up.'

Barlow looked at him like he'd two heads. 'It can't have. It's an open-and-shut case with a full confession in writing.'

But apparently not, Barlow finally understood. The original confession and Charge Sheet had gone missing. They weren't in the papers that he, Barlow, had given Wilson to take into court. Neither were they in the folder, which Wilson found on top of a filing cabinet in the Clerk's office.

'Where I put it myself,' said Barlow.

Wilson had tears in his eyes. 'They were in it when I left the station. I could swear to it.'

Barlow looked grim. 'I know you young boys. How often did you take those papers out of the folder to check that they were all there? Twenty? Wilson said nothing; he looked guilty. 'Then the twenty-first time something happened and you got distracted.' Barlow shook his head in despair. 'This will damage your career. You know that.'

He spat on his fingers and rubbed them together to get rid of a sticky residue. 'Okay, let's go try sort things.'

He levered himself to his feet and tramped out of the tea-room and along the corridor. Grimaced in distaste at the trail of damp footprints on the terrazzo floor 'Is it raining again?'

'What?' asked the distracted Wilson.

'Raining?'

'I think so. At least… '

Wilson was still muttering about the state of the weather when Barlow led the way into No 1 Court.

Judge Donaldson sat on the bench. Donaldson had a certain reputation for exactitude and protocol, and a short fuse for inefficiency or attempted bluff.

'Never in my longest day… Gross incompetence… '

Every person in the courtroom had their heads bowed, letting the judge's invective flow over them. Anything else would risk a charge of contempt.

Harvey spotted Barlow. Relief flooded his face. 'Did you find them? Good man.'

'I'm afraid not, sir.'

Harvey turned on Wilson, his face mottled with fury. 'You're for the islands. You'll live with the seals and the descendants of wreckers until you retire or die of old age.'

Wilson looked like he wanted to cry. Barlow motioned for him to go and sit down, and indicated a bench well away from Harvey. Barlow himself continued to stand and marvel at Judge Donaldson's command of English.

Even so, it was a relief when Donaldson stopped talking and the Defence Counsel, with deliberate languidness, rose to his feet to address the court. The Defence Counsel was a tall man, with a good golf swing. He also had the ability to hold his drink and still be effective the next day.

'Your Honour, this situation is highly irregular and most unsatisfactory. My client is of considerable standing in the county. He has suffered a grievous amount of embarrassment and adverse publicity because of the ridiculous charges levied against him.'

The Defence Counsel forced his lips together to stop himself from smiling. 'Now I find that my client has no case to answer. No charge sheet. No *alleged* admission of guilt.' His tone changed to one of utter disbelief. 'In *writing*?'

Harvey bounced up. 'I took down the statement myself.'

Colonel Packenham was standing in the dock. With the dark day and the poor lighting in the court, he'd been almost forgotten about. He gave a polite cough. 'Perhaps if I may say something.'

The Defence Counsel interjected with a swift, 'Certainly not!' He looked horrified at the very thought of his client daring to address the court.

Packenham persisted. 'Surely a verbal statement would suffice?' He nodded at Barlow. 'After all, I gave the Sergeant my word.'

'Be silent,' roared the Defence Counsel.

'It's the law, sir. It's got nothing to do with justice,' said Barlow from the other side of the courtroom. Crossed his fingers that Packenham would obey Counsel, and stay silent.

Donaldson hammered on the bench with his paperweight. 'This is not the ladies' knitting circle. The next person to speak out of turn will be given a custodial sentence.'

Harvey's face went from mottled to white. He pointed a finger at Barlow and hissed. 'Your hand's in this, right up to your neck. You'll get jail if I have my way.'

Barlow looked shocked and hurt at the allegation.

Donaldson again hammered for silence. 'Mr Harvey, all remarks are to be addressed to the bench.'

'Your Honour, I apologise for the interruption.' Harvey could hardly get the words out through gritted teeth.

Donaldson looked around the court. 'Gentlemen, this is most unsatisfactory.' He waited until he had everyone's undivided attention. 'No proper paperwork relating to the case. No alleged admission of guilt in writing.' He nodded to Defence Counsel as if acknowledging the validity of his disbelief.

Counsel for the Prosecution lumbered to his feet. The cartilage in his knees cracked and egg stained the swell of his waistcoat from that morning's breakfast. 'Perhaps His Honour would grant us an adjournment of one week?'

Donaldson hesitated.

While he waited for the decision, Barlow looked across at Wilson and asked, 'Where's the evidence?'

Every eye went from Barlow to the empty evidence table, then to the table occupied by Counsel for the Prosecution, which was equally bereft of wallets.

Harvey's white face darkened down to the colour of death.

'Well?' thundered Donaldson.

'Your Honour, you see...'

The Defence Counsel said, 'Don't tell me that the *alleged* evidence has gone missing as well. And where are the witnesses? The people you *allege* lost these mysteriously missing wallets.' He looked like he was enjoying his day in court.

Not too much, Barlow hoped. Otherwise, he would find himself stopped some night coming from the golf club and be up in court himself for "driving under the influence".

Harvey stuttered that the defendant had made a full admission of guilt. For that reason he'd considered it unnecessary to summons the victims of the crime to give evidence. They were busy men, with large organisations to run. As for the evidence...

The Defence Counsel popped up and said in a loud voice, '*Alleged* evidence of an *alleged* crime.'

The alleged evidence hadn't gone missing: it's just that it was no longer in Harvey's actual possession.

Judge Donaldson's tone and bearing became regal. 'Perhaps, District Inspector, you would care to explain to the Court how you managed to misplace the evidence in this case.'

Barlow stepped up beside his superior. Wilson joined them, but stood with Barlow between him and the District Inspector. Harvey glanced at them both, his face a mixture of relief for their moral support, and pure, unadorned hate for landing him into this embarrassing position.

His tale to the court was simple, but interspersed with excuses and apologies. The two stolen wallets... The Defence Counsel readied himself for another bounce-up and Harvey quickly corrected himself. The two allegedly stolen wallets had been found in the possession of Colonel Packenham. As the Colonel had made a full confession in writing he, Harvey, could see no reason why he shouldn't give the Mayor, Alderman Fetherton, his wallet. In fact, the Alderman had been quite insistent about getting it back.

The Defence Counsel rose to his feet again. 'Your Honour, contaminated exhibits are not admissible evidence.'

Donaldson glared at him. 'Perhaps, sir, you will allow me the honour of making the decisions in my own court.'

The Defence Counsel wisely apologised and sat down.

Barlow whispered to Harvey. 'There's always Captain Denton's wallet, sir.'

Harvey's face went beyond death into decay. It appeared, as he had to admit to Donaldson, that Captain Denton, had withdrawn his complaint of theft against Colonel Packenham. In fact, Captain Denton had accepted the Colonel's explanation that he'd found the wallets and was in the process of returning them to their rightful owners when he was arrested by the police.

After Harvey had finished speaking, the only sound in court was that of rain beating off the high windows. The Defence Counsel went puce as he struggled to hold back a raft of "submissions" for a mistrial.

Colonel Packenham was weeping and didn't appear able to find a handkerchief. Barlow tip-toed over and gave him his.

'Sergeant, I'll be forever in your debt,' Packenham whispered.

'Sir, we old soldiers have to stick together.'

'But we had an agreement… '

Barlow dismissed the objection with a wave of his hand as Judge Donaldson began to speak. He spoke at length about the total unprofessionalism of everyone concerned.

The paperweight slammed down one final time.

'Case dismissed.'

30

Once Judge Donaldson had dismissed the Packenham case for lack of evidence there was no reason for Barlow to remain in the courthouse. Harvey had designated Sergeant Pierson as Duty Sergeant for the day so there was no need to head back to the station. The rain had stopped so, with a wary eye on the sky, Barlow decided to stretch his legs.

He avoided puddles in the cement-flagged pavements and stepped wide of overflowing gutters. 'Loose water should be like loose women, laws against it,' he muttered, as he selected an imaginary Victory V to suck on.

He stood at the top of Church Street, where he had a view of the tin bridge and the river. The rain had deterred shoppers and he quickly spotted Mrs Harvey, the District Inspector's wife. She was walking downhill, away from Barlow. Her head kept turning, as if looking out for someone. For no purpose other than a natural curiosity he took station behind her. Mrs Harvey stopped and stared in a shop window, then started in surprise, and hurried her step.

Barlow eased himself into a handy doorway, that of Woolworths store, and watched. She rushed to catch up with Mrs Carberry, who had appeared out of Linenhall Street. Mrs Carberry spotted Mrs Harvey, and waited for her. They walked on together and crossed the bridge.

'Now why would two women, at least one of whom has money in her purse, head away from the shops?' Barlow wondered to himself. He wondered even more when he noticed that Mrs Harvey's posture was by now no longer hunched forward. Furthermore, she was quick to laugh at things Mrs Carberry said.

Her laughter seemed unpractised. 'I'm not surprised, married to a man like that,' he muttered.

He followed the two women. He was headed in their general direction anyway. He stopped briefly to look in the window of Murrays, the chemists, where Mrs Harvey had paused earlier. He shrugged at that and stayed behind the two women as they crossed the bridge, their feet thrumming on the steel plating. They carried on up the Larne Road and eventually turned right into a warren of houses in the industrial area of the town.

Why slum, he puzzled, and then he remembered that Mrs Carberry made her living from renting houses. 'Must be rent day.'

He went back to the bridge and followed the road and the river in its meandering curve to Curles Bridge and to Edward's tar and paper hut under the dry arch. The hut was dry but smelled musty. No milk or butter in the cool box, the bread in the tin box down to the last heel. Barlow was too annoyed to even shake his head. He went back to the station where he found Edward pacing the kitchen, waiting for him.

'The hut's like you, bucked,' Barlow informed Edward.

'You've been snooping again.'

Edward went to sit in Barlow's favourite chair. Barlow thumbed him out of it. 'Tramps and drunks in the cells.'

'Really, my dear chap, your humour is ill-timed.'

'My humour is off duty, like the rest of me.'

Edward paced quickly around the kitchen, his coat tails flying after him like a broken flag. 'Grace is coming,' he informed Barlow.

Barlow played it calm. He poured the tea. 'So you already said.'

Edward took another sweep around the kitchen.

'Get the milk the next time you pass,' said Barlow.

For all his apparent casualness, he was watching Edward, concerned at his obvious distress.

Edward obliged with the milk from the fridge and kept sweeping. Barlow poured the milk and spooned sugar into each cup. Took a look at Edward, and added another.

He asked, 'Have you eaten today?'

'How can one think of food at a time like this?'

Sergeant Pierson's lunch was sitting on the draining board. Barlow gave it to Edward. 'Wrap yourself around that. And sit down before you make me dizzy.'

Edward slumped into a chair at the table and picked miserably at the greaseproof wrapping paper. Barlow took the pack off him and opened it out. Edward shuddered at the sight of food.

'Well if you don't want it then,' said Barlow, and bit into a rough-cut sandwich.

'Grace…' began Edward.

'I know, your sister, the Duchess of Hoity-Toity.'

'Has written again. She's coming home next month, flying into London, and she thinks…' Edward's hands flapped over his faded army overcoat.

Barlow shook his head. He hadn't see Miss Grace since before the Second World War. She had gone off and married some rich Australian. Now, she was coming back to see her brother and, from the panic Edward was displaying, she didn't know that he was the town drunk.

'So what does she think you're doing?' he asked.

'Directorships and things.'

'Not much then.'

Edward's head came up and he sniffed as if at a lesser being. 'Then there's the family trust, of course.'

Barlow stiffened in surprise. He hadn't known about the trust. 'Can the trust not cough you up a few bob?'

Edward's mouth opened and closed. It obviously hadn't occurred to him.

He tried to cover. 'The trustees are very tight. However… Perhaps?'

Barlow made Edward finish the sandwiches, then he picked up his cap. 'Come on.'

'Where are we going?'

'The trustees.'

31

The trustees were the firm of Combertons, solicitors. Or more properly, Mr Comberton, a quiet little man with a respected clientele. Captain Denton was a client for all conveyancing matters. He used less upright firms for his sharper practices.

Mr Comberton was in and would see Major Edward Adair. Barlow got the impression that Mr Comberton was expecting them. Perhaps a little surprised that they hadn't called before.

Once Edward was in and seated in a deep leather chair, he ran out of words.

Barlow said, 'His sister, Miss Grace, is coming home. You couldn't lend him enough out of that trust fund to buy a house and find himself a job?'

Mr Comberton smiled, pleasant as ever and slightly amused. 'I'm afraid not, but it could run to a new suit and some shirts and things.'

Edward became all stiff and indignant. 'Are you telling me that the Adair Trust Fund…? Petty cash! Petty cash!' He stood to go.

'Sit down,' said Barlow, and he did.

Edward sat quiet until a budget had been agreed between Mr Comberton and Barlow, then he found his voice again. 'Cash in hand would be most acceptable.'

Mr Comberton shook his head.

'No bloody way,' said Barlow.

Mr Comberton made a phone call, after which Barlow escorted Edward to the premises of *Dunlop & Carson, Gentleman's*

Outfitters and Tailors. A speedy job was promised; the suit would be ready long before Miss Grace arrived.

Edward licked dry lips and started the next round of panics as soon as they left the shop. 'But where is Grace going to stay? I can hardly… '

Barlow nodded. A tar and paper hut under the dry span of Curles Bridge was not exactly what Miss Grace was expecting.

He asked, 'What about Mrs Anderson's guest house?'

Edward's head vibrated a categorical no. 'For all its charms, Mrs Anderson's establishment is hardly Grace's normal standard.'

Barlow wanted to shake the man to knock some sense into him.

He said, impatiently, 'I can't see her returning to the castle, not now that they've built a factory on the lawn.' He looked Edward up and down. 'A bath wouldn't hurt you, and if you played your cards right, Mrs Anderson might scrub your back for you.'

A flush started in Edward's neck and burned up his cheeks.

Barlow envied him.

32

Barlow abandoned Edward to his worries about Miss Grace's imminent arrival and headed down town. His destination: the offices of the Ballymena Brewery Company Limited.

The brewery was a tall, almost windowless edifice built of dark lava stone. It reminded Barlow of Dartmoor Prison, although he had never actually been there.

He took the "Visitors Only" stairs up to the office suite, a long barrack of a room, which ran the breadth of the factory. The office had a high ceiling, antique dust and unstable stacks of paper on every desk. Captain Denton's office was at the far end. It had two large windows. One overlooked the office and the women clerks. The other provided a clear view of the bottling plant and the loading bays. From the loading bays came the sounds of wooden crates being hefted around, the rattle of bottles and the shouts of the workers.

Barlow looked through the internal window and saw that Denton was alone in the office. He knocked on the doorframe.

'Mr Barlow,' protested the nearest clerk, Mrs Anderson, who doubled as secretary and office manager.

Barlow ignored her. He opened the door and walked in.

Captain Denton was a big man, with more chest and girth than Barlow. His hair was darker than it should have been for his age and was beginning to thin at the temples. Even in age-faded clothes, Colonel Packenham looked a gentleman. In a pinstripe suit straight out of Bond Street Denton could still be mistaken for a butler.

Denton gave Barlow a long, hard stare. 'This is most inappropriate.'

Mrs Anderson rushed to close the door. Denton said, 'Leave it.'

As she backed off, Barlow told her. 'Do me a favour and ring the station. Tell Constable Wilson to meet me at your front gate ASAP.'

'I've had Harvey on the phone making serious allegations against you. Bribery and corruption is the least of them,' said Denton.

Barlow stood easy: legs apart, hands behind back, spine ramrod straight. He fixed his eyes on Denton's only personal item on show: a photograph of his primary school class.

'Sir, I'm here to see you about Edward.'

'In what respect?'

'Miss Grace is coming home.' Barlow proceeded to explain about the letter she'd sent Edward.

At the mention of Miss Grace, Denton had started and appeared uneasy. Barlow didn't blame him. Miss Grace was likely to be snooty about socialising with her former under-gardener.

Denton asked in an unsettled voice. 'What can I do?'

Barlow looked pointedly at the open door.

'Oh close it if you want,' said Denton, looking relieved at being able to revert to his usual brusque manner.

With the door closed and his at-ease stance resumed, Barlow said, 'Miss Grace doesn't know about Edward and his problems. She has no idea that he's a hopeless alcoholic. She believes him to be a successful businessman.'

'Then she's in for one hell of a shock.'

Barlow chose his words carefully. 'Sir, you worked up at the castle. You know what Miss Grace is like.'

'Don't I just,' said Denton. 'She'll gut the poor sod.'

'So, I was wondering if you could help.'

Denton looked impatient. 'I can hardly magic Edward a business out of fresh air.'

'No, but you could give him a directorship. One of your companies, it doesn't have to be important.'

'You're asking a lot, Sergeant.'

'You've never let Edward down yet.'

It was a nasty dig, a reminder that Denton owed his commission in the wartime army and his subsequent career to Edward having a quiet word with the right people.

Barlow prompted, 'The Honourable, Major Edward George Charles Adair: George Cross, Military Cross, has got to look good on your headed notepaper.'

'Not so good when he's up in court, charged with being drunk and disorderly,' snapped Denton.

'Leave that to me,' said Barlow.

He nodded to Denton and left.

33

Hours later, tired and weary-footed, Barlow trudged back to the police station to sign off-duty for the day. Frank Wilson limped alongside him.

They found the building ablaze with light. Every floor-board and joist reverberating with activity.

'What's got into you lot?' Barlow asked Sergeant Pierson.

Pierson shrugged. 'The DI came back from the court like a bear with a sore head.' His voice took on a bitter note. 'Would you know anything about my missing lunch?'

'Me?' asked Barlow.

'Yes, you.'

'Never.'

'And the DI wants to see you both.'

Barlow walked on. In every room, every hidden corner, people were pretending to do paperwork. Not a head lifted when he appeared. 'IN' trays were being rapidly depleted. It was already past shift change time, but no one seemed willing, or perhaps didn't dare, to sign off for the day.

Detective Sergeant Leary came trundling out of Harvey's office. Normally, the two men passed each other with little more than a grunt in greeting. This time, however, Leary stopped and shook his head sympathetically. 'Barlow, hell would be cooler than the trouble you're in.'

'You think so?'

Barlow tapped the District Inspector's door and he and Wilson went in. Harvey sat at his desk, a new brass desk lamp was angled to illuminate the pages in front of him.

Instead of the usual automatic glare, Harvey gave Barlow a blank look that changed slowly to one of apparent incomprehension.

'Did I ask for you?'

'Yes, sir.'

Harvey's look of incomprehension changed to one of anger. 'You're wrong, Barlow. I never asked for you. I've been trying to get rid of you since day one.'

'Sir?'

'And now I think I have.'

'Indeed, sir.'

Harvey pointed to his watch. 'To start with, where have you been all day?'

Barlow indicated for Wilson to answer.

Wilson said, 'Sir, we spent the afternoon calling at public houses and reminding the licensees of their obligations under the Licensing Act 1921.'

'We kept going until we'd visited the lot,' interjected Barlow, anxious that Wilson didn't say anything else.

Wilson had his notebook out. He held it up for Harvey to see. 'The establishments we called at and the names of the people we spoke to.'

'Good job.' The words nearly choked Harvey. He turned on Barlow, looking severe. 'Today's debacle in the courthouse can be laid solely at your door.'

'I see the missing papers have been found,' said Barlow.

With his usual stance of toes hard against the desk, and bending forward, he was actually looking down at Packenham's written confession.

'Yes, when it's too late.' Harvey jumped to his feet and all but shouted. 'Behind the filing cabinet in the Clerk's office.'

'They must have fallen,' said Barlow. 'That was most unfortunate.'

'Not "fallen". Inserted.' Harvey held the pages up to show their thickness. 'There wasn't enough room for them to fall, so the cabinet had to be moved and the papers pushed in behind.'

Barlow tut-tutted. 'The things Defence Counsels will do these days to get a client off.'

'Rubbish, complete and upper rubbish,' roared Harvey, his control finally gone. His fingers formed a hook, as if preparing to rip the stripes off Barlow's sleeve. 'Let me tell you this. I intend to re-investigate every case you have ever handled. When – and I mean when – I find evidence of knavery on your part, I shall take the greatest pleasure in arresting you myself.'

Barlow looked affronted. 'I object most strongly to remarks of that nature. They question my…' He took his time searching his memory for the correct words. 'My probity and honesty.'

'Get out,' screamed Harvey. 'Get out!'

Barlow nodded and left, with Wilson treading on his heels in case Harvey turned on him as well. A wary eye peered out from the WPCs' office.

Barlow told WPC Day, 'You start studying for those sergeant's stripes or I'll make your life hell.'

He walked on. In the Enquiry Office he stopped before Pierson, who didn't know whether to be triumphant or to look embarrassed. Barlow stared straight into Pierson's eyes, forcing him to ask, 'Is there anything I can do for you?'

'Aye, tell your wife to put more filling in her sandwiches.'

'I knew it was you,' said Pierson.

'And I always knew you to be an arse-licking gabshite.'

He swung his cape around his shoulders and left for the day.

34

Barlow would never admit it to anyone else, would hardly admit it even to himself, but Harvey's display of pure, unadulterated hatred had shaken him. He went home because there was nowhere else to go to on a dreary Thursday evening except a bar, and that, he felt, was no solution.

Daisy had a meal cooked and waiting for him when he arrived at the house. Leg of pork. Not the haunch, but the lower leg, with its pink flesh that dissolved in his mouth at first bite. And white sauce, and potatoes bursting out of their jackets. Daisy liked to talk, getting a conversation going with him and encouraging Maggie to join in. Half the time that evening he'd looked at Daisy blankly, not remembering what she'd just said. Eventually, she turned on the television to cover the silence that was enveloping the house.

Maggie spoke even less than usual, and seemed to cock an ear whenever Barlow or Daisy made a comment. She went to bed early. He didn't suggest they share a hot toddy before she went up, though it made her sleep better. Right then, he needed a drink but he couldn't trust himself to stop at one.

As soon as Maggie's footsteps sounded above them, Daisy slipped into the scullery. Was back in a moment, nodding at Barlow, the six knives were all accounted for.

What a bloody way to live, he thought: the events of his day seemed to have infected the entire house.

Daisy leaned forward and put a hand on his knee. 'John Barlow, what's the matter?'

Of all the women in the world, he knew he could trust Daisy not to blab about his troubles. But some of the secrets weren't his to tell, so he shook his head. 'Police stuff.'

She slid her hand away. He immediately missed the comfort of its warmth on his leg.

Over a final cup of tea Daisy talked about the hardware shop where she worked, and of her boss, Mr Gardiner Senior. How kind he was, how thoughtful. Never letting her walk home on a dark night, even if it meant her taking a lift in one of his lorries. She giggled at that and, in spite of himself, Barlow started to warm to the stories of her work: the people there and the funny things that happened. Mr Gardiner Senior was a widower. Unconsciously, she echoed her own loneliness when she talked of Mr Gardiner spending long evenings and weekends at the firm. Of how he kept her back from getting the books squared, by wanting to talk.

'He never remarried?' asked Barlow.

He hadn't, although his wife had been dead for several years. Her voice dropped in pitch as she shared a confidence. Mr Gardiner travelled on a regular basis to Dublin where he met a certain person. Not that she, Daisy, was supposed to know that.

'A lady friend?' asked Barlow.

'There's a financial arrangement,' said Daisy, a hint of tartness in her voice.

'Ah,' he said and asked the question more by way of a jibe. 'Would the two of you not... you know…?'

'John Barlow!' she said like he'd just taken the Good Lord's name in vain.

Her protest was too vehement.

He bit down a "and why not?" It was none of his business.

35

Barlow heard a car pull up outside the house. The noise of its engine invaded his dreams and it became a Stuka dive bomber screaming down to release its bombs. Bombs he had to de-fuse in mid-air before they hit his home and blew up Vera's schoolbag. A schoolbag that held a cottage with flowers in the garden. That's how he knew it was a dream: he'd never waste ground on flowers when he could grow vegetables.

The Stuka bombs hit the ground in a series of explosions. BANG, BANG, BANG. He struggled with the last bomb. It went right down the chimney, shot through the range and landed on the new settee. Vera stood, hands on hips, giving out about the dirt.

BANG.

He struggled into a sitting position, shaking sleep from his head. *There's someone at the door.* Checked the clock. *Barely six.* His heart started to thump. This early, something had to be wrong. *Dear God, not Vera.*

He stumbled out of bed. Looked over at Maggie, who was asleep. Saw his first-ever dressing gown hanging from a hook on the door and remembered Daisy in the next room. Pulled it on before opening the door, belting it tight as he headed for the stairs.

Daisy was awake. Sitting up in alarm, the bedclothes held to her shoulders.

'Don't worry,' he said. 'The world's ended and they can't cope at the station without me.'

He went down the stairs, deliberately not showing haste. Toby came hard on his heels, growling.

BANG. BANG.

Someone called out, 'Sarge, it's me, Gillespie.' His voice sounded strained.

Lord, anything but Vera.

He opened the door. Gillespie and Frank Wilson stood on the doorstep. Toby knew Gillespie. He showed him his teeth, annoyed at being disturbed so early, and aimed a growl at Wilson who backed off a step. Toby dived past the two officers and went for Sergeant Pierson who sat in the front passenger seat of the car, with the door open. Pierson slammed the door shut before Toby could reach him. Toby jumped around the car, snapping and snarling.

Things had to be bad because Gillespie didn't mutter about Toby damaging the paintwork.

There was a pause, the other two waiting for Pierson to join them. Pierson had no intention of getting out of the car with Toby there.

Finally, Gillespie spoke in a low voice, so that the neighbours couldn't hear. 'Sergeant John Barlow, I am arresting you on a charge of misusing your position as a serving officer in the Royal Ulster Constabulary, for personal gain.'

Not Vera. She's okay. His first feeling was of relief.

Gillespie continued. 'Anything you say may be taken down and used against you in evidence.' He held up a sheet of paper. 'I have a warrant here, authorising us to search your house.'

Barlow stood in the doorway, frozen. He knew he should step aside and grant the officers access. He knew he should take the warrant and examine it carefully to see the limit of the police's authority to search his home.

'It's Friday,' he said, like the day of the week mattered. Friday, the last day before Daisy went home and Vera returned. The last day in a tiring week when, day by day, he could feel the station turn against him.

'John Barlow, what's wrong?'

Daisy stood on the bottom step, her dressing gown wrapped tight around her.

He nearly said 'It's all right', but it wasn't, as she would soon find out. 'Trouble,' he said.

Gillespie pointed to the built-in cupboard beside the range and said to Wilson. 'The spare uniforms will be in there. Seize them.'

Barlow stepped aside to let Wilson past. Wilson kept his head down, so as not to meet his eye.

Gillespie lowered his voice to a whisper. 'Is there anything you don't want us to find?'

Barlow shook his head, grateful for the offer.

Gillespie spoke in a more normal tone. 'Where's your weapon?'

'In my locker at the station.'

No way did he dare bring a revolver and ammunition home. Not with Maggie the way she was.

Daisy looked as shaken as Barlow felt. Even so, her voice came out determined. 'Constable whoever you are, stay down here until I have finished dressing.' Her finger pointed at Wilson. 'And you, young man, put the kettle on.'

She disappeared upstairs.

Barlow went and sat in his chair. But not before Gillespie had checked under the cushion and made a show of tapping Barlow's dressing gown pockets by way of a body search.

'Proper pyjamas?' said Gillespie. 'I thought you were a long johns man?'

'I let Vera loose with my money,' said Barlow, grateful to Gillespie for risking the paintwork of his beloved car to keep

Pierson out of the house. Pierson might guess how frugally the Barlows lived, but he didn't want the man to see it first hand and gloat over it.

Daisy came downstairs dressed and made him a cup of tea. He found his hands shaking. Wilson had a look around the scullery and the yard, and then carried Barlow's uniforms out to the car. He heard the car boot open and close and Wilson telling Toby to bugger off. He came back in, rubbing a licked hand against his trousers.

Daisy sat in a chair at the dining table. She reached out and took Barlow's hand in hers. 'Is there anything I can do?'

He shook his head.

'If you need money for a solicitor, John Barlow, I've got some saved.'

He shook his head again, not trusting his voice. Her hand was comforting on his. So long as it stayed there, he'd be okay. *That's daft thinking.*

Gillespie's boots sounded on the floorboards upstairs. Barlow could tell he was walking around for effect rather than looking at things. He heard him talk to Maggie and Maggie speak in reply. She knew Gillespie, and wasn't startled at seeing him in her bedroom. *Is that normal?* Decided he hadn't time to worry about Maggie. He'd do better trying to work out what Harvey thought he had on him. Gillespie's hint in the caution of "personal gain" gave him some idea. *Bollocks and bother.*

Gillespie came downstairs, bringing fresh civilian clothes for him. Daisy slipped into the scullery while he dressed, then they went out to the car. He was put in the back seat with Wilson.

Toby was still trying to get at Pierson.

'If that flaming dog has scraped my paintwork...' threatened Gillespie, reverting to his normal self.

Toby piddled on the wheels, and they drove off.

36

Sergeant Pierson and Constable Gillespie marched Barlow in through the front door of the police station.

Harvey stood waiting for them. 'Why isn't this man in handcuffs?' he demanded.

Gillespie butted in before Pierson could speak. 'Sergeant Pierson said that he would personally secure Barlow and read him his rights.'

'You idiot,' blazed Harvey at Pierson. 'Now we can't inter-rogate him off the record.'

Barlow didn't like the reference to "him". Nor the fact that Leary was waiting in the Enquiry Office with his fingerprint kit at the ready.

'Barlow's dog attacked me,' said Pierson.

That at least pleased Harvey. 'Get the animal put down then. Add it to the charges. Failure to control a dangerous animal.'

'Pierson stayed in the car. The dog never got near him,' said Gillespie, disdainfully.

'Toby kept licking me,' said Wilson, and again wiped his hand on his trousers.

Harvey glared at Pierson, who slunk off into the back-ground while Barlow was being fingerprinted.

'I object to this, and I intend to complain to my Federa-tion about your humiliating treatment of a senior officer,' said Barlow.

'You'll get to make your phone call in my good time,' said Harvey.

His good time wasn't then. Barlow was paraded through the station, taken down to the cells and locked in the one nearest the toilets. The cell was six foot wide and ten foot long with a high, sealed window. The air held an odour of urine and bleach which made that particular cell almost uninhabitable. Barlow only used it for wife-beaters and dirty old men.

He could hear voices in the adjoining cell and he recognised the speakers as the Hart brothers. They'd obviously sobered up from the previous night's drinking because, while they cleared their throats a few times, they didn't actually start singing. *For such small mercies may God be thanked.*

Someone knocked on the door. He ignored it. In his station you didn't knock on cell doors, you opened them. Another knock.

'Come in,' he said.

WPC Day came in carrying a tray. She'd been crying, her eyes were red. 'Oh, Papa Bear.'

'Aye.'

She'd brought him a mug of tea and an Ulster fry. The tea he was grateful for. He choked down some food rather than have her worry any more about him.

After a long delay Sergeant Pierson escorted Barlow to an interview room where Harvey waited with WPC Day.

Barlow sat across the table from Harvey and Pierson. WPC Day sat to the side, an open notebook on her knee.

'WPC Day, record date and time,' said Harvey and then added more formally: 'Interview with Station Sergeant John Barlow by District Inspector Laurence Harvey and Duty Sergeant Woodrow Pierson. WPC Susan Day in attendance to take notes.'

'Barlow, your actions and your approach to your work have concerned me from the day I first arrived at this station.' He stopped and looked across at WPC Day. 'Did you get that?'

'Yes, sir.'

'All of it?'

She looked apologetically at Barlow. 'Yes, sir.'

Barlow knew he was being stitched up. Even so, he didn't know what to do. Appear to be innocent and concerned by answering Harvey's loaded questions. Or refuse to answer anything until he had legal representation, which always looked bad.

Someone tapped the door and came in.

'Ah, here's the Duty Solicitor,' said Harvey, looking all surprised.

'I heard I was needed, and naturally I came immediately,' said Moncrief.

Harvey beamed. 'Barlow, now that your solicitor is present, we can begin.'

Moncrief was a tall man, with his frame softening and turning to fat. At rest, his jaw hung crooked. Straightened, his face looked even more sour than usual.

With Moncrief allegedly on his side, Barlow knew he was as good as hung. He wondered if he should wait and see what the charges were, or go for throats.

The Federation solicitor, when he arrived, could be trusted to do his best for him. Meanwhile? *Go for the throat,* he decided.

'Mr Moncrief, does your firm just happen to be the Duty Solicitor for today?'

'That's right,' said Moncrief. 'And it's a pleasure to act on your behalf, Sergeant.'

'And for the first time in years you came yourself. You personally, the senior partner, and not one of your juniors?'

'Barlow, you can sort this out later,' snapped Harvey. 'You've got your legal representation. I insist that we begin.'

'Begin what?' asked Barlow. He pointed to Moncrief. 'The last time that bastard was in the station I had arrested him for attempting to pervert the course of justice.' He swung the finger around to point at Harvey. 'Add to that criminal damage and possession of an illegal weapon. Cases that you, Mr Harvey, failed to pursue through the courts.'

Actually, for his own reasons, Barlow had told Harvey not to proceed with the case, but two could play dirty.

Harvey yelled at WPC Day, 'You're not to write that down.'

Barlow said, 'Oh yes you do. I want you to record every word spoken. This is an official interview under caution.'

He leaned over the desk, surprised at the fury which was now threatening to burst out of him. Sergeant Pierson backed off, Harvey sank down in his seat.

Barlow said slowly and distinctly, giving WPC Day time to write it down. 'District Inspector Laurence Harvey, I now give you a formal caution that every word said by you or your lickspittle sergeant here will be taken down and will be used by me in a complaint of mal-administration and victimisation of a subordinate.'

'There's no need for this,' said Harvey, trying to regain control of the situation.

'No need!' Barlow swung around to Moncrief, who wisely had stayed near the door and a quick escape. Barlow used Harvey's name deliberately, so that his guilt would be clearly recorded. 'Mr Harvey, as you know full well, Mr Moncrief and I are first cousins. His uncle seduced my mother and then abandoned her. You, Mr Harvey, also know that instead of helping my mother through her subsequent pregnancy, the Moncriefs called her a whore and left her to die in the Workhouse. And, in addition, that this excuse for a solicitor has spent a lifetime trying to destroy me.'

He looked over at WPC Day. Her pencil was flying over the page as she tried to keep up.

'Interview ends.'

Barlow flung Moncrief and the door aside, and stormed back to his cell.

37

The day passed slowly for Barlow. The representative from the Federation came and talked to him and departed again. Lunch he passed on, but not the regular cups of tea. Lay and stared at the ceiling. He began to understand why prisoners revolted out of sheer frustration: sought to break up their cells. Smash anything they could get their hands on.

The sun dipped down to evening.

Finally, the door opened to reveal Sergeant Pierson, backed up by two of the strongest constables in the station. Also the stupidest, best kept for weekends and aggressive drunks.

'Out,' said Pierson.

A reasonable request, Barlow decided, but took his time straightening his clothes and finger-combing his hair into a parting.

'Get him out of there,' said Pierson.

Barlow looked at the two constables. They stayed where they were.

Barlow left the cell and followed Pierson through the building. The two constables followed behind.

One of them muttered. 'We know where he drinks. You only have to say the word.'

'Nah,' said Barlow, although the idea of Pierson hospitalised as a result of an injury pleased him. *Something painful, like broken toes*. He sucked on an imaginary sugared almond while he thought about it.

Pierson opened the door leading into Harvey's office. Barlow walked in and back-heeled the door shut in Pierson's face. Heard a yowl of pain before the door opened again. Pierson limped over to a corner and stood rubbing a knee.

In the room were Harvey, acting the cock sparrow behind his desk; the Federation representative, Inspector Foxwood; WPC Day to take notes and... *Thank the Good Lord*... Captain Denton.

Denton sat against the back wall, to the side and out of Harvey's vision. That way, he couldn't be accused of being more than an interested observer. Barlow wondered if the chair had come with bow legs or had it developed them after Denton started to use it.

Harvey glowed with pleasure at having Barlow where he wanted him. Foxwood sat upright, stiff. Occasionally, his eyes flickered to the right, towards his own office through the wall. Barlow always made sure that the man had a week's paperwork on his desk. It kept him too busy to go looking for trouble.

Proceedings started with Foxwood re-reading him his rights. Barlow stared at the portrait of the Queen on the wall behind Harvey. He felt disappointed in her.

Harvey tugged a crinkle out of his cuffs. 'Barlow, I hope that a day spent cooling your heels in the cells has taught you to be more respectful to your superiors.'

Barlow said, 'My formal caution of you and Sergeant Pierson still stands.'

The Federation man grimaced and rested his head in his hand. Captain Denton flicked fluff off his suit.

Barlow looked over at WPC Day. 'You are getting all of this down?'

'Yes, Sergeant.' She gave him a wink that crinkled her nose.

'Then, Mr Harvey, you may carry on.'

That "Mister" was the nearest thing to respect he intended to give Harvey that evening. Not one "sir" would pass his lips.

Foxwood asked, 'Do you know what the charges are against you?'

'No,' Barlow said, giving no ground. An admission of being able to guess the charges could be taken as a tacit admission of guilt.

Harvey's lips shaped into a smirk as he summarised the first charge. That he, Barlow, had concealed evidence that one Geordie Dunlop had operated an unofficial car park at the recent point-to-point meeting. The bookie, Neeson – a very reputable man in spite of his occupation – had recounted the story of Geordie Dunlop and the ten-pound bet to everyone in the City Club.

In a formal written statement made regarding the incident, Neeson also stated that he had informed Barlow about the bet and the direction Geordie had come from. In addition, several upright citizens were willing to testify that they had given Geordie money to get parking their cars on Whithead's land.

Harvey finished by asking, 'What do you have to say about that, Barlow?'

'I told you at the time. Nobody was willing to testify.'

'You threatened them into silence.'

Barlow shook his head in stubborn denial. 'They knew it was crooked, but they couldn't resist a bargain.'

Harvey went rigid with indignation. 'You are talking about some of the leading businessmen of the town.'

Barlow shaped his lips into a thin line. 'Who have now been offered immunity from prosecution if they say the right thing in court.' He found himself breathing deeply and made himself relax. The charge of aiding and abetting Geordie was weak enough to be laughable, but the more mud they threw, the more likely that some of it would stick.

'Barlow, you'd argue your way into hell. And right now you're well on your way there,' said Inspector Foxwood.

Harvey sat back in his chair and his nose wrinkled as if he was getting a bad smell. 'The second charge relates to money missing from the wallet of our Mayor, Alderman Ezekiel Fetherton.' He made a play of looking at the papers before him. 'Fifty pounds to be precise.'

Barlow kept his eye on the young Queen. He wondered what she thought she was doing, letting paper-pushers run the country.

'Have you anything to say?' demanded Harvey.

'Alderman Fetherton mentioned it to me as well.' Barlow agreed. 'However, there appears to be a problem of proof.'

Harvey spluttered through what appeared to be a statement from Fetherton. 'An over-looked entry in the books... Easily done in a cash business... Now made good and the money properly accounted for.'

He looked up. 'Well, Barlow?'

'There's nothing I can say.'

Harvey beamed. 'So you admit your guilt?'

Barlow lowered his eyes from studying the portrait of the Queen until they met Harvey's. Whatever Harvey saw there made him push back his chair.

'It's not for me to say, but our Mayor is a load of wind and fart,' said Barlow.

38

Barlow kept leaning over Harvey's desk. He loved the way the man always backed off when he did that. Right now, Harvey looked like he was having a heart attack.

'Barlow, you're not taking this matter seriously,' said Inspector Foxwood.

'But I am. Wasting police time is a serious matter, and I've better things to do than stand here and listen to this load of nonsense.'

Harvey's colour went from burning red, to white, to a high pink. Barlow was disappointed. Some of the bombs he'd dealt with during the war had exploded with less provocation.

He listened to Foxwood giving out, saying that that sort of attitude didn't help his case. He knew Foxwood was buying time while Harvey recovered his composure.

Eventually, Harvey fistled and shuffled through a new batch of papers. He'd obtained a fresh statement from Colonel Packenham, he said. In it Packenham stated that he'd seen the wallet drop from Mayor Fetherton's possession. By the time he picked it up the Mayor had disappeared into the crowd. Not being able to find the owner himself he was pleased to pass the wallet on to Sergeant Barlow. No, he hadn't looked in the wallet and, no, he didn't know how much it contained.

Barlow nodded at the last part, the bit about Packenham not knowing the contents of the wallet. The rest was pure invention.

A second statement, this one made by Constable Wilson, said that Barlow had given him the wallet at the police station and later reminded him to list the contents. On counting the money, he had arrived at the sum of one hundred and fifty pounds.

Harvey seemed more like his usual arrogant self as he looked at Barlow over the papers. 'Which is fifty pounds less than when the wallet contained when it came into your possession.'

Barlow chose his words carefully. 'Constable Wilson is as honest as the day is long. If he says there was one hundred and fifty pounds in that wallet, then there was one hundred and fifty.'

Even Harvey nodded at that.

Barlow continued. 'The Mayor, however…' Harvey tried to interrupt but he ploughed on. 'Any man that waters down milk…?' He shrugged.

'An unfortunate incident caused by a leak,' snapped Harvey.

'That affected only the schoolchildren's milk – for weeks.' Barlow gave a derisive laugh.

Harvey jumped to his feet and tried to dominate Barlow over the desk. 'You've got it in for the Mayor.'

'And he's got it in for me.'

Barlow found himself breathing hard. Angry at a system geared to protect the rich.

Inspector Foxwood gave a discreet cough. 'Perhaps we should move on to the third and final offence?'

Harvey took the hint and subsided into his chair. His hands shook as he leafed through the bottom sheaf of papers.

Barlow's aggressive fight back had sapped much of Harvey's confidence. Even so, he started hard. 'Lastly, the vital papers relating to the Packenham case, which disappeared while in your possession.'

'I dispute that,' said Barlow who, in an odd way, was starting to enjoy himself.

'Those missing papers were put behind the filing cabinet in the Clerk's room.'

'Fell,' Barlow let the word ring around the room.

'Put,' snarled Harvey. 'How much did Packenham pay you to pervert the course of justice?'

Barlow frowned at the portrait of the young Queen. 'Colonel Packenham is a gentleman with clear notions of good form.' He stared at Harvey. 'He would never offer a bribe to get himself out of trouble.'

Harvey flushed. It seemed to start at the root of his toes and work its way up his body. 'What do you mean by that?'

'Just what I said.'

Barlow wondered what weak spot he'd hit in Harvey. Was it the gentleman bit, the reference to good form, or the reference to a bribe? There had to be some way of finding out.

Harvey sat still as the seconds ticked on. Inspector Foxwood looked curiously at him.

Eventually, Harvey said, 'Inspector, take Barlow outside and book him. I want him remanded in custody. Dispute any bail application.'

Captain Denton coughed gently into the side of his hand. Harvey and Foxwood's heads jerked around in his direction. They'd forgotten he was in the room. Barlow had seen Denton cough that way to gain the attention of the nobs years ago, when he worked at the castle. Denton had gone from under-gardener to footman and then was fired for being rude to a guest. The guest, feeling guilty for her part in the argument, had got him a job in her father's brewery and, after a more-off-than-on courtship, married him.

Denton said, 'I think we have a problem here.'

Which didn't surprise Barlow. The man had an opinion on every subject and it wasn't like him to be silent for so long.

Denton eased himself upright in his chair. 'Since the time I was an under-manager in the brewery I've dreamed of this day.' He wagged a finger at Barlow. 'Five bob you cost me for not having a light on my bike. Don't think I've forgotten that.'

Denton got to his feet. Out of politeness Harvey and Fox-wood stood as well.

Denton stumped about in annoyance. 'The under-manager in me wants his revenge. Wants you in the dock for a change. Unfortunately, as Chairman of the Local Policing Board I've got to think of the good of the force.'

He stopped in the middle of the room. 'It's all very specula-tive and circumstantial.'

'But the money,' interrupted Harvey. 'The missing money is a matter of fact.'

'It's Barlow's word against the Mayor's.' Denton was plainly irritated. 'If only Fetherton had come forward at the time. But he waited a week before reporting it missing. A good barrister would make hay of that delay.'

He stopped beside Barlow and peered at Harvey, acting the short-sighted and disbelieving counsel. 'Where and when did you first make this complaint to Mr Harvey? In the City Club, you say? In the evening, you say? The subject just happened to come up?'

He made as if to remove the glasses. 'The City Club? Is this where you once swore that you'd happily sell your soul to the devil if it got Sergeant Barlow jail?' He replaced the pretend glasses. 'Perhaps you decided that fabricating evidence under oath was a less – shall we say – onerous way of exacting your revenge?'

'It wasn't like that,' protested Harvey.

'That's the way it would sound.' Denton went back and sat in his chair, from where he gave Barlow a cool up and down appraisal. 'Barlow, I could swear on a stack of Bibles that you took that money. Unfortunately, we can't prove it to the satisfaction of any court.'

Denton turned to Harvey. 'In my opinion, Mr Harvey, the best we can do at this point is suspend Barlow pending further enquiries.' Harvey gave a reluctant nod, the Federation man a more enthusiastic one.

Denton pointed at the door. 'Get out, Barlow, and remember we're watching your every move.'

Barlow held down a shrug rather than add insolence to the charges already against him. He walked out of the room. Pierson came scurrying after him.

From behind the closed door they heard Harvey roar. 'Foxwood, from now on Barlow's your responsibility. I never want to lay eyes on that man again.'

'Unless it's at his hanging,' added Denton.

'Yes,' said Harvey. 'And I hope it goes horribly wrong.'

Barlow walked on. Better Harvey thought that he and Denton were at each other's throats than for him to learn the truth. Barlow and Denton had been friends from primary school and had gone through the war together. Barlow had even been the best man at Denton's wedding because they couldn't trust Edward to stay sober.

Pierson caught up with Barlow. 'Did you really do Captain Denton for not having lights on his bike?'

'He was only a junior manager then and he wouldn't listen to sense.'

Barlow walked faster. He needed fresh air before his head exploded.

Pierson was breathless with admiration. 'You done him anyway?'

'I did, and every other boss I could get my hands on.'

The admiration turned to horror. 'Are you a Communist?'

Barlow stopped and looked at Pierson with studied patience, 'I'm not for sharing anything I make with people too feckless to work for themselves.'

He ploughed on through the Enquiry Office. Waited while Pierson and Foxwood completed the paperwork, then escaped into the blessed relief of the evening air.

39

Barlow walked home. His pace faster than that of a foot patrol, but slower than the double-time march of the local regiment, the Royal Ulster Rifles. He approached Mill Row obliquely, by way of the better housing favoured by Gillespie and many of the married policemen. The walk home involved off-duty policemen and their families disappearing from view rather than being seen talking to him.

They can't say I'm hiding from them.

His strength and his resolve faded as he approached his own front door. He went in, forgetting his now customary knock, so that Daisy would know he was coming.

Maggie stood at the range, stirring something in a pot. 'You're back early, Mr Barlow. Tea's not ready yet.'

For a moment he thought his mind had slipped with the strains of the day. Maggie up and doing things. Maggie talking to him without having to be prompted. And looking "alive". The last time she'd showed that amount of energy, she'd stabbed him. Tried to murder him.

Daisy appeared from the scullery. 'We've had a great day,' she said in a voice that carried both pleasure and a warning.

'What about yours?' she asked as he sank into his chair and closed his eyes.

'Bad. I'm suspended from duty,' he whispered.

He twitched with the shock of the impact as Toby jumped up and curled into his lap. He put his hand on the dog and felt the warmth radiating from its body. Someone tugged at his boots. Opened his eyes to find Daisy crouched down unlacing them for him so that they could talk without Maggie overhearing.

'The District Inspector is determined to get rid of me, one way or another.'

He said it bluntly in a low voice. After his arrest that morning, Daisy was entitled to know the truth, and Maggie would have to be told sometime.

Maggie turned from the stove and said, wistfully, 'Do you remember we used to take off Papa's boots for him when he came home from the Lodge?'

Barlow and Daisy looked at each other, startled.

'And do you remember the laugh we had the night we found a hole in his sock and his big toe sticking out?'

'I do,' said Daisy. She pointed to the scullery. 'Would you check the potatoes, they should be ready about now.'

Maggie disappeared into the scullery. Daisy eased off the first boot. He sighed at the feeling of freedom and wiggled his toes.

'I don't think she took in what happened this morning,' Daisy said. 'We've spent the whole day spring-cleaning the house and washing all the dirty clothes.'

He had to tell someone. 'They said I stole money. They said I took a bribe.'

She stopped with the second boot half off. 'You're the most honest man I've ever met.'

'The only thing I ever took for myself was a free pint for doing someone a favour.'

Maggie came back with the drained potatoes. He held the dog carefully as he stood up and set it on his chair, with instructions to lie there and keep the cushion warm.

'You spoil that dog,' said Daisy.

'Me?'

Maggie said, 'Papa used to lift us out of bed and carry us around the house. Even when we were big.'

Either the tablets were starting to work at last, or Maggie needed to see a doctor urgently. He didn't know if he dared share a bed with her that night and yet he ached for the oblivion of sleep. Daisy looked equally concerned.

Daisy had thoughtfully given him less food than usual, yet he couldn't clear his plate. The tea things washed and put away, he took his chair by the range while the sisters shared the settee. Toby lay entangled in Barlow's legs. Maggie talked incessantly about her wonderful childhood in Donaghadee. At nine o'clock Daisy turned on the television, saying she wanted to watch the news. Barlow kept an eye on the clock, wishing it was Maggie's usual bedtime.

After the news, Daisy pulled the kettle onto the hotplate, fetched the whiskey out of the cupboard and poured it into three glasses. Held the bottle up to the light and shook the amber liquid around. 'What's left isn't worth keeping.' She drained the bottle into the glasses. Barlow noticed that Maggie got the biggest share. *Good on you.* Hopefully, the strong drink would knock her out for the night.

Maggie finished hers and went up to bed. Barlow slid his feet into his boots. *For a penny I'd sit on.* This was often the best time of the evening, him and Daisy sitting over a final cup of tea, putting the world to rights.

'You're not going out at this hour?' asked Daisy. She looked disappointed.

'I have to. I gave my word on something.'

40

With Maggie safely tucked up in bed for the night, and the sharp knives counted, Barlow slipped out of the house and headed down to the Bridge Bar. There was no moon that night and the recently installed electric street lighting obscured most of the stars.

On the way he passed a two-man foot patrol. They nodded and walked on. Normally, they'd have stopped and given him a verbal report. He made a mental note to keep those two on nights until they'd learned some manners.

The Bridge Bar was at least warm and welcoming. An open fire blazed in the grate against the dank chill of threatening rain. Heads turned his way and nodded a greeting. Curious eyes watched, so word was out that he was in trouble.

'Look what the cat's dragged in,' shouted a man leaning against the bar counter.

'Evening, Geordie,' said Barlow.

He kept moving rather than be seen talking to Geordie. Stopped when he saw how the Guinness mirror on one wall and the Tennent's mirror on the other reflected an infinity of Edwards in a corner seat. Lined up in front of Edward were an equal number of pints and chasers.

Edward pretended to hunt in his pockets for change. 'Is it my shout or yours, Sergeant?'

His voice was slurred. He could have been on his first or his fourth drink. After four he was incapable of stringing a sentence together.

Barlow looked at the barman. 'I spoke to you earlier this week,' he said.

The barman said, 'You did.' He wouldn't meet Barlow's eye.

'So long as you know,' said Barlow. He walked out of the bar and went straight to the police station where he found Gillespie manning the Enquiry Office.

'What are you doing here?' asked Barlow.

'Acting Station Sergeant Pierson made me Acting Duty Sergeant,' said Gillespie, and shook himself like a turkey cock ruffling its feathers. 'Which is more than you ever did.'

'I'd more bloody sense.'

Gillespie dropped his voice. 'What can I do for you, Sarge?'

'I need personal stuff out of my locker, and is young Wilson still working?'

'He's in the Squad Room, studying for his exams. He never quits.' Gillespie looked embarrassed. 'I'll have to go with you and check that you take only personal items.'

'And while we're there, tell Wilson to gear up. He's going on foot patrol.'

Gillespie laughed, easing the tension between them. 'God help whoever ate your wee bun.'

Wilson jumped at the chance of getting away from his books. Promotion to sergeant involved knowing the contents of two loose-leaf volumes on law and procedure: each of them four inches thick. It also required a good conviction record. Gillespie's hint that Barlow was out for blood had Wilson reaching for his notebook and pen before he thought to pick up his cap.

'Where are we going, Sergeant?'

'Not for a drink, that's for sure.'

Barlow nodded, pleased. If the young constable was worried about going somewhere with a suspended officer, it didn't show.

Barlow took Wilson in a long curving walk through the town until they came to Bridge Street. They stopped across from the Bridge Bar and compared times. Their watches disagreed by a minute.

'How accurate is yours?' demanded Barlow.

'It's right by the pips.'

Barlow nodded. It would be of course; Wilson was like that.

'Then we're okay,' he said and they slipped into a doorway to get out of the biting wind.

In the stillness of the night they could hear the murmur of voices coming from the Bridge Bar across the street. Only a handful of pedestrians passed. The hour was late and people had an early start for work the next morning. None of the passers-by spoke to them. Most ducked into their collars and hurried on.

Wilson kept twitching. With curiosity, Barlow assumed, because he'd told him nothing.

The young constable surprised him by saying. 'Sergeant, I've got a problem.'

'She's up the spout?'

Wilson spluttered with indignation. 'Eleanor's not like that.'

Barlow looked stern. 'Keep away from that one or your career will come to a bad end.'

'But she'd nothing to do with her father being a villain, you said.'

'I did,' admitted Barlow. 'And she buttered you up nicely.' He didn't like that budding romance. Didn't like the thought of Wilson and Eleanor sharing confidences. The sort of confidences that would add to his problems. At the same time, he remembered his own early days in the force and looked at the young officer kindly. 'In this game, son, a scowl can mark a covert friend as easily as a smile can hide an enemy.'

'The truth is, Sergeant…'

Barlow grabbed Wilson's arm, and pointed at a box-shaped van approaching the bridge. 'That wouldn't be our friends again, would it?'

The van trundled over the bridge and rattled up the hill. Barlow moved into the middle of the road. Wished the town's new lighting was even brighter. Wilson joined him.

The van's lights changed to full beam. Its engine roared as the driver dropped down a gear and accelerated.

Barlow said to Wilson, 'If I say "jump" don't think, just do it.'

He held up his hand indicating to the driver to stop. Wilson did the same. *Good lad, he's standing firm.*

The van veered to their left as if trying to slip past on that side, then it swung sharp right into Linenhall Street and disappeared.

'Damn,' said Barlow. Not that he was particularly surprised. He'd found those van men a slippery lot.

'They're not clear yet,' yelled Wilson.

The young officer ran up Bridge Street to the crossroads, and sprinted down Mill Street, which paralleled Linenhall Street.

'Bugger,' said Barlow and took off after Wilson.

He found Bridge Street tough going with the hill against him. Mill Street sloped gently in his favour. Even so, Wilson's feet had wings compared to Barlow's lumbering gait. At the first junction, Wilson stopped and looked down Pat's Bray towards Linenhall Street.

Barlow barely had time to feel relief that he could stop running when Wilson was illuminated by the lights of an oncoming vehicle. The lights got stronger. Wilson stood in the centre of the narrow street, holding up his hand for it to stop.

Again, Barlow heard the engine race as the driver accelerated. He ran harder, faster, until he seemed to be running into a world made of cold light. In the middle of the light stood Wilson, his hand still in mid-air. Barlow jammed his foot hard against the edge of the pavement and dived through the light. His flying body caught Wilson, and his weight carried them both clear. They rolled and tumbled, barley clear of the wheels of the speeding vehicle.

The van kept on going, heading straight up Wellington Street towards Broadway, where five streets converged, giving the driver a choice of escape routes out of the town.

Everything about Barlow hurt. Especially his arm. He was sure his wound had opened up again. That he'd bleed to death this time. He crawled onto his hands and knees.

Wilson was already on his feet. 'Did you see that, Sergeant? They didn't stop.'

'You buck eejit.' Decided he wasn't fit to stand. He sat with his head resting on his knees, sought for breath to say more. Pointed across the street at a pub, The Farmer's Rest. 'Go in there and ring Gillespie.'

Gillespie wasn't like that idiot Pierson; he could trust him to make all the right phone calls.

'But Sergeant, it's after opening hours. It'll be closed.'

These new officers, they're all bloody boy scouts.

'Go in and make your phone call. And mind your own damn business while you're about it.'

Barlow was back on his feet by the time Wilson reappeared, pointing backwards. 'Sergeant there's maybe half a dozen… '

'I don't want to know. The owner's a decent man trying to make a living. And he's just done you a favour.'

41

Barlow limped back to Bridge Street and his shelter in the shop doorway across from the Bridge Bar. Wilson walked alongside him, mercifully quiet. Barlow hoped the young man realised how close he had come to being killed, and in future would temper courage with a bit of sense.

They were barely back in the doorway when a trickle of people came down the covered passageway leading from the back door of bar and set off in the direction of their homes. The bulky shadow of the last man to leave filled the opening. The man stopped and spat.

'Right,' said Barlow and started across the street. Wilson went with him.

'Well if it isn't the wrong arm of the law,' slurred the shadow.

'Shut up, Geordie.' He nodded towards the bar. 'Is Mr Edward still in there?'

'Aye, and well lit.'

'Get him out of it.'

Geordie straightened until his bulk hung over Barlow. 'Is that the Sergeant Major I'm hearing?' He pulled his sleeves back and flexed his fists. 'And not that shite in blue?'

Barlow stood easy, ignoring the implied threat. Wilson reached for his nightstick.

'Yes, Rifleman Dunlop,' said Barlow.

'Right,' said Geordie.

He turned and, with careful footsteps, disappeared down the passageway. He was back in a minute with Edward dangling from his hand like an empty sack. 'Now what do I do with him?'

'Put me down,' demanded Edward.

Barlow jerked his head in the direction of the Town Hall. 'Take him to the top of the street and hold him there until I arrive.'

He waited until Geordie and Edward were well away before he flexed his shoulders and gave a sigh. 'I remember when they were both tight men.' He stood on a bit longer, watching the two make their uncertain way up the hill, before drawing the nightstick he'd retrieved from his locker.

'Come on,' he ordered the young constable.

With Wilson hard on his heels, he bulled straight into the bar. A lot of faces turned his way. His slap of nightstick on the counter made sure they paid full attention.

He made a play of looking at his watch. 'By my H Samuel, ever-right watch it is now forty minutes past closing time.'

The barman threw a cloth over the draught beer handles. Barlow caught it with the point of his nightstick and pushed it away.

He nodded at Wilson. 'Constable, take all their names and addresses with a view to prosecution.'

Once he was sure the customers were telling Wilson the truth and not giving Mickey Mouse names and addresses, he turned his full invective on the barman.

'I told you, didn't I? I warned every bar in this town and every man behind it. Not a drink is to pass Mr Edward's lips until I say otherwise.'

'You did,' said the barman.

Barlow frowned at the sulk in the man's voice. 'Maybe now you'll heed me. Mr Edward is not to be served alcohol.'

The barman said, 'After tonight, that goes for you as well.'

42

Ten minutes later Barlow took the still protesting Edward into his personal custody. The cold wait had sobered him up.

'Where's the young shrimp?' asked Geordie.

'It's past his bedtime.'

'He's not bad for a Rozzer, nearly human.' Geordie made a play of looking at his watch. 'Now I've a man to see about a dog.' He headed off downhill.

'And I shall depart for my abode,' declared Edward.

'Yes you are. At Mrs Anderson's.'

Edward looked shocked. 'You wouldn't disturb the good lady at this advanced hour?'

'Try me,' said Barlow and hustled him along Meeting House Lane and across the bottom of Broadway Avenue.

With every step of the way Edward protested at being kidnapped. Barlow ignored him and was glad when they came to Farm Lodge Lane. He was tired to the point of exhaustion.

Mrs Anderson's house was in darkness. He rang the bell.

Edward tried to wriggle clear of his grip. 'Really, my dear chap, you are being most inconsiderate.'

'You're one to be talking. The bigger the words, the fuller the drunk.'

The landing light came on. It glowed through the curve of glass above the door.

Barlow shouted through the letterbox. 'It's Sergeant Barlow with Edward.'

Mrs Anderson came downstairs and opened the door. She was the senior clerk who had tried to stop Barlow from walking into Captain Denton's office unannounced. She wore a pink dressing gown and looked frightened and still a bit sleepy.

'What's wrong? Is Edward all right?'

'He just needs to sleep it off,' said Barlow.

'One is perfectly capable…'

'Shut up,' said Barlow.

'Edward, go to bed,' said Mrs Anderson and pointed to the stairs.

Edward slunk out of Barlow's grip and made his uncertain way up the stairs. At the turn he tried to protest, but steely glares from both Barlow and Mrs Anderson silenced him before he could even start. He disappeared from view.

Barlow listened. He heard Edward's footsteps on the landing, a bedroom door opening and closing and further, muffled, footsteps. Bed springs creaked, then there was silence from above.

Mrs Anderson kept the door open. 'Come in, Mr Barlow. I'll make us a cup of tea.'

Barlow said, 'I wouldn't mind a few minutes in front of that range of yours.'

He stepped into the house, the sort of house he dreamed of. He loved the wood-panelled hall and the fact that the stairwell was broad enough to hold pictures. The rug on the red tiled floor made for comfort.

'A grand house,' he said. He always said that.

He checked his boots for mud. Found they were clean, but wiped them on the doormat anyway and followed her into the kitchen. He sat at the table, on the chair nearest the range, and eased his sports coat open. His eyes closed.

'You're tired,' she said.

He jerked himself fully awake. 'It's been a long day.'

She busied herself making tea and buttering some bread. He looked at the pictures on display: a primary school class, the same as the one on the wall of Captain Denton's office. And another photograph of the same boys, a dozen years on, all wearing the uniform of the Royal Ulster Rifles.

'No finer bunch of men,' he said.

She stopped on her way to the table with a pot of raspberry jam, and studied the picture as well. 'You thumped enough of them in your day,' she said.

'Isn't that why I had to join up in England?'

Barlow and Mrs Anderson took their time over the late supper. From upstairs they could hear the rumble of Edward's snores.

'I hope you don't mind,' he said and nodded to the ceiling.

She shook her head over the top of her cup. 'No. I like a man about the house.'

They sat relaxed in each other's company. A friendship that went back to their childhood days in Clabbor Avenue. Where they used to climb into a hayloft and plan wonderful futures for themselves.

All the women in my life, how the hell did I end up with Maggie?

'You've stopped taking in guests?' he asked by way of an opener.

'I've no need to now. The house was never my own.' Nor was she safe from groping hands, he guessed. She was a fine woman who wore her years well. Any lines on her face came from laughter or pain. If she had a sour bone in her body he had yet to come across it.

He picked delicately at the subject in his head. 'Edward's sister, Miss Grace, is coming home for a visit.'

'I know. She wrote to me.'

The cautious way she said it stirred his professional instincts.

'It wouldn't be the first time she sent you a letter?'

'We keep in contact.'

'And you tell her...?' Now the edge to his voice rang clear.

She matched his gaze, but without the hardness. 'When Edward has a cold. What's going on in the town. Things like that.'

He nodded, satisfied that he could trust her not to say the wrong thing. At the same time, he felt uneasy. He hadn't known about the letters and couldn't control them.

He asked, still searching for information. 'What if she wanted to stay with you?'

'She knows what she's coming to.' Mrs Anderson looked around her kitchen with its little warm touches of plumped cushions and throws for a chill night. 'She might have been reared in the castle, but when you remember where I came from, this place is a palace.'

'Good on you,' he said.

'Anyway,' she said. 'Edward's bounty money at the end of the war bought this house for me and Arthur.'

'He'd have drunk himself to death otherwise.'

She smiled at Barlow. 'And you helped furnish it.'

'The bedroom stuff,' he said.

'You're incorrigible,' she said and got up and moved restlessly, touching things: lifting photographs to have a better look.

She looked closely at the men in their Royal Ulster Rifles uniforms. 'When Arthur joined up with the rest of you I was terrified that he would be killed. I never thought of him coming home choked with tuberculosis.'

He nodded. 'Edward reckoned that bomb disposal in England would be safer than hitting the Normandy beaches when the time came.'

'Was it that safe?' she asked.

'No, but he liked to do the really dangerous ones himself.' He buttoned up his jacket prior to leaving and looked again at the photograph. 'We made quite a team. Big Geordie humping stuff, your Arthur on the radio, and the quartermaster stealing whatever we couldn't get through official channels.'

She stood up with him. 'And your job, Mr Barlow?'

'Like always. Keeping Edward alive.'

43

In spite of the lateness of the hour, the light was still on in the house when Barlow got back to Mill Row. Daisy sat curled into a corner of the settee. She wore a nightdress and dressing gown and had her slippers kicked off. An open Bible sat on her lap. Daisy had a quiet belief in the goodness of man – a belief that Barlow envied.

'You didn't have to wait up for me,' he said.

'I wasn't tired.'

He knew that was a lie, and that she wanted to talk about something, Maggie probably. But he was past dealing with other people's problems. It had been one long, difficult day and the muscles he'd hurt in flinging Wilson clear of the Bedford van were beginning to stiffen.

'In the morning,' he said. 'Sorry.' And noted that she almost looked relieved.

He stumbled up the stairs, through Daisy's bedroom and her waiting bed, into his own room. As usual, Maggie lay at the far side of the bed, a dim hump against the night sky.

He pulled off his clothes, too weary to do more than let them drop in a heap. Reached under the pillow for his pyjamas. He was starting to come round to the idea of pyjamas: fresh, cool cloth against his flesh instead of long johns that held the sweats and worries of the day.

Clambering into his pyjamas he became aware that Maggie was awake. He stood frozen, hoping that she would go back to sleep, but she turned restlessly and saw him.

'Papa,' she whispered.

Other than WPC Day and her "Papa Bear" nickname for him, Barlow had never been called "Papa" before. Not even by Vera in fun. He made no reply. Maggie sounded dopey from the night-time Valium. If he kept quiet she might nod off again.

'Papa,' she repeated, louder this time, and he had to go to her.

He perched on the edge of the bed. Her hand came out from under the covers. He was careful not to touch it.

'Papa, can we not do that sore thing tonight? I'm very tired.'

He puzzled, *what sore thing*? 'You had a busy day,' he said, keeping his voice low. 'You need your sleep.'

Should he take her hand and put it back under the covers?

She whispered. 'You don't mind?'

'No,' he said, aching for the Valium to work properly so that he could get into bed and turn off his own day.

The dark shape of her head came off the pillow. 'You won't do it to Daisy either?'

What the "sore thing" was hit him with the force of a half-brick between the eyes. 'Oh Christ! Oh Jesus, no.'

The loudness of his voice and its sharpness brought her half sitting up.

'I won't,' he said, hastily.

'Promise.' Her hand slipped between his legs.

He jerked away from her. Thought he was going to vomit over the bed.

'No, I just came up to say goodnight.' Realised his voice was tight with tension and made it relax. 'God bless.'

He found himself in the kitchen. How he got there he didn't know.

'That old bastard. The dirty old goat. I'll… '

There was nothing he could do to a man long dead.

He'd forgotten about Daisy. She was looking at him, knuckles hard against her mouth. So she'd heard. *Enough anyway*. Knew he was going to be sick. Fled to the scullery and out into the yard. Hung against a wall and let the sick come. Again and again until acid welled up to burn his throat.

He leaned his forehead against the stone wall and tried not to think. The weather had turned chill and he was shaking with the cold. Decided to stay there and freeze. Better that than moving and having to start making more decisions.

Something soft folded over his shoulders, Daisy's dressing gown. Warm hands circled his chest.

Daisy whispered. 'I'm so sorry, John Barlow, I was afraid of this. The whiskey and the Valium, and all that talk about when we were young. It stirred memories best forgotten.'

Memories? *A nightmare*. His stomach heaved again.

She passed him a little handkerchief to wipe his face. 'Come on inside.'

The D for Daisy stitched into the corner of the handkerchief snagged his bristles. He wanted a real physical hurt, an arm smashed with a crowbar. Anything to take away the pain in his head.

He let her take him by the hand and lead him back into the kitchen. Let her sit him down on the settee. Let her hold him against the warmth of her body. Felt the comfort of her breasts with only a thin nightdress separating them. Put his arms around her to make sure she wouldn't abandon him to the horror in his head. Daisy's eyes leaked tears. He wouldn't let his out, fought them back.

Gradually, he warmed up, and his body stopped shaking from the shock. Daisy still held him, he held her. They didn't speak. They would have to at some stage, but not yet. Because there was only emptiness where his brain should be.

Time slipped by. He must have dozed, slept even. The dressing gown had fallen off. Daisy had slid sideways, he ending up half on top of her, a hand resting on her left breast. One of her hands lay trapped low between their bodies. Their lips only a fraction apart.

Somehow their lips met. Hers must have parted in surprise because his tongue felt the barrier of her teeth, the confines of her gums. Tasted the residue of the hot whiskey she'd taken earlier.

Even as he gripped her to him he knew that the settee was too small. Upstairs on Vera's bed, with Maggie in the next room? *Impossible.* His hands were already under her nightdress. Her muffled groans matched his. Her nails scoured his flesh.

Where? The floor would be too hard for her.

He stared into her eyes and saw a look he knew only too well.

The first tear came as he untangled himself from Daisy. Stood speechless before her, hands out pleading for forgiveness, his face wet from the stream of tears. Somehow, her arms had slipped out of her nightdress, it hung around her head and shoulders like a cowl. He stood on, unable to move. Knew he should turn away, hide in the scullery while that good woman made herself presentable again.

'What have I done?' he asked more of himself than her. Collapsed into his own chair as hard aching cries tore at his chest.

Instead of leaving, Daisy came to him. Hugging him, crying with him, saying it was all her fault and not to blame himself. Tucked her dressing gown around him.

She could say what she wanted, but he knew the truth. He had forced himself on a kind, God-fearing woman. And worse than that – all that talk about "Papa" taking them out of their bed and carrying them around the house.

Into Papa's own room. Into Papa's own bed to…

The look in Daisy's eyes as was the look he'd seen in Maggie's eyes throughout their married life. He sank to his knees. Stretched out his arms, praying for someone or something to kill him, to put him out of his agony.

It burst out of him in a cry of pain. 'All these years, I've been raping my wife.'

44

'You'll take a cup of tea, Mr Barlow?'

Barlow struggled his eyes open. Maggie stood before him. She was dressed, ready to go out: coat on, her hair combed. Motes of dust danced in the sunlight streaming in the window. *I'll be late for work.* Remembered there was no work for him now, and might never be again.

He still sat in his chair, a blanket tucked around him instead of Daisy's dressing gown. Something warm lay on his feet. Toby. Barlow looked up at Maggie. She gave an uncertain smile and backed off. He looked at Toby, who bared his teeth.

Barlow felt… He didn't know how he felt. Like every bone in his body had been pounded into dust. Like his insides had been ripped out and wrung dry.

'Aye, love.'

He'd never use that title "love" with her again. Had no right to.

All these years? He should have known. Should have realised. Too busy being *Station Sergeant Barlow*, the man the town liked to fear, to realise the damage he was doing in his own home.

Maggie turned away to pour the tea. He slid a hand along his leg as far as the knee, checked the other leg. Felt material the whole way. At least his pyjama were on, he was still decent. *I deserve that cell near the toilets with all the other dirty old men.*

He took the proffered mug and sipped the tea. 'Great, love…' Corrected himself. '…ly, thanks.' Noted how his hand trembled, and steadied the mug on the arm of his chair.

He heard Daisy come down the stairs and forced himself

to look her way. She was dressed, ready to leave, *aye Saturday already*. She carried her suitcase. *It couldn't be that time.*

'Maggie's taking Toby for a walk. She wants me to come with her.'

She sounded normal, her usual chatty tone. *Thank the Good Lord for that.* He'd inflicted enough hurt on Maggie without her discovering about last night.

'Well it's a grand day for a walk.'

Was that me speaking? Had to be, he was the only one in the house with a Ballymena accent, saying "wook" instead of "walk".

Toby climbed off his feet, submitted to the lead and collar and set off with the two sisters. Barlow finished his tea, which brought a tincture of strength to his pulverised body. He staggered out to the toilet. Someone, *Daisy bless her*, had thrown buckets of water to wash his vomit down the drain.

They had to talk. Trust him to sleep in the day Maggie was up early. He washed and dressed, had another cup of tea while he waited for them to come back. Couldn't face food. Became anxious about Daisy missing her train and was standing in the doorway when they finally arrived back at the house.

'We had a lovely walk,' said Maggie.

Daisy looked weary. She puffed out her cheeks to show exhaustion. *So she's not trying to avoid me.*

Maggie up and about and doing things, worried him. *What will it lead to?* He wanted to be somewhere else the next time she hit a downer.

He picked up Daisy's case. He'd already checked that she'd left nothing behind. Maggie picked up her knitting bag. It bulged with things.

'We'll be back in twenty minutes,' he said.

She said nothing, but her lips tightened into a stubborn look he knew so well.

He held out his hand to carry the knitting bag for her. She grasped it tight to her chest. He didn't mind, wasn't sure he had the energy to carry Daisy's case. When Daisy got onto the train, Vera would get off. *And she'll have to be told I've been suspended.* Better him telling her than those old bitches of police wives with their vindictive tongues.

They set off for the station. Maggie brought Toby, who'd looked longingly at his bed as he was dragged out for another walk. They walked the Ballymoney Road and the Galgorm Road, with little said between them. What had passed between Barlow and Daisy the previous night merited more than a discussion about the weather. With Maggie there, he didn't have the chance to apologise.

Nearing the police station he sensed things were happening. Of people in a hurry and no levity. One of the stupid constables who'd escorted him to Harvey's office the previous day came striding out of the police station.

Barlow grabbed his arm. 'Who's hurt?'

The constable glanced anxiously behind him. Said, 'None of us.' Shook his arm free and walked on.

Which told Barlow everything and nothing. At least it wasn't one of his men. *I should be there.*

They were in the railway station before he could bring his mind back to the problem of Daisy and the need to speak to her. But the train was already pulling in, with Vera spilling out of the carriage and starting a round of hugs. He admired her suntan, a decent colour without being sunburnt.

'Ma!' said Vera suddenly.

Maggie had climbed into the carriage and sat down, the knitting bag held firmly on her knees. Toby stood anxiously at her feet, looking out at Barlow.

'I'm going home,' said Maggie.

'But, Ma, this is your home.'

Maggie shook her head. Vera tried to pull her out of the carriage but Maggie refused to move.

The porter was already walking the length of the train, slamming the doors shut.

Daisy linked her hand in his. 'John Barlow, I did something terrible to you last night. But after Papa, I had to know if I could give Mr Gardiner what he needs from that woman in Dublin.'

She kissed Barlow, a brief touch lip on lip. 'I should have married you myself all those years back. I could cope with being Papa's "wife". Maggie couldn't.'

Then she was gone.

45

Barlow and Vera stood on the platform and watched the train pull out. Nobody waved out at them. They stood on until the last remnant of smoke had shredded itself in the sky.

'I don't understand,' said Vera.

He had no words for her that could even start to explain.

They walked down the ramp from the raised platform and through the tunnel under the railway tracks and out of the station. The sound of his boots and the patter of Vera's lighter footsteps set up an echo around the now empty building.

On the way home he made one attempt at conversation. 'How did your week in Portrush go?'

'That bloody bitch Angela.'

He didn't correct her language. Wished he didn't have to dump more pain on her.

Once home, he built up the courage to make her sit and listen while he explained about him being suspended from duty. The charge of aiding and abetting Geordie Dunlop was laughable, he told her. Issuing a caution before those men signed the statements was the right thing to do. It wasn't up to a mere Station Sergeant to guarantee law breakers immunity from prosecution. As for the missing money? As Captain Denton said, Fetherton's delay in making a complaint, coupled with his widely expressed hatred of Barlow, would have the charge thrown out of court.

'You don't have to tell me that, Dad,' Vera said. 'You've never taken a penny that didn't belong to you.'

All the same she cried.

As for the Packenham case, he said, being accused of hiding papers to get the man off. Why would he do such a thing?

What did worry Barlow, although he didn't mention it, was the danger of Frank Wilson sniffing around the Packenhams. What if Eleanor boasted of her criminal past during one of their romantic trysts? Admitted to helping her father steal the wallets? Information that Barlow had deliberately withheld from his superiors.

The boy had tried to tell him something before the van appeared at the bridge. It couldn't be an admission of passing on tittle-tattle from Eleanor to Harvey. If Wilson had done that, then he'd already be in the cells with Harvey drooling over the charge sheet. If it wasn't Eleanor and the wallets, then it had to be an admission of a personal nature. Barlow thought he knew what that admission was and nodded in approval at the boy's honesty and, by implication, his growing trust in his sergeant.

Even so, the possibility of Eleanor saying the wrong thing made him restless. He left Vera sorting through things that needed washing after her week away and went upstairs. He needed to see what clothes Maggie had packed into her knitting bag. It might give him an idea of how long she intended to stay in Donaghadee. And maybe he should ring the Donaghadee police station and warn them that if Daisy rang looking for help, then it really would be a matter of life or death.

Instead of searching in drawers, he sat on the bed. He felt so hurt, so tired of fighting: his battles, other people's. Was tempted to give Harvey his way: offer to resign in exchange for all charges being dropped. Learn to live on a pittance of a pension. His very bones ached from the weariness of worrying about other people, of trying to do the right thing by them. *Like Maggie, like Daisy herself.*

Daisy had taken the blame for last night, but he was on her like a man possessed. Only her eyes had stopped him from violating her. He could only be grateful that her fear was of failure to please, not of what he was doing to her body.

It felt a million lifetimes back: his second date with Daisy had seemed promising. Her kisses stayed well inside "respectable" but were definitely encouraging. The following weekend she wasn't free to go somewhere he'd planned, *the pictures or something*, and she suggested that Maggie went with him instead. Eventually, he took the hint that Daisy wasn't interested in him, but Maggie was. And he, a young man preparing to go off to war, was anxious to leave something of himself in case he didn't come back.

She did that, threw away a chance of love and freedom, rather than leave her sister trapped with that monster of a father.

It made the worries about his own problems seem selfish somehow.

Vera came looking for him to say lunch was ready. He pointed. She sat on the bed beside him and cuddled into him in her sudden grief.

On the dressing table sat Maggie's wedding ring and the little silver and diamond ring he'd given her to mark their engagement.

It hurt to see confirmed what he'd already guessed. Maggie wouldn't be back. His marriage was over. Almost half of his lifetime wasted on the wrong woman.

46

The scrambled egg and bacon for lunch had long since gone cold before they thought to go down and eat it.

Vera pointed accusingly at the envelope half hidden by the clock on the mantelpiece. 'You didn't go to the Credit Union for me.'

He'd forgotten about it, and that gave him something else to worry about. Those money lender boys took no excuses. Payment on the nail or else a huge fine, or increased interest, or something more serious.

'Look, I'm sorry, I'll go with you next Friday night. If there's anything extra to pay…'

She was laughing at him. 'Dad, you make them sound like loan sharks, with their enforcers ready to kick down your door if you miss a payment.'

He had made it sound like that, he admitted to himself. And she'd started to call him "Dad". A bit of gentrification had gone on in Portrush, he guessed, but right then he needed the old "Da' back. Too many changes were happening all at once.

He asked, 'Where do you hear all these words "enforcers, loan sharks"?'

'The pictures.' She shook her head in disgust at him. 'When were you last at the pictures? Years ago. Well Friday night, after the Credit Union heavies have beaten me to within an inch of my life, I'm taking you to the pictures.' She hesitated. He could almost feel her count her sparse salary before continuing. 'Followed by a fish supper in Caulfields.'

She was trying for both their sakes to give them something to look forward to other than a home empty of a mother. His daughter was going to treat him – and out of her wages. That felt good. Made him feel – not old exactly – mature, getting on. A man with his seed stretching out into future years long after he himself had passed on. That too felt good. *So long as she doesn't do any premature seeding with that pimply Cameron boy.*

After two trying days he felt his shoulders square off, firm themselves in readiness for the next knock.

Vera laughed. 'That's of course if our landlord's enforcer hasn't sorted you out first.'

Barlow had to smile at her depiction of the landlord's enforcer, the rent man. Davy Cotters: five foot and little else, thin as a rake and a soft touch for any sob story.

'No decenter man ever walked the earth,' he said. He'd go see Davy later. Sitting on the bed with Vera he'd suddenly become aware that she was a desirable woman as well as his daughter. Finding out about the abuse Maggie and Daisy had suffered had brought it into his head. *But still!*

With Davy's permission he could do something about the shower room Vera had asked about. Give her somewhere to bathe and change in private.

'You're not listening,' said Vera. She was on her feet, searching for her long-abandoned schoolbag.

'I *am* listening,' he lied.

She gave him a glare of disbelief that brought a reluctant smile to his lips.

'As I was saying,' she said pointedly, dragging the bag out from under a pile of spare clothing. 'Talking about rent made me think of Mrs Carberry and the others. You asked me to keep an eye out for them. What with getting things ready for Aunt Daisy coming, and one thing and another, I didn't get around to telling you.'

'Tell me what?'

'Mrs Carberry lets out houses. Some for herself and some for Camilla Denton.'

'You told me the first bit before.'

She searched in her schoolbag, pulled out a notepad and tore off the top page. 'She does short lets to get round the Rents Act: single people – like bank clerks – who are only going to be in town for a couple of years at most and want the place furnished.'

She handed the list to Barlow whose eyes squinted as he focused on the words. If he didn't know better, he'd think he needed glasses.

There were six houses in Mrs Carberry's name and eleven in the name of Camilla. Against each house was the name of the tenant and where they worked. Two were currently empty.

Barlow lit a cigarette while he studied the list. Vera raised an eyebrow in surprise. He seldom smoked in front of her, especially with all the recent talk about tobacco causing lung cancer.

He pointed to one address. 'That's the house I saw Mrs Carberry and Mrs Harvey going to. The one off the Larne Road.

She checked over his shoulder. 'It's let out to a clerk with the Provincial Bank. He's just moved into town.'

He nodded and took a slow pull on the cigarette. 'Mrs Carberry must have been on her way to get the house ready for him.'

She asked, 'But why Mrs Harvey as well, there's nothing in it for her?'

'That's a good question,' he said, and she smiled at the compliment.

He tapped the list. 'How did you find all this out?'

'Och, Da,' she said forgetting her gentrification. 'I asked for the addresses at the rates office. The junior clerk used to be at the Academy and he fancies me something rotten.'

'And the names of the tenants and the empty houses?'

She feigned casualness. 'I got the names by selling raffle tickets, door to door. Some of the tenants even told me what their rent cost.'

He closed his eyes and dreamed of reaching for her throat.

'A good enquiry, well executed,' he admitted in the end. His eyes opened. 'Did you have to take time off from work to do all this?'

'Dad, I can't be working all the time,' she said, before adding casually 'A couple of the men invited me in.'

It was only a red herring to distract him from her taking time off and losing wages as a result. But he couldn't resist a lecture on strange men and the dangers they posed. He could only seethe as she nodded in agreement in all the right places, and struggled to keep a smirk off her face.

47

The knock at the front door was timid, more by way of a mouse scratch. Vera was watching television and pointedly didn't notice it.

'Don't worry,' I'll get it,' said Barlow, equally pointedly, and went to the door.

Mrs Gillespie, Constable Gillespie's wife, stood there, her eyes darting up and down the street in case anyone saw her. She wore a scarf as if that would stop people from recognising her.

She said, 'Sammy had a late lunch.' As if the vagrancies of the work shifts explained the reason for her call.

'Come in,' said Barlow, standing back and holding the door open.

Her head shook in fear. 'Any man talks to you, they get posted to the Fermanagh lakes. That goes for their wives too.'

'Right,' he said. If Gillespie was willing to risk his family being uprooted to get a message to him, then it had to be important.

'He told me to tell you. Geordie Dunlop's on the run. He killed old Jordan Montgomery. Jordan was guarding Mayor Fetherton's house. They're away somewhere.'

It seemed like a million years back, but the night before Geordie had hurried off, said he had to see a man about a dog.

Barlow realised his mouth was open, and closed it.

Mrs Gillespie was already sliding away. She checked her step. 'Oh, and somebody shot Mr Whithead. He's dead as well.'

She hurried off.

Barlow stood on, still holding the door open for Mrs Gilles-pie to come in. *I should be down at the station.* All hell had to be going on with two deaths and Geordie on the run. *Harvey's the sort to totally overreact.*

He couldn't go to the station to find out what was going on. He doubted if they'd even let him in the door. Illogically, he blamed Harvey for the deaths. Ballymena had been a quiet posting until he appeared: drunks on a Saturday night, the odd thieving. The last murder had been way back in the early fif-ties, a domestic dispute. This was the fourth and fifth murder in nearly as many months. *That man's a scunner.*

Barlow went back into the house and fetched his jacket.

'I'm away out,' he told Vera, swung a leg over his bike and set off through the town and across the tin bridge. Kept to the Antrim Road until the turn into Victory Park.

Geordie's house was one of a cluster of temporary wartime prefabs. The cramped front garden had a lawn and a hedge, and trellised roses growing at the front door. A woman's muddy shoes sat on the doorstep.

He rang the doorbell and waited. After a short pause, an age-ing woman opened it. She wore slippers and a wrap-around apron.

She gave Barlow a cold look that took in his flannels and jacket. 'Who's calling?'

'The Sergeant Major,' he said.

'Not that bastarding policeman?'

'And not that bastarding policeman,' he agreed.

'Come in then. The tea's fresh made.'

He followed her down a tight hallway into a small kitchen and took a chair at a drop-leaf table. Shelves and the window ledge were crowded with ornaments. A spider plant dripped tendrils off a high shelf. Much of the furnishings were faded and cheap to start with. The smell of Mansion House polish irritated his sinuses.

Barlow shook his head. If Geordie had put half as much effort into honest work as he put into rouging…

'What's going on, Connie?' he asked.

She stopped pouring tea. 'I wouldn't know, Mr Barlow. Geordie left for England yesterday morning, looking for work.'

He said, 'Geordie was in the Bridge Bar last night.'

'It couldn't have been him. Wasn't he getting a lift from someone? Away first thing, he was.'

'Connie, I was talking to him myself.' He made his tone sharp, disbelieving.

She gave him his tea and folded into a chair across from him. Leaned her heavy bulk on the table. 'Our Geordie wouldn't hurt a fly, you know that Mr Barlow.'

'So what happened?'

'You see, he went… ' She paused. 'I'm only guessing and I know nothing. But Geordie… If it was Geordie, mind… he went to Fethertons to see old Jordan about something.'

'Like nicking things?'

She was too well trained over the years to react to the taunt. 'And he found old Jordan tied up.' She peered at Barlow trying to gauge his reaction, but found him slightly out of focus because she never wore her glasses in company. 'I'm guessing here, you see. Geordie released Jordan, but the man was having a heart attack, so Geordie phoned for an ambulance. Old Jordan asked him to stay with him, and then he died.' The last bit came out in a rush of words as she ran out of breath.

'Where is he, Connie?' he asked.

'England, Mr Barlow. Honest to God.'

'He'd do better coming in. They're calling it murder.'

'England, honest he's in England.' She started to cry. Brought up the hem of her apron to hide her tears.

Over the years, Barlow had many a good row with Connie. Ducked flying ornaments more than once, but he'd never seen Connie cry before.

The doorbell rang. One short polite buzz.

'I'll get it,' he said in relief and went into the hallway.

Edward stood on the doorstep, carrying a small bunch of flowers. He wore an ancient pinstripe suit. The suit was over-tight at the shoulders and the turn-ups had been unstitched to add another inch to the leg.

Barlow was sure he'd seen that suit before. 'Isn't that Arthur Anderson's wedding suit?'

Edward sniffed in disdain at his apparel being questioned. 'I am here to offer the good lady of the house my condolences in these trying times.'

'Oh are you now?' he said with a smile that took away the sourness of the words. 'Well the good lady's in the kitchen and she could do with some of your nonsense.'

'One is obliged,' Edward said and walked past him into the kitchen, where he made a little ceremony of kissing the 'good woman of the house' and presenting her with the flowers. When Connie offered him a tipple of whiskey, he said, 'Perhaps on another occasion, dear lady,' and gave Barlow a pained look.

Barlow sat down at the table again. Became aware of looks and covert signalled questions passing between Connie and Edward.

'I'm not stupid,' he growled. 'Edward if you're involved in hiding Geordie you'll be an accessory after the fact.'

'My dear chap.'

'Bugger the "my dear chap". Where's Geordie?'

'One could not say with any degree of certainty. England perhaps.'

Edward had probably talked one of the brewery drivers, another old soldier, into giving Geordie a lift to Belfast and the boat. Maybe the other way, Waterfoot to Cairnryan?

'Bollocks!'

He sat on and drank his tea and ignored Connie's scowls. If Edward didn't want to tell, there was no way of making him talk.

'Bollocks!' he said again and became aware of car engines at the door, two at least. Both with the comfortable growl of well-maintained engines. Edward heard them as well and raised an eyebrow in query.

Barlow asked Connie, 'Were the police around earlier, searching?'

'Aye, and ignorant too, that man who replaced you.' She looked grim. 'Could you see Geordie hiding under a baby's cot? But they woke the wee bairn anyway and searched under her pillow, as if he might be hiding there as well.'

A thunderous knock came to the door. Barlow went to open it. As soon as he released the catch Pierson burst in, shouting, 'Police.'

Barlow blocked Pierson from going any further. Behind him stood Wilson and some of the other constables.

'What are you doing here, Barlow?'

'What are you doing here?'

Pierson held up a piece of paper and tried to push past. 'Search warrant.'

Barlow held his ground. 'Did you have a search warrant when you forced your ignorant way in this morning?'

'I could do you for obstruction,' said Pierson.

Barlow used his bulk to nudge Pierson back a step. 'This search will be done by the book.' He gave Pierson another shove back. 'You will not enter this house until Mrs Dunlop's solicitor is present.' A final shove put Pierson over the doorstep.

Barlow slammed the door shut.

Found he was trembling.

Hated Pierson for his bullying misuse of the powers vested in him. Hated all senior officers who condoned the actions of Pierson and his ilk.

He walked back into the kitchen and vented his anger on Connie. 'What the hell did Geordie think he was doing?'

Connie said, 'He was getting back at Fetherton for causing all that bother.' She spat the last words, 'That two-faced old crook, getting decent people into trouble.'

Barlow scratched his head in puzzlement. 'When did Fetherton ever do anything on Geordie?'

'Not Geordie, Mr Barlow.'

She looked surprised that he didn't know the answer already. 'You.'

48

Barlow's knees gave way and he folded into a chair. Geordie had killed a man because of him? Getting back at Fetherton, for him? All the horrors of the previous days were nothing compared to this.

He listened as Connie recounted for Edward's sake what she thought had happened. Obviously, Geordie had told her all this when he ran home to pack a bag. One thought gave Barlow comfort. Maybe Jordan had agreed to Geordie tying him up. That way, he wouldn't be blamed for the theft. Maybe he got overexcited and that brought on the heart attack.

The doorbell rang again. A moderately long ring, quite firm, by someone comfortable in their authority. Barlow did doorman again, half expecting to find Gillespie advising him to step aside and let the search party in. Instead, Inspector Foxwood stood on the doorstep, cap in hand to indicate that he wanted to talk.

'May I come in?' Foxwood asked.

'Of course, sir.'

A number of policemen stood grouped around the gate. Behind them, neighbours had started to gather, their mood sour. Many of them were known to the police. Barlow pointed at Wilson and WPC Day and indicated for them to come in as well. The Inspector was entitled to have colleagues along as witnesses in case of a later dispute.

They all crowded into the little kitchen. Barlow made the formal introductions. Foxwood refused a chair and the offer of a cup of tea. He remained ultra-polite and addressed his remarks to Connie. Obviously, the information was for Barlow's benefit as well. To Barlow's astonishment he talked not about the death of old Jordan, but the murder of Whithead.

Mr Whithead always took the last fortnight of July off work. Usually, he and his wife went away somewhere, leaving the house unattended. This year, being concerned at the latest outbreak of burglaries, he sent his wife and her sister off to Italy for a week while he stayed to guard the house. According to Thompson, the stockman, this was a last-minute decision. Also, according to Thompson, Mr Whithead kept a loaded shotgun beside the bed at night. It would appear that he heard the burglar or burglars break in and then confronted them.

Having met Whithead, Barlow could guess the rest. Whithead was an impatient man with a quick temper. Just the sort stubborn enough to take on the burglars singlehanded. Barlow also knew that any normal man might threaten burglars with a gun, but it took a different sort of man to actually pull the trigger. Whithead had hesitated too long and paid for that hesitation with his life. He'd been shot with his own gun. The burglar or burglars had left, taking with them the shotgun, a Purdy worth several hundred pounds and Mr Whithead's collection of Victorian era postage stamps.

'What makes you think that Geordie Dunlop murdered Whithead?' Barlow asked. It seemed a reasonable question.

Foxwood replied. 'A rear window was forced open from the outside and then reclosed. We found fingerprints on the window frame and on the inside wall where someone had pulled themselves through. The prints are Geordie's.'

He sounded astonished.

Connie set up a howl of anguish and appeared to be on the point of collapse. WPC Day took Connie into a bedroom to lie down. Foxwood sent Wilson out to the cars to call for a doctor. Edward made a fresh pot of tea and took a cup into the 'good lady'.

Once they were on their own, Foxwood turned to Barlow. 'That idiot Pierson creates more problems than he solves. I wish to God you were back on duty.'

49

Barlow chewed hard on an imaginary crunchy sweet as he cycled homewards. There was nothing useful that he could do for Connie Dunlop and, with Foxwood supervising, he could trust the police to carry out the house search causing the minimum of fuss and damage in the process.

Two burglaries in one night. Two men dead. Geordie was a total idiot. All those years spent protecting the man from himself, wasted. If the authorities didn't hang him, he'd stay in prison until they carried him out in a coffin. *If he's that lucky.*

An all-points bulletin had gone out to every District in Northern Ireland and every police station in those Districts: George Aloysius Dunlop. Wanted for questioning in respect of two suspicious deaths. Probably armed, possibly dangerous.

Barlow knew the instructions he'd give his men. Don't take any chances. If he even looks sideways at you, shoot.

Once home, he prowled the house. Vera announced that sharing a cage with a hungry lion would be more restful, and headed 'out'. Barlow told her to call to Esler's on the way and ask Terry to call in if it was convenient.

While he waited for Terry, he changed into old clothes. Leaving the front door open, so that Terry would know to walk in, he went out to the yard and stood for a while having a think to himself. Beyond the scullery extension was a small storage area now converted into a coal shed. Across from the scullery and the small coal shed was a long shed, hardly wide enough to hold Barlow's bike. Right at the bottom of the yard was the outside toilet.

He retrieved tools and some old hessian sacks from the narrow shed and started to bag the coal. He was well into the job and warmed to the task when a voice said, 'You were looking for me?'

He turned and saw Terry Esler. Terry was a year or two younger than Barlow. He didn't work Saturday afternoons or Sundays, so he was dressed in fresh jeans and a white shirt. Terry was about five-nine, his medium-build body layered with muscle.

Terry picked up a sledgehammer and swung it casually off one hand. Terry said, 'My Dad always said that the best way to get anything knocked down in a hurry was to get you into a bad mood, give you a sledgehammer and stand well back.'

Barlow nodded, still too annoyed about Geordie to pretend a laugh. 'Your Da taught me to keep my temper.'

Barlow had run away from the Workhouse at the age of twelve and had lived rough for years. Eventually, Terry's father had taken him on as an apprentice. The older Esler quickly realised that the young Barlow couldn't afford a week's food on an apprentice's wage, so his wife started to fill her husband's tin box to overflowing. 'If it's not eaten to the last crust, I'll be in all sorts of bother at home,' he'd say as he forced food on the hungry but proud young Barlow.

'So what can I do for you, Mr Barlow?' asked Terry.

Barlow pointed to the coal shed. 'I want that converted into a shower room for Vera.'

'It's not as easy as all that,' said Terry and he began to poke around. Barlow continued bagging the coal.

They went inside and raided Vera's schoolbag for blank paper and a pencil.

'You've the sledge out and you're in the mood for knocking things, so let's do it properly,' said Terry.

'I'm not looking for the Taj Mahal,' said Barlow, acutely aware that his salary would stop following his dismissal from the force. Hopefully, the Federation would meet his defence bills, but still…

The 'still' was Vera, not the money itself. All her life Vera had been made to do without. Every spare penny had been spent on getting Maggie private treatment.

Barlow had wanted a say in things, especially in being able to say no to electroconvulsive therapy. He didn't want Maggie plugged into the mains and her brains fried. But once Maggie became violent, the State took over responsibility for her treatment and his savings account had begun to swell. He couldn't risk moving to a better house with a high rent, so giving Vera her bathroom seemed the better option.

Terry sketched as he talked. 'You'll want access from the house. You can't have access to a ground floor bathroom without a vestibule between it and the main structure.' Barlow was about to argue about the waste of space but Terry said, 'It's the law.'

'So,' said Terry, 'we replace your current back door with a window and put your sink there. The scullery window becomes a doorway into the vestibule.' He indicated doorways with lines joined to the main structure by an arc. 'The vestibule has a new door leading out into the yard and a doorway leading into the new bathroom.' He kept sketching. 'A bathroom big enough to hold the toilet as well as a bath.'

Barlow was now really worried about cost. 'There's a fair bit of money in that? New this, new that. New the other.'

'Na,' said Terry. 'Wood for the joists, together with the doors and windows, can be got from the second-hand dealers in the

Fair Hill. The bath will cost nothing. People are chucking out old-style baths in favour of these modern, panelled things. As for the wrecking?' He looked at Barlow. 'There's no better man than yourself.'

Barlow nodded. He'd spend the rest of the day reorganising things in the yard and have that word with Davy Cotters, the landlord's agent. Come Monday he'd take the sledgehammer to the coal shed.

Terry stood up to leave. 'Anytime you need a hand, just shout.' He made a play of checking his watch. 'My charging time starts from here.'

Barlow said, 'Will this cost me more than a pint?'

Terry laughed. 'Which I didn't get and I'm not likely to now. Word has it you're barred from every pub in the town.'

50

Good as his word, on Monday morning, first thing, Terry Esler had a trailer and a wheelbarrow waiting at Barlow's door.
Every day Barlow filled the trailer and every evening Terry
emptied it and had it back ready for the next morning.

On the Monday, Barlow stripped the slates and rafters off
the coal shed roof. He cleaned the slates and put them aside
for reuse. Over the week that followed the lava stone wall was
demolished, the concrete floor was dug up and a layer of quar-
ry stone was laid as the base for a new floor. Foundations were
dug and the limestone grouting on the party wall was chipped
out so as to give the plasterwork a better grip. Barlow swung
harder, chipped deeper as the days went by and still no news
came of Geordie being captured.

Vera helped in the evenings when she got home from Woolworths. She was so excited about having her own bathroom
that she would have kept them working in the moonlight.
Fortunately for Barlow the sky clouded over every night and
they had to stop as soon as the heavy dusk settled. That was
one week she didn't complain about 'people' being untidy or
leaving things in a mess.

Barlow slept soundly at night in spite of aching muscles
and his ongoing worry about Geordie. Geordie, in Barlow's
opinion, was sly and had an eye for the main chance, but no
way had he the intelligence to make a successful criminal. Yet,
Geordie had evaded the police and, as Connie kept assuring
everyone, had made it safely to England. Geordie would be

back, of that Barlow was certain, because Geordie was a home bird. The fact that he had gone on the run would make things worse for him when the case got to court.

On Friday afternoon, Barlow, Terry and Terry's son poured concrete for the foundations of the new bathroom. As soon as they finished laying the concrete he boiled the kettle twice for hot water and bathed in the tin bath, ready for his night out with Vera.

Vera had it all planned: first to the Credit Union to pay her dues, then to the State picture house for the first show. The State rather than its rival, the Towers, because the Towers was right beside the police station and neither of them wanted to head that direction. After the picture, a late supper in Caulfields and home. Funnily enough, Barlow felt excited about spending an evening with his daughter, now a young woman with opinions of her own and an inexhaustible supply of chat.

Vera arrived home from work, changed into a pointedly modest skirt and blouse and they set off for the Credit Union office in William Street. They climbed the narrow stairs and went into the front room. Barlow recognised the man and woman behind the desk. They were the couple he'd escorted as far as the Provincial Bank the night Unwin Kirker's window got smashed.

While he and Vera waited their turn in an impressively long queue of people clutching pass books, he looked around. Could see no sign of heavily built men acting as enforcers. *Maybe they keep them in the back room?*

When their turn came, the man stared over his glasses at Vera. 'You missed last week, young lady.'

'Not my fault, Mr Clarke,' said Vera a bit more cheerfully than Barlow would have liked. It paid to be respectful to moneylenders.

Vera jerked at thumb at Barlow. 'He forgot to deliver it.' She held up the overlooked envelope.

Barlow said, 'Any extra interest or whatever, I'll pay.'

Mr Clarke sucked air through his teeth then counted on his fingers. 'Last week's interest plus this week's interest, PLUS the missing capital sum of ten shillings.' He sucked through his teeth again and kept counting. 'That's twelve pence in interest, young lady, plus the ten shillings. Plus this week's ten shillings of course.'

Vera put her hands over her face and pretended to sob. 'And there's me with six wanes to feed and not a penny in the house.'

She paid up. Barlow hustled her out as fast as he politely could. He felt an utter fool about all his worries over the unpaid debt. Whatever the Credit Union people were up to, he'd open a savings account there himself once the nastiness with Harvey had been sorted. *If it can be sorted.* People like that deserved support.

They walked down William Street, crossed the road into Springwell Street and followed the slope to the Ballymoney Road. Under the shading trees at the Castle Arms Hotel, they met Edward and Mrs Anderson strolling arm in arm from the opposite direction.

'It's a lovely evening, so we thought we'd head home this way,' said Mrs Anderson with a hard stare at Barlow to take the hint.

'That's a good idea, after being stuck in an office all day,' said Barlow, with a quick glance at Edward who seemed almost desiccated. Mrs Anderson's chosen route would bring them safely home without having to pass a single pub.

Edward said, almost desperately. 'Grace is arriving on Wednesday morning by boat.'

'Good luck,' said Barlow, and meant it.

'You'll be there. I mean there's a reception at the Town Hall.' Edward's voice quivered into silence.

The last thing Barlow needed was to be surrounded by the nobs of the town, his declared enemies. Especially now when he was vulnerable. He compromised. 'I'll be outside the Town Hall if I'm needed.'

They separated, Mrs Anderson and Edward on their way home to a plate of Irish stew, Barlow and Vera across the road to the State Cinema. At the door Barlow looked back at Edward, his silhouette flickering in and out of sight between passing cars. His feet dragged as Mrs Anderson linked him further and further away from the Bridge Bar. *Five days until Miss Grace is due and she plans to stay for a week?* Barlow shivered.

'What's wrong?' Vera asked.

'Someone just walked on my grave.'

They joined the queue to buy their tickets. Barlow's feeling of unease persisted.

51

The film showing that night, *The Big Circus*, was not exactly Barlow's idea of entertainment. Far less did he approve of Victor Mature filling the screen with tight swimming trunks over a leotard in the presence of his daughter. But, surprisingly, the strangeness of the experience – he hadn't been in a picture house since he took Vera to see *Snow White and the Seven Dwarfs* – made it enjoyable. Vera paid their way in. The poor woman with 'six starving wanes at home' had a fair bit of money in her purse. Barlow bought sweets at the kiosk and ice creams at the interval.

He spent the second half of the evening worrying about the pulse of unease in his head. He recognised that pulse for what it was: a feeling of something about to happen. A feeling that old policemen and petty officers and sergeant majors seemed able to pluck out of the ether. Normally, he'd put on his uniform and hang around the station until the call came or the feeling left him. All he could do now was eat a late tea of fish and chips in Caulfields, and pretend to enjoy himself.

The evening had faded into darkness when they left the café. To the right was home. Barlow indicated left. 'Do you mind if we go this way? My legs could do with a stretch.' With a bit of luck he'd run into a foot patrol, hear what was going on.

At the crest of Church Street he turned, on a sudden impulse, into Bryan Street and then at the derelict Guys School, turned right into Wellington Street.

Wellington Street looked absolutely normal, but Barlow's feeling of unease had almost become a headache. Unwin

Kirker's display of work clothes shone brightly through the new plate glass window. The lights of the Marquis Hotel were muted, the entrance leading to the Gospel Hall dark. A handful of corner boys hung around Broadway. *All Regular.* Absolutely nothing there to worry him.

A man and a woman appeared around the corner at the top of the street. Walked past McKillen's dress shop and disappeared into the recess at the Provincial Bank. Barlow ignored them, no problem there. Mr Clarke and his female sidekick from the Credit Union, using the night safe.

Car tyres squealed. A car raced into sight. The smell of burnt rubber reached Barlow as it slid to a stop beside the Provincial Bank. Two men jumped out. They disappeared into the bank recess. Barlow heard loud shouts, screaming. A voice cried out, 'Don't sh…' Then the heavy boom of a shotgun.

The sound of the shot echoed down the quiet street. Barlow found himself running. Another shot intensified the echo. The screaming stopped.

Vera ran with Barlow. 'Stop, go back and hide,' he said.

She fell back, yet he sensed she was still following.

Two figures, men, appeared from the Provincial Bank recess. One struggled with an L- shaped object in his hand. *The bugger's reloading.* The gun swung in his direction. Barlow slammed to a halt. *No good committing suicide.* Ached for his revolver, now under secure lockup at the police station.

The men piled into the car. It was already moving before the doors shut, screaming around in a tight circle to go back the way they'd come. A window came down, the gun barrel appeared.

He's going to shoot.

Barlow threw himself to the ground. The gun boomed. Somewhere nearby wood splintered and glass shattered. The car kept turning until the boot showed. Barlow felt safe: at that angle the gunman couldn't see him. Jumped to his feet. The car reached the top of the street and turned right, giving the gunman the chance of a snap shot. He took it. The spread of pellets howled past Barlow. He flung himself down on the ground again. The car disappeared around the corner, engine racing as the driver whipped through the gears.

Barlow scrambled to his feet. Vera lay curled into the pavement behind him. *Good girl, she knew to duck.* 'You're safe now, love,' he said and ran to the Provincial Bank. The Credit Union couple lay on either side of the night safe. *The cash bag's gone, nicked,* noted Barlow, his mind reluctant to take in what he had to deal with. The woman had been shot in the throat. Her head lay detached from her body. Mr Clarke was whimpering, his left leg at an impossible angle.

Barlow knelt beside Mr Clarke. It hadn't rained in days yet that the ground felt wet under his knees. Blood. It pulsed out of Mr Clarke near the top of his thigh. Barlow unbuttoned his jacket, threw it away. Tore the shirt off his body and stuffed it and his fist into the hole in Mr Clarke's thigh. Felt bone move.

Vera stood nearby. She looked ready to collapse.

Barlow shouted. 'Don't stand there. Use the kiosk at Broadway to get help.'

Vera staggered off. The corner boys arrived. Stayed well back, but offered their shirts and vests to help staunch the blood. Barlow knew that Mr Clarke had died seconds after his arrival, but he kept pressing into the wound until an ambulance arrived.

The ambulance men took over. Barlow used the metal railings to pull himself back onto his feet. Saw a crowd had gathered to gawp at the horror. The first police car pulled up. Officers jumped out.

'You're wallet's safe, Mr Barlow, we made sure no one touched you coat,' said one of the corner boys.

'Thanks.'

Barlow looked around, trying to spot Vera, disappointed that she hadn't come back to help.

Spotted her at last. Lying on the ground outside the telephone kiosk.

He forced his way through the crowd. A policeman tried to stop him, 'Sarge.' He ran on.

Vera lay on her side. Blood trickled through fingers clamped to her side.

'I'm okay Da,' she whispered.

He lifted her hand clear and saw the fresh blood and the tear in her blouse. 'Oh my love, my sweet love.'

He scooped her up. 'You're going to be all right,' he kept telling her.

Halfway across Broadway he saw a second ambulance come speeding down Broughshane Street, bell clattering. He stood on in the middle of the street, waited for the ambulance to screech to a halt beside him. The driver rolled down his window.

'Gunshot,' Barlow said succinctly.

In seconds it seemed, Vera was on a stretcher in the back of the ambulance. The driver did a U-turn and sped back the way he'd just come. The ambulance man cut away Vera's blouse and held a pad to the wound. *There's not too much blood,* Barlow realised and didn't know if that was a good thing or bad. Vera kept sobbing. Each sob hurt her side and she cried out in pain. He held her hand and keep saying, 'You're going to be all right, love.'

He remembered doing the same thing, saying the same thing to one of his constables with gunshot wounds. Constable Jackson.

And Jackson had died.

52

At the hospital they rushed Vera into the Emergency Ward. Nurses tried to get Barlow onto a trolley as well and took some convincing that he wasn't hurt. One nurse walked into the ward, saw the blood running off him, and fainted.

His trousers hung heavy with blood. Blood also caked his arms to near his elbows and across the front of his vest. He wanted to be with Vera, to hold her hand while they treated her. Knew he'd only be in the way, so he followed the nurses' to the shower area. Consigned his clothes to a black plastic bag held out by the Ward Sister herself. The Sister, a woman who had gone prematurely grey while working in the Emergency Ward, left him when he covered his face and started to cry.

Barlow cried for the little girl he'd nearly lost that night. For running to the bank to attend to strangers while she might have bled to death where she lay. For the way she had tried to help other people even though she was badly hurt herself.

The Ward Sister came back with hospital pyjamas and a dressing gown and helped him to dry himself. His arms wouldn't coordinate with what his mind was telling them to do.

'Your daughter's in X-ray. She's conscious and her vital signs are good, so she should be okay.'

As soon as he was dressed she led him to a cubicle and made him lie down. Covered him with a blanket because he was shaking with the cold.

Barlow would have sworn that he wouldn't sleep, couldn't sleep. Yet, when he suddenly snapped awake, he found Constable

Gillespie sitting in a chair beside the bed.

'Vera?' Barlow asked.

'The Sister's away to get an update.' Gillespie's voice trembled. Vera was a special favourite of his.

Barlow remembered what had brought him awake. In his dream he'd again been standing on the steps at the State Cinema. Except in his dream he wasn't looking at Edward, but at the cars passing. One car had registered.

He grabbed Gillespie's arm. 'Ring the station. Tell them to look out for a Hillman Super Minx, colour red. A driver and one passenger.' *Where the hell did the third man come from?* 'It's the same people, the ones in the green van.'

'Are you sure?'

'As sure as I'm breathing.'

Gillespie rushed off. Barlow lay back and tried to create an image of the men in the car: height, weight, build, colour of hair. Came up with nothing near a useful description, but it was them because …their heads had turned to stare at him, then just as quickly turned away, so that he couldn't see their faces. *I should have noticed that at the time.*

The Ward Sister came back with good news. Vera was fine. The charge of shot had scraped along her side. None had invaded the chest cavity although a couple of pellets remained lodged between her ribs. Mr Hanna, the surgeon, said he'd excise them on Monday at some Christian hour. Meanwhile, he for one was going back to bed.

'I want to see her,' said Barlow. Sister had a wheelchair waiting. 'I can walk.'

'The wheelchair or you're going nowhere.'

He knew when he was beaten. Knew he couldn't go charging through the hospital at that time of night trying to find Vera. He swung himself out of bed. His legs buckled. Sister grabbed his elbow and stopped him from falling. She guided him into the wheelchair. Gillespie arrived back in time to push him along corridors and into the lift to take them to the first floor.

Vera lay in a private ward overlooking the hospital grounds. The bed was metal framed, the walls a soft cream. She looked pale and shrunken in the bed.

'They've given her something to make her sleep,' said Sister in a quiet voice.

Vera's hands lay outside the covers. Barlow took one in his. He started to cry.

When he had himself under control again he apologised. 'I don't know what's wrong with me, I've gone all to pieces.'

Gillespie placed a comforting hand on his shoulder. 'Sarge, it's been one thing after another for you recently.' The comforting hand became a friendly grip. 'It's like battle fatigue, the body can only take so much before you crack.'

Barlow spent the rest of the night at Vera's bedside. He wanted to be there when his little girl first opened her eyes.

She woke up and was fine. They talked, she laughed at him in his hospital pyjamas. She had tea and toast for breakfast.

Then she started to cry. 'I'm going to be so ugly. What will people say when they see my big scar?'

'It's not like you wear a bikini,' he said to be comforting. Saw a gleam in her eye and could imagine her in a bikini and Kenny in swimming trunks, lying together. Short of castrating every boy in the area he wondered what he could do to keep his daughter safe. *An injection that would put them off the notion.*

Knew he needed something else. Something more urgent than an injection.

Said it into himself where there'd be no witnesses. 'What I need is a gun.'

53

Wednesday morning found Barlow, like the day, bright and sharp because there was talk of Vera getting out of hospital. Vera's own little world was sunny. Kenny had come rushing back from Portrush and the dreaded Angela, to be with his wounded love.

That morning, Barlow kept his promised appointment with Edward. Miss Grace was due in on the Liverpool boat. Captain Denton had sent Edward in the Rolls-Royce to collect her, with an offer to put her up in his own house. Harvey had ordered a police car to be stationed on the Belfast road. They were to escort the Rolls on the final leg of its journey.

Around nine o'clock Barlow dug an old envelope out of a concertina of personal papers and left for the Town Hall. The Town Council had insisted on holding an official reception to welcome home Miss Grace. Or more formally: The Honourable Grace Alexandra Elizabeth Montmercy, née Adair, onetime barons of Ballymena and its domains.

He arrived at the Town Hall just in time. The dignitaries had left their sherries and were assembling on the front steps.

Harvey stood in the midst of them, wearing a new uniform and flashing his wartime medals. He scowled when he saw Barlow. 'What are you doing here?'

'Mr Edward asked me to come. Sort of moral support.'

'Make the most of it, Barlow. We expect to charge you formally next week.' He showed his teeth in a false smile. 'A man of your experience unable to give a description of the men who killed Mrs and Mrs Clarke? It was Geordie Dunlop, and you're covering for him, as usual.'

Harvey backed off, scowling. Barlow positioned himself to the side where he could see what was going on, without being caught up in the welcoming committee. He felt like he was standing out of his body, watching himself do things for the last time. Eyes that normally wouldn't meet his now stared back, and he sensed a snigger. All the people standing there knew he was in trouble. Awkward he might be, and maybe cantankerous, but he got things done and kept crime within reasonable bounds. Why they should hate him so much was beyond him.

He stared back, refusing to be intimidated. He noticed that Captain Denton alternated between swallowing dryness out of his throat and wiping sweat from his forehead. He and the mayor, Ezekiel Fetherton, shuffled politely around the other, each angling for the precedent position. All the men kept checking their ties.

'It's coming,' said Barlow, not making it plain which of the dignitaries he was speaking to. He could see the Rolls crest the hill on the far side of the tin bridge.

More shuffling for position ensued. Mrs Denton took her place beside her husband, blocking Mayor Fetherton in the process. She held Denton's hand as the Rolls-Royce pulled up at the Town Hall. Barlow stepped forward and opened the door. Edward was first out. He licked dry lips and his eyes burned in anguish.

Miss Grace followed Edward. She might have aged and put on weight, but the age had given her a sweet maturity and the weight had created a voluptuous body. Barlow would have known that pinched Adair nose anywhere. Miss Grace's eyes looked through him as if he was invisible, then she smiled and held out her hand in greeting.

'Charles.'

Denton blushed in pleasure at being recognised. 'Miss Grace… Grace… Mrs…'

'And Camilla.'

She and Denton's wife hugged and air kissed each other. Barlow remembered that they used to gad about town together.

Finally, she looked back at Barlow. 'I see you've still got that policeman here?'

Barlow took the faded envelope from his pocket and handed it to her. 'Court Order, Miss Grace. You never did pay that driving fine.'

'Barlow! This is most inappropriate,' snapped Harvey.

Miss Grace's lips went tight. 'I thought I had you posted to the Outer Hebrides?'

'Donaghadee, but I came back after the war.'

Harvey made all sorts of cringing apologies. Denton cut him off and introduced her to the Mayor and all the local dignitaries. The men crowded around her and vied for her attention. The women got pushed to the back.

The three ladies: Carberry, Harvey and Fetherton stood together. Their fixed smiles never reached their eyes. Mrs Harvey spent most of the time looking at the ground. That day she seemed particularly faded.

Miss Grace had left before the war, yet she stepped into the Town Hall without once glancing around to see how the town had changed in those twenty odd years.

Edward looked chill and thin without his usual overcoat.

Barlow stopped him as he went to follow the group in. 'Are you all right?'

'I am in withdrawal due to your interfering offices,' replied Edward stiffly.

'Good man, yourself,' said Barlow and went on about his business, which was to do nothing but stand in a Woolworths doorway and wait for the reception to be over. Something about the three ladies, Carberry, Harvey and Fetherton, had caught his attention. With nothing better to do, he thought they might be worth following. Anyway, he wanted a word with Mrs Fetherton and needed witnesses in case the lady claimed intimidation or worse.

He found it a chill wait. The crossroads at the Town Hall seemed to attract every stray draught of wind. His writing hand twitched at all the fancy cars parked on yellow lines.

Two WPCs tried to sneak out the lower Woolworths door without being seen.

'Good on you,' he said. 'Trying to discourage shoplifters.'

'That's what we were doing,' agreed one of the girls.

'Bollocks.'

'It's not like you to be in a good mood,' said the other one who knew him better.

'It goes with a blue moon. Now clear off.'

They did, very hastily, just as people started to drift away from the reception. Mrs Fetherton and Mrs Harvey were among the earliest to leave. Mrs Harvey seemed reluctant, but Mrs Fetherton encouraged her along. They got into a Rover 75 and drove off.

'Bollocks,' said Barlow again.

He watched the car go down the hill. At the bridge it turned left.

'Aha.'

That route didn't lead to any of the ladies' homes. Barlow opened his wallet and took out the list of rental houses that Vera had given him. He ran his finger down the list. The road the ladies were on took them in the direction of one of the vacant houses. He set off on foot.

The house that Barlow headed for sat on the edge of the town. It formed part of a development of new houses abandoned at the outbreak of war and never recommenced.

The house was a three-bed semi, with a separate garage: an old wooden structure that canted against the boundary wall. The Rover 75 sat in the driveway and there was no sign of life through the front windows.

Barlow had a think to himself, then he walked up the drive, past the Rover. If it had been one of the ladies' own houses, he would have rung the bell and asked to speak to Mrs Fetherton, *but a rented house*? A quick look in the front window confirmed there was nobody in the sitting room.

He decided to have a nosey around and to see what the ladies were up to before he announced his presence. At the back of the house he eased against the wall and peered cautiously through the windows. He could see no one in either the scullery or the kitchen. Sliding closer he saw a bottle of gin and a Schweppes tonic sitting side-by-side on a worktop.

From up above he heard a cry of pain.

54

Barlow heard the cry again. Definitely that of a woman hurt.

The only thing he could think of was the Belfast men in the green van. The women must have stumbled on their hideout. If he stood there and let the DI's wife be murdered, he'd be in all sorts of bother.

He tried the back door. Found it bolted and the windows snibbed shut. Ran for the front of the house. As he did so, he heard a car door slam and footsteps on the driveway.

Coming around the side of the house he saw the trailing edge of a coat heading for the front door. A second car now stood at the gate. He became cautious. Tiptoed to the front corner of the house and listened.

A key turned in the lock, the front door caught slightly as it was pushed open and leather heels clipped on the tiled hallway.

Mrs Carberry's voice shouted. 'Hello.'

Barlow stepped into the house.

Mrs Carberry spun around, hands shooting to her face in shock. 'Mr Barlow…' She sounded frightened.

I'll deal with her later. He rammed past Mrs Carberry and took the stairs on tiptoe. *No need to warn the buggers I'm coming.*

'Please…' Her voice trailed away.

Barlow pushed open the bedroom door.

Mrs Harvey's and Mrs Fetherton's clothes lay in a jumbled heap on the floor. The two ladies were in the bed, the bedclothes pushed down until he could see their naked backs. They hadn't seen or heard him enter the room.

Barlow's mind was so fixed on the Belfast men and murder that it took a few seconds for him to realise that he shouldn't be there, shouldn't be watching as Mrs Harvey whispered, 'There there, my love, my sweet,' as Mrs Fetherton's cries eased into groans of pleasure.

Suddenly, the two women became aware of his presence. They rolled apart and clawed the bedclothes over their nakedness.

'Oh, Sweet Lord,' whispered Mrs Harvey.

Barlow dragged his eyes away from their horrified faces, stepped back into the landing and closed the door. He was shaken not by what he had just seen, but by the clinging sadness in the way the women held each other.

He found Mrs Carberry waiting for him. She was white faced and holding grimly onto the banisters half way up the stairs. A lifetime of experience kicked in. He tried to adjust a uniform cap that wasn't there and hauled on the belt of his trousers.

'I'd like a word,' he said, and indicated towards the kitchen. Hopefully, the other two would run and he could pass the buck up the line to Foxwood and the WPCs. Some things a man shouldn't deal with, and this was definitely one of them.

A telephone sat on the hallway table. He tried it in passing and got no dial tone.

'It's disconnected until the next tenant,' she said.

'Aye, it would be.'

He replaced the receiver and thought of the two WPCs window-shopping in the town. If only he'd brought them along.

Mrs Carberry hesitated at the kitchen door. 'Do you have to make this official?'

'It's against the law.'

It was no answer, but right then he only had his training kept him going.

They went into the kitchen. It was comfortable and warm, with a lick of sun angling in the window. Mrs Carberry poured herself a gin and tonic. A stiff one, he noted. She drank it in quick gulps and pored herself another. Neither of them spoke. They listened instead to quiet sounds of the lovers making themselves presentable again. Barlow made a point of turning to examine every corner of the room. It helped quell his embarrassment at what he had witnessed upstairs.

The kitchen was the sort of kitchen in the sort of house that he ached to live in. Room to swing a cat and somewhere to go and sit in peace when family life got too much for him. A house like that with a patch of a garden back and front might have done Maggie more good than all the doctors he'd wasted money on over the years.

Eventually, they heard footsteps on the stairs and then the front door opening and closing. A single set of high heels clicked along the tiled hallway towards the kitchen. The door opened and Mrs Harvey walked in.

Barlow forced down an image of her succulent body, now hidden by a high-buttoned coat. 'Where's Mrs Fetherton?'

She wouldn't meet his eye. 'She left. She had an important... She couldn't wait.'

'Aye, I could see she was in a hurry.'

He motioned for Mrs Harvey to sit across from him. Mrs Carberry poured her a gin and tonic while he pulled out his notebook and opened it. He turned the pages slowly until he came to a blank one. He wouldn't have minded a fortifying drink as well. A pub fight on a Saturday night was nothing compared to this.

'Is this necessary?' asked Mrs Harvey, pointing to the note-book.

She wasn't crying, he noted, and embarrassment had brought a bloom to her normally drawn face.

He said, 'I'm making enquiries. Seeking information, you might say. I'm not cautioning you first, so anything you say cannot be held against you in court.'

Both women shivered at the implied threat of prosecution. He felt comfort in the repetition of the well-worn phrases, though with his warrant card withdrawn, he didn't think he had the right.

Mrs Carberry reached out and took Mrs Harvey's hand. 'I know Sergeant Barlow. He's a reasonable man, but we've got to be honest with him.'

'Is that what you think?' asked Barlow. He knew a bit of buttering-up when he heard it.

Mrs Carberry said, 'Captain Denton told me that you can always be relied on to do the decent thing.'

Barlow looked at Mrs Harvey and sensed an aura of her husband about her. 'And a fat lot of good it did me.' He poised his pencil over the notebook and spoke bluntly, steadying himself for the interview to come. 'Mrs Carberry, can you explain why you were providing accommodation for illegal acts?' Perhaps even participating in those acts yourself? Acts of gross indecency in contravention of…'

For the life of him he didn't know what Act of Parliament, never having had to worry about it before.

Mrs Harvey took a sip of gin and put the glass down again. Mrs Carberry's own drink was finished. She picked up Mrs Harvey's glass and took a good gulp. She deliberately drank from the lipsticked side used by Mrs Harvey. Barlow grimaced.

Mrs Carberry put the glass down with a thump to indicate that she was ready to start. She was less nervous than she'd been on the stairs and an edge of anger had come into her manner.

'Before the war I was young, and innocent and an heiress. One of the officers in the regiment,' her voice became derisory, 'swept me off my feet and married me with hearts and flowers and an archway of crossed swords.'

She took another drink. 'You've no idea how appealing that sounded to a silly young girl.' She drank again. 'That officer and gentleman stayed with me long enough to spend every penny I possessed, then he left.'

'I don't remember a Carberry in the regiment,' said Barlow.

'It's my maiden name.'

'You should've divorced him,' he said.

'I did. Just in time for the bastard to get killed in Korea, so I lost out on a widow's pension.' Her hand came out in a sweeping gesture to indicate the house. The swift infusion of gin nearly made her fall off her seat.

She steadied herself. 'The rents from this and a couple of other houses I inherited is what I have to live on.'

She reached for the gin bottle.

'Go easy on that,' said Barlow.

She paused in the pouring. 'Why? Men only want one thing. But women...' She nodded at Mrs Harvey. 'We go shopping together and talk about things. Sometimes we want to feel loved for ourselves.'

'I could see that,' said Barlow, dryly. He tried to take the bottle off her. 'You've had enough.'

She fought back against his pull. Mrs Harvey put a hand on hers. 'Please, Louise, you really shouldn't.'

A look passed between the two women, a look that Barlow couldn't fathom. In a way he found it more disturbing than what he'd seen upstairs. Mrs Carberry let go of the bottle. He put it well away from her.

'You don't spend every night staring at walls without a sinner to talk to,' said Mrs Carberry.

'I might as well,' said Mrs Harvey. She looked directly at Barlow for the first time. 'My husband has all these meetings in Belfast.'

'Yes,' he said, guessing what was coming next.

'Her name is Marie. She used to be his secretary. He set her up in a flat in Atlantic Crescent. He also pays child maintenance to a former WPC.'

He nodded rather than speak and disturb her flow of words.

'He takes this Marie to Wynne's in Dublin for weekends.' Mrs Carberry now had her arms around Mrs Harvey, comforting her. 'The best I ever get is the odd day in Portrush with the children.'

She started to cry and stopped herself.

'And Mrs Fetherton?' he prompted.

'We all married bastards!'

He jerked in surprise at the bitter words and the vicious way she'd said them.

The pencil was still in his hand although he hadn't taken any notes. He put it away and closed his notebook. 'Are you sure about your husband and those women?'

'I've got the spare key to his filing cabinet at home.'

All this time he'd thought of Mrs Harvey as a mouse of a woman. It was Mrs Carberry who leaned on her for help, not the other way around.

'Mrs Fetherton is bad news,' he said.

Mrs Harvey said, 'Maybe, but she's got her own problems.' She fiddled with her fingernails. 'I promised Mrs Fetherton I would say this. If it's a question of money?'

'All you bloody nobs. You think everyone's got their price.'
He fought to control his temper. 'It's my last days in the Force.
I'll finish the way I started.'

He stood up and walked out of the kitchen.

Mrs Carberry ran after him. 'But what about us?' She indicated Mrs Harvey. 'He'll divorce her and take the children.'

'No money, broke, needing a job? Join the club,' said Barlow.

But maybe not. The threat of Mrs Harvey being charged with 'unnatural practices' would bring Harvey to heel, force him to drop the charges. Either that or have him become the laughing stock of the police force. Even if Harvey didn't have to resign, he'd never get another promotion. Find himself in some dead-end job, pushing papers in endless circles.

'The children,' whispered Mrs Harvey. She wrapped her arms around her chest like she was crushing them to her. 'The children.'

'I'll have to think about things,' he said and walked out.

55

Barlow called into Caulfields for a cup of espresso coffee, hoping the hot milk would settle his unease. He found himself sitting at a table next to the woman police constables. They smiled at him, giving the appearance of sweet innocence.

'Aren't you two supposed to be on foot patrol?' he asked.

Their smiles became ingratiatingly sweet. One of them fluttered her eyelashes at him. 'We thought we'd take an early lunch.'

'I'm not in the mood for flannel.'

An untouched pastry was pushed his way. 'Pretty please. It looked like rain and I've just paid a fortune to get my hair done.'

'Oh all right.'

He forced himself to sound grudgingly pleasant. Really, he wanted them to go away and let him sit over his coffee and try to make sense of what he'd just seen and heard. No way did he want to take those images home. There was enough sadness there already.

'I'm getting old. Some things are way beyond me now.'

The WPC nodded. 'Way past it. You were the only one who didn't lick around Miss Grace.'

'What?'

'The rest of the men, didn't you see them? Their tongues were hanging out.'

He had, but not that way. Not the way of a husband or a wife seeing their spouse dream of being unfaithful. He'd be angry if it happened to himself and he could see others seeking comfort for their hurt if it happened too often. Looked at that way, the sex between Mrs Harvey and Mrs Fetherton made sense.

The WPC looked concerned. 'Sarge, are you all right?'

He shook his head to clear it. 'It's been a bad day.'

He sat back and closed his eyes to indicate that he didn't want to talk anymore. Sipped his coffee, had a second cup and ate the WPCs' pastry. He started to feel better when he thought of the hidden strengths of Mrs Harvey. Her husband thought he had married a compliant mouse, but some day that mouse would turn. Barlow hoped he'd be there to see it happen.

With that cheerful thought in mind he began to plan his own future.

Harvey had said that he'd be charged next week. With Judge Donaldson on the bench, he'd be put on remand without the option of bail. First things first. The house had to be finished for Vera. The sub-floor was in and the new walls were at wall-plate level. Water, gas and sewerage pipes in but not connected up to the mains. Today, he had to scutch the old stone walls and render the new ones with cement. If Terry cemented the bathroom floor this evening, they could finish the roof, and do the internal plasterwork and connect up all the fittings over the weekend.

Which created its own problems, because Vera was due home from the hospital. No way did he want her living in dirt with an open wound. And on top of that, they'd have no electricity, gas, water or even a toilet for much of the weekend. He supposed they could go to a boarding house, but Mrs Anderson had Grace and Edward staying. He hated the thought of having to move in with strangers and them wondering at his comings and goings.

Having given himself a plan of action he strode purpose-fully home, changed into his work clothes and used the edge of a shovel to burst open the first bag of cement. Really what he wanted to do was to pick up the sledgehammer and knock down a few walls.

An image of Mrs Harvey and Mrs Fetherton in the bed-room kept coming to mind. The smell of fear in the kitchen and the desperate loneliness of those two woman sharing the bed. If only Mrs Harvey would hurry up and take a stick to that husband of hers. *A big stick, weighted with lead.*

At three o'clock he cleaned himself up and went to visit Vera. Kenny Cameron was by her bedside. He seemed to live there.

Maybe she could stay with Kenny's people for a few days?

Didn't think that was a good idea. Not the way Vera sat cross-legged on top of the bed, her dressing gown gaping open bot-tom and top. "Get Well Soon" cards hung off the bedrails and cluttered the windowsill. Many of them from her school friends and many, pointedly, from individual policemen, including Detective Sergeant Leary. Public opinion in the station, if that counted for anything, was on his side in his fight with Harvey.

Kenny stayed for a polite couple of minutes and then sidled off. He always did when Barlow appeared. Hung around the foyer until he left, and then went straight back up to the ward.

Vera slid under the bedclothes and became the demure daughter while Barlow gave her an update on the new bath-room: did this, planning that, doing the other.

He decided not to broach the subject of where to stay over the weekend. He'd have to find digs somewhere, and that in itself created a problem.

Vague thoughts were forming in his head about the spate of thefts, the killing of old Jordan and Mr Whithead and the cou-ple from the Credit Union. The man who had shot Vera. *He'll get my special, undivided attention.* He needed space to think, not be trapped in a cramped house with strangers.

He was so busy thinking that he hadn't noticed Vera go quiet as well.

'Dad... about Mum.'

"Dad" and "Mum" he still found them unusual coming from her.

She picked at her bed cover. 'Have you heard anything from Mum since she left?'

'Just the card from your aunt saying that things were fine.'

He forced himself not to move uneasily when Vera said, 'Dad, I'm not stupid.'

Her eyes, he noted, were wet.

His heart faltered a beat. 'What do you mean?'

'It's been a long time since I had to block my ears at night.'

'You hear too much, young lady.'

He knew she deserved better than a snapped reply. He bought time by tidying the cards on the window ledge. 'Your Ma and I...'

He didn't know how to continue.

She nodded, apparently understanding. 'A wartime romance. You stuck with her even when her mind left you.'

At long last he found the words to explain their marriage. 'We both wanted a family.'

'And you got big, fat, ugly me.' Her voice came faintly mocking.

He was proud to have raised such a daughter, and ached to have the innocent child of his memories back. 'You made it *all* worthwhile.'

He placed great emphasis on the 'all', and was back at home before he realised that he'd been speaking of his marriage in the past tense.

56

The next morning, Thursday, Barlow woke with the first glimmer of dawn. He did a whole-body wash at the sink in the scullery and then went hunting for fresh clothes. He changed the sheets on his bed and washed the soiled ones and all the dirty clothes in the house. Hung them out on the line. By then, shafts of sunlight streaked across a cloudless sky and shadows sat long and heavy on dewy ground.

Barlow cleaned both bedrooms: brushed, dusted, flicked spiders out open windows. Polished the linoleum-covered floors. Worked down the stairs doing the same and got stuck into the living room and scullery, taking down and washing every ornament in the process. Got out the blacking and freshened up the old range. When he finally finished, he made himself a saucepan of porridge and a generous pot of tea and sat at the table having a good think to himself.

He had ideas, but they kept swirling around in his head in a formless way. Frustrated, he fetched Vera's writing pad from her schoolbag and a pencil.

Slowly wrote the word 'Ideas' at the top of the page.

Then 'People and facts' and began to list:

PEOPLE ROBBED
Mo Hunt
Unwin Kirker
Mayor Fetherton
Mr Whithead

Mr and Mrs Clarke
Made himself a fresh pot of tea. Looked at the names.
Added in *Unwin Kirker* for a second time.
Began a second list.
PEOPLE INVOLVED
The men in the green Bedford
The men in the red Hillman
Geordie Dunlop (alleged)

He was convinced that the men in the Hillman and the men in the Bedford van were the same people. He had seen two men when the Hillman passed him on the Ballymoney Road, yet three were involved in the robbery: the two who got out and the driver.

He made one final addition to the list:

The man who got into the Hillman after it passed me.

Then he started to think in terms of the known movements of the vehicles.

He'd first seen the green Bedford speeding down Wellington Street, heading south having (presumably, he wrote) just robbed Mo Hunt's house to the north of the town.

The second time, the time he and Wilson had given chase, the van was on the Galgorm Road, again heading south. He made a special note that the driver had avoided a potential trap at the bridge in Toome. Which gave at least one of them local knowledge. The night Wilson was nearly run down, the van was coming into town from a southerly direction.

As for the car, it had been heading north past the cinema, heading out of town. He put a question mark against that. Wrote: Detouring around the town centre and if so, why?

After six o'clock on any evening the town centre was all but deserted, with little or no chance of them being held up in traffic.

The next question: What were the men doing between me seeing them outside the cinema and the attack on the Credit Union couple?

Had another think. Found himself chewing hard on an imaginary wine gum. Those men wouldn't have spent the intervening hours in a pub. *Looking for other places to rob?* He wrote that down as well.

Having got that far he sat back and looked at the page. *All questions and no answers,* he decided. Kept the point of the pencil touching the next line down. Somehow, that physical contact always stopped his mind from sparking off in useless directions.

His eye was drawn to the heading "PEOPLE ROBBED".

Robbed, yes, but what of? Unwin Kirker he knew had suffered a huge loss of collectable items. But what about the rest of them? He started another list on a fresh sheet of the writing pad.

Mo Hunt – Morris Openshaw Hunt, whose eccentric father, in naming him, had correctly predicted that young Morris would someday become the Master of the Hunt and entitled to the letters MoH after his name. The fact that the Hunts kennelled the hounds on their lands had helped Hunt Senior come to that conclusion.

Old family, old money. Lived like lords of the manor, with most of the lands sold off to meet death duties. Mo Hunt claimed to have lost several generations of collectable items.

Unwin Kirker? *They made a killing there.* Wished he hadn't thought of that expression. He'd been at Kirker's house before the burglary. Maybe he should call again? Certainly, he needed to see the murder scenes in Mayor Fetherton's house and in Whitehead's. Literally get the feel of things.

Someone knocked at the front door, a hard authoritative knock.

Barlow stood up to answer it, surprised at how stiff he felt. Glanced at the clock. He'd been at the table a long time, writing and thinking when he should have been out doing.

Constable Gillespie stood at the door. He was wearing his cap. The knock and the cap warned Barlow that this was official. Constable Wilson stood behind Gillespie. Barlow knew he was being paranoid, but he could almost feel Wilson's notebook out recording what was done and said.

Gillespie said, 'Station Sergeant Barlow, we'd like a word.'

Barlow stood back and held the door open. Said nothing. *Let Wilson record that.*

Gillespie took off his cap and walked in, looked around and indicated for Wilson to sit on the settee. He himself sat at the table, on the chair Barlow had been using. Gillespie glanced down at the writing pad and said, 'It's surprising all the bits and pieces you need for an extension.' Closed the pad and flipped it over. Nodded at Wilson to start.

Barlow settled himself with his back to the range. Wilson, he noted, kept turning his cap around and around in his hands. *So he feels guilty at shafting a fellow officer?* Thought about having a suck at an imaginary Mint Imperial, and decided not to.

Wilson began. 'District Inspector Harvey ordered us to call.' The cap got a couple of turns. 'He instructed us to say that your behaviour yesterday at the Town Hall was unacceptable.

In his opinion it was designed to embarrass both the Town Council and an honoured guest of the town.'

Gillespie butted in. 'They're giving Miss Grace the Freedom of the Town...'

Barlow said, 'Her ancestors didn't need bits of paper the time they nicked it.'

Gillespie stared significantly at Wilson, and then added. 'Mr Harvey says you are forbidden to do anything in your official capacity as a policeman. And you are not to involve yourself in any current investigations.'

Wilson added, 'Any interference, and he'll charge you with attempting to pervert the course of justice.'

'As if I would,' said Barlow, sounding annoyed at his integrity being questioned. Stared over at Wilson. *Write that down.*

Instead of taking notes, Wilson produced a paper from an inside pocket. 'Mr Harvey wants you to sign this as acknowledgement of having received an official warning.'

The page was almost solid with black typescript. Barlow kept his hands well clear of the page, in case touching it implied acceptance. 'Send it to my Federation. If they say to sign it, I shall do so gladly.' *Write that down as well, you wee bugger.* 'Anyway,' he said airily. 'I'm away for the weekend, and you lot should have everything sorted before I get back.' Saw Gillespie raise his eyes to the heavens. *So that's how bad things are?*

The two officers got up to go. Barlow sat on the edge of the range and folded his arms to show casualness. 'I'm worried about the Credit Union robbery. It didn't say in the papers how much was much taken. Vera has a fair bit of money lodged with them.'

Surprisingly, it was Wilson who answered. 'This time of the year, Sergeant, nearly as much money goes out as comes in. People going on holidays and so on.'

'That's a relief. The child's worried in case she loses everything.'

'It's a pity Clarke and his Missus didn't go for that cup of tea,' said Gillespie, sounding genuinely sad and frustrated.

'Aye,' said Barlow.

A cup of tea? He had a quick suck on an imaginary wine gum. Now he knew where to go to ask more questions. Was sorry that he'd missed the Clarkes' funeral, but he knew his men would be there in force and he didn't want to embarrass them with his presence.

He walked the two officers to the door. Gillespie went around to the driver's side of the car.

Wilson hung back. 'Sergeant, those fingerprints on the steel ball bearings. I couldn't match them to any of the juvenile fingerprints in that cabinet that doesn't exist.'

He smiled at his own levity. Stood on, waiting for Barlow's reply.

Barlow frowned, genuinely puzzled. Was this another attempt by Harvey to set him up for something? *I wouldn't put it past him.* Like Wilson volunteering information on the Credit Union robbery. Anything said in reply could be taken as interference in an ongoing investigation.

He nodded towards the car where Gillespie had the passenger door swung open. Turned on his heel and went back into the house.

58

Barlow stood in his hallway and waited until he heard the passenger door slam and the police car drive off. Waited until the noise of its engine had faded into the sounds of a busy town going about its day.

He checked his watch as he pulled on his jacket. Maybe time for one call before he was due to pick up Vera from the hospital. He deliberately chose a route that took him along Ballymoney Street towards Broadway. Luck was on his side for once. He met one of the Misses Magill coming out of the only private house in the street. Two sisters, their mother and two corgis lived in the house. The women were as plump as the corgis. The sisters were very alike. Whenever he met them on their own, Barlow was never sure which one he was talking to.

'It's not like you to be out without one of the wee corgis,' said Barlow.

She held up a shopping basket. 'They don't like them in the shops.'

He nodded, pretending sympathy for the dogs. 'That poor Clarke couple, you'd have known them of course.'

Her eyes glistened with tears. 'If only they'd come in for that cup of tea.'

Barlow adjusted his pace to that of Miss Magill's and prompted her for the full story.

The Magill sisters were giving the corgis a last run out before bedtime, when they met Mr and Mrs Clarke, she said. They walked together to the Magill's house: the Clarkes and the

Magills had known each other for years. It was late on a Friday night. The Clarkes were tired after a long week, and said they'd call in for a cup of tea another time. Right then, all they wanted to do was lodge the money and head home.

He prodded her memory gently, trying to take her step by step from the moment they met the Clarkes to when they separated. Who they'd encountered, who they'd seen but not spoken to. People in passing cars. Where the dogs stopped to relieve themselves, and did they use lampposts or car wheels?

With the best will in the world Miss Magill had little new to tell him, but she remembered a car roaring past them on William Street when they stopped to greet the Clarkes. 'It was right outside the Credit Union office. I had to raise my voice to be heard,' said Miss Magill.

All this allowed Barlow to speculate with a reasonable degree of accuracy. The men in the Hillman had waited in William Street. They'd planned to grab the Credit Union money when the Clarkes appeared, but were foiled by the unexpected arrival of the Misses Magill. Rather than try to cope with a man, three women and the dogs they'd driven around to Broadway and waited for the Clarkes to reappear.

'God rest their gentle souls,' said Miss Magill as she and Barlow parted.

'Aye,' he said and pushed his way into Shalko Adair's office.

The door needed a good shove to get it open. The rust-coloured carpet was faded, worn down to a bare thread where customer heels had drummed while they waited to see Shalko. The secretary wore a black dress designed to camouflage her expanding girth and had her greying hair caught up tight in a bun.

She took off her glasses and concealed them on her lap while she squinted at Barlow. 'Can I help you?'

'Sergeant Barlow. I'd like a word with Mr Adair.'

She telephoned the adjoining office even though the party door was ajar. Shalko's voice carried clear. 'Send him in.' He spoke in the tight tone that people adopt, wondering if the call is about police business or something more social.

Barlow settled himself in a chair across the desk from Shalko. 'I was wondering about a bit of insurance,' he said to make the man relax. 'The house is rented but I'm building on a bathroom with my own money.'

Shalko nodded over steepled fingers. 'It's unusual to insure only part of a building, but give me a minute. He made a few phone calls. Put a price of £1,000 pounds on the extension.

'It won't cost anything near that,' said Barlow, startled at the possibility of getting a huge bill from Terry Esler.

Shalko put his hand over the receiver. 'That's because you're doing a lot of the work yourself. Pay a proper contractor and it would cost that, and maybe more.' He carried on with his phone calls, negotiating for the best price.

Barlow sat and listened in. Wondered how Shalko knew that he'd done much of the work himself. *Maybe he saw me run a wheelbarrow of rubble into the trailer?*' Not that it was a secret, but what would bring Shalko up Mill Row? It only lead into a warren of new houses.

'It was good of you to see me without an appointment,' he said when Shalko finally put down the receiver.

Shalko made a dismissive gesture. 'It's always a pleasure to talk to you Mr Barlow.'

'And you a busy man with all these insurance claims.'

'Yes, unfortunately.' Shalko looked profound.

Barlow stretched his feet out, making it plain that he was in no rush to leave. 'As your cousin Edward would say "for my edification and knowledge". How do you go about working out an insurance claim? You know, some place like the Hunts. Do you take a round figure or do you have to list everything?'

'Item by item. And put a value on them as well.'

'Rather you than me.' Barlow flexed the hand cramped from a morning's writing and filled out a cheque for the insurance premium. 'But it takes quite a skill to value a farm one day and, say, Mr Whithead's stamp collection the next?' He shook his head in admiration as he handed over the cheque. 'That must require some brainpower.'

'A lifetime's experience, Sergeant,' said Shalko, moving uneasily in his chair.

'Heavens is that the time?' exclaimed Barlow, pretending to glance at his watch. He hopped to his feet. 'If there's nothing else, I'll get going. I've got Johnny Scullion and his taxi expecting me. Vera's being discharged from hospital this morning.'

'Call on Monday morning. The policy will be in by then,' said Shalko, looking relieved.

Johnny Scullion and his taxi were sitting outside Shalko's office.

Barlow slipped into the front passenger seat, and sniffed. 'You and Paddy Murray were out marking greyhound pups this morning.'

'How do you know?' asked Johnny, who spent enjoyable days driving the local Irish Coursing Club Steward around the countryside.

'I've a nose for that sort of thing.'

59

Vera eased herself gently out of the taxi, careful not to brush her injured side against the car door. In the hospital she'd looked great, bouncing on the bed with impatience to be discharged. Outside her own home, Barlow noticed a twist to her stance that hurt him more than it hurt her. She looked pale and shaky, though she pretended she was fine.

'You go on in, I'll get the bags,' Barlow told her and turned to settle the more than reasonable fare with Johnny Scullion. Johnny did so many good turns for people, Barlow wondered how he made a living at all.

Johnny drove off. Barlow followed Vera into the house. She wasn't in the living room. The doors leading to the scullery and out into the yard were wide open. He ran up the stairs and put Vera's case on the bed, so that she wouldn't be tempted to carry it up herself, and followed her out into the yard.

He found her standing, hands over her face, tears trickling between her fingers. He felt a failure, with the new walls only roughly plastered and the window frames and the bath lying in the yard.

Careful not to cause her any pain, he put a comforting arm around her shoulders. 'It's the best I can do, love. It's a bit rough at the minute, but wait until Terry and the boys get at it over the weekend.'

'A bathroom. A real bathroom,' she whispered. 'It's beautiful.'

He held her until the crying stopped and she told him she was just being silly.

Her tears had shaken him more than he dared admit. He'd been so busy over the years thinking about Maggie and saving for Maggie's medical costs that he'd never seriously considered Vera's feelings and wishes. Nor had he thought properly about the strain she'd been under the last few days. She'd seen people she knew murdered in the most gruesome fashion and had been shot herself.

Scarred for life as a result of shotgun wounds, a madwoman for a mother and a father likely to end up in jail. He realised that if he didn't put a tight lid on his emotions he would also begin crying. Realised that right then Vera was extremely vulnerable. No way could he put her into a guest house among strangers.

He went back into the house, undecided what to do next. Vera couldn't stay in the house, there'd be no water, no bathing facilities and dirt everywhere. She'd be in the workers' way plus she risked getting all sorts of infections with that open wound.

Normally, the Gillespies would have made room for her, with a heart and a half. But that was impossible with him suspended and facing charges. Mrs Anderson's guest house was full and Vera needed something better than a put-up bed.

Barlow sat over a cup of tea and shared Vera's leftover biscuits from the hospital. Her mood had swung the other way. Now, she was full of plans for the bathroom: colours, tiles around the bath, tiles on the floor, mirrors. He began to think that Vera and her gewgaws would cost more than Terry and his building work.

Eventually, Kenny came knocking. Vera dragged him out to see the new bathroom. Barlow checked his pocket for change and walked down to the nearest call box. He had two choices: beg a bed off Mrs Cameron, Kenny's mother, for the weekend, or ask Mrs Denton.

He found his heart pounding as he dialled. 'Big, brave John Barlow,' he muttered, disgusted with himself. He could be as ignorant to people as he liked and it didn't take a fidge out of him. But if he needed to ask a favour…

'Dentons,' said a voice.

Oh God. Miss Grace. He should have known she'd be there when Mrs Anderson was at work.

'May I speak to Mrs Denton, please?'

'Whom will I say is calling?'

Her way of pronouncing 'calling' had stretched out the syllables.

He cleared his throat. 'Sergeant John Barlow.' Cleared it again.

She said nothing. He heard the receiver being placed on a table, the creak of a door hinge and distant voices. After what seemed like a long pause, the receiver was picked up again.

Clarissa Denton identified herself, an edge of caution to her tone. Now he knew for sure that he'd made a mistake. He struggled through an explanation of why he'd called. Throughout, he got a stony silence from the other end. Finally he ended with, 'I'm sorry. I realise now I shouldn't have asked.'

'John, when your wife first took ill and you were left to take care of an infant, who did you come to for help?'

'It's different now… I'm in trouble… It could compromise the Captain's position on the Policing Board…' Found himself repeating. 'I'm sorry, I shouldn't have asked.' Placed a hand on his knee to quell a spasm of nerves.

'Tell Vera to have her bag packed and be ready to leave at ten o'clock tomorrow morning. Grace and I are going shopping in Belfast. She can come with us; she's got a good eye for colours.'

He didn't know what to say. He wasn't used to people do-ing him a kindness and this was a big one. Clarissa Denton was the only person in the world who called him John. Not John Barlow or Mister Barlow or Sergeant Barlow. But plain 'John'.

She cut through his stuttered thanks. 'I've pastries burning in the oven. Tomorrow morning, ten sharp.'

He heard the receiver click. The line went dead.

60

By ten past ten the next morning Vera was on her way to Belfast, with enough money in her pocket to buy herself an outfit in Renee Meneely's dress shop. Barlow reckoned that if he was going to drain his savings account, he might as well do it in style.

He picked up his overnight bag and an old fishing rod dug out of the attic. He left the front door on the push for Terry Esler and swung down the road with a spring in his step that surprised even him. He was going to Portstewart for a couple of nights.

Barlow's route took him down the Galgorm Road, past the police station. He passed no one, saw no one. Not that any officer would dare stop and chat outside Harvey's window. Geordie Dunlop hadn't been caught yet. According to the television news, the police were following definite lines of enquiry. An arrest was expected at any time. Barlow had to give Geordie credit where credit was due. He'd expected the man to be picked up within days, probably in the Battery Inn, the first pub on the road to Larne Port and the ferry to Scotland.

Once under the railway arch, Barlow walked on straight instead of turning right into the railway station. From that point on the housing changed from terraces to detached and semi-detached monoliths or the gated entrances to estates. Not far up the road he turned in through the gateway of a grey cement-faced house standing on its own grounds. The sitting room alone was probably the size of his own house.

He rang the bell. The door was opened by Mrs Fetherton. She wore a housecoat that had never seen cleaning or cooking.

'I knew you'd come,' she said.

She left him standing at the door and went back to the hall table. Returned, carrying her handbag. Glancing anxiously behind her, she said, 'I can give you thirty-five pounds now. If you want more you'll have to wait.'

'I didn't come for money,' he said.

She became flustered and tried to push the notes into his hand. 'It's a loan between friends. Things are tight for you at the minute. Pay it back when you can.'

She kept winking as if to say "That'll keep us both right if anyone asks."

He pushed her hand away. Repeated. 'I didn't come for money.'

She stiffened and her lips tightened into a thin line. 'Surely you don't mean…?'

Barlow understood what she meant all right. Obviously, she didn't do casual sex, and certainly not with someone as common as a policeman.

'Mrs Fetherton, I want to talk to you about the night Jordan Montgomery was killed.'

He didn't know whether she believed him or not, and he didn't care.

Mrs Fetherton put her nose in the air and walked away from the door. He followed her down a hallway the length of his own house and yard combined. Everything was fresh and new, the carpet under his feet springy, the paintwork shining. Somehow though, the reds and greens and golds of the decor didn't quite work, glared off each other instead of creating a harmonious whole.

Mrs Fetherton pushed through a door into the kitchen. 'Get out,' she told a woman busy mopping the floor.

'I'm not finished yet,' protested the woman.

'It will do.' Mrs Fetherton checked her watch. 'You'll owe me an extra half hour on Monday.'

The woman picked up the mop and bucket and walked stiff-backed into a room off the kitchen. After a pause, the back door slammed shut and Barlow heard footsteps on the gravelled drive-way. Rather than wait and not be invited to sit down, he pulled out a chair at the kitchen table and made himself comfortable.

Mrs Fetherton sat across from him, holding the handbag close to her chest as a barrier. 'What do you want to know about Jordan Montgomery?' Her tone was 'who cares?' She clearly thought Barlow's visit was merely a ploy to get into the house and her purse, if not into her bed.

'Where was he found tied up?'

'Here in the kitchen.' She pointed to the door the cleaning lady had disappeared through. 'He had a fold-up bed in there and the use of facilities in the yard.'

That sort of attitude, that way of treating decent, hard-working people always put Barlow's teeth on edge. But he'd sat in on too many interviews to let his temper surge.

'And who knew you were on holidays?'

'Everyone.' The tone implied "everyone who counted". 'We'd flown to the Algarve for the week. That's in Portugal, you know.'

'So it is,' said Barlow, knowingly. He'd never heard of the place before in his life. What he did know was that Mrs Fetherton and her husband would boast for weeks about their upcoming "foreign" holiday. The chances were the Fethertons were still boring everyone with unending tales of their time in Portugal.

'Did the burglars get much?' he asked. Walking through the hallway he'd gained no impression of ornaments missing, or of gaps on walls from which paintings had disappeared.

'Things Ezekiel and I had collected over the years. Valuable things.' Her voice changed, and suddenly he was hearing the real woman. 'A little Davenport my mother left me.'

'Maybe you'd show me.'

'The Davenport?' she asked, showing a bit of spark.

'The other rooms. Tell me what was taken.'

They started with the dining room. The dining table was still there. The twelve Chippendale chairs gone, together with a silver service and silver ice buckets. Casual tables had disappeared from the sitting room, along with a chaise longue and a set of figurines bought when the contents of Adair Castle were auctioned off.

They went back into the hallway.

Her hand was at her throat, playing nervously with her pearls. 'Do you need to see upstairs?'

Barlow stared at her slab face, breathed in the reek of stale drink on her breath. Nearly said 'I'm not that desperate', but changed it to a, 'No.'

Relief flashed across Mrs Fetherton's face, quickly followed by an air of disdain. 'If you're quite finished.' She indicated the front door, for him to leave.

Barlow ignored the hint and did a quick summary in his head. The burglars had taken about half a vanload of items. All of them easily sold, nothing of any particular value, other than the chairs. And absolutely not the sort of stuff Geordie would take. Geordie liked things that could be easily carried and flogged off for a pound or two in the pubs.

'Mrs Fetherton, were any small bits and pieces taken? You know, silver thimbles and things?'

She sniffed. 'That friend of yours, Dunlop, he left most of them on the kitchen table.'

He would, thought Barlow. Nick things as he went through the house, then dump everything as soon as he found Jordan and realised he was in big trouble.

'I suppose he only left the silver plate…what about the sterling silver?'

'Obviously his friends… '

'Obviously.' He nodded and went to the front door. 'Thank you for your time.'

She said, anxiously, 'What are you going to do…?' She didn't dare be specific about what he'd seen and heard in the rented house.

He turned with the front door open. 'I haven't made up my mind.'

She made to go back into the kitchen for her handbag. 'You've forgotten the money.'

'You lot might think otherwise, but I've never been bought yet.'

He slammed the door behind him.

61

Barlow caught the train and bus to the seaside town of Portstewart. Checked into Mrs McGarry's guest house on the Promenade, just up the street from the bus stop.

The tide was wrong for fishing. Even so, he picked up his rod and went across the rocks to try his luck. Later that evening he treated himself to a sirloin steak in the Montague Arms Hotel and sank a few pints in the Anchor Bar with men of his own ilk.

It was Sunday morning before he allowed himself to reflect on his problems. The way certain people rejoiced at his troubles really irked him. These were the men who regularly misused their position in the community in order to line their own pockets. The fact that they hid behind the respectability of the Masonic and the City clubs as cover for their dirty little deeds really irritated him.

Shalko Adair was one of those men. Outwardly a respected member of the community and yet... That 'yet' was the fact that Shalko always seemed to be around, to be involved in some way with the people who were robbed. Barlow's call to Shalko to insure his new bathroom was only an excuse to see the man in his own setting. Prior to that, Barlow had been doubtful: Shalko was just one more person to check out. Now, however, as he lay on his bed in the Portstewart guest house, any doubts evaporated. *Those Belfast men have to get their information from somewhere.*

He hunted in his coat pocket for his list of people robbed and ran his finger down the names while he had a think about Shalko. In the case of Mo Hunt, he was not aware of a connection between the two men other than, perhaps, the City Club and the local hunt.

Mo Hunt was robbed when he was away organising the next day's point-to-point; his role as chief organiser was one he assumed every year. Mayor Fetherton and his wife had irritated everyone with their talk of the holiday in the Algarve. The one thing they'd probably never mentioned was the fact that they'd hired poor old Jordan to guard the house while they were away.

Barlow tapped his pencil against his teeth while he thought of Mr Whithead. *God rest his soul.* Did Shalko know the house was supposed to be empty? He certainly knew about the contents, the stamp collection in particular.

As for Unwin Kirker? Shalko had been there when Unwin said he planned to join his family at the coast for the weekend. That covered the big robbery. But how could Shalko have known that the house was empty on the Friday evening when Unwin was at the shop sorting out the broken window?

He reckoned he should start talking to people, but just then his stomach rumbled. A quick look at his watch had him hurrying to dress in time for a late breakfast.

62

Johnny Scullion and his taxi were waiting when Barlow came striding out of Ballymena railway station. Barlow threw his case into the back and swung into the front beside Johnny.

'You're getting awful grand, taking taxis here and there and everywhere,' said Johnny.

'If you don't want the job I can always ring Sam Henry,' said Barlow, mentioning Johnny's biggest rival and also one of his best friends.

'Now stop trying to make a man annoyed,' said Johnny as he slipped into first gear.

Barlow indicated for him to turn down Waveney Avenue. 'Go by way of Farm Lodge. I want to pick up Mr Edward.'

At the end of Waveney Avenue Johnny turned to the right, up Bridge Street. Barlow shouted at him to stop and jumped out of the car.

Edward stood in the archway leading to the rear of the Bridge Bar. He wore his new suit and regimental tie and was freshly shaved and washed.

'What do you think you're doing?' asked Barlow.

'Stretching one's legs after one has done one's religious duty.'

'At the Bridge Bar? It's shut on a Sunday.'

'Where one can inhale the residue of other people's enjoyable weekend.' Edward sounded more desperate than bitter.

Barlow thought Edward looked shrunken in his new suit, which had fitted him perfectly in the shop. Maybe being made to lay off drink and coping with Miss Grace's visit, all at the same time, was too much for him?

'Edward, there's plenty of loose drink about the brewery. Why don't you have the odd snifter to keep you going?'

Edward gave him a look of utter contempt. 'That, my dear chap, would be a betrayal of trust.'

Barlow felt almost smacked down as he held open the rear door of the car. 'If you're not praying and you're not drinking, you might as well make yourself useful.'

Edward's shoulders squared off until they almost filled the material again. 'My dear chap, why didn't you say?'

The house Barlow was heading for belonged to Mo Hunt. The house had forty-six rooms and was reputed to be haunted. Barlow couldn't swear to the haunting, but he could swear to the ivy crawling through the window frames and the moss and weeds dripping from the guttering.

They pulled up at the front door. Barlow got out and looked into the car again. 'We could be a while.'

'Your time is my money,' said Johnny, and made himself comfortable.

Barlow rang the bell repeatedly until he heard someone come stumping along the flagged hallway to answer his ring.

Mo himself opened the door. He was middle-aged, somewhere between fit and falling apart from too much alcohol. His clothes stank of dogs and kennels.

'Yes?' Mo didn't even try to sound polite.

Barlow stepped into the hallway. Mo moved hurriedly back to avoid his toes being trampled on. 'It's Sergeant Barlow, sir. I'd like a word.'

'You're suspended,' said Mo. He seemed to enjoy that recollection.

'Which gives me more time to recover your stolen goods.'

'Does Mr Harvey know you're here?'

Edward appeared from behind Barlow's shoulder. 'Morris, old boy, the good sergeant is obliging me by personally looking into the matter.'

'I'll be making my own report,' said Barlow, keeping it vague. Not specifying who he'd be reporting to. He pulled out his notebook and flicked to a fresh page. 'Now if you'd show me where the burglars got in. And if it's not too much trouble, give me a quick tour and describe to me what was taken, and from where.'

Barlow muttered the words as he wrote in the notebook. 'Sunday – it's the thirty-first, isn't it, sir? Time: 14.32. Interview with the Master of the Hunt, Mr Mo Hunt.' Looked up. 'This is very good of you, sir. I know you're a busy man.'

With Mo outmanoeuvred, he took time to look around the hallway. Noted marks on the wallpaper where family portraits had originally hung. Noted light, modern tables set against the walls when he had expected to see heavier, more venerable furniture.

'Oh my goodness,' breathed Barlow. 'How terrible, to lose all those lovely things.'

He walked the length of the hallway to get a closer look at the gaps in the furnishings.

'It's a heartbreak,' said Mo in a tone that could only be genuine. He followed Barlow, describing what had been taken and from where.

Barlow tut-ted in annoyance at himself. 'And here's me without the list. Would you have a copy yourself, sir, of the items that were stolen and their value?'

Mo went off to fetch the list and came back with a frown on his face. The time away from Barlow had given him the space to wonder why a suspended and much reviled policeman was doing detective work for Harvey.

Mo withheld the list from Barlow. 'If you don't mind, I think I'll phone Mr Harvey and confirm that you're supposed to be here.'

A telephone sat on one of the modern tables. Barlow gripped Mo's arm before he could step over to it. 'Before you make that call, sir, a question.'

The list of items taken was contained in a thin booklet with a sky blue cover. The name of the valuer was printed in the bottom right hand corner: Shalko Adair & Co: Auctioneers, Valuers and Estate Agents.

He pointed at the booklet. 'Is this the list of items stolen and the individual values you supplied to both the police and the insurance company?'

'Yes!' Mo pulled his arm free. 'I think you should leave now.

From an adjoining room Barlow heard the unmistakable clink of a glass stopper being placed on a silver salver. He looked around. *No Edward.* 'Damn.' He rushed through the semi-open door and found himself in an oak-panelled dining room. Edward stood at a giant sideboard, holding a decanter half-filled with a dark amber liquid.

'What do you think you're doing?' demanded Barlow.

Edward ignored Barlow and addressed the accompanying Mo. 'It's terrible, terrible, when one's standards have to drop so far.'

'What are you talking about?' asked Barlow.

'The brandy. Not of the first barrel, nor of the second, one suspects.' He put the stopper back in the decanter and the decanter back on the sideboard. His hand lingered before he could pull it away. 'One has to blame the Land Acts. This was once a twenty thousand acre-estate with hundreds of tenant farmers. Now there's hardly enough land left to graze decent herd of cows.'

He walked over and gripped Mo's hand. 'My dear chap, you have my sympathy. First, the rents stop, then an ancestor squanders the pittance the government gave us for the land. One loses one's servants and, piece by piece, family trinkets disappear into the auction houses.' He wrung Mo's hand again. 'I've been there myself, my dear chap, been there.'

Barlow left them and went back into the hall and had a good nosey around. Ducked down and checked the floor along one of the skirting boards. Dipped his fingers in a grey residue, then wiped it off.

Stood up when Mo reappeared. 'Barlow, leave now. At once!'

Barlow stood on. 'There's dust around those replacement tables. It's been there a long time.'

Mo vibrated with anger. 'How dare you criticise my household!'

Edward said, 'It's most improper for visitors to notice certain shortcomings.'

Barlow ignored him and stepped closer to Mo. 'If we compared that list of things you say were stolen with your transactions over the last few years with…' He looked to Edward for help. 'Auction houses, big ones?'

'Christie's and Sotheby's in London,' said Edward. 'Real gentlemen. Not what one would expect in trade. I remember…'

Barlow cut off Edward's reminiscences. 'In Christie's or Sotheby's in London, would we, by any chance, find duplication?'

Mo stood frozen. Barlow moved closer to him, 'I wouldn't mention my visit to Mr Harvey if I were you. He'll want to know what I was doing here. Then he might take a good look at your amended schedule of items taken and begin to think in terms of an insurance fraud.'

He walked to the front door and opened it. Looked back. Mo was standing where he'd left him. He looked defeated.

Like a man who had been depending on that insurance money to maintain a house that was crumbling around him. Barlow felt sorry for Mo. Wondered would he have turned a blind eye if it had been Edward instead. But he also knew that was a decision Edward would never ask anyone to make on his behalf. Edward had sold up in 1939, paid his debts, sent the few pounds left over to Miss Grace and gone to war with the expectation of never returning.

Barlow closed the front door behind him. Wished he had the authority to revoke Mo's gun licence and seize all the shotguns and ammunition in the house.

63

Barlow's stomach bubbled with nervous excitement as the taxi turned into Mill Row. He was coming home to a real bathroom. To a bath large enough to wallow in. Could lather and soak and stretch to his heart's content.

He teased himself by postponing the pleasure. Waited to see Johnny Scullion drive off. Then pushed the front door open. Found all the furniture stacked near the window and Vera and Kenny Cameron busy painting the back wall.

'Dad!' Vera came flying over. She had the sense to hold back and stretch out a paint-japed face for a kiss. The last thing he wanted was paint on his good clothes.

'What are you doing?' he asked.

She said with studied patience, as if he should know the answer anyway. 'We can't paint the bathroom until the plaster dries, so we thought we'd make a start in here.'

She was doing more than spreading cream emulsion over Maggie's choice of dark green paint. She was admitting to herself that Maggie wouldn't be back, and therefore would not get upset at the changes made to her original choice of decor.

'It'll brighten the place up no end,' he said and let her lead him through the scullery into the new vestibule. Showed him the new gas boiler and the shelving underneath it to air clothes.

'Voilà!' she said theatrically and flung the bathroom door open. It was long and, even with the bath and the other fittings, there was still space for a man to dress in comfort.

He had to touch things for himself. The wash-hand basin and toilet. The bathmats and fluffy towels, the laundry basket and the soap rack she'd spent his money on instead of buying herself a dress in Belfast.

Paint tins were produced from behind the laundry basket. 'Rose pink for the walls and white gloss for the doors.' She looked anxiously at him. 'Is that all right? Mr Lowry said I could take them back.'

'Pink walls,' he said thoughtfully, looking at the grey cement. He toed the bare concrete underfoot. 'What about cork tiles instead of linoleum? They're bound to be warmer.'

He enjoyed her bubbling plans for the house while they tidied up and she served tea. Afterwards, she and Kenny went off to some friend's house to listen to records.

'Have you work tomorrow?' he asked, trying to be tactful.

'I won't be late,' she promised and swung out the door, with the quiet Kenny in tow.

At last he had the house to himself. He didn't mind the abandoned part-painted wall. It would take more than one coat to subdue the green paint. The whole house needed to be freshened up.

He turned on the gas boiler and unpacked his suitcase while the water was heating up. Then he looked out fresh pyjamas and went down the stairs, moving slowly, teasing himself with anticipation. He ran a bath and undressed and climbed into the steaming water. Vera had bought him a present, a bottle of Matey bubble bath. He swirled a capful of that into the water and flexed his back to make waves of water run up and down his chest.

Darkness had settled on the house by the time the water eventually cooled. He climbed out of the bath and towelled himself down with one of the new towels Vera had bought.

Dressed in his new pyjamas and dressing gown and slippers, he went and sat in his favourite chair and felt quite the gentleman. The street lights angling in the window were all he needed to enable him to see what he was doing while he made himself a cup of tea. He didn't bother turning on the television. Tried to ignore the sound of neighbours talking at their front doors and their children playing under the lampposts. Something was working in his mind, troubling him. Something he'd missed. Something obvious.

He went through the list of names in his head: Hunt, Kirker, Fetherton, Whithead. Remembered the Clarkes with sadness. Why rob them? It wasn't an opportunist robbery. They'd waited for the couple, followed them, and carried out the robbery and, *God help us*, murdered them for a handful of change.

He became aware of the quietness outside. Not the quiet of people drifting off to their beds but the quietness of people suddenly alert to something. He heard the rumble of a car engine at his door but no car lights. *A police car? Mo's complained to Harvey.*

He saw the hole in the window as pain exploded in his head. His body arched out of the chair. Darkness, then a vague light. Something sparkling...The sound of a car speeding away... The light still sparkled – like an electric bulb gone mad. Voices outside. 'What the hell?' A woman's voice. 'Is the wain all right? Get the wain.'

Tried to move. Heard a sound he'd heard before. A spitting fizz. *A sparkler, some bastard's thrown a sparkler.*

Registered the solid shape behind the spitting flame. *A banger.* If that goes off, I'll have a headache for a month. Crawled onto his hands and knees. His hand slid off a half-brick. *Bastards for throwing that!* Saw the flame was attached to a tube the size of a Roman candle.

Dynamite!

Blood from his head dripped onto the flame. It didn't go out. The fuse was burnt down, short seconds from the detonator.

He focused hard. This was a bomb. This was what he'd been trained to deal with all those years back. He picked up the stick of dynamite, made to lob it back through the broken window. Heard voices outside. Heard a man ask, 'Is there anyone in the Barlow house?' and someone reply. 'They'll rue the day they broke the sergeant's window.'

'Bloody right,' said Barlow. If only his head would stop spinning long enough for him to think.

He let himself collapse onto his back. Head towards the front door, feet towards the scullery. He put his arm over his head and threw the stick of dynamite as hard as he could towards the far window. Watched the burning fuse tumble through the scullery, ricochet off the door-jam and skid into the new bathroom.

'On, bloody hell!'

He rolled clear of the doorway and towards the range. A fierce crump of air lifted him and smashed him down onto the hard floor. The settee cartwheeled through the air and landed on top of him. 'Shite.' He could only think the curse, hadn't the breath for words.

Acrid smoke billowed around him. He smelt something strong and sweet – fumes from the exploded dynamite. *Some other smell?* Sharp and irritating in the lungs.

Gas!

He threw the settee off and crawled to the front door. Over rubble, then the banisters lying like a thrown-down ladder. The front door hung outwards. There seemed to be nothing in the air but gas. Then he was on the pavement, crawling onto the road. A whump of burning air played pitch and toss with his body. Found himself sliding along a ground that sloped downwards. Stopped with an arm and a leg in the millrace. Pieces of Bangor blue slate speared into the ground all around him.

People came and spoke to him. At least he could see who was speaking, even if he couldn't hear a word they said. Didn't dare shake his head in case it fell off. The gas made him violently sick into the millrace. He decided not to move until the firemen came with their steel shovels to scrape up his body.

A group of policemen who lived in the adjoining estate came running up. Constable Gillespie arrived last, but used his girth to bull his way to the front. 'Vera?' Gillespie asked.

'Out... visiting... friends.'

The effort of speaking promptly made him sick again.

The ambulance arrived. Police officers stood in the mill-race, holding the stretcher just above the level of the water while they rolled him onto it.

Once on his back he could see his house. Flames were leaping out of the windows and the door, and the roof had caved in. Neighbouring houses were burning as well.

Gillespie walked beside the stretcher. He asked, 'Sarge, by any chance, does someone not like you?'

64

The prematurely grey Ward Sister was on duty again when the ambulance men wheeled Barlow into the Emergency Ward. Thanks to the oxygen they'd pumped into him he could breathe again, which gave all his other agonies a chance to announce their presence.

'Where are you sore?' Sister asked once they'd eased him off the stretcher onto the bed.

'My head and my arse.'

She peered under the gauze pad covering the cut on his head. 'How did that happen?'

'A half-brick.'

He wiggled his fingers to show they were still there and operating. Sister looked on while a doctor checked down his body for any obvious injuries. 'You've got the lives of a cat,' she told him. Counted his toes and asked him to wiggle them as well.

'I'm not fit to wiggle anything in between,' he told her.

Before he could stop them, Sister and a young nurse cut off the remains of his pyjamas and dressing gown.

'You're right about the middle bit,' she said and draped a blanket over him. The doctor asked him to turn onto his side so that he could check his back. Sister started to laugh.

'What's so funny?' he demanded.

She gave him a poke in the buttocks that really hurt. 'You're right about your arse. It's covered in flash burns. You're going to need nappy cream.'

With that, the doctor sent him off to the X-ray Department. The gentle rocking of the trolley as they wheeled him through the hospital made his eyes close. The pain in his head started to recede.

Sister shook his shoulder. He snapped back to full consciousness, his head hurting worse than ever.

She told him. 'You've got a head injury. Don't you dare go asleep.'

They X-rayed his head: no fracture, no sign of internal bleeding. Then his lungs: no permanent damage. Merely smoke and fume inhalation. He'd probably feel off-colour for a few days until the fumes worked their way out of his system. Take a week off on the sick.

It wasn't so funny when people treated him the way he treated others, with casual indifference. The next time he put a troublemaker in a cell he'd give them a sympathetic pat, and then shove.

They wheeled him back into the Emergency Ward and put a stitch in his head. Then rolled him into a private room opposite the nurses' station where Sister could keep an eye on him. She made him sit up. Most of his weight crushed down on the tenderest part of his anatomy. A painkiller for his headache and a cup of tea made him think she wasn't totally heartless. A second cup, and he counted her among the angels.

His headache hurt too much for him to think logically. A touch of concussion, according to Sister. He sat upright in the bed, his head unsupported. That way, if he tried to sleep his head would flop forward. The jerk would ignite his headache and bring him awake.

Inspector Foxwood called to see him. Barlow could only confirm that he'd seen and heard nothing until the half-brick came through the window. That the brick hit him, stunning him. That he regained consciousness lying beside a stick of dynamite with its fuse spluttering. Foxwood seemed impressed that he'd chosen to throw the dynamite into the rear of the house instead of back into the street.

'That should earn you an official commendation, Sergeant,' he said and then coloured, remembering that Barlow was facing jail.

Foxwood asked Barlow who would want to kill him.

Barlow said, 'It's those men in the green Bedford van that Mr Harvey doesn't think exists.'

'What do you know about them?'

'Sir, when I've names or anything concrete to go on, you'll be the first to know.'

But he did tell Foxwood to check out Shalko Adair. His finances, where he socialised and who with.

'The City Club,' said Foxwood, who'd been there as Captain Denton's guest.

'It's not the only place in this county where crooks meet,' said Barlow.

Surprisingly, instead of being annoyed, Foxwood laughed. 'They're not all crooks.'

'That's what Lot told the Good Lord, and look what happened to Sodom and Gomorrah.'

Foxwood said he'd start ringing around in the morning. See what he could find out about Shalko Adair. Barlow suggested he start by finding out why Shalko had resigned as Secretary of the Golf Club. A job like that was usually a lifetime sinecure.

Foxwood said that they'd checked out every green Bedford van in Northern Ireland. Every owner had an alibi for the nights in question. The police had also examined every vehicle. None of them showed damage consistent with running Frank Wilson's car off the road.

Barlow asked, 'What if they changed the colour of the van to green and never bothered telling the vehicle licensing people?'

Foxwood nodded. 'And if they've any sense, the van will now be back to its original colour.'

By this time, Foxwood was on his feet, gathering up his hat and notebook prior to leaving. He sat down for a moment. 'Barlow, before I came to Ballymena I asked around about you. Do you know that you're a legend up in RUC Headquarters? Several inspectors and above said they'd started their careers under your tutelage. You taught them real policing. Afterwards, they learned what the law actually said.' Generously, he held out his hand for a shake. 'But I'm afraid you've gone too far this time.'

Another cup of tea helped settle Barlow's headache. Then Vera came flying in and the pain exploded again with a huge hug.

He held her at arm's length so as to have a good look at her, wondering where she'd been all this time. 'No tears for our wee house?' he asked.

'Dad, you're my house.'

Now, *he* wanted to cry.

65

Barlow woke to find the hospital Pathologist standing over him. The Pathologist was a tall, lean man who had done his post-medical school training in Changi Prison, under the watchful eye of brutal Japanese guards. After that experience, little could annoy or rattle the man.

'Doc, I hope you're being a bit premature.'

'Doctor,' said the Pathologist and pulled up a chair for himself. Checked Barlow's pulse, pulled down the skin under his eyes and stared at the irises. He seemed satisfied. 'Head?'

'I can nod without wishing I hadn't.'

'Chest?'

'Sore.'

'Throat?'

Barlow asked. 'Do you often tour the wards, touting for business?' He found his throat had a dry croak.

The Pathologist said, 'You've been known to break out of a hospital ward to talk to me, so I thought this time I'd save you the trip.'

Barlow eased himself up into a sitting position and helped himself to a glass of water. Sitting upright irritated the raw areas in his buttocks. Sister hadn't been joking about the nappy cream. He wouldn't have minded another application. 'So, you thought I'd want to talk to you?'

'Four murders, and you haven't called.' The Pathologist shook his head. 'With most people, the last thing that goes is their hearing. With you, Barlow, it'll be your curiosity.'

Barlow nodded. 'Tell me about Jordan Montgomery and Mr Whithead.'

'Without all the big words?'

'Doc, I never use Latin before breakfast.'

'Doctor,' the Pathologist reminded him.

'Doctor,' agreed Barlow and listened while the Pathologist listed Jordan Montgomery's injuries.

Old Jordan had been battered about the head and ribs, maybe even kicked before he'd been tied up.

Barlow's forehead furrowed in thought. 'The way Mr Harvey sees it, Geordie Dunlop beat Old Jordan to pulp and tied him up. Then he untied him and called for an ambulance and applied resuscitation until the ambulance men got there. Now what sort of idiot would do that?' he asked.

'A thick idiot,' replied the Pathologist.

'A brutal, thick idiot,' said Barlow building on the image.

'Or two different people,' said the Pathologist, knowing where Barlow's prodding was leading to.

'And Mr Whithead?'

'That's where your friend Geordie has the real problem.'

The Pathologist stood up and put a hand to the side of his face as if holding an injury. 'Whithead was standing like this when he was shot. The shotgun pellets tore along the inside of his arm and struck his chest. Death was instantaneous.'

Barlow said, 'I'm guessing there was a fight and Whithead took a thump to the face. And he must have lost his gun, or he wouldn't have stood like that.' He imitated how someone's hands would move while struggling for possession of a shotgun. 'Could the gun have gone off accidentally?'

'I can't answer that,' said the Pathologist. 'But the man who pulled the trigger was at least six feet back from Whithead.'

Barlow nodded. 'They've hung people for less.' He had another think. 'What about times of death?'

The Pathologist said, 'Jordan Montgomery was pronounced "dead on arrival" at the hospital at eleven-forty. Whithead's wife rang and spoke to him near ten. So, somewhere between then and threeish.'

'So having killed one man, Geordie went straight off and killed another?'

'Apparently,' said the Pathologist, refusing to commit himself to an opinion.

He told Barlow to 'get well soon' and left the ward in a slow walk that would have been perfect for a man on the beat.

Sister was straight in carrying a bundle of clothes. 'You're being discharged as soon as the Surgeon has a look at you.' She dumped the clothes on his legs. 'Unwin Kirker left these in. He says he knows your sizes and you'll get a good discount on anything you need.'

Barlow nodded, grateful. He'd been prepared to fight to get out of hospital. And now he had something better to wear than a borrowed dressing gown.

He asked, 'How did Unwin know I was in hospital?'

Sister did like the Pathologist, checked his eyes and his pulse. 'The switchboard's going mad with people ringing wanting to know how you are.'

'They'd be happier checking the time of the funeral,' he growled to hide a thrill of pleasure. *I must be getting old and soft when I worry about other people and what they think of me.*

'You're a terrible man,' said Sister and went off to organise a late breakfast for him. She also sent in the youngest and most beautiful nurse on the ward to apply more nappy cream.

Barlow promised himself, *I'll do that woman for jaywalking if nothing else.*

At that point, Sister, with perfect timing, went off duty. Barlow dozed until the Neurosurgeon examined him and autho-rised his discharge.

The effort of dressing made him short of breath and his knees shook. At least the clothes were a good fit, the flannels and jacket the sort of thing he'd have chosen for himself.

He went out to the nurses' station to ring for Johnny Scul-lion and his taxi, and found Mrs Carberry waiting there. She stood up. She was wearing a light raincoat and scarf against the chill of a damp morning.

'My car's right at the door,' she said.

'Look Mrs Carberry… ' He intended to refuse any favours from her. It could be a set-up and taking a lift from her would compromise his independence.

She interrupted him, glancing nervously at the nearby nurs-es. 'Please, Captain Denton sent me. I couldn't refuse with-out… you know.'

He nodded. The woman did a lot of things for Denton. This had to be one of the less distasteful favours.

By the time he arrived at her car he was in a cold sweat and glad to fold into the passenger seat. Mrs Carberry started the engine and drove out of the hospital grounds. About half a mile down the road, she pulled into the pavement and parked.

'Mr Barlow, if you have anything to say to me, say it now.'

He liked that direct approach, nearly as much as he disliked the stale smell of gin off her breath.

'The notebook, even if I had written things down… ' He couldn't bear to think what those "things" were. 'It got de-stroyed in the fire, so that evidence is gone.'

'Have you told anyone else?' She looked strained and anxious.

He said nothing. Didn't dare tell her that, suspended or not, he could be accused of dereliction of duty for not having re-ported the offence immediately.

'Helen and the children?' It came out as a plea.

He saw a tear glisten in the corner of her eye. *A hell of an actress, or she really cares.*

If he did tell Harvey what he'd seen, Harvey would have to drop the charges against him or risk ridicule and the destruction of his own career. Harvey would divorce Helen in revenge, and she'd lose the children.

Barlow said, 'God help me but I'm tempted.'

66

Barlow and Mrs Carberry picked up Vera from Constable Gillespie's house, where she'd spent the night. Both Barlow and Vera knew the house the Dentons proposed renting to them: a pebble-dashed bungalow on the Ballymoney Road, close to the postern gate leading into the Convent grounds.

Even Barlow became excited when Mrs Carberry drove through the gateway. *Me with a driveway for a car?* Vera and Mrs Carberry disappeared into the house. He walked the garden, marvelling at having a front and a back lawn, a detached garage and an outbuilding. *A man would have room here to take up a hobby.* He'd started life as a carpenter and always dreamed of something better than nailing down floorboards.

He felt nervous at walking in the front door without knocking. Felt a man like him should go in the back way, and knew he never would. The hallway had a tiled floor. *Even better than Mrs Anderson's,* he told himself and inspected a sitting room, a dining room, a kitchen with a breakfast table, three spacious bedrooms *each with their own door* and a bathroom. The bathroom was bigger than the one he'd lost, but meant nothing to him. Someone else had built it, had left their mark on it.

The decor and the painting looked fresh, though he assumed Vera would want her bedroom redecorated. The furniture was in good condition. The kitchen held every item of equipment needed, from teaspoons to a twin-tub washing machine.

'Now, I can have my friends around,' said Vera.

That comment hurt a lot more than his chest. One of those big things missing in her life that she'd never complained about.

He found fresh food in the fridge and in the store cupboard. Before he could object, Mrs Carberry said, 'Touchy, touchy,' and handed him a bill from McHenry's grocery shop. 'The Manager, Mick Killough, says if that's not paid by the weekend he'll send in the grippers.'

Barlow smiled, folded the bill and put it in his breast pocket. The Barlows and the Killoughs had been friends for generations.

He suggested that Vera make them a cup of tea. Took Mrs Carberry by the elbow and guided her into the hallway.

'What are the terms of the lease?' he asked. Anxious, because he didn't know how much money he'd have left by the time all the bills were paid.

'You pay Mrs Denton monthly in arrears.'

That said a lot. The Dentons would know money was tight and were willing to wait until the next payday. Barlow also knew that if the worst happened, and he ended up in jail, Vera would have a home. The Dentons would never ask her for the money.

Vera shouted that the tea was ready. She'd set the kitchen table with cups and saucers and plates from the sideboard. The new Woolworths range of crockery: white with circular blue stripes. Not exactly Barlow's style, but Vera seemed to like them. Plus the cups held a decent amount of tea. Biscuits supplied by Mick Killough were arranged on a fancy plate. Barlow missed the old biscuit tin they'd had since the early days of his marriage.

The tea helped revive his flagging energy.

'Are you all right, Dad?'

'It's my internal battery. It's gone a bit faulty after last night.'

He didn't dare look near the sitting room as they headed out again. The thought of stretching out on the settee drew him like a magnet. Mrs Carberry kindly dropped them off in Wellington Street. He sent Vera ahead of him into Kirker's to buy clothes. Anything he picked would be subject to her approval, so she might as well select them in the first place.

He made a point of striding past Shalko's office. Doing that going uphill, the effort nearly killed him. He staggered into the Provincial Bank and leaned heavily on the counter while a clerk fetched him a replacement chequebook and a current statement. The balance looked good, but outstanding bills were stacking up.

Out of the bank, he forced his legs to walk again, this time downhill. *Thank God.* Nearing Shalko's office he held himself straighter, slammed the tight door open and strode through the reception area into Shalko's private office. The secretary barely had time to whip off her glasses.

Shalko sat at his desk. He jumped to his feet. Appeared apprehensive. 'Mr Barlow!'

'We've a few things to sort here, Mr Shalko Adair, haven't we?'

Moisture stood on Shalko's top lip. 'I don't know what you mean?'

'The fire. The explosion.' Barlow sat in a chair and folded his arms. 'That insurance I spent good money on had better pay out.'

'The insurance? Right... Of course... Dreadful accident... I was in the City Club at the time... lots of other people there... heard the explosion. Dreadful. Dreadful.'

That's his alibi established, thought Barlow.

Shalko sat down again. Shuffled the papers on his desk. Put some into his briefcase. Shuffled again.

Barlow said, 'There has be a form or something to fill up.' Checked his wrist for the time and realised that he'd lost his watch in the fire. A watch given to him by a certain young lady on the day he reported to RUC Enniskillen for basic training in 1934.

First Maggie then our wee house and now the watch. It's like my life's being ended piece by piece.

Shalko was cowering in his chair. Barlow realised that he must have scowled at him while he was thinking of the lost watch. He replaced the scowl with a stare and sat silent until Shalko felt forced to ask a question. 'I heard you were in hospital?'

'Barely touched,' lied Barlow. 'But if my daughter had been at home she'd have been killed.' He dropped his voice, as if letting Shalko into a confidence. 'Something I'll bear in mind when I meet the men responsible.' He massaged the knuckles of his right hand.

The anger he felt at times with Harvey was nothing to the fury threatening to overcome him. He wanted to reach across the desk to Shalko and pound his bones into powder.

'About these forms…' he said. Shalko searched a drawer for a form. 'A preliminary claim at the minute,' he informed Barlow. 'A quantity surveyor will survey the property and determine the cost of rebuilding the bathroom. He forced a smile. 'It will be up to us to arrive at a value for the personal items lost in the explosion.'

Barlow got a sense of "nudge nudge, wink wink" coming from Shalko. He wouldn't be asking any searching questions about what Barlow claimed he'd lost in the fire or their value. Barlow allowed himself what passed for a grateful smile in return and agreed that he and Vera would prepare a list of furnishings and the personal items destroyed. The amount of compensation for the extension to the house was complicated because the house was rented rather than owned outright.

'But I'm sure that between us and the landlord and the surveyor we'll come to a reasonable settlement.'

'Aye,' said Barlow in a sour tone. Shalko hadn't mentioned that complication when he took out the insurance.

Shalko made himself busy completing the form. Eventually he asked what Barlow considered to be a loaded question. 'Your temporary address for correspondence purposes?'

Barlow had a vision of a gunman storming into their bungalow on the Ballymoney Road and not worrying whether it was Vera or him they shot.

He lied through a red haze of anger. 'I've taken a room in the Section House at the police station. Vera is staying with friends until we get things sorted.'

When he signed the preliminary claim form, he noted that Shalko's writing was shaky. He made his own signature broad and confident.

As he stood to leave, Shalko asked in a voice high-pitched with anxiety, 'Have you any idea who is responsible for all these robberies?'

Barlow was tempted to say, 'I have a bloody good idea', but he had Vera's safety to think of. 'I understand the detectives have a name, but they're not saying who it is.'

Shalko's face went ashen. Barlow nodded and walked out.

The tensions and raging emotions he'd experienced in Shalko's office took their toll. Even the short walk downhill to Kirker's shop left him shaking and drenched in a cold sweat. He nodded his approval at what Vera had picked for him and wrote the cheque while Unwin Kirker rang for Johnny Scullion to come and collect him.

The drive to their new home seemed interminable. Barlow left Vera to struggle with unloading the shopping and went into the sitting room. The settee was somewhere between cream and a faded blue, a three-seater. He dumped a cushion and his head at one end, stuck his feet out the other end and was immediately asleep.

67

The next morning, Tuesday, Barlow discovered the one truly annoying thing about the new house. It didn't have Vera's schoolbag with its writing pad. All that had gone up in the fire. A search of the house turned up no writing paper or pens. Not even the stub of a pencil.

'And you a policeman,' said Vera.

He sent her across the road to Harkness's sweetie shop to see what she could get. As she hurried out the front door he shouted after her. 'Watch for the cars, that's a main road out there.'

'I'm a big girl, Dad.'

'All the easier to hit.'

She grunted impatiently and ran on.

She's nearly eighteen, he told himself and worried unnecessarily until she finally came back with a primary school writing pad and pencils.

They sat at the kitchen table and started by listing the furniture lost. The first thing he wrote down was the settee she'd bought with her own money. Beds, bedding. His clothes.

'For heaven's sake, Dad, most of your stuff was only fit for the bin.'

'They've still got to be replaced.'

She nodded in agreement. 'We'll try the charity shop this afternoon.' Ducked under his swipe at her ear.

He tore a page out of the centre of the jotter and let her get on with the listing of pots and pans while he did his own thinking.

He sat and looked at the wall for a while. In the old house, staring at the range used to bring him inspiration. Here, the only thing worth looking at on the wall was the clock, and its hands kept moving on, reminding him of time flying when he had none to waste. Noticed that Vera's listing of things lost in the fire had reached a third page. *As much as that?* They really did need the insurance money in order to straighten out their finances. Said a prayer of thanks that his chest was now much easier, even though the wickerwork seat was making an uncomfortable impression on his tender backside.

Finally, he started as he'd done before, with Unwin Kirker

He double-underlined that. Then wrote down Unwin's name a second time, then the rest of them.

Against Unwin Kirker's first entry he wrote "only the people around the shop and friends".

Beside the second Unwin Kirker entry he placed a tick. Unwin had told Shalko that he would be away that night and, by implication, that the house would be empty. Wrote down what he knew of the other victims of the burglars:

Mo Hunt	Traditionally out of house on eve of the point-to-point/City Club member
E Fetherton	Told everyone he'd be away/Never mentioned security guard/City Club Member
Mr Whithead	Should have been away/Shalko Adair is his insurer

He drew another double line across the page before making his final entry:

Mr and Mrs Clarke – Routine lodgement,
same day and same time

Shalko's business as an insurance agent gave him a unique
knowledge of the contents of people's houses. Even if he didn't
act for people like Fetherton, they shared the same club and
the Fethertons weren't averse to boasting about what they had.

Inspector Foxwood had drawn a blank so far in tracing the
green Bedford van. He could trust Foxwood to have every
Bedford in the country checked for signs of being resprayed.
With four murders and the killers still untraced, all the other
Districts would be more than happy to cooperate in the search.

As for Shalko? Foxwood would give priority to checking
out Shalko's finances and the people he associated with.

Barlow sat and stared at the list until Vera plonked a plate
down on the page. 'Watch out,' he said.

She said, 'You wanted lunch early. You said you were going
out.'

He stared at the list as he ate. It was all there in front of him
and he wasn't seeing it.

68

This time Johnny Scullion had come prepared for a long sit, with the *Irish News* to read and an apple for a snack.

'It's not the Antarctic we're going to,' said Barlow as he swung into the passenger seat. He felt irritable with himself because there was a time when he could have jogged to Whithead's farm and hardly broken sweat. Right then, with his chest still hurting – although he denied it to Vera – he didn't trust himself to walk to the end of the road.

Johnny crunched the car into gear and they set off. Barlow hoped to catch Whithead's son at the house. He was working on the assumption that young man would come home for his lunch.

Whithead's profession as an accountant was evident from the front gate onwards. Everything was orderly and neat. Fencing rails regularly oiled as protection from the weather, the driveway brushed clear of debris and farm dirt. The farmhouse itself was old, late nineteenth century. A substantial extension had been added to the back of the original building, creating both a windbreak and a sun trap. A battered Land Rover stood at the door, and at the door itself, a pair of green wellingtons.

Barlow got out of the car and peered in all the front windows before he rang the bell. Somewhere deep in the house a bell chimed electronic notes. While he waited, he examined the front door: the gloss paint smelled new and felt tacky to the touch.

'Aye.'

William Whithead came to the door. He was about thirty years of age and had his father's broad shoulders, but he wasn't quite as tall. He wore old army camouflage trousers and stood in his stocking feet.

William, the eldest of the late Mr Whithead's sons, had gone to Greenmount Agricultural College. The second son, Simon, was currently at Sandhurst Military Academy, and the youngest son worked with Frank McKeown & Co in Ballymena, training to be an accountant like his father.

'Mr Barlow, please come in.'

It wasn't often that Barlow got invited in with a smile that appeared genuine and was accompanied by a friendly handshake.

Barlow expressed his regret at the passing of Whithead senior. At the same time his eyes were on the back wall where no amount of fill and fresh paint could cover the damage caused by shotgun pellets.

William said, 'It's very good of you to call, Sergeant. Now you're here, you'll have a cup of tea?'

'If you don't mind, young William, maybe you'd show me where things happened.'

William looked uncomfortable. 'I'm not being awkward...but I find it difficult to... Well, the whole thing's hard to get over.'

'I know that too well,' said Barlow soothingly. 'Haven't we all got our own troubles?'

He measured distances with his eye. Front door to the bottom of the stairs and wall to wall, about ten feet each way. He noticed replacement spindles in the banisters. The turned wood not quite matching the design of the original ones. A dent in the bannisters themselves could have been caused by a rifle butt.

William stood on undecided.

Barlow prompted him. 'Maybe if you told me what you think happened?'

William said, 'The pantry window was warped and wouldn't close properly We used a fly screen up to keep flies away from the fresh food.'

He padded down the hallway, showing Barlow into a huge farmhouse kitchen. *The old kitchen and as much again added on,* Barlow guessed. The kitchen held a giant AGA, padded chairs for sinking into after dark, and a dining table, and still left plenty of room to move around.

William slid the kettle onto the AGA hotplate as he passed. 'Mum's staying with us at the minute,' he said as if apologising for the poor hospitality on offer.

'You'll give her my best wishes,' said Barlow.

William nodded and carried on through the scullery to a large pantry. He sighed, 'I know it sounds daft.' He nodded past Barlow into the scullery. 'It never occurred to any of us to fix the window until....'

Barlow stood in the doorway and had a good look around the pantry. The window sat between two wooden slatted shelves. It was now properly closed. The shelves held only tins of fruit and dry goods like flour.

He reached between the shelves and opened the window. 'I want you to do me a favour. Go out into the yard and climb in the window.'

William shook his head. 'I can tell you now, I wouldn't make it.'

'Are you sure?'

For the first time, William's aura of sadness lifted as he re-membered a fond memory. 'I tried to get in that way one time after a night out, and damn near got stuck. My sides and hips were scraped to blazes.'

Barlow nodded. 'I'm bigger than you and Geordie Dunlop is my height, but he's running to fat.'

They went back into the kitchen. Barlow sat at the table while William made the tea.

Barlow said, 'It appears that Geordie Dunlop tried to get into the house through the pantry. When that didn't work, he jemmied open the front door. The noise disturbed your father, who came charging down with his shotgun. The two men fought, Geordie got control of the gun and shot your father.'

William nodded. 'They found Dunlop's fingerprints all around the pantry window.

'But nowhere else in the house,' said Barlow.

This time William didn't nod. He looked puzzled. 'When you put it that way, Mr Barlow...' He put milk and sugar and a packet of digestives in front of Barlow. 'So how did his fingerprints get there?'

Barlow shrugged, he'd no answer for that either. William sat across from him and they sipped their tea.

William stayed quiet, which suited Barlow, as he recounted in his head what had been stolen from the Whithead home: some silver plate – all modern – china figurines from the hallway, and the stamp collection, of course. From what he'd seen by peeking through the windows into the two front rooms, the burglars had missed out on a vanload of stuff worth taking. The late Mr Whithead and his wife had an eye for quality.

William crumbled a biscuit in his nervousness. 'Mr Barlow, the last time you met my father he was rude to you.'

'The gentleman was a bit annoyed at the start, but there was no harm done.'

William shook his head in disagreement. 'He was sorry afterwards for his bad temper, but anything about the hunt always set him off.'

'I know why, and I don't blame the man,' said Barlow. 'That Geordie Dunlop would annoy a saint.'

William looked up and gave a reluctant smile. 'To be honest, me and my brothers – we thought it hilarious at the time. Not that we dared say.'

The last thing Barlow needed was to be delayed while William talked at length about family life with the late Mr Whithead. He'd got what he'd come for and, while hiring Johnny Scullion's taxi was cheap, it still cost good money.

He worked at finishing his cup of tea and deftly changed the subject: 'You married into the horsey set yourself. I understand your wife has a couple of useful jumpers.'

William smiled. 'The day I told my father that Mary Jo and I were getting engaged, he reminded me that he'd sworn an oath that not one horse would ever set a hoof on land owned by him. Then he handed me the deeds of the out-farm and told me to put them in my name.'

Some little nerve ticked in Barlow's brain. He found himself asking, genuinely surprised. 'Your father kept important papers like deeds in the house?'

'Oh no,' protested William. 'My parents suspected that the ring would appear at Christmas, so he got them out of the bank and had them waiting. He liked giving people surprises.'

Barlow drained his cup and stood up. 'Maybe on the way out you'd show me where these deeds were kept?'

William shrugged and led the way out of the kitchen and across the hallway into a room fitted out as an office. Forms and invoices lay around in heaps. Some stained by the fingerprint powder spread around liberally by Detective Sergeant Leary and his men.

William walked to the back of the room and opened a cupboard door to reveal a safe. He twisted the safe handle and it opened.

'You don't keep it locked?' asked Barlow.

William said, 'The key snapped in the lock years ago, but it's fireproof. It's useful for keeping important papers short term in case of a fire – and the stamp collection of course.'

'Aye,' said Barlow. 'The stamp collection.'

'Their value meant nothing to my father. He'd bought most of them as a youngster, for pennies. Every stamp had a story: of people's kindness to him, of his own childhood.' William's face went red as he fought down tears. He turned away from Barlow and stared out the window. 'If you could find them, it would mean a lot to my mother.'

69

Barlow had Johnny Scullion drop him off at the bottom of Mill Row. It seemed funny to walk up that little street for the last time as a resident. When he stood outside his now wreck of a house – and the destroyed homes on either side – his sense of loss surprised him. He knew all the neighbours by name and nickname. Had watched them when they first moved into these houses, remembered some of them being born, growing up, leaving home or staying put, growing old, dying. Had given some people references, so that they could get a job; warned others as to their future behaviour. These people were the nearest thing he'd ever had to family.

A lorry stood parked against the houses. Terry Esler and his men were gingerly standing on what remained of the roofs, stripping off slate and joist. Terry saw Barlow and came down the ladder, brushed his hands clean on the seat of his jeans and shook Barlow's hand as if sympathising over a bereavement. Which it was in a way.

'A terrible thing,' he said.

'Aye.'

A workman threw a handful of slate. It crashed down into the lorry. Externally, Barlow remained impassive. Internally he shuddered at the abrupt ending of a large part of his life.

Terry said, 'I don't know if the landlord will ever rebuild them.'

'I was thinking that.'

'The good thing is, Mr Barlow, we found your bike.'

'Did you begod?' said Barlow, thinking of all the money he'd wasted on Johnny Scullion.

'The paint's a bit blistered, but otherwise it's fine. The blast went past it.'

Terry fetched Barlow's bike. He'd even washed it down and re-oiled the chain. Then they argued over the bill for the bathroom extension. Not so much the amount – on principle, Barlow demanded a discount – but *when* Terry would be paid. Terry said there was no rush for a day or two. Barlow said he'd money in the bank and a chequebook in his pocket. In the end, he wrote a cheque for the agreed amount and blew on the ink even though he was using one of those new-fangled Biro pens. All the time, he was conscious of a car stopping behind them and of someone getting out.

'That'll keep things handy for you between now and Christmas,' Barlow said as he watched Terry fold the cheque, then fold it again before putting it in his wallet.

Terry said, 'It soon thins out when you've other men to pay.'

Barlow frowned because something in Terry's remark clicked in his brain. *All those clicks in my head and no solution.* He turned away to find Miss Grace, Edward's sister, standing, tight-lipped behind him.

She wore a two-piece suit in soft pink, and was holding out the keys to Camilla Denton's shooting-brake. 'I want you to drive.' She drew herself up to her full imperial height. 'Now.'

He stared into her eyes. A moment passed before he said, 'Aye,' and took the keys.

He left his bike against the wall a couple of doors down, knowing it would be safe there. He turned in time to see Miss Grace slide into the passenger seat, and he could now see what the WPCs had been referring to. The years had been kind to Miss Grace and the extra weight she carried did make her appear voluptuous and desirable. He hadn't spotted it first off for himself. That failure made him feel old.

'Get in,' she said. He obeyed her and adjusted the driver's seat to let his legs stretch.

'When you're quite ready.'

He looked at her. She stared him back.

'You haven't changed a bit, Miss Grace,' he said.

'And you're as rude as ever.'

She looked forward. He started the engine and drove off. At the bottom of the street he hesitated.

'Where to?'

'Just drive.'

70

Barlow and Miss Grace were silent after that. He took the car in an intricate pattern of roads and streets that encompassed the Adair estate without actually encroaching on it. At one point her eyes closed and her head nodded on her chest.

Barlow braked sharply to avoid a pedestrian. She jerked into full consciousness and sat bolt upright.

'Show me where Edward lives.'

He drove to Farm Lodge Lane. She looked at him. She looked at Mrs Anderson's house. 'That is where I am currently staying. It is also Edward's postal address.' The Adair nose tightened into a thin line. 'I asked you to show me where he lives.'

Barlow drove her along the river. Parked up where she could take in the scenic view of Curles Bridge, and behind it the old copse: the pathetic remains of the Adair fortune.

They got out of the car. She stood at the embankment wall, staring down at the tar and paper hut under the dry arch. The river was high and the hut seemed to float in its own water-garden.

She said, 'Is this the best you can do for Edward Adair of the Adairs, onetime barons of Ballymena?'

'Your family bled us dry long enough.'

She stared at him coldly. 'You are insufferably rude.'

'Blunt, Missus. The rest just think it but daren't say it.'

She stormed back to the car. He blocked the door with his body. 'Mr Edward got me through the war. He's picked his death. All I can do is make his going as easy for him as possible.'

She went around to the driver's side, got in and started the engine. He reached for the passenger door, but she rammed the car into gear and drove off, leaving him standing.

He shouted after her. 'Don't you go making waves. Edward wouldn't thank you for it.'

It started to rain, heavy drops that increased in size and tempo until it could have been machinegun fire ripping up the tarmac. He retreated to a sheltering hedge at a bus stop and smoked a cigarette while he waited for the rain to let up.

He was on his second cigarette and thinking that he might have to catch a bus after all, when Miss Grace came back. She drew up beside him and pushed the passenger door open. He got in without speaking. They remained silent while she drove back to Farm Lodge Lane. She parked in Mrs Anderson's stunted drive. The rain was still pelting down, so they sat on rather than get soaked while running to the house. He offered her a cigarette.

She shook her head. 'I don't now.'

'Would it make any difference at this point?'

She glanced at him in surprise and looked quickly away. In that brief instant he saw that her eyes were red from crying. Her fresh-on make-up caked with moisture.

He picked up her handbag and shook it. Something rattled.

'Indigestion tablets,' she said, and grabbed the bag off him.

'I'm betting morphine or a morphine derivative.'

She started the engine again. He thought she was going to drive somewhere, but she switched the heater to full.

'I get cold very easily,' she said.

'Aye, it's a big change after Australia.'

The windows were opaque with rain. She stared as if trying to see someone or something through them. 'It's early spring in Australia. We've rented a house on the coast. There's something restful about the sea crashing onto the rocks.'

She stared into the window for a long time. Eventually, she turned her face to Barlow and drew a line with her finger, from the top of her nose, over the forehead and down the side of her face to the dimple on her jawline.

'If I let them cut this away I'll live for another year, maybe eighteen months.'

He dared take her hand in both of his. She let it stay.

He said, 'I knew something was wrong that first day at the Town Hall.'

'So you fought with me?' Something of her old spark showed.

'You started it.'

She smiled. 'It was either fight with you or burst into tears. You've no idea how much I missed home. I just had to see it again.'

'I knew that too.'

She pulled her hand free and used the rear-view mirror to finger-brush her hair tidy. 'How could you?'

His heart was breaking for this brave woman.

'Because you've got eyes like your brother. They show pain.'

The rain eased slightly and they ran for the shelter of the front door. He fussed, brushing raindrops off his jacket in the hallway while she went on into the kitchen. He heard the tap run and the unmistakable rattle of pills out of a bottle. He followed her in when he heard the kettle refilled and slapped onto the range.

He stood in the doorway and said to her back. 'Is there any way the family trust could increase its payments to Edward? It would make things a lot easier for him.'

She turned from putting out cups and saucers and faced him directly. 'There is no trust. It's all I can afford from my part-time salary.'

'Surely, your husband's family…?'

She laughed. It was a pleasant laugh that brought a smile to his lips although he didn't understand why. When the laughing stopped she carried on making the tea. He sat down.

Now that she'd brought it to his attention, he could see the cancerous growth starting to show: pushing one eye shut and bulging her cheek out.

'Aye,' he said.

She brought a plate of tray-bakes to the table and sat with him while the tea drew. In a way, he found it unsettling, sitting with a long-time enemy who had become someone absolutely charming. He wished she would snarl again. At least then he would know where he stood.

She said, 'I'll tell you in case Edward ever has to know the truth. My father-in-law was a docker and a wonderful man. My husband, Frederick, was a schoolteacher with a grown-up family. He was Frederick, not Fred or Freddie or any similar diminutive. I think that's why I loved him. He spends most of his time in a wheelchair now. His pension is good but not that wonderful.'

'So London wasn't about business?' he asked.

'No.' She sighed. 'I knew it was a waste of money, but Frederick insisted that I see the best specialists in Harley Street. The doctor made me spend a few days in hospital doing tests.'

'That must have cost a right few bob?'

He knew he was prying; the old policeman instinct to know everything.

'Our house,' she said bluntly.

That didn't make sense to him. 'But where will you live?'

She said, 'We've enough left over to pay for our holiday at the seaside. After that…'

She got up and poured the tea. He marvelled that her hand was absolutely steady.

71

The rain had stopped by the time Barlow was ready to leave Mrs Anderson's house. He insisted on walking because Terry's remark about the cheque 'thinning out' when he'd other men to pay was racing around in his head.

Nearing Mill Row he stopped and looked again at the list of names. Recast them in the light of what he knew of the value of goods taken.

Unwin Kirker:	£489-5-4 1/2

Unwin Kirker:	A good haul of things
Mo Hunt:	A lot less than claimed
E Fetherton:	Little worth taking
Mr Whithead:	Main loss the stamp collection

The Clarkes:	Not a lot of cash

The way he saw it, the burglars had robbed four homes and the Clarkes. The only robbery worthwhile to the burglars was the raid on Kirker's house. Mo Hunt had already sold anything of real value and the thieves had ignored Fetherton's modern junk. Grabbed what they could at Whithead's house and ran in case he called the police.

To start with, they knew what they were looking for, which made at least one of them a professional in the antiques trade. They were also ruthless, having left an old man tied up and in distress, and they'd gunned down three people. He tried not to think of Vera shot and scarred for life. Hate and anger would cloud his thinking.

Instead, he counted things off on his fingers: Split over two or three people, the value of the stuff they'd stolen hardly justified the risks they'd taken. And they had nerve. They'd hit two houses in one night, trying to make the trip from Belfast worthwhile. Even after killing two people, they'd tried for the Credit Union lodgement. Unfortunately for them, they'd chosen the wrong time of year. Later on, with people starting to save for Christmas, there'd be a lot of money going into the night safe.

They'd be back. He was sure of that in his bones. Why else try to kill him unless they were afraid that he was getting close? He could see Harvey sitting in the City Club, gin and tonic in hand, while he recounted the story of Barlow and the phantom Bedford van, and Shalko's ears flapping as he listened.

There would be one last robbery, and this time they'd pick their target carefully. Be sure of who they were hitting and what they were likely to get. This time they'd plan to make a killing in cash terms and God help anyone who stood in their way.

The question was: who would they hit and when?

He found himself on the Ballymoney Road, near his new home, wheeling his bicycle along by the handlebars instead of riding it. He didn't even remember being back in Mill Row to pick up the bike, which shook him.

There'd be no leaving the bicycle at the front door of the new house. This wasn't Mill Row with watchful neighbours. Too many chancers went up and down the main road. He wheeled the bicycle into the backyard and went into the house by the back door, something he'd promised himself he'd never do.

The tea was on. At least something was cooking in the oven, and it smelt good. He shouted that he was home and Vera shouted back. He found her in the sitting room, curled into the settee. He nearly asked her what she was doing when he realised she was enjoying the stretch of the house and the fact that she could retreat into a room and be with her own thoughts.

He sat with her, even though he was anxious to go down to the station and have a word with Gillespie and some of the older officers.

'There's a suitcase in the hall?' he said, to break a long, restful silence.

'I'm babysitting for the Dentons. The Town Council are giving Miss Grace a party before she leaves tomorrow.'

He clapped his hands to his head. *Idiot that I am. It'll be tonight.*

'What's wrong Dad?' Vera looked anxious.

'Early senility, that's what's wrong.'

Now he couldn't leave the house until Captain Denton had picked up Vera. *Not with those bastards in town.* He thanked God he hadn't given Shalko his address. All the same, he'd be happier if she was elsewhere for the night.

While Vera served up tea: brown stew, baby potatoes and onions all cooked in the one pot, he went through the house. Made sure every external door was locked, every window closed and snibbed shut. Checked every room for an emergency weapon. Sitting room: the poker. Table lamps, ornaments. Anything that could be lifted and flung, or used to smash in heads. When eating his tea he changed his table knife for a steak knife with a serrated edge.

'The meat's not that tough,' protested Vera.

He shrugged. She sulked through the meal and went off to touch up her make-up. Pointedly, left the washing up for him. With Vera out of the way he wrapped the steak knife in a tea towel and carried it with him into the sitting room. He turned an armchair around so that he could keep an eye on the gateway and the road beyond. Hid the knife down the side of the cushion. Vera joined him and they watched television while they waited for Captain Denton.

Denton arrived at nearly eight o'clock, sweeping his Rolls into the drive and braking sharply to a halt. Barlow went to the car with Vera, just in case something happened to her in that short distance. Anyway, he was curious. Denton had his tie off, which he never did in public, and his hair was crimped as if he'd been gripping it.

Straight off, Denton said, 'Edward's gone missing.'

Right then, Barlow didn't care about Edward and the fact that he'd gone missing. He'd worry about Edward when Vera was away from the house and safe. He did concede to himself that he'd been neglecting Edward at a time when he needed support: forced off the drink and having to cope with a judgemental big sister.

There's only one of me. He'd had his own problems and worries, been in hospital and in all sorts of bother with Harvey. *Still…*

'I knew he was falling apart, but I kept hoping he'd last until tomorrow,' said Denton.

'When did he go missing?'

'Lunchtime, with a full bottle of whisky. I've people scouring the countryside for him.'

Barlow thought of Miss Grace. What that woman needed to get her through the next few months was good memories of her visit to Ballymena. A final evening when she was again chatelaine of her home town, not the sight of her only brother lying in a pool of vomit.

'I'll see what I can do,' Barlow said, wondering if he would find the time.

72

Barlow balanced his bike against the wall and went into the police station, with barely a glance at the setting sun. Constables Gillespie and Wilson manned the Enquiries Office. From deep in the building he could hear Sergeant Pierson brief the new shift.

'God speaks from on high,' he murmured.

'Can I help you, sir?' asked Gillespie in the dry go-away-and-stop-annoying-my-head tone he adopted with the general public.

Barlow asked, 'Are you on tonight?'

'Only to chauffeur the DI and Mrs Harvey to and from the Castle Arms Hotel.'

Aware of Wilson listening in, Barlow was careful to use ranks. 'What about Sergeant Pierson?'

'On all evening.'

'And the DI?'

'Away getting himself dickied up for the dinner dance.'

'And the inspector?'

Gillespie's head tilted, like a grouse on the moors sensing danger. 'Somewhere in Belfast. He isn't back yet.'

Barlow nodded and waited. Ignored Gillespie's anxious frown and Wilson looking curiously between the two of them. Noticed that Wilson wore a black armband, the sign of someone close having died. Before he could ask who, the sound of Pierson's voice was replaced by the shuffle of booted feet on linoleum as the briefing ended.

Pierson tramped into the Enquiry Office and started at the sight of Barlow standing at the counter. 'What do you want, Barlow?'

Pierson wore his best uniform. The tips of his boots gleamed and he carried his ceremonial gloves. Pierson, Barlow guessed, intended to ingratiate himself with the nobs of the town by supplying a one-man honour guard at the Castle Arms Hotel.

'I need a crime reference for my insurance claim,' said Barlow.

'I'm just getting it for him, Sergeant,' said Gillespie and made himself busy flicking through the Incident Book.

Pierson grandstanded, blocking the door into the street, holding back the men going off shift. He said, 'Get it, Barlow, and then clear off. We don't want your sort hanging around the station.'

He stalked out the door, slamming it in the faces of the men.

Barlow looked at the constables. They refused to meet his eye, shuffled their feet in embarrassment.

Barlow said, 'Boys, stay near a phone tonight. You might be needed in a hurry.'

'What sort of hurry?' asked one.

'Green Bedford vans,' said Barlow.

The constable who'd spoken said, 'I think I'll stay back and service my revolver.'

He headed back down the corridor into the locker room. Most of the men followed him. The others said they had to go home but would be straight back.

Gillespie muttered into Barlow' ear, 'They wouldn't do that for Pierson.'

'Bollocks, they're in it for the overtime,' he said out loud.

The spokesman constable, who'd nearly as many years served as Barlow himself, shouted back, 'One minute Pierson wants to be our friend, the next minute he's down our throats over nothing. The thing about you Barlow is that you're plain, straightforward ignorant.'

'So long as you know,' said Barlow. He told Gillespie to call the patrol cars back and send them out again with four men in each instead of two. Keep circling their District Area.

Gillespie said, 'I'll throw a couple of rifles in the cars. They might come in handy.'

'You need an inspector or above to authorise that.'

Gillespie said, 'What they don't know won't hurt them. And if anything does happen they'll take the credit for issuing them in the first place.'

'You'd make a good sergeant,' said Barlow.

After that he followed the constables into the back of the building. He needed privacy while he made a few phone calls. Once the corridor was clear, he slipped into Harvey's office. He thought he might as well be comfortable while he made the calls, and Harvey had the best chair in the building.

He started with the police stations and manned sub-stations scattered around Ballymena, then the Belfast stations to the north and west of the city. On each call he insisted on speaking to the Duty Sergeant or the Senior Constable on duty. Each man was asked to tell their patrols to keep a close eye out for a green Bedford van, or red, or white or blue, or any other colour. Registration unknown but believed to be a Belfast one.

He warned every sergeant or constable he spoke to, to re-member that these men were wanted for questioning in con-nection with four violent deaths. They were merely to observe and report back to either himself or Constable Gillespie at the Ballymena station.

'Now we wait,' he muttered, and wished he'd thought to make himself a mug of tea before starting the calls.

He made one final call to Mrs Anderson's house. 'Any sign of him?'

'Not yet.' She'd been crying.

'I'll see what I can do.'

He sighed and left Harvey's office. Looked longingly towards the kitchen and that mug of tea. Sighed again and strode into the Enquiry Office where he found Gillespie cleaning his gun and Wilson leaning on the counter staring at the empty fireplace.

Barlow asked Gillespie, 'Have you run the DI to the Castle Arms yet?'

'Not yet.'

'Stay here as much as you can. Take any phone calls coming in for me.'

'What phone calls?'

'You'll know when you get them.' Barlow scooped out Wilson's cap from beneath the counter and jammed it on his head. 'Instead of standing there like a wet weekend, take a walk up the town and annoy a few innocent citizens.'

He left the station and was putting on his cycle clips when Wilson followed him out.

'Barlow asked, 'Who's dead, son?'

'The Colonel.'

Barlow shook his head, but he wasn't surprised. He'd been round too many wartime hospitals, visiting injured friends. It got so he could tell who wasn't going to make it.

He asked, 'A heart attack?'

'No.'

'One of those foreign bugs he picked up in the tropics?'

'Not that either,' said Wilson. 'Though he had enough of them.'

'What then?'

'An aneurysm on the brain. Eleanor says it's no wonder he's been acting funny. Doing things he normally wouldn't do, like stealing.'

The information bubbled out of Wilson. 'We'd just had dinner. Eleanor and I cleared the table and did the washing up.'

There was a hint of uneasiness in his manner. Barlow reckoned that more than the washing up had gone on in the kitchen.

'I went to ask him if he wanted coffee. I thought he was asleep so we left it for half an hour. But he was dead. Just like that.'

Wilson's voice trembled. He bit his lip and turned away. 'Sorry.'

Barlow said, 'A sudden death is a shock at the best of times, and harder still when it's someone you know.'

He was astride the bike and ready to push off when Wilson said, 'Eleanor told me what really happened that day at the point-to-point.'

Barlow hoped Wilson wouldn't pass on that titbit of information to Harvey. He rode off without replying.

Doing that bitch a good turn will get me hung.

73

Barlow started with the pubs. No, they hadn't seen Mr Edward. Give him a drink? They wouldn't dare. Which left a few unlicensed shebeens he wasn't supposed to know about, and a retired chemistry teacher whose hobby was distilling the mash of various products. 'Solely in the interest of science,' the teacher claimed. Occasionally, he gave Barlow a bottle of experimental brew for his considered opinion.

No matter where he looked, Barlow drew a blank. Nobody had seen Edward and they'd no idea where he might be. Barlow had a look-see in Edward's hut under the dry arch, even though he was sure Denton would have already checked there.

He made his way back up the crumbling bank and stood looking down at the hut while he wondered where to go next. The hut had a decided cant. He reckoned that a good push would send it flying into the water, which would solve one problem.

'And who would have to build the new one?' he asked. He already knew the answer to that, and decided to leave well enough alone.

The only other place left to look, other than the river itself, was the remains of the once-proud Adair estate.

He cycled along the river to the back of the estate and a long-abandoned gate lodge. It sat squat, its lava-stone walls almost invisible among the encroaching trees. Barlow put a foot to the ground for balance and swung the bicycle light onto the gate lodge. Its front door lay open, forced wide enough to let a thin person through. He looked closer and saw the dark shadow of someone inside.

The door crunched and squealed as he shouldered it back against the wall. The bicycle light and the last of the sun flooded in. The shadow became a man sitting on an upturned crate. Edward neither moved nor acknowledged Barlow's presence in any way. He sat looking at a bottle of Johnny Walker Red Label on the floor before him. His new suit was muddy and smeared green where he'd brushed against algae.

Barlow stood on. Eventually, Edward looked at him, with a face that was more bone and sunken eyes than anything else. 'There'll be drink all around me tonight.'

'There's drink in the brewery and you've survived that.'

'I stay away from the bottling plant.' He waved vaguely at the bottle. 'So why bother trying?'

'Putting yourself through needless torture for nothing,' agreed Barlow.

He noted that the seal on the whisky bottle was still intact.

'I like to drink,' said Edward, with all the conviction of a connoisseur of fine wines. 'I am a convivial social drinker.'

'You drink because you're gutless.' Barlow said. 'The widows and orphans from the war get on with things, there's nothing else for it. But you…?'

'People died because I made mistakes.' Edward started to sob.

The ghosts of the dead walked before Barlow's eyes. Sometimes his job had been to collect enough body parts to make a funeral.

He spat into the corner. 'People die in a war. It goes with the job.'

'But I killed them.' Edward's sobs tore at his throat. 'Me.'

Barlow moved into the room. He didn't want to because it put the ghosts of his imagination between him and the door.

He pulled up a spare crate and sat sideways on to Edward, contemplated the unbroached bottle of whiskey. Eventually, Edward's sobs eased and stopped.

Barlow held his hands out to the whiskey bottle as if warming them before a fire. 'The people with us were unlucky. Sometimes they got careless. Sometimes they weren't good enough. Sometimes the job was beyond them.'

He felt bad. It was the worst of luck criticising the dead.

He looked at Edward. 'Do you remember the cellar in that bloody factory? A full day we spent up to our necks in freezing water, with a bomb that persisted in trying to tick. We could have been blown to hell a dozen times, and what did we get? Pneumonia and hypothermia.

'Anderson died.'

'Anderson was chesty. Anderson had TB.'

Edward made a fist and struck the palm of his other hand. 'I should have known he wasn't well.'

'You weren't his mother.'

The ghosts of Barlow's war service faded and disappeared.

Edward wiped away the last of his tears. 'Grace is going to kill me.'

'Bollocks Grace.'

'She hates me for living in Farm Lodge Lane.'

'Did she tell you that?'

Edward said nothing.

'So she didn't.'

Barlow looked at him grimly. 'You've enough problems without inventing them.'

Now the shadows had gone, he felt safe throwing his memory back.

'You spent the war pretending that you didn't care who died or when or how, so long as the job got done.' Subtlety wasn't in Barlow's makeup, but he tried raising an eyebrow. 'This time you'll be the only casualty.'

Edward raised a smile. 'That tongue of hers could flense you.'

They sat silent after that, staring at the bottle. Finally, with the sun waning below the horizon, Barlow shifted himself and stood up.

He stretched. 'Mrs Anderson's worried about you. Apparently, you missed an important meeting.'

'Oh the board meeting,' said Edward in a dismissive voice.

'A board meeting? Now that sounds awful grand, and you go and miss it?'

Edward raised a faint smile. 'You, me, Corporal Anderson and RQMS Denton. We used to get more work done over a pint.'

'Not too difficult then?'

'Difficult enough,' said Edward with a sudden snap of indignation. He stood up as well and brushed at the mud on his clothes. 'Ninety percent of the problems are personnel related. The men come to me with their concerns.'

'Good on you.'

'Damn!' said Edward with sudden vehemence. 'I intended to raise a couple of issues under "Other Business".'

Barlow walked to the door, hoping that Edward would follow.

He said, over his shoulder, 'So you don't just sit there at these important meetings with nothing to say?'

'Certainly not.'

Barlow collected his bike and stood waiting. He said, 'These last few weeks have been like the journey to an exploded bomb, exciting in a way. Now we're here, everyone's scared and gone quiet.'

He canted his head up and looked towards the heavens. Venus shone bright in the sky and the moon was fighting the last rays of the sun for dominance. The path home beneath the trees lay in deep dusk.

Barlow said, 'I don't know about you, but I stopped shaking once I touched the bomb.'

He breathed in the scents of the evening while he waited.

After a few minutes Edward walked out of the house and handed him the bottle of whiskey. 'Are you comparing my sister to an exploded bomb?'

'Don't I still have the scars from that time I booked her for speeding?'

74

'What about these phone calls I never got?' asked Gillespie sourly when Barlow arrived back at the police station.

Barlow eyed a bottle of Buckfast on the counter. 'So you turned to drink while you were waiting.'

Gillespie gave him a cold look. 'Wilson arrested the Harts.'

'The Harts? What did they do this time?'

'They were walking a white line to see how drunk they were.'

Barlow held down a smile. 'The one in the middle of the road?'

'Singing like lords they were before you arrived,' moaned Gillespie. 'And them without a note between them.'

'Feed them up, sober them up and throw them out.'

'That's exactly what Wilson's doing. And, anyway, who are you to be giving me orders?' Gillespie brushed disdainfully at his sleeve. 'Me, the Acting Sergeant while Pierson is at the hotel.'

'Well act that bottle off the counter and into the bin,' said Barlow in as surly a tone as he could manage.

Gillespie picked up the bottle. One of those little clicks went off in Barlow's mind.

He asked, 'That bottle the night Kirker's window was put in, what happened to it?'

Gillespie said, 'It's probably still in the Evidence Room.'

'Get it.'

Barlow roared down the corridor. 'Wilson!'

A door opened and closed. Wilson came hurrying. 'You wanted me, Sergeant?'

'Gillespie will give you a bottle. Check it against that fin-gerprint you got off the ball bearings.'

The two officers hurried off. Barlow trusted that no one would rob the Enquiry Office while it was unmanned and went into the Squad Room. It was empty. All the constables on standby had adjourned to the kitchen. Going by the rancid smoke seeping out, more than the Harts were being fed.

Barlow perched on the edge of a desk and stared at maps of the area. One set showed the streets of Ballymena, the other the rural area incorporated in the Ballymena Policing District.

The door opened and Gillespie came in.

He said, 'Wilson's manning the Enquiry Office while he works. Going by the size of the fingerprint he's looking for someone thirty foot tall.'

Barlow said, 'Or someone drunk enough to be stupid, and enough bad blood in his system to be vindictive.'

'JD threw that bottle, so you think it was him who put in your window and nearly killed you?' Gillespie asked.

'If it's not him, I'll be starting on my supposed friends next.'

Gillespie gave a shiver that wasn't all mock. 'That young gentleman takes after his father. When you go to arrest him, you're on your own. I'm not that brave – or stupid.' He stared at the maps. 'What are we looking for?'

'Places these Bedford van men are likely to hit.'

Gillespie sighed. 'I thought of that too. Do you realise there are more millionaires per head of population in the Ballymena area than anywhere else in the United Kingdom?' He made a sweeping motion with his finger. 'We can't guard them all.'

'I know, I know.'

With their meal finished, the Harts cleared their throats and once again began to sing.

Barlow shuddered as the out-of tune roaring grated in his head. 'It'll be a long hour until there's enough blood in the alcohol to throw them out.'

With nothing better to do they stood on, gazing at the map.

After a time, Wilson put his head around the door and nodded at Gillespie. 'Sergeant Pierson's back. He wants to know where you are.'

Gillespie said to Barlow, 'You'd better slope out the back door.'

'Aye,' said Barlow who'd no intention of going anywhere.'

Gillespie pulled his uniform jacket straight and left with Wilson. Barlow waited until they were out of sight before he slipped down the corridor towards the back of the building. By now, the Harts' singing was appallingly loud. He slipped into Harvey's office and opened the new drinks cabinet and hesitated over the selection on offer: whiskey, gin, a bottle of vodka more than half full, mixers. A Special Reserve Brandy.

He lifted out the brandy and went back to the door. Checked carefully that the corridor remained free of passers-by before striding quickly down to the cells. He lifted the keys off their ring, unlocked the door of the Harts' cell and replaced the keys before going in. Pushed the door shut behind him and made sure the lock engaged. In the enclosed space the screaming sound that the Harts took to be singing made his brain vibrate. They wore matching canary yellow waistcoats and woollen ties under jackets stained with ancient drink.

Barlow splashed brandy into the dregs of tea in their mugs. 'Here, boys, have a real drink.'

'God bless you, Mr Barlow.'

They knocked back their drinks in one gulp and held out the mugs for a refill.

'Not until you've sung me something,' he said. 'Something rousing.' He gave them a quick splash of a refill and started them off. 'We're public guardians, bold but wary… '

They took up the refrain of the *Bold Gendarmes*. Roared it lustily in the confined space until Barlow thought his head was going to burst. He retreated as far back from the brothers as he could and set the brandy bottle carefully in the corner. Wrapped the knuckles of his right hand in his handkerchief. Waited.

From a distance he heard a roar of rage and the pounding of feet. He squared his shoulders against the corridor wall and blew on his bound knuckles. Drew his fist back when the key rattled in the lock. Pierson pushed on the door even as he turned the key. The door swung open, Pierson stumbled into the cell. Barlow unleashed a blow he'd ached to let rip for a long time. Pierson folded to his knees, bowed forward until his forehead rested on the floor. Fell sideways.

Barlow said, 'Ohhh.' Gripped his injured hand in his armpit and again said, 'Ohhh.'

The Harts stopped singing and watched, fascinated.

'Sing, boys, sing.'

They started again. '*When the foeman bears his steel, tarantara, tarantara…*'

As far as Barlow was concerned, Gilbert and Sullivan were as good as anything. 'Louder boys, louder.'

Pierson lay groaning, barely conscious. Barlow gripped him by the collar and dragged him clear of the door. With Pierson stretched out on his back, Barlow splashed a little brandy into his mouth. Pierson spluttered and wiped at the liquid with his hand. His eyes fluttered prior to opening. Barlow set the bottle of brandy at Pierson's head and stepped into the corridor. Watched as the Harts dived forward and fought over the almost unconscious Pierson for the bottle.

Barlow slipped into the corridor and closed the door behind him. Leaving the key in the lock he returned to the Enquiry Office.

'Where's Sergeant Pierson?' asked Gillespie.

Barlow made his shrug long and casual. 'He must have left.'

Wilson stared at him in surprised disbelief. With Wilson looking in Barlow's direction, Gillespie scooped Pierson's cap off the counter and lobbed it into a cupboard.

From the prison cell triumphant voices disclaimed, '*I belong to Glasgow, dear old Glasgow town…*'

75

Over the Harts' singing came the metallic rumble of someone pounding weakly at a steel door.

'They can't even beat time to the tune,' said Barlow in disgust.

Wilson asked, 'Do you want me to go down and tell them to shut up?'

'You're busy fingerprinting,' Barlow reminded him.

Wilson looked pleased with himself. 'I'm done, Sergeant. It's the same fingerprint – thumbprint actually – so far as I can tell.'

So it was JD who had fired the ball bearings through his window. No real surprise there. *Like father, like son.* Given time he'd find a way to teach that young tyke some manners.

'Right,' said Barlow, searching for ideas to keep Wilson busy and out of the cell block. The last thing he wanted was for the young officer to worry what he should tell Harvey if asked. *Preferably nothing.*

'Now that we've got a spare pair of fingerprints, and we know who they belong to, why don't you check them against the unidentified prints in all those robbed houses?'

Wilson beamed. This was real police work. He collected his fingerprint cards and hurried off to disturb the sleeping Duty Detective Constable.

'That'll keep him busy,' said Gillespie with a grin.

'And you can ring around all the stations and make sure they're on the lookout. If those boys are coming to rob to-night, it'll be any time now.'

Gillespie made a face. 'And here's me planning a quiet night.' A third voice had joined in with the Harts, shouting rather than singing.

'What did you do to Pierson?' Gillespie asked while fashioning his fingers in the shape of a cross and holding it in front of his face, as if to ward off evil. 'I don't want to know.'

He was grinning as he reached for the phone.

Barlow left him to it and went searching for that long-delayed mug of tea. The men on standby had adjourned to the Radio Room, and were telling the men in the patrol cars that it was now their turn to get out and about. They pretended not to see Barlow because he was barred from the station, and if they didn't see him, then he wasn't there in the first place.

Barlow poured two mugs of tea, checked the oven for leftovers and managed to salvage a satisfactory plateful of fried bread and bacon. He was barely back in the Enquiry Office when Inspector Foxwood walked in.

Gillespie was in the middle of a phone call to Toome police station, so Foxwood knew exactly what he was up to. Barlow was badly caught holding a mug of tea, his mouth full of fried bread and bacon.

Almost instantaneously Foxwood went from drained exhaustion to burning fury. 'What the hell are you doing here?'

Gillespie crossed fingers behind his back and said, 'Sir, there's a good chance those burglars will strike again tonight, with everyone at the hotel.'

'Where I should be,' said Foxwood bitterly.

'So, I was just ringing around to see if anyone had spotted a green Bedford van.'

Barlow knew that story would only hold until Foxwood thought to ring a couple of stations. He shoved Gillespie's mug of tea into Foxwood's hands. 'Without telling anyone, especially Acting Sergeant Gillespie, I made the first round of calls. Gillespie thought that now that people are looking out for the Bedford van, he might as well keep them at it.'

Foxwood looked from one man to the other, plainly disbelieving them. He seemed to realise he was holding a mug of tea and drained it in one go. The Harts were still in full voice and now a third one had joined in, clearly shouting 'help!'

'And what the hell is that noise?' Foxwood asked.

'The Harts,' said Gillespie.

'Tell someone to go and shut them up.'

Gillespie disappeared rapidly down the corridor, leaving Foxwood and Barlow standing face to face.

Barlow asked quickly, before Foxwood could launch into a rant of temper. 'Any luck with the Bedford van?'

Foxwood slumped against the counter, overcome by a mixture of exhaustion and disappointment. 'We traced it. At least we think it's the one we're looking for. The registered owner is as honest as they come. He traded it in for a new van earlier this year and the dealer sold it on for cash. The buyer called himself Michael Campbell and gave a false address.' He nearly spat the words. 'Do you know there are nearly as many Campbells in Northern Ireland as there are Smiths in England?'

Barlow pushed the plate towards him. Foxwood lifted a slice of fried bread and savagely bit into it. Said, through a mouthful of food, 'Barlow, you're in enough trouble as it is. Get out of here.'

A strong waft of alcohol preceded the arrival of Sergeant Pierson, with Gillespie at his heel. Pierson's tie was gone, his shirt pulled open at the collar.

'Somehow sergeant Pierson locked himself in with the Harts,' said Gillespie. He held up the brandy bottle behind Pierson's back. 'And this,' he added in a disapproving voice. He turned the bottle upside down to show it was empty.

'Somebody hit me over the head and knocked me out,' said Pierson, rubbing at a swelling on his jaw.

'Mr Hennessy,' said Barlow, pretending not to notice Foxwood's disbelieving glare.

'What happened?' Foxwood asked Pierson.

'The Harts were singing. I went down to shut them up.' Pierson looked at Barlow accusingly. 'Somebody hit me as I walked in.'

'So you weren't drinking yourself?'

'No,' said Pierson. 'No.'

Barlow said, 'You were at the Castle Arms Hotel. Captain Denton always sends out a drink to the men at the door.'

'So you *were* drinking Pierson,' Foxwood snapped

'And on duty,' said Barlow in a tone of righteous indignation.

Foxwood returned his attention to Barlow. Knew he was involved somehow and intended to get to the truth.

Barlow was saved by the sound of running feet. Wilson came bursting into the Enquiries Office, his face burning with excitement. 'We've got it, Sergeant. We've got it.' He saw Foxwood and crashed to a halt, breathing hard.

'Are you sure?' asked Barlow, uncertain that he was hearing Wilson correctly. He'd only sent him to check the fingerprints to keep him out of the way and busy.

'Sergeant, the fingerprints match. And the detective confirmed it.'

'What fingerprints?' asked Foxwood, looking like he wished he'd stayed in Belfast.

Wilson gulped. 'Unwin Kirker's house. The first night, the night the money was taken. We've got a match.'

'Who was it?' Foxwood asked, fixing Barlow with a gimlet-eyed stare, knowing that he was somehow involved in this as well.

'JD,' replied Barlow, still not quite believing it in spite of Wilson's nod in agreement.

Of course JD. Unwin Kirker's had kept complaining about his weekend at the caravan ruined and the next day JD claimed to have won a lot of money at the point to point.

'JD who?' Foxwood asked.

'James Donaldson.'

'Not the son of…?'

'Yes,' said Barlow.

He knew he should celebrate getting his revenge on a man who had given him a lot of grief over the years. He also knew that an arrogant, vindictive youth had just ruined his own future.

Foxwood closed his eyes. If today was bad, tomorrow would be ten times worse when it came to arresting Judge Donaldson's son. 'Dear God, let this day end.'

76

The police station, like the night outside had gone quiet. Each man preoccupied with his thoughts: triumphant or apprehensive. The only thing Barlow knew for certain was that tomorrow, when it came to him being arraigned, Judge Donaldson wouldn't be on the bench. A personal interest, the attack of the judge's son on Barlow's house, would disbar him, which gave Barlow a decent chance of getting bail. *If it gets that far.* He didn't hold out much hope that it wouldn't.

The telephone shrilled, breaking the silence, making everyone jump.

Gillespie answered it, 'Police, Ballymena.' Listened, then held out the receiver for Barlow. 'It's your old friend from Randalstown.'

Pierson tried to reassert his authority. 'No private phone calls, Barlow.'

Barlow ignored him and took the receiver.

'What have you got for me?' he asked.

'The sweetest brew I've tasted in years, but besides that…' The old constable knew how to play an audience by pausing. 'Not the green Bedford you've been going on about. A bigger job, a dark blue truck.' He paused again.

Not the green Bedford, a blue truck. Barlow should have been shouting 'false alarm' but the old constable wouldn't be phoning unless something about the blue truck had caught his attention. He let the old constable have his small victory by asking, 'What about it?'

'A nice job, new, engine sweet as the glass of nectar in my hand.'

If he didn't hurry up and tell, Barlow swore that first chance he'd ram the glass down the old constable's throat and hold it there until he choked.

'Two or three men in the cab,' continued the old constable. 'But the back was the bit that caught my eye. No tail lights, no light over the number plate.' Barlow heard him take a deep breath as he savoured the bouquet from the glass of brew. 'Now it could be heading for Derry, or Magherafelt, but if I was a betting man I'd say Ballymena.'

Barlow slammed the phone down. 'They're on their way.'

He told Foxwood and the rest what the old constable had said. Ordered Wilson to tell the men on standby to gear up. Tapped the map to show Foxwood the approximate position of cars currently out on patrol. Then he had to stand back and grit his teeth in frustration as Foxwood took over. The patrol cars were to go here and here. Men were to be called in off duty to provide backup. Other stations asked to cover the edges of their area and be on the look-out for the dark blue truck. At this point Foxwood stopped speaking and blinked in amazement as the men on standby tramped into the Enquiries Office. 'And rifles, we need rifles,' he said.

Gillespie produced a clipboard and pen. 'Two rifles per car and three clips of ammunition per rifle,' he said.

'My car as well,' said Foxwood as he signed the authorisation to withdraw rifles and ammunition from the armoury.

Barlow opened a cupboard door to reveal two rifles resting comfortably among the stationery.

'I'm glad I planned things well ahead,' said Foxwood in a dry tone, missing Gillespie's sardonic lift of an eyebrow.

Pierson detailed men. 'You two come with me and the Inspector.' His stabbing finger deliberately skipped Barlow.

'You've been drinking,' said Barlow.

Pierson snarled. 'Someone hit me over the head and locked me in that cell. It had to be you Barlow.'

We're going into a situation where we need a steady hand and cool judgement,' said Foxwood. He seemed happy ordering Pierson to stay in the station. 'I'm not risking other men's lives to a drunk.'

A senior constable was delegated to go in Pierson's place. Gillespie was told to take over in the Radio Room, coordinating the movement of the patrol cars. Pierson could man the front desk.

'And deal with all the grannies,' muttered Gillespie.

Barlow knew he would be left behind, but it still hurt when Foxwood stopped at the door and said. 'Sorry, Barlow, but not when you're suspended.'

Wilson was standing equally bereft. Pierson had deliberately excluded him as well when detailing men their duties. Sympathetic pats from the constables as they passed him was no consolation. But it told Barlow one thing, the men were starting to like and trust the young officer.

He asked Wilson, 'Is that crappy yoke of yours back on the road?'

Wilson seemed to grow six inches, 'It's fixed and Gillespie has it running like a racing car.'

'Right,' said Barlow and hauled Wilson out the front door before Pierson could order him to empty all the wastepaper baskets or do something equally useful.

Wilson was in the old A5 and revving the engine hard before Barlow had even reached the backyard. At the exit from the station car park Wilson stood on the brakes.

Barlow had to fend himself off windscreen. 'I thought I told you to get driving lessons,' he grumbled.

'Which way, Sergeant?'

A good question. The other patrol cars had already left, so there was no chance of tailing one of them. Worse, the old A5 didn't have a radio, so Barlow and Wilson had no way of keeping up to date with the latest developments. They needed some way of communicating with Gillespie in the Radio Room.

'Left,' he told Wilson and felt himself being catapulted back into his seat as the old A5 took off. 'Are you using aviation fuel?'

Once Wilson had the car roaring down the road at an incredible sixty miles an hour he took a hand off the steering wheel and patted his side. 'At least I've got my pistol this time.'

He sounded excited, like he was going into a real life Cowboys and Indians film. Barlow felt naked without his gun. There'd been no chance of sneaking it out, not with Pierson around. Just himself and an inexperienced officer against two or three armed and ruthless men. He didn't like the odds.

'Where are we heading?' asked Wilson as he tried to coax sixty-five out of the old engine.

'Captain Denton's house,' said Barlow.

Vera was babysitting for the Dentons. They could use that as a base and have Gillespie phone through with updates. Also, when he thought about it, the Denton Demesne was in the area where the truck was headed. *At least that's what we hope.*

'The house itself?' exclaimed Wilson.

'Do you want a long wait in a muddy field?'

Barlow looked over at the young constable. He was clearly hyped by the coming confrontation with armed men. Wilson could have the muddy field if he wanted. Personally, Barlow preferred to wait in a warm room, with a mug of tea to soothe his jangling nerves.

Again, something pinged in his brain. Mud, muddy fields. Mud on Connie Dunlop's shoes in a garden so small she could do most of the weeding from her front door.

He thumped the dashboard with his fist. 'Stop! Go back! We're going the wrong way!'

Wilson stood on the brakes. The A5 slewed to a halt. 'What do you mean the wrong way?'

Barlow said, 'We need someone for backup, and I know just the man.'

77

Wilson drove back through the town. He stayed within the speed limit after Barlow warned him, 'Killing an innocent citizen is not a good career move.'

On the Ballymoney Road cars were parked from the Pentagon to well beyond the Convent's postern gate. Wilson double-parked outside the Castle Arms Hotel. Deep in the hotel a band was playing a quickstep.

Barlow hopped out of the car. 'Get her turned and then wait here.'

He was about to run up the steps into the hotel, when he spotted Edward standing beside a tree. He wore a hired dress suit and a bow tie.

'What are you doing out here?'

'Regardless of modern mores, a gentleman does not smoke in front of the ladies.'

'You don't smoke'

'Neither does one drink.'

Edward intended it to be humorous, but it came out more like pain. Barlow felt for him, having to sit at the function surrounded by alcohol, with people drinking it, spilling it, slobbering over it. Having to pass bottles up and down the table.

He grasped Edward by the arm to prevent him from slipping away. 'Tell you what, come and show me where Geordie's hiding out.'

'My dear chap, Rifleman Dunlop has relocated to England.'

Barlow changed his grasp to a double-handed grip of Edward's lapels. 'Edward!' he snarled.

Edward brushed at Barlow's hands the way he would cigarette ash. 'One has given one's word.'

'If Geordie Dunlop is going to get out of this mess, I need him with me tonight.'

Edward threw his head back so he could look Barlow straight in the eye. 'Is it the Sergeant Major who speaks?'

'The Sergeant Major,' agreed Barlow and let go of the lapels.

'Then one needs to accompany one to the residue and remainder of the Adair Estate.'

Barlow said, 'All these big words. I think I preferred you drunk.'

Wilson arrived back with the car. Barlow ran into the hotel. He asked the Receptionist to tell Captain Denton that Edward had gone to assist the police with their enquiries, and not to worry. Then he rushed out again. He needed to get back to Wilson's car as quickly as possible. No way could he risk Edward saying the wrong thing to Wilson.

He bundled Edward into the back of the A5 and told Wilson. 'Mr Edward has an idea where Geordie Dunlop might be hiding out. Drive out to Curles Bridge and he'll guide you from there.'

Mercifully, Edward stayed quiet in the back. Barlow didn't like the way Wilson unclipped his holster and eased the pistol loose.

At Curles Bridge, Edward directed Wilson through a disused gateway and on up a muddy lane to a row of houses once used by estate workers. Barlow got Wilson to swing the car around in an arc, spotlighting each house one by one. They were all uninhabitable, with roofs and walls almost completely fallen in.

From there they set off on foot. Edward led them through darkness, with tractor ruts guiding their feet along the lane.

Brambles tore at their clothes, unseen branches whipped their faces. The town and its lights lay well behind, traffic only the faintest hum.

A hard, choking cough cut through the silence.

Barlow stopped suddenly. Wilson cannoned into him. Through the darkness a glimmer of light hardly bigger than a dying match showed.

'Bloody hell,' said Barlow eventually. 'I should have twigged.'

He whispered to Wilson, 'It's the old Ice House.'

They walked on, stepping more quietly now. The light grew brighter, became a concealed candle flame flickering in wafts of air. They stopped in front of a low doorway.

Barlow shouted, 'Geordie Dunlop, it's Sergeant Major Barlow. We've got you surrounded. Come out with your hands up.'

Geordie shouted back, 'Come and get me Barlow. I've got a shotgun here and… ' He coughed again. 'And plenty of ammunition.'

Barlow heard Wilson drawing his pistol. Grabbed his hand and forced the pistol back into its holster.

'But, Sergeant, he's armed and dangerous.'

'Really, my dear fellow,' said Edward reprovingly to Wilson.

'Bollocks to you and your gun,' shouted Barlow to Geordie. 'If you don't come out right now, I'll go in there with a stick and beat you out.'

Edward raised his voice slightly. 'Rifleman Dunlop, come out at once.'

Geordie appeared, crouching to get through the low doorway, then stood fists bunched. 'Come on, Barlow. I can beat you and your stick with one hand tied behind my back.'

He started to cough again, held his arms to his chest to ease the pain.

Barlow laughed. 'Stay there and die of pneumonia, for all I care, or come and give us a hand to catch the real killers.'

'It's taken you long enough to find them,' said Geordie and marched forward.

'Well, you were no great help. Hiding out here like a big sissy.'

Barlow sensed Wilson's fear at a suspected murderer coming close, and him with his gun still in its holster. He liked the fact that the young constable held his ground, ready to back him if it came to a fight.

'Go on in and check the Ice House,' Barlow told Wilson, and earned a scowl from Geordie.

Wilson kept well out of arms reach as he stepped past Geordie and disappeared in through the doorway.

Geordie was shivering even though it was a mild night.

'Come on,' said Barlow and led Edward and Geordie back towards the derelict houses and the car.

Wilson appeared a few moments later empty handed.

'Where are all the machine guns and bazookas he threatened us with?' asked Barlow.

'There aren't any,' said Wilson.

'Didn't I tell you he's all talk.'

'I've got a Swiss army knife,' volunteered Geordie, and coughed again.

'Oh choke to death,' said Barlow.

78

Captain Denton's house was lit up like a Christmas tree. Barlow eyed it balefully as they swept up the long drive. 'It must be great having money to burn.'

'We can't all be tightwads like you,' said Geordie.

His hacking cough had settled down into an occasional throaty choke.

Wilson drove with one eye on the road and the other on the rear mirror. He was clearly uneasy at having an alleged mass murderer behind him: unsecured and unsearched. He took the car in a large sweeping curve before pulling up at the front door.

'You're good at navigating fancy driveways,' said Barlow.

Wilson didn't reply and didn't look uncomfortable either at the oblique reference to him dating Eleanor Packenham. As soon as they were out of the car he drew Barlow aside. 'Sergeant, there are children in there. Shouldn't Dunlop be handcuffed?'

'He should,' agreed Barlow as he headed for the front door of the house, leaving Wilson to wonder if he was expected to secure Geordie single-handedly.

Barlow ran up the steps and rang the bell. Listened to the sound of tiny feet tripping down the stairs. A little girl with golden ringlets opened the door.

'Shouldn't you be in bed, young lady?' asked Barlow.

'She should, but take your eye off her for one second and she's gone,' said Vera appearing from a back room. She frowned

at Barlow. 'What are you doing here Dad?' She started in surprise when Geordie appeared on the doorstep. When she saw
Wilson she finger-brushed a stray lock of hair and tidied her
blouse

Barlow said, 'We need to use the phone.' Saw her hesitation
and added. 'The Captain won't mind. It's business.'

He walked across a carpeted hallway the size of his new
sitting room to a telephone and dialled the station number.
WPC Day answered on the first ring. She informed him that
the WPCs had been called in to help and wanted to put him
through to Gillespie but Barlow made her ring him back so
that the call wouldn't be charged to Denton.

Gillespie hardly had time to talk to Barlow, what with cars
flying here, there and everywhere. Checkpoints being set up,
and then moved. He was of the opinion and – as he informed
Barlow grandly – Inspector Foxwood agreed with him that, by
this time, the burglars were probably between the cordon and
the town. The question was, should they tighten the cordon
in the hope of constricting the burglars or wait and grab them
when they made a dash for Belfast and home.

'Your call, not mine,' said Barlow, and found that he was
talking to himself.

Gillespie had hung up on him. *The man's busy,* thought Barlow to excuse the annoyance he felt. Started to walk away
from the phone then thought, *maybe not.* He tried the number
of the police station again. There was no dial tone. The line
was dead.

He looked at the table the telephone stood on. Looked
around the hall and through an open doorway into a long living room. Saw a fortune in pictures and porcelain ornaments,
and glass-topped cabinets displaying family mementoes.

Up the drive came a large vehicle at speed.

The little girl was in 'Uncle Edward's' arms, holding her nose and saying 'he smells' as she pointed at Geordie.

'Shit!'

The telephone suddenly dead and a large vehicle flying up the drive. It had to be the burglars in the truck, all presumably armed. Against them, four men, one pistol and a house full of children. Barlow tried not to think that these criminals never left witnesses alive and able to talk.

He said to Wilson. 'Do a John Wayne. Go and stand in the front door and look twenty foot tall.'

He felt it was a good gamble. On seeing one armed officer they might assume the house was full of them and back off. A real patrol car would have looked more convincing *than that beat up A5.*

Vera took the little angel with the golden ringlets into her arms. He said to her, 'Gather up all the kids. Lock them and yourself in the furthest bathroom.'

She nodded, white-faced, and ran up the stairs.

'Good girl,' he called after her and wished he'd had the wit to send the children off in Wilson's car when he had the chance.

He found he was breathing deeply in long, slow stretches. His heart pumping oxygen-rich blood throughout his body in anticipation of the huge effort that lay ahead.

He looked around him checking things. Wilson stood in the doorway, legs apart, thumbs hooked into his weapons belt. The truck lights were trained on him.

The bastards are still coming.

Edward stood at his shoulder. 'Orders, Sergeant Major?'

'What do you want me to do?' asked Geordie.

'There's a gun cabinet somewhere. We need anything you can lay your hands on.'

'It'll be locked. I'll need the key.'

'You're the burglar. Find it!'

Edward and Geordie went off together.

He told Wilson to come in and secure the door. Switched off the hall lights to give themselves the cover of darkness. Sprinted for the kitchen and the cutlery drawer.

79

The kitchen had been extended by incorporating old pantries and stores to create a huge working area. It held more drawers and cupboards than Barlow could count in a hurry.

'Bloody hell!' he breathed and, working on the premise that anything sharp would be kept away from little fingers, he searched high. The drawers ran on steel bearings. His pull nearly ripped the first drawer out of its unit. *Pastry forks.* Second and third drawers: napkins and dishcloths. He noticed a butcher's block in the corner and tried the nearby cupboard. Found a meat cleaver and carving knives. Grabbed a handful and ran.

From a room deep inside the house he heard thumping and banging, Geordie trying to break into the gun cabinet. The children upstairs: their voices squeaky with excitement, the patter of bare feet.

Wilson stood between the stairs and the door, legs slightly bent, pistol held two-handed. Barlow juggled the knives into one hand, grabbed Wilson and flung them both against a side wall. A panel of the front door disintegrated. Something tore the air as it howled past them. The carpet on the stairs sprouted a large smoking hole. The hallway filled with choking cordite and splinters of wood that slashed at their faces and clothes.

Barlow tried to tell himself that it was like old times, handling bombs that insisted on going off. He'd always walked away from those. But this was scarier: Vera could get hurt.

'Shoot!' he shouted at Wilson as the burglars' shotgun roared for a second time.

The door lock disintegrated, the door swung open. A thickly built, hooded man stood in the doorway reloading. Barlow flung the meat cleaver, Wilson fired. The bullet caught the door and slammed it shut again. The meat cleaver buried itself in the wood. Unimpeded it would have buried itself in the gunman's chest.

'Bugger,' said Barlow as he grabbed Wilson by the collar and hustled him across the hallway to the opposite wall. Those seconds out in the open, seeing vague masked faces through the hole in the door, seemed to last forever. He heard the *click, click* as the gunman loaded fresh shells into the shotgun. Outside, voices argued among themselves. The shotgun hinged shut with a metallic snick.

Barlow shoved Wilson into the comparative shelter of a doorway and ran for the front wall. Pressed tight against it. The shotgun roared again. Roared a second time, followed by the crescendoing echo of other shotguns being fired. If Barlow and Wilson hadn't changed position when they did, they'd have been shredded by the blasts that tore chunks out of the wall.

Wilson shouted, 'This is the police. Throw your weapons down and put your hands on your head.'

Barlow didn't dare even whisper in case he was overheard. What he wanted to do was take the rule book and ram it down the young officer's throat for revealing his location. Outside he could hear spent shells being ejected and fresh ones being slid in.

Wilson fired a warning shot through the doorway. The flame of light from the exploding gunpowder lit up the hallway for a fraction of a second. Barlow saw the outline of a face pressed hard against the glass side-panel, staring in. He gripped one of the carving knives as hard as he could and stabbed the man, backhanded through the glass. The man screamed. The feeling of the knife grating on bone made Barlow's stomach heave.

Once again the shotguns roared, this time the blasts and the hail of shot aimed in Wilson's direction. There was a yell from Wilson, a thud as he hit the floor and then silence.

The burglars had to be reloading. Barlow took a chance and ran for Wilson's doorway. Swung into the room, out of the direct line of fire. His toe caught on something that groaned.

Off balance, Barlow crashed to the floor, jarring his elbows. Lost the grip on his knives and heard them slide away across the wooden floor. Wilson was crawling around on his hands and knees.

Barlow crossed his arms and rubbed at his elbows while he whispered, 'Wilson, are you all right?'

'I've lost my gun.'

'Well bloody find it then.'

He scrambled to his feet, using first a chair, then the edge of a table for leverage. *This has to be the dining room.* Over the sound of his racing heartbeat he heard footsteps in the hall-way, coming from the direction of the front door. He looked around in the near darkness, trying to find the shape of a possible weapon to defend himself with. Then he heard the sound of other, lighter footsteps rushing towards them from the back of the house.

A little voice saying, 'Go away. This is my daddy's house.'

And Vera further back, hissing, 'Rachel, come back.'

Barlow didn't take time to stop and think. Vera being there and in danger was enough. He flung himself out the doorway. Saw the dark shadows of the burglars at the bottom of the stairs.

Grappled with one of the men and tried to throw him against the second shadow. Barlow and the two burglars stumbled against the banisters, clawing at each other for possession of the guns. Hit the hall table. The telephone tinkled gracefully as it fell, then tinkled discordantly as someone's foot kicked it, sending it flying. One of the burglars pulled a trigger, the blast momentarily lighting up the hallway. Vera was scooping little Rachel into her arms. And between them and the burglars stood Edward, with Geordie coming bursting out of a doorway. The first shot tore spindles out of the banisters. Barlow grabbed at the shotgun as it fired a second time. Geordie yelled in pain and spun to the ground.

Barlow had been holding the barrels of the shotgun when fired. Now his hands were numb and from the vibration of the blast. The burglar who had fired stepped back. The second burglar stepped forward, his gun coming up to fire into Barlow's chest. Barlow's shoulder still worked. He drew his forearm back and smashed it into the burglar's face.

'Vera, run!' he screamed.

A pistol cracked out a shot. *Let it be Wilson*, he prayed. Glass shattered. *It is.*

The burglar he'd hit was off balance. Barlow pushed him against the wall and kneed him in the groin. The burglar screamed and doubled over, clutching himself. Barlow stepped back and drove his boot into the man's face. The man arched backwards to the ground and lay still.

The burglar who had fired turned and ran. The front doorway showed the bulk of his figure, then only the night sky. Barlow heard feet running over gravel. He and Wilson reached the door together. The truck's engine roared. Its wheels spat gravel as it accelerated down the drive. Someone lay groaning at their feet. Before Barlow could stop her, Vera switched on the lights.

The man at their feet wore a combat jacket. The jacket had a stain of fresh blood high up on the shoulder. Barlow whipped off the man's mask. He didn't know him. *Thank God he's still alive.* 'Cuff him,' he told Wilson and rushed back into the house.

Vera was standing near the kitchen with little Rachel crushed into her arms.

In spite of her obvious shock, she gave him a smile. 'I'm okay this time, Dad.'

She walked backwards until she reached the servants' stairs so that Rachel wouldn't see the carnage in the hallway. Mounted the steps to check up on the other children hiding upstairs. Tears of pride popped into Barlow's eyes. *This wonderful young woman is my daughter.*

Geordie sat with his back against a wall, bloody hands clamped over the upper thigh of his right leg. Barlow banged his hands together to get some feeling into them and examined the wound. Extensive flesh had been torn away but the bone was intact. The bleeding heavy, but from damaged muscles, not arterial.

Barlow remembered seeing a first aid kit in the kitchen. He fetched it and bound Geordie's leg with a compress pad. Doing something practical made the recovery from a raw-gut sickness much easier. He'd never killed a man, not even in wartime. The feel of that knife crunching into that burglar's chest would stay with him for a long time.

Edward helped by holding Geordie's leg up while Barlow bound the wound. Barlow remembered him standing between Vera and the gunmen, sheltering her with his body. He put an arm on his shoulder. 'Edward, I'll owe you forever.'

'My dear chap.'

Geordie said, 'I go through the war without a scratch and now this.'

He started to cough again. One hand holding his chest the other the injured leg.

Barlow said, 'If that gun had fired six inches to the left and forty years earlier and there'd be no young Dunlops to cause me all sorts of bother.'

The burglar Barlow had kicked groaned as he began to regain consciousness. Barlow went into the dining room and came back with a candlestick. Handed it to Edward. 'Don't hesitate to thump hard.'

He pulled off the burglar's hood. He didn't know him either. Another of the Belfast men, he supposed. The man who'd shot at Vera and got away had to be Shalko. Barlow's mind flashed back to that night outside the Provincial Bank. Mr Clarke must have torn off Shalko's mask in the struggle. He hadn't shouted, 'Don't shoot', he'd shouted 'Don't Shalko'.

Barlow told Geordie, as much to imprint it in his own mind as anything else, 'Shalko Adair's a ruthless bastard. I'd never taken him to be more than a bit shady in his business dealings.'

Geordie laughed through a cough. 'Who do you think bought the bits and pieces I nicked over the years?'

'I don't want to know,' said Barlow and jumped to his feet as Wilson shouted, 'Sergeant, come here quick.'

The truck had almost reached the bottom of the long and winding drive. But on the county road, coming in both directions were cars with blue flashing lights on their roofs. Gillespie had come to the correct conclusion about the lost telephone connection.

'Too late as usual,' muttered Barlow, thinking that he owed Gillespie a pint.

It was a toss-up who would reach the front gate first: the police or Shalko.

Barlow stood tense as the lights converged. The truck got there first. Swung out the gates, turning to the right and the road to Belfast. The oncoming police car skidded to a halt, sideways on, creating an improvised road block. The truck swatted it aside and drove on.

Barlow went cold. That was his men down there and some of them were bound to be injured. The second police car stopped, its road ahead blocked by the damaged police car.

The truck disappeared around a bend, its lights gradually fading as it sped away.

80

Barlow had a quick decision to make. If he wasted time searching the injured Belfast men for ammunition for their shotguns,
the truck would be long gone, or…He grabbed Wilson and
dragged him down the steps.

'Where are we going, Sergeant?'

'That bastard's not getting away with it.'

They ran for the A5. Barlow shoved Wilson towards the
passenger side.

'It's my car,' Wilson protested.

'You're not qualified for high-speed chases, remember?'

Barlow crashed into the driver's seat. The key was still in the
ignition, the engine fired first time. He spun the car around
and headed down the side of the house.

'Where are we going, Sergeant?'

'By the back road.'

The back road was designed more for tractors and Land
Rovers than for cars. With the boot to the floor and going
downhill, the A5 seemed to spend more time in the air than
on the ground. Barlow kept his head buried in his shoulders
and his mouth tight closed in order to lessen the impact of the
ricochets over the bumps. Paling posts and tight-strung wire
guided them to the Demesne farmyard and on down a con-
creted stretch to the county road.

Wilson held the gate open while Barlow drove onto the
county road, then Wilson jumped into the car. Barlow made
him go back and close the gate behind them. Denton would

rather risk Shalko getting away than have his prize Aberdeen Angus cattle stray onto the road.

They drove on, with no car lights to be seen other than their own headlights. With two police cars drawn to Dentons there had to be a gap in the cordon that Shalko could exploit. The A5 struggled up to sixty-five miles an hour and the water gauge climbed steadily towards the red line. Even if it wrecked the young officer's car, even if he had to pay for the repairs himself, Barlow had no intention of easing up until either they caught up with the truck or the engine of the A5 seized.

They came to a junction. Straight on towards the Antrim Road lay darkness. To the right a vague glimmer of headlights showed in the distance. Barlow hauled the A5 around in a screaming turn and all but stood on the accelerator, willing the car to find another mile of speed.

He looked over at Wilson, whose eyes were now fluorescent with fear. 'Have you reloaded your pistol yet?'

'No.' Wilson rummage in his pouch for spare ammunition and began loading the pistol.

The muzzle dug into Barlow's leg. Barlow turned the pistol around in Wilson's shaking hand until it aimed out the passenger door. 'Steady, son.'

'Sorry, Sergeant.'

They were catching up with the truck faster than he thought they would. He reckoned it had been damaged in the collision with the police car.

'I was thinking,' Barlow said, 'We were in the car talking and you said that if Geordie hadn't committed the murders and if he hadn't gone to England as the wife said, and if he wasn't hiding out in a friend's house, then where could he be? It was you who jogged Edward's memory of the old Ice House. That way you get the credit for Geordie's arrest.'

'That's not the way it happened,' said Wilson.

'It'll help your career, son.'

'I don't tell lies.'

Barlow concentrated on flicking the car around tight corners, with a sharp drop into a field if he got it wrong. They'd be on the Randalstown Road in a minute, he reckoned. Shalko was in a panic and taking a known route to the city and safety.

'I tried to tell you that night outside the pub,' Wilson said.

Barlow remained mute.

'You know my mother lives in Malone Park in Belfast?'

Barlow nodded.

'Well, she doesn't own the place. She's the live-in housekeeper. The family allow me to stay over anytime I want.' He put emphasis on the next words to make sure Barlow understood their significance. 'In the *servants' quarters*.

'My father,' he said, almost spitting the word, 'is a career criminal. A wide-boy, an informer, a con artist. You couldn't believe his oath if he swore it on a stack of Bibles.'

He was breathing hard as if he'd run a distance. 'I thought you should know why I don't tell lies.'

Barlow said, 'I already knew all that, son.'

'You did?' Wilson sounded doubtful. 'How could you?'

'I'm your Station Sergeant. It's my job to know these things.'

At least Wilson was no longer nervous. A good thing because the truck was right ahead of them, disappearing around the next bend. Without any tail lights for guidance Barlow found it hard to judge the exact distance. His leg was cramping from standing hard on the accelerator. The truck headlights disappeared.

Barlow jiggled the steering wheel, 'On, on.'

They seemed to fly around the bend, the old A5's weak lights picking out stark roadside hedges. Ahead, instead of seeing the truck's lights Barlow saw only the dark road and the vague dome of light in the sky that was Randalstown. And something else, a solid darkness where the car lights should have faded into the earth. The truck had stopped with its lights out, waiting to ambush them. Waiting for the A5 to smash into its rear, and probably slide under its chassis, decapitating them.

Barlow spun the wheel even as the headlights finally illuminated the truck. The B Class county road was narrow, too narrow for the car to pass a truck straddling the middle of the road. The ditch separating the road from the fields too high to try and bump over. He spotted a gateway, with the ditch angling down sharply at the opening.

Barlow aimed for the slope of the ditch. On Wilson's side he had the truck. On his own side the wheels rode up the sharp-angled ditch until the car teetered at an impossible angle. Barlow wrapped his arms around the steering wheel, trying to keep his weight to his own side, but the gradient made him slide into Wilson. They were over too far. *We're going to roll.* The edge of the car roof hit the side of the truck, got knocked back over the point of no return, and then they were past the truck and coming off the ditch.

Somehow, he fought the car to a stop. He was breathing hard, his mouth so dry he didn't dare try to speak. The lights of the truck bore down on them, glaring in the back window. He glanced over at Wilson, his face bloodless, frozen with shock.

The lights of the truck got stronger, seemed to burn into his eyes. He didn't dare let Shalko get level. If he did, he'd probably blast them with the shotgun.

Barlow crunched the car into gear. It moved forward slowly. Something underneath gave a metallic scream at every bump. In third gear, with the boot to the floor, it wouldn't go any faster than twenty-five miles an hour.

The truck tried to come level, he swerved into its path. Shalko rammed the A5 trying to drive it off the road. The impact sent Barlow crashing back in his seat. His neck hurt. In the side mirror he saw a shotgun barrel poking out the window, aimed straight at him.

He thumped Wilson's shoulder to knock him out of his stupor. 'Use your gun before he gets level or he'll blast us to bits.'

Wilson wound down the side window.

Barlow swerved again to block the truck. This time Shalko's impact was more aggressive and the car nearly went sideways. If that happened, they were as good as dead.

He thumped Wilson again. 'Out the side window you'll only hit some innocent cow. Shoot through the back window. Aim for the engine block.'

Wilson clambered around in his seat. In passing, the gun barrel scraped Barlow's scalp. 'Thanks.'

The truck had dropped back, now it was coming again, using a greater speed to make the ramming more effective. Wilson started to fire. The sound of the gunshots boomed in the confined space. The truck was nearly on them again. It hit them. The push and shove of the truck forced the car to slew sideways.

Wilson continued to fire. Steady, aimed shots, Barlow noted as he gritted his teeth and jerked backwards and forwards in his seat trying to squeeze every possible advantage out of the old car. His head hurt from sound the gunfire, the smell of burnt gunpowder made him want to throw up.

They were nearly at a forty-five degree angle to the truck and rocking wildly. Soon they'd be sideways on and the truck would crush them. He saw a flicker of flame in the rear mirror and thought they were on fire. Realised it was too far away, it had to be the truck.

Wilson and that cross-eyed shooting of his.

One of his shots had missed the engine and hit the truck's petrol tank.

The violent shoves of the truck slackened. The truck drifted to one side, mounted the bank and ever so slowly toppled over. It lights went from two parallel beams to one on top of the other. Sparks flew from somewhere. By now it was no longer a truck but a fireball pursuing them down the road. Touched the rear bumper and fell back as the A5 limped clear of the carnage.

With the car engine switched off they could hear Shalko's screams. Fuel from the burst petrol tank had pooled around the front of the truck. The burning petrol roared into the cab through the open window. The cab was already a mass of flames and they could see a blackened figure trying vainly to climb out by the passenger door. Barlow held Wilson back from splashing through a puddle of burning petrol to rescue the trapped man.

Found himself praying for the screaming to stop. Praying that God would forgive Shalko, although he himself couldn't.

81

A patrol car from the Randalstown station drove Barlow home. Before they left Randalstown, Barlow found a private office for the traumatised Wilson and insisted that he ring Eleanor Packenham.

'I don't care what hour of the night it is, son, you need to hear her voice.'

At the Ballymena station, Barlow let the young officer out of the patrol car, but didn't go in himself. Lights burned in every window. Every man and woman in the District had been called back on duty. Harvey would be there for sure and Barlow didn't want to run into the man. He might decide to lock him up until the time came for him to be formally arrested and charged.

He stepped out of the car at his own gate. He was surprised to find people going to work, the postman doing his rounds. 'All Regular,' he muttered, falling back on the old police mantra.

Every part of him hurt and keeping his eyes open required major effort. He knew if he went to bed he'd sleep through to the next day. Didn't even trust himself to lie in the bath. Had a cold shower instead and emptied his trouser pockets before throwing them out. Anticipated Vera's tonguing at the state of his new jacket. A brush-down only seemed to highlight the rips and tears in the material. Stood in the kitchen and drank tea until it was time.

Miss Grace was booked on the noon flight to London. Before leaving Ballymena for the airport she was the honoured guest at a coffee morning hosted by Captain and Mrs Denton. Barlow waited in the shelter of the Castle Arms Hotel doorway. He wore an old police cape to keep out a shower of rain that seemed set to last all day.

Edward emerged first and sidled up to Barlow.

'She knows,' whispered Edward.

'What makes you think that?'

'Because she didn't ask any questions.'

Barlow said, 'You never were a good liar.'

Harvey appeared, still receiving plaudits from his peers for a 'job well done'. Barlow understood that Harvey was still at the hotel, in blissful ignorance of all the dramas taking place, until well after the truck had crashed and burned itself out.

Harvey took advantage of a pause in the congratulations to drift close by. 'Eleven o'clock, sharp, Barlow. I'll soon wipe that smile off your face.'

'Very good, sir,' said Barlow, who wasn't aware that he was smiling.

Miss Grace appeared, flanked by an entourage of admirers. In spite of the rain she stopped to say a formal goodbye to them all. The rain began to lash down. Barlow pointedly went and opened the car door for Miss Grace. The men took the hint and let her move out of the rain.

At the last moment Miss Grace stopped and took Barlow's hand. 'Take care of my little brother,' she whispered.

He looked into eyes filled with a pain that opiates couldn't cure. 'Don't I always?'

She hugged him. The murmur of goodbyes came to a shocked stop.

Miss Grace got into the car and was driven away. Barlow used the rain as an excuse to backhand water off his face.

82

Harvey sat at his desk. He looked ready to purr in pleasure at his final destruction of Barlow. Inspector Foxwood stood beside him and Captain Denton had his usual seat to the side. Barlow stopped in front of the desk. Never was he so glad to see Denton.

Barlow must have looked as exhausted as he felt because Denton cleared his throat. 'Inspector, perhaps you would get Sergeant Barlow a chair?'

Foxwood ran to get one. The chair he selected was hard and caused some discomfort to Barlow's almost forgotten burns. Barlow settled himself slowly onto it and let the cold, hard wood anaesthetise the pain.

'Barlow, your actions have caused me no end of embarrassment, and as for stealing money off our respected mayor...' Harvey began.

'He'll not be so respected when he goes to jail for tampering with the children's milk,' Barlow retorted. He didn't even try to tone down the contempt in his voice. 'You lot have run this wee country to suit yourselves from time immemorial, but the free education you gave the working man will destroy you in the end.'

Harvey's mouth disappeared into a white line. 'Are you threatening me? Inspector, do you hear that? He's threatening me.'

'Predicting,' said Barlow, and deliberately left out the "sir".

Denton gave another tactful cough. 'Could we press on? At the minute I'm dealing with a very upset wife and children...' He mouthed at Barlow. 'Shut up.'

'Yes…right…sorry.' Harvey looked through the papers on his desk. 'Barlow, you are charged that on…' His spiel was interrupted by a knock on the door. 'Come in!' he yelled.

Barlow heard the door open and Wilson's voice at its most hesitant. 'Sir, could I have a word?'

'Not now, Wilson.'

'It's about one of the charges.'

Harvey brightened. 'Yes of course. If you've anything to add.' He beamed in satisfaction at Barlow.

Wilson came in and stood beside Barlow. One of his legs was visibly shaking. 'Sir, I had dinner with Colonel Packenham and his daughter the night he died.'

'And?'

'After dinner we drank toasts: the Queen, family, the usual sort of thing.'

Wilson drew a deep breath. The deep breath seemed to give him strength and he continued in a stronger voice. 'Colonel Packenham proposed a toast to Sergeant Barlow, here. He said that he was one of the most honourable men he had ever met.'

'Get out,' snarled Harvey.

Wilson retreated a step. 'Eleanor's willing to testify as well.'

'Out!'

The door banged and Wilson was gone. Harvey's breath came in rolls of shuddering indignation.

Barlow reckoned that the toast to the Queen and family was the only truthful part of Wilson's statement. He nodded in satisfaction. He'd taught the boy well, but he'd never be a convincing liar.

Denton said, 'Unfortunately, that corresponds with a telephone call I had with Colonel Packenham. I rang him a day or two before he died.' He looked Barlow up and down as if examining something that had gone off. 'I wasn't going to mention it, but now…He moved restlessly. 'Packenham denied offering Barlow an inducement. Neither did Barlow ask for or hint that a sum of money would make those papers disappear.'

'But he did it,' said Harvey. 'We've got proof, the fingerprints.'

Denton said, 'Hang him anyway you want, but hang him clean.'

He was staring at Barlow. Barlow stared him back.

Foxwood cleared his throat. 'Sir, about the Dunlop case: the trespass on the late Mr Whithead's land and the criminal damage to a hedge.'

'Yes,' snapped Harvey, plainly annoyed at another interruption.

'Captain Denton thought that we should go through the paperwork again,' said Foxwood.

'What's the problem? It's all there.'

'That is the problem, sir. There are notes of all the interviews in Barlow's old notebook. In addition, the original complaint by the late Mr Whithead, as taken down by Barlow, is a masterpiece of organised facts.'

Foxwood looked to Denton for confirmation.

Denton growled his disgust. 'In the circumstances, we feel that it might be difficult to prove collusion or an attempt to cover for Dunlop.'

Barlow gave a nod of thanks in the direction of Denton, who nodded back. Then Barlow watched Harvey shrink into himself with tension. If his muscles came loose again in a hurry he'd explode. At least, that's what Barlow hoped.

Harvey said, between gritted teeth. 'He threatened witnesses.'

Foxwood was sweating hard. 'According to the notes, it was Constable Wilson who cautioned the witnesses, not Sergeant Barlow.'

'He encouraged Wilson to do it,' said Harvey.

The threat in his voice made Foxwood go silent.

Barlow stared at the portrait of the Queen as Harvey began formally to read out the charges.

At each one he stopped. 'How do you plead?'

'Not guilty.'

Harvey made great play with the charges relating to the fingerprints and Ezekiel Fetherton's missing money. The ones relating to Geordie Dunlop and the unofficial car park he hesitated over, and then slowly, reluctantly, bitterly pushed them aside.

Barlow knew that the next step was the cells. Laces and tie and belt removed and pockets emptied. He'd often slept in one when he was on nights. They weren't very comfortable but right at that moment he'd have given anything to just lie down and sleep for a few hours.

He lumbered to his feet and stood swaying with exhaustion.

Foxwood took his arm and held him steady. 'You should be in bed.'

The phone rang. Harvey answered it with a beam on his face. It disappeared. 'Tell her I'm busy.'

He hung up. 'Right, Foxwood, take Barlow away.' He pushed the charge sheets across the desk. 'Sign these off. Oppose bail. I want Barlow remanded in custody and make it as public as possible.'

83

There was a faint knock on Harvey's door, then it burst open. Barlow slowly twisted around to look and saw Mrs Carberry push Gillespie before her into the room. Whatever the reason for her arrival, there'd be a delay before he could get to the cells and lie down. He eased himself back into his chair.

Gillespie said to Harvey, 'Sorry, sir, I couldn't stop them.'

Mrs Carberry wore a short-sleeved summer dress with a slim belt to emphasise her waist. Mrs Harvey came tiptoeing in behind her.

Harvey snapped, 'Helen, I told you I was busy.'

'I know, dear,' said Mrs Harvey in a surprisingly confident voice.

'We've got something to tell you,' said Mrs Carberry. 'We were talking to Mrs Fetherton last night at the dinner.'

'She got drunk,' said Mrs Harvey. 'I told her not to mix her drinks, but you know what she's like.'

'Tell her to do one thing and she'll do the complete opposite just to spite you,' continued Mrs Carberry.

Mrs Harvey continued, 'Anyway, what with one thing and another…' She stuttered to a stop under Harvey's seething glare.

Mrs Carberry's nerves also showed, but she managed to finish the story. 'Anyway, when she was drunk, she admitted to stealing that fifty pounds out of Ezekiel's wallet.'

Harvey closed his eyes.

He opened them again. Vein throbbed in his head as he said, 'We'll have to speak to Mrs Fetherton about this.'

Mrs Carberry said, 'She won't dare deny it.'

Barlow caught the scent of evasion.

A hand rested on Barlow's shoulder. From the perfume he knew it was Mrs Harvey. Even that light pressure made him wince. Mrs Carberry's hand brushed the back of his head.

'Are you all right, Mr Barlow?' asked Mrs Carberry.

'I've felt better,' he said in a growl because he couldn't trust his voice. He wasn't used to people being concerned about him, especially nobs.

'Get away from the prisoner,' said Harvey to the two women. He pointed from Foxwood to Barlow. 'Put him in the cells and complete the paperwork.'

'Oh no,' said Foxwood. 'No way.'

He looked startled, as if he couldn't believe that he'd been so blunt with his superior. He backed off from the desk as if it and everything on it was contaminated. 'We're down to fingerprints on a filing cabinet that's even older than Barlow. How many cups of tea were spilled over it and when? Those prints of Barlow's could go back to the thirties.'

'Nonsense!'

Denton coughed. 'Today's news bulletins are full of Barlow's gallantry. There's even a quote from the Chief Constable saying that his actions are in the highest traditions of the RUC.'

'He deserves a medal,' said Mrs Carberry.

She was standing where Barlow could see her. She gave him a wink, not a very good one because it screwed up her nose.

'Dear,' said Mrs Harvey. 'If you annoy the Chief Constable, we'll never get a posting back to Belfast.'

Harvey's face blazed fury. 'I'll speak to you later.'

'Do you have blood pressure?' asked Mrs Carberry.

'You should get it checked out,' said Denton, as he stood up. 'I'm wasting my time here.'

At the door he turned. 'Barlow, can I give you a lift somewhere?'

'Aye,' said Barlow, his eye on the baffled Harvey. '*The Observer* office. I'd like their readers to know how I've been treated here today. Not a word of congratulations, not a question about my injuries.'

His temper was up. He ached to take Harvey behind the bicycle shed and paste him. 'All I've got is insults, accusations and pure spite.'

'You can't speak to *The Observer*, Barlow. Think of the good of the force,' said Denton.

'I know the Chief Constable. He hates being made a fool of,' added Mrs Carberry.

Mrs Harvey's hand trembled on Barlow's shoulder, but her voice was steady. 'If only you could get posted back to Belfast. I'd love to live in Atlantic Crescent, I think the houses there are gorgeous. Isn't that where your former secretary lives, dear?'

Harvey went white.

84

It felt good to wear a uniform again. To feel the stripes on his sleeves and the weight of the gun belt around his waist. Barlow stood before the mirror in the Squad Room and brushed at an imaginary piece of fluff. Pretended to be annoyed at the state of his uniform. Everything had been flung into his locker. Every item would now have to be taken home and ironed.

'But not today,' he told himself. Today, Station Sergeant Barlow would stride the town letting everyone know that he was back on duty. Criminals beware.

'Or maybe tomorrow,' he muttered. Bed and sleep were an enticing short mile away.

The door opened and Wilson came in. Eleanor was with him, almost supporting his wobbly legs. Shalko's screams in the burning van and the smell of roasted flesh had got to the young constable. Had also upset Barlow a lot more than he would care to admit.

'Are you not away yet?' demanded Barlow.

'In a minute, Sergeant.'

'If I see you back here before Monday, I'll put you on foot patrol.'

'No danger of that,' snapped Eleanor.

She still didn't like Barlow. Which was okay. He didn't particularly like her either, but she was good for Wilson.

Barlow nodded goodbye and walked out. Realised his own legs weren't that steady either. Had to concentrate hard as he walked up the corridor.

Foxwood called from his room. 'Barlow, a minute please.'

Bloody hell. The thought of a detour was exhausting but the sight of a chair to sit on enticing. Barlow went in and sat down.

Foxwood said, 'I won't keep you too long.' He checked his watch, 'If I'm not at the front door in ten minutes my wife is going straight to the solicitors and suing for divorce.'

'Never marry a policeman,' said Barlow, wishing Foxwood would get on with whatever he wanted to see him about.

Foxwood said, 'First, Sergeant Pierson. Mr Harvey has suspended him for a week for being drunk on duty.'

'Terrible thing that,' Barlow said, and refused to meet Foxwood's gaze.

'Second, Geordie Dunlop.' Foxwood tapped a bulging file. 'He got drunk and tried to break into the late Mr Whithead's house, and couldn't get through the pantry window. He tried to burgle Mr Fetherton's house and found the front door already open. Did he go in to steal or did he go in to see what was going on? I know what a defence lawyer would claim. Either way, he stole nothing and stayed to take care of a dying man.

'As for the unofficial car park at the point-to-point, Mr William Whithead, acting as the Executor of the late Mr Whithead's Estate, has withdrawn the complaint.'

Barlow said, 'Which leaves the complaint by the Hunt Committee.'

'Barlow, you got to Mo Hunt as well,' Foxwood said with a sudden sharpness.

Barlow allowed himself a frown of puzzlement as he stood up, 'Well, if that's all, sir?'

Foxwood let him reach the door before saying, 'It's funny how the sum of fifty pounds keeps popping up.'

'Sir?'

'Mo Hunt was telling me that a few days after the point-to-point someone posted a letter to the Hunt Committee. He said that the envelope contained fifty pounds in notes and a note saying "Restitution 6453". The sender hadn't thought to include their name or address so they don't know who to thank.'

'Funny that, sir,' said Barlow edging backwards.

'The odd thing is, that number is also the last four digits of Geordie Dunlop's army number.' Foxwood lifted Geordie's file and stuffed it into his out tray. 'Sergeant, some day you'll go too far.'

'Sir,' said Barlow and went on.

He stopped at the front door and carefully stretched his stiffening body. Eleanor was easing Wilson into the passenger seat of the old Humber. He knew they would spend the coming days locked in each other's arms. He himself ached for the comfort of that sort of healing trust. He'd never had it with Maggie.

He chose an imaginary sweet to chew on the weary walk home, a mint he thought, and squared his cap on his head. Hardly noticed a car pull up beside him or a window being rolled down.

A woman's voice said, 'John Barlow. John, are you going my way?'

He blinked to bring his mind into focus and saw Mrs Carberry leaning out the car window. A fine woman, he thought. Kept her figure neat, dressed stylishly on a small budget and had been through enough rough times to know when someone else was suffering.

Barlow said, 'I could be Mrs Carberry – Louise. I could well be.'

ACKNOWLEDGEMENTS

I'd like to thank my wife, Patricia for her constant help and patience when my head is full of writing instead of something important – like family life. My children, Lucie and Daniel. It's really something when children are proud of their dad. Kevin Hart for his constant mentoring and Sammy Gillespie for the use of his name and the good bits of his character.

My sisters, their husbands and their children and their families for their support. Ditto the extended McAllister family and our many friends for their encouragement. I was so pleased and honoured at the numbers who came to my book launches. And a sincere apology to the Rev Patricia McBride whom I omitted to invite.

People gave willingly of their time and expertise to help with this new book: Professor Ciaran Carson and the fellow members of the Queen's University Writers Group, the Seamus Heaney Centre. Dr Stella Hughes for being on constant call to answer any medical questions, Owen Milligan and Stephen Day for their technical help, Ian and Izzy Orr for keeping me right about Ballymena of the 1960s, and Mark Kennedy of the Ulster Transport Museum. A big thanks to them all. To Larisa of Dufour Editions for going that extra mile for me

And of course an even bigger thanks to my publishers: Andrew Mangan and Arlene Hunt of Portnoy Publishing, for their unstinting support, and Brenda O'Hanlon for her incisive and inspired edit.